I have so many people to thank. First my family, who have put up with me working on this on every spare minute, and not strangling me when I spend hours glued to a laptop. My wife, Jill, who has encouraged me to keep going, and was the first to read the initial, very rough, draft. My son, Jake, my inspiration in all things, watching him grow and learn is a gift, and, of course, his best buddy Blue Dog. To all the others who offered encouragement, free editing services, or just put up with me, you know who you are, and thank you! This book is as much you as it is me. I hope you enjoy my first crack at writing, and I am already working on volume 2 of The Tyrant's Cycle.

J.Robert Byrd

I0452747

A Tyrant's Whisper

Table of Contents

Part One

Chapter 1

Teridon Jace was inspecting the fences around Lord Baelin's estate. The days had begun getting longer and warmer. Winter had finally broken; though it had not the brutally cold season of most years, even a mild winter was long and dark this far north. It was invigoration to be free of his little cabin, despite what that freedom meant. Planting season was right around the corner. Early spring was an extremely busy time of year. Winter's damage needed to be repaired, and the fields needed to be prepared for planting.

He was not thinking about any of that though; his head was elsewhere, as it usually was when he was bored. He always had a hard time focusing on tasks that bored him, and riding fences was about as boring as work on the farm got. Staring off at nothing in particular; he tried to concentrate on the fence, but was failing at that simple task. 'Ouch!' His hand shot to his cheek in response to the sudden pain, he tried to rub the pain away. It felt like he had been hit, then stung, by a bee. That made no sense. It was too early in the season for bees. 'What was that?' He felt moisture on his fingertips. Pulling them back, blood shined red on them.

He studied his fingers when he heard a thud. His horse reared; he pulled on the reins, desperately trying to control the stallion, but the horse's panic was too powerful. Teridon landed hard on his shoulder, sinking slightly into the soft ground, moist from the winter melt. He sat up quickly and looked around. While nowhere close to an expert horseman, he had never been thrown before. Jerking to the right, towards a flash in his peripheral vision; someone disappeared into the forest. Jumping to his feet, Teridon hurtled the fence and gave chase. The forest engulfed him as he hit the tree line. Trees flashed by as he ran, they were thin in this area, so he was able to run at full speed, but whomever he was chasing had quite a head start.

He stopped, sliding on the slick carpet of hemlock needles. Patrick Lueless stood across the small clearing; all color absent from his, already, pale face. The boy was nose to nose with a giant panther.

The cat was black as the darkest night; its jowls were pulled back exposing huge yellowed fangs. It growled, a low, ominous, sound that vibrated from deep inside its muscled chest. What was the cat doing in the forest fringe?

The great cats rarely left the cover of the deep forest, and never during daylight. The cat pulled back onto its haunches, sizing up the short, spindly, boy. Lueless stood completely still, frozen in fear, a leather sling hung from his fingers. Before he could think better of it, Teridon sprinted towards the Lueless, ripping the machete out of its sheath as he ran. Teridon's feelings for the arrogant boy aside, the giant cat would tear him apart, no one deserved that. He was lucky, the cat stayed focused on Lueless, so was able to close most of the gap between them by the time it noticed him.

The Machete was heavy in his hand. The blade was made for harvesting crops, its heavy tip meant for building momentum to cut wood, not balanced for fighting. It did not move quickly, or easily, so blocking would be difficult. It was too late for second thoughts, one last step completely closed the distance, bringing him into the range of the cat's giant claws; it took a casual swipe at Teridon, not bothering to turn its body, not finding him much of a threat. He dodged left, the claw just missing his shoulder. He reached back and pushed Lueless out of the way, the boy stumbled backwards before falling heavily onto his backside.

Patrick pushed himself backwards along the ground, trying desperately to get away, but not able to look away from the scene playing out in front of him.

Teridon stabbed, the blunt point striking just behind the cat's left eye. The blade was not designed for stabbing, so this did nothing but anger the cat, and convince it that he was the true threat. It slowly wheeled on him, nose flaring, and muscles tensed. Sinking onto its haunches, it pounced, flying at him with claws extended.

Out of desperation, he dropped flat to his stomach. The cat flew over his prone body, its rear claws catching his cloak and tearing it off. Teridon pushed up, jumping to his feet as the cat wheeled on him. He had been lucky so far, but that luck would only last so long. He could not fight this animal for very long, it was too fast, too powerful; if he did not end this soon, he was dead.

The cat sat back onto its haunches, a low growl vibrating from deep inside its chest. The panther's eyes stared through him, the elongated black irises narrowed as the animal sized him up. Its shoulders tensed, his respite was over. The cat jumped again, this time diving at his chest, not giving him the space to drop to the ground.

Desperately diving to his right, the cat flew past, swiping at him as it did. Landing in a shoulder roll, he snapped back to his feet. The cat landed and slid on the slick forest floor.

This was his chance. The cat had given him its flank as tried to stop its slide. Seizing the opening, he took a huge overhead cut, swinging with all the power that he could muster. The machete's heavy tip cut deep into the cat's shoulder, sinking into the flesh, cutting through muscle, stopping when it hit the hard bone underneath. The machete stuck in the shoulder and the giant animal's momentum tore the weapon from his hand. The cat unleashed a screech like Teridon had never heard. It went through him, and reverberated throughout the forest.

Teridon and the cat stood, staring at each other, chests heaving. The machete hung out of the animal's shoulder, slowly falling towards ground. After a heartbeat or two, the animal decided the two boys were not worth its trouble, turned away, and bounded into the forest. As it left the clearing, the machete hit a tree and fell to the ground with a dull thud.

***

Teridon stood in the center of the clearing, his chest heaving as his pulse raced. After taking a moment to gather himself, he walked to the edge of the clearing, and picked the machete up, then cleaned the blood of the blade on the ground.   He looked deeper into the forest; following the path the cat had taken, wondering what had brought the cat so close to civilization. Typically, the only men that saw the giant forest cats were hunters and trappers, who ventured into the deep forest and, even then, it was extremely rare. Lueless had not moved since Teridon knocked him out of the way, he sat leaning on his elbows.

Judging by his stark white face, he was too scared to move. That will happen when you stare death in the face. Teridon reached down to help the boy up.

"I don't need your help, " Lueless sneered, as he snapped back to reality, he slapped Teridon's hand away before getting up.

Typical Lueless, Teridon saved his life, and the boy could not muster a shred of gratitude. Teridon did not bother to reply, he just shook his head and walked away.

He needed to get back to the fields and his work. Unlike the ungrateful prick that he just saved, he didn't have daddy's money to spend, and the work needed to get done.

Chapter 2

Teridon left the canopy of the forest, and walked the short distance to the fence, then jumped over the top rail. His horse, Lord Baelin's horse to be more accurate, stood where it had thrown him. His Lord's horses were extremely well trained, so the animal rearing like it did was unusual, and was something he would have to speak with the stable master about.

He was about to swing into the saddle when he saw the perfectly round stone lying next to the horse, right next to the shallow depression his shoulder made in the soft earth.

'That prick!'

That was why Lueless had the sling. The gash on his cheek and the thud he heard were from the tiny round stones; stones that Lueless had slung. He threw the stone into the woods. He should have let the cat eat him.

He mounted the horse and scanned the field. The field was surrounded by tall, straight, hemlocks, their high canopies swaying in the crisp breeze. The fields had all been cut out of the forest, and if they ever stopped trimming it back, the farmland would be reclaimed in a short time.

The north was just coming out of winter; the sun still stayed low in the sky, and a distinct chill still hung in the air, especially in the shade. It would be more than a month before the fields got full sun. For now, the trees cast long shadows, all day long.

The long, harsh, winters, and short cool summers, made for a short planting season. Work had to begin as soon as winter broke, and had to progress quickly. If the fields were not prepared in time, or not planted immediately after, an entire season could be missed. Potatoes were the region's main crop. Whatever they grew could not be fragile, and potatoes, being tubers, were not. They could survive a frost or two.

They also held up well in transport, which was extremely important. Barnstable sat in the North West corner of the empire, and if a crop did not travel well, there would be no way to bring it to market. They were a week from the closest market, and several weeks from the large markets in the south.

The first order of business was to make sure that the fences were intact after the winter so they can let the cattle out into the fields. The store of feed and hay was mostly depleted, like it was at this time every year. They needed to let the cattle start grazing, lest they run out of feed. That would be disastrous for the area. The cattle were counted on for the area's meat and dairy. If they ran out of feed, the milk would dry up and the cattle would become emaciated before they died.

Westin Forrest covered most of the continents northern tip. Barnstable was on the western edge, where the forest was mainly hemlock groves, so it was relatively open, with little undergrowth. The forest got deeper and thicker as you moved east or north, the sparse softwoods gradually changing to old growth hardwoods. Parts were so deep, that they remained uncharted to modern day.

The forest was a dangerous place, a fact Teridon had just been reminded of, like a hammer reminds a nail of its place. But, as dangerous as the outer forest was, the deep forest was doubly so, only hunters, trappers, and woodsman braved it. The softwoods in the outer forest were worthless, so the woodsmen didn't have a choice; they had to get the hardwoods deeper inside. In addition, the fur trade had exploded over the past decade, making the dangers of the deep forest were worth it for the hunters and trappers.

The fur trade had always existed, but as fashion in the larger cities had changed, the demand for furs had risen. The economy of the area had blossomed; bringing people like Lueless to the area.

'*I guess you take the good with the bad.*'

He got back to work, kicking the horse into a trot along the fence. The entire estate, including the fields, was ringed with fence. He will be at this a good portion of the week.

It was a stout fence, built with three crossbars, inserted into posts with rough cut mortis joints, wooden planks were buried in the ground, so animals could not dig under. The forest's predators made the strong fence a necessity. One of those large cats could decimate an entire heard of cattle in a night and they were just one of the predators. There were bears, wolves, even foxes.

As he continued along the fence, until he saw a large branch lying across the fence. He kicked the horse and trotted towards the damage.

Teridon was a contract farmer on Lord Aerick Baelin's estate. He, and his mother, served at the Lord's pleasure, and they were provided quarters, and rations, as payment. Still, Lord Baelin was a good man. He demanded a lot during planting and harvest seasons but when the work was done, they had ample downtime; he even gave bonuses for good work. Good man or no, he would not be happy if Teridon's work was not done, so he had to get moving.

***

What he thought was a branch, from the distance, turned out to be a small tree, large enough that he could not wrap his hands around the girth. He reined the horse to a stop, grabbed the bow saw from the saddle horn, and swung out of the saddle.

He cut the tree in half, the two pieces dropping off to either side of the fence. The top rail was cracked but still mostly intact, it could be patched. He fetched a hammer and nails from a saddlebag. The sun was diving toward the treetops; the shadows had stretched completely across the field. He had to be back before dark, and dusk approached. Damn, if Lueless had not been such an idiot, he would have been done already.

He rode Lord Baelin's horse and used Lord Baelin's tools, so he lived by Lord Baelin's rules; everything had to be checked in at the stables by sundown. If the clerk started his count before he checked them in, he would be fined.

It was not just a fine he was worried about; the choosing approached, and he needed time to train.

The choosing was his way out of servitude, and he needed to be ready. He was not sure exactly when it was starting, but it was would be soon. Unfortunately, he did not have the luxury of spending his days training; he had to squeeze it in after his work was finished. He had dreamt of serving in the military since he was small. Unfortunately, he was neither noble born nor a landed citizen, so he could not just join the military.

Only nobles, or landed citizens, could directly petition for enlistment. His only choice was to win the Choosing, or at least impress someone enough that they gave him special dispensation. Either way, his only path into the military, and off the farm, lay through the Choosing. Teridon caught himself before he was fully into his flight of fancy; there was work that needed doing.

He held three cut nails in his hand. They were iron, soft and easy to bend. These were the last of his nails, so he needed to be careful. If he bent them, he would have to ride out here tomorrow to finish the repair.

He laid the rail on the ground, his mind still on the Choosing and not his work. He placed the longer piece on top of the shorter. Holding the pieces together with his left hand, he took a big swing with the hammer, missing the nail completely, and smashing his finger.

He yanked the hand into his gut, cursing as his thumb began to throb, the tip already turning black. This has been quite the day. Behind him, hoof beats thundered, vibrating the ground under his knee. He turned, a smile spreading across his face when he saw the rider.

Jakes dismounted, he was Teridon's best friend and, at seventeen, was a year older. The son of Barnstable's blacksmith, he was going to be entering the Choosing as well. His father owned a business and land, so he could enlist without going through the contest, but there was good chance the petition would be denied. If he wanted to have a guaranteed slot, and any chance of becoming an officer, he had to win the Choosing.

Jakes called out to him, "What's taking so long T?"

"I'm going as fast as I can, some of us have actual work to do!" Teridon called back.

He rubbed and flexed his hand, trying to get blood back into his smashed thumb. Once the throb settled down a bit, he finished the repair with three quick swings. The nails secured the two pieces together. He wrapped rough hemp twine around the repair to reinforce it, then putting it back in place.

"All done!" he yelled back to Jakes.

Jakes rode up and jumped off the deep black horse.

"Jakes, where did you get a horse? And, why didn't you tell me about it?"

Jakes' family was well off, by country standards, but a horse was beyond them. In the country, only nobility could afford to own horses. He explained, "Baelin made a big order with my dad. He asked for the horse as part of the contract".

Teridon was impressed; he knew that things had been going well for the Pints', Jakes family, but not this good. Even with getting the horse as payment, they still would need to feed and board it. Horses were expensive animals, no matter how you acquired the animal itself.

While happy for his friend, Teridon's thoughts were elsewhere, "Wow, that's great Jakes. I'm done for the day, can we go train? Or, do you want to rub your fortune in my face some more?" He, jokingly, chided his friend. He had been itching to get out to the training grounds all day long, and was finally done for the day. The choosing loomed and Teridon would be ready.

Jakes stood kicking at the dirt, looking back and forth, anywhere but directly at him. Jakes was not as aggressive as he was, but he was certainly not passive. He held something back.

"Spill it Jakes, what's going on?"

His friend let out a long soft sigh, "my father offered me a deal, and the horse is part of it. He doesn't want me joining the military. He wants me to stay here and take over the shop. He wants to keep the shop in our family. The long and short is, I get the horse if I agree to stay. "

Teridon was never good at covering emotions, his eyes had softened and he was moving his mouth slightly, like he was trying to figure out what to say. He had just been punched in the gut, they were supposed to do this together, the Choosing, Basic at the Forge, everything.

Jakes saw the pain on his friend's face, "Relax, I haven't committed to anything, I only said I'd think about it. He let me ride the horse as incentive, but it is still his. I'm going to compete and see what happens."

While his friend offered a glimmer of hope, Jakes was extremely close to his family. Teridon did not doubt that he was seriously considering staying. No use dwelling on the negative, "It doesn't matter, you aren't beating me anyway!" Teridon punched him in the shoulder, as they shared a tense laugh.

They both mounted up, and kicked the horses, started towards the road. It was some distance to the stables, but they were both on horseback, so he had plenty of time to get back.

Silence hung between them as they trotted along the fence, making their way to the road. Teridon was not really sure what to say, so he said nothing, choosing uncomfortable silence over forced conversation.

They reached the road and turned towards Barnstable proper. The only sound was the clicking of the horses' hooves on the hard, light stone road. After a few moments, the tension was too much; Teridon pulled the reigns, turned towards the woods and kicked his horse into a gallop. He crouched in the saddle, feeling the horse's muscles working under him, allowing the ride to distract him.

The woods engulfed him, he never slowed as he pulled the reigns left, then right, navigating the wide spaces between the hemlocks.

Jakes had been waiting for Teridon to speak; he was shocked when his friend galloped away. He pulled the reigns, and, already several lengths behind, kicked his own horse into a gallop. Wind whistled over his head as he weaved through the trees. Tears rolled from his eyes; he wanted to shield them from the wind, but the ride required his full attention.

Beyond taking his mind off things, he had to concentrate on navigating the trees without hurting himself, or the horse, cutting through the forest was more direct, so it made the ride a bit shorter. The challenge calmed him, and once he was thinking clearly, he pulled the reigns back, slowing the chestnut gelding. If it was returned hurt, he would have to pay for its care or replacement, money he did not even come close to having.

Once Teridon eased his pace, Jakes was able to catch up. Pulling even, he slowed to match his friend. Taking Teridon's cue, he stayed silent. He did not want to push his friend, but he wanted to be there to discuss the situation when Teridon was ready.

Teridon's mind was still whirling, even the throbbing of his rapidly blackening finger hadn't made it stop. The Choosing was supposed to be the start of a new life for both of them, and now Jakes was going to stay in this hole of a town.

He had never been satisfied as a simple farmer, he wanted nothing more than to leave this place and be something greater. But, it would be bittersweet, Jakes was supposed to be at his side. He had to get past that, though; if Jakes stayed, that was his choice, and he had something to stay for. He deep was inside his thoughts, when he felt a tug on his cloak, he snapped his head around, "What?"

Jakes had stopped, and was pointing through the trees. Teridon pulled his horse to a stop, and following his friend's finger with his eyes. Through the trees, several large wagons were rolling past, surrounded by mounted men.

The forest was quiet, they could hear the clip clop of horse's shoes and the scraping of the Wagons' wheels metal treads on the stone road.

Teridon turned to Jakes, the tension between them was broken by the excitement of the scene, "The recruiters are here!" Teridon'a heart leapt. The day was here! This was the beginning of his future. He kicked his horse and started towards the road, hoping to catch a glimpse.

Jakes kicked his horse, and the chase was on again.

***

It was a short gallop before they pulled the reigns, the horses sliding to a stop. They did not want to get in the way of the procession, so they stood along the side of the road. Up close, the column was even larger, and more impressive, than they had imagined. Several rows of soldiers rode three abreast at the head; pure black warhorses' canter was in perfect unison. Their polished mail gleamed in the dying sun, the stark white, doublets stood out against the deep black mounts. The doublets were emblazoned with an indigo hammer, the sigil of the Aragonian military. The fading sunlight danced off the crown of the polished helms.

The helmets wrapped around their faces, leaving a small gap in front of the men's' mouths, while a post hung down over their noses. Under the helmets, pieces of black cloth protected them from breathing in road dust and insects.

Standard empirical short swords hung from their belts, the short, thick, blades bouncing with the horses' movements. Shields were strapped to the horses' flanks, each bearing the soldier's individual crest.

Teridon was in complete awe of these warriors; he wanted to be up there, riding on the powerful warhorses, wearing the shining uniforms, and part of the perfect formations.

So engrossed in the scene, he did not notice that he had been inching forward. Another tug on his cloak snapped him out of the trance. Pulling the reigns, he backed the horse off the road.

"Thanks."

Behind the rows of soldiers rolled the wagons, large timber freight wagons towed by gigantic brown draft horses, their manes tightly braided and tied with polished bangles that clinked against the huge polished black leather harnesses. The wagons were covered with canvas tarps. Each wagon had a single driver with no security. They must be carrying supplies for the choosing, if they were anything valuable, there would have been guards on the wagons, even in a military procession.

The column proceeded like this, soldiers interspersed with wagons, no wagon markedly different from another. Nothing changed in the pattern until the gloss black stage coach passed. Pulled by four large white horses, the doors had no markings and the windows were covered with black curtains. The beautiful vehicle had to be carrying the commanders. It was surrounded by eight grizzled soldiers, their faces and hands covered with scars, hard eyes were focused on the forest, like hawks searching for mice.

The stage rolled by slowly, the curtains completely obscuring occupants. The men behind those curtains held his future in their hands. It took all of his will not to run up and look inside. Teridon's mouth hung slack, like he was some sort of dullard. He could not do anything but gape at the lacquered beauty of the stage. A tap on the shoulder startled him. He needed to get his head out of the clouds before he ends up hurting himself.

"T, look at the sun, you need to get going."

Jakes was pointing towards the trees, the sun had slipped even lower in the sky, and was now half buried behind the treetops.

"Gotta go! Meet me at the stables."

He could not afford the fine for being late, and the horse needed to be back by sundown. He whipped the reins and kicked the horse's sides, galloping back into the woods, making time to the stables.

Chapter 3

General Ambrose Moore was Aragonian Military's head of recruiting, and he hated coming out to these small, far-flung, villages; it was a complete waste of time. The recruits, for the most part, were completely worthless. Even the nobles were infantry fodder, at best. The commoners were not even that useful, most would never make it past basic training. He let out a long, slow, sigh. A military would always need an infantry, but times have changed, and the military's needs had changed with them. There hadn't been a true war in over forty years; the military had become more of a police force than an instrument to project empirical power. The modern mission called for small battalions of educated soldiers that could move swiftly and responded with diplomacy rather than steel. This new mission flew in the face of the military's antiquated construction. It was still built for an old war, huge infantries smashing into each other on great fields of battle, fighting wars of attrition.

The transition from the latter to the former has just begun, but the recruiting process did not yet reflect the new mission. They were still recruiting low born country folk that would end up as nothing more than mouths to feed.

The two men sitting across the carriage from him were knights, nobles who had distinguished themselves in service to the empire, and were given the title of knight by the three. Like him, they got this assignment as a boon before they retired. He could not believe that he had actually been excited about being named commander of recruiting. He had no clue that it meant spending endless days traveling from one backwater village to another, watching overweight children of minor lords attempt the Choosing, and pretending that they did well, when they barely completed the course. Recruiting 'soldiers', knowing that they were barely competent and would only amount to fodder when war returns to the world

General Moore shifted, trying to get comfortable; his ass was numb from the ride. It has been three days travel from the last village, whose name he had already forgotten. Even in the stage, comfort was relative. The cushion he sat on had been long crushed. He was, essentially, sitting on the hard wood bench.

The forest had begun to thin and they were starting to come across farmer's fields and homesteads. They were getting close to the next village.

General Moore pulled back the curtains and gave the order to stop. Alain wheeled his horse and passed the order to the nearest wagon drivers. The order filtered through the column and it ground to a stop. These small towns had certain expectations of the officers, and three old men riding in a carriage what not the image they wanted to portray. All three were decorated officers, and they had to look the part. For most of these villages, the choosing was the only interaction they had with the military; they were expected to put on a show, and leave an impression. Military service was considered glamorous, a path of upward mobility within society. Besides recruiting, one of the secondary purposes of the Choosing is to reinforce, even strengthen, this notion. If the bumpkins were left wanting, they risked losing recruits. Though, given the current state of things, would that be such a bad thing? The coach groaned and shook, as it rolled to a stop. He looked across the stage, to Sirs William Shanin and Nidan Loorie, the two knights were his assistants, for the purpose of recruiting.

"Ready?"

The two men nodded and exited the carriage.

"You really hate this don't you?" Sir Loorie asked as he followed the general out the door.

"Unqualified, arrogant, and lazy sums up the majority of the country nobility. Their children are even worse."

Sir Loorie nodded, and could not disagree. He, however, held out hope that somewhere in those lumps of coal was a diamond waiting to be exposed.

Three squires drove a supply wagon up. The tradition of keeping individual squires had largely fallen by the wayside, though it did happen on occasion. What were called squires, now, were company assistants, there to assist anyone who needed it.

The three boys, probably twelve or thirteen, pulled back the tarp, revealing three neatly arraigned suits of polished plate armor, packed in straw.

They stood in the wagon disassembling the suits, brushing the packing straw off the leather, then handing them down to the officers, piece by piece.

The three men donned the ridiculous ceremonial armor. The armor was nothing that could ever be worn on battlefield. It was meant worn during long ceremonies, so it was built for comfort.

The polished plate was not thick enough to provide any real protection, and would crumple if struck. It only had single leather straps to hold each piece on, so even if the plated could withstand a strike, the thin straps would break.

While they were changing, Alain, their protocol officer, began briefing them on the minor lord of the day, "Sirs, the sovereign of this region is Lord Aerick Baelin. He is lord of the north, and Westin Forrest. His seat is Barnstable. His wife is Mildred, and they have no children."

"Well at least we won't need to pretend his kid was a good candidate." General Moore said derisively, laughing slightly. Sir Loorie cringed, but silently agreed, especially given the useless lump that the last lord's progeny was.

Alain cleared his throat, bringing the attention back to his briefing, "Aerick Baelin was installed by the three, so he does have more of a pedigree than the country nobles you have been dealing with. Moving on, Barnstable is the largest town in the area, its primary economy is based on farming and the fur trade. According to reports, winter has broken early, so we are interrupting preparations for planting season. I recommend that we get set up and move things along, to minimize interruption."

General Ambrose snorted, "Oh, I plan on moving things along, I don't want to be here any longer than necessary. I want to get home."

The three men finished buckling the leather straps, with the squire's help. There were no mail undergarments; the plate was worn over a simple cotton shirt and thin cotton leggings. The ensemble did its job, the polished metal was impressive, and was far more comfortable than battle gear.

Their warhorses were led to them; the black horses wore polished ceremonial armor on their heads, and hanging in front of their chests. The three commanders mounted up, the dress armor was light enough that they did not need a hoist. General Moore looked at Sir Loorie, on his right hand, and, Sir Shanin on his left hand, "Ready for the masquerade?"

The two men answered with simple nods, and kicked their mounts into motion.

***

It was a short few moments before the three men cantered to the head of the procession. General Moore called, "FORM UP." The banner men came to the front of the line, and stopped next to the two knights. Once the banner men were in place, He called, "MOVE OUT." The column haltingly surged ahead.

The three commanders rode at the front of the column, flanked by the two banner men. Helms tucked under their arms, so as not to show disrespect to Lord Baelin. Riding on a lord's manor with faces covered by armor implied aggression and would have been a show of great disrespect. The commanders set an easy trot, trying not to get too far ahead of the mass that followed them.

Chapter 4

Lord Aerick Baelin stood at the top of the manor's front stair. He needed to be ready; the recruiters would be arriving any time. From his vantage, he would be able to see their approach on the road. He moved his weight from foot to foot, while pulling at his cape, anything to ease the tension of waiting. His efforts were futile, however; his mind constantly went over the preparations, were they ready? He always received dignitaries with a touch of trepidation; he did not have the facilities to properly put up such men. The estate was large for the outlying territories, but it would nothing more than an outbuilding on the estates around the capital. Barnstable had a thriving economy, but it was a pale comparison to the industrial centers of the empire. Aerick was always fighting thoughts that guests laughed at him when he was not looking. All the trepidation would not change anything, they were coming, and he would receive them.

The manor house had been built using materials local to the area; it had very little stone, mostly grey and black fieldstone in the chimneys and foundation. No, the house was primarily wood, which, given the proximity to the forest, the area had in abundance. The home stood two stories tall. The living, dining, cooking and office areas were on the first floor, and sleeping quarters on the second.

Built in the style of the area, logs were stacked on top of each other and locked at the corners. Instead of the garish paint found in other areas, the logs were allowed to weather naturally, turning a light grey color; a mix of white mud and straw packed the voids between logs, insulating and sealing the walls. The house was built with small windows, a concession dictated by the area's harsh winters. In the south, windows were openings to the world, allowing light and fresh air into a building; in the north, they are openings to the weather allowing heat out and harsh weather in. The roof was black and grey slate; broken by several large chimneys, which serviced the homes many fireplaces.

The temperate climate of the south allowed for architectural beauty, but the weather of the north gave no room for such luxuries. Buildings were function first; form came a distant second.

No one would call the thick log walls and white mud of the manor home's walls beautiful, but they were not meant for beauty, they were meant to keep heat inside while keeping ice and snow out, and they did these jobs exceedingly well.

Tall maples lined either side of the road, standing straight and proud, giving Lord Baelin's guests a proper entrance to regional seat of government. Aerick straighten as three mounted men rounded the corner and started up the long straight approach. The column of men, horses, and wagons, began coming around the distant corner behind the mounted men.

Mildred ran out of the house to give Aerick a final once over; she spread the thick dark green cape over his shoulders, and adjusted the gold clips that attached it to the dark red wool tunic. His clothes kept with the style of the north, dark, rich, colors. He had been preparing for this for the last several months, the choosing was the biggest event in the outer territories, and he was going to make sure it was perfect.

The three men were impressive, they rode beautiful black warhorses, polished dress armor shining in the sun and, flanking the commanders, rode the standard bearers, on the left side, the flag of the Aragonian empire, the star over the globe, and to the right the flag of the Aragonian military, a hammer. The column stopped well short of the house, while the three men continued right to the base of the stairs. Pulling the horses to a stop, the officers dismounted in unison.

The lead man was slightly taller than Aerick, broad shouldered with a chiseled face, only the lines around his eyes and mouth showing his age. The man removed his leather riding gloves and held out his right hand, "Lord Baelin?"

Aerick reached his hand out and grasped the other hand tightly, "I am, sir." The men shook hands as the general replied, "General Ambrose Moore, pleased to make your acquaintance and, please, call me Ambrose. Allow me to introduce my assistants, Sir Nidan Loorie and Sir William Shanin". Lord Baelin stepped in front of each and shook their hands. The general continued, "Unfortunately our time is short, and we need to get set up immediately."

"Of course, we have cleared several paths in the Forest. We followed the diagrams that were sent ahead. We did have to make some changes, unfortunately, the fields are being prepared for planting so, we can't risk them getting torn up. Because of our short season, it would mean a complete loss of a planting season"

Ambrose nodded, "I understand. I am sure what you did will be fine, might even give another dimension to the games."

He turned to Aelin, who stood at the base of the stairs, "Get the engineers moving, I want work started this afternoon."

"Yes, sir, I will make sure of it."

Ambrose turned back and nodded to Lord Baelin, who took the cue, and opened the heavy oaken door. He held his hand out, guiding his guests into the door. They nodded and walked inside.

The three men stood inside the entry foyer, Areick shutting the door and moving to stand next to them. The stairs were on either side of the entry way and led to the second floor and the first floor opened up, leading to the living areas. The foyer was actually fairly impressive for a backwoods village.

Aerick turned to the men, "Please, you are my guests; my home is your home. My staff will show you to your rooms and once you are settled in, I have prepared a feast of local fare. It would be my great pleasure to show you the simple, but delectable, foods of this area"

"It will be our pleasure." Ambrose said, as the three men were led up the staircase to their rooms, on the upper floor.

***

About an hour later, the four men sat chatting in Lord Baelin's study. The door creaked open and Ambrose stood, as Mildred walked into the room. She addressed the men, "Dinner is ready sir. Would you, and your men, please follow me to the dining hall?"

They followed her down the long hallway to the dining hall. Inside, a long rectangular table was covered with local vegetables, cheeses and bread, but the centerpiece of the meal was the huge roast boar sitting in the middle of the table, dressed and the skin had been crisped to golden perfection. The golden skin ended at the head, which still had the large, angry, tusks attached.

Aerick faced the three men, his pride swelling because of the spread that he was able to provide. The trepidation he had been feeling largely faded, "this boar was taken down in Westin forest, about a mile from here. All of the cheeses, and vegetables, are from my farm and the bread was baked this afternoon."

"It looks delicious" Sir Shanin interjected.

The table was fashioned from a single slab of wood, and was striking, the heart wood in the middle was almost black and it faded to a light brown towards the edges. There were long benches on either side, and heavy padded chairs stood at both ends. The knights took their places on the benches and, Lord Baelin took a seat at the head and General Moore took the seat at the foot. The table was lit by the candles hanging off the large iron chandelier that hung overhead. The smoke was allowed to exit through several vents in the vaulted ceiling.

The men ate, chatting causally all the while, not talking about anything important. After finishing the meal, Ambrose leaned back in his chair, the meal had been fantastic and his stomach was tight against his belt.

The company had been surprisingly pleasant up until now, but he needed to turn the conversation to more pressing business, "Aerick, this meal has been fantastic. I fear business looms, how many candidates do we have?"

"Of course, General, I understand the import of this. We have fifteen contestants. There are no contestants from the nobility, and only one lowborn; a huge boy that has been living with his mother as a contract farmer. The boy is a good worker and, if he wins, I'll be sorry to see him go."

The general leaned back on his chair, unbuckling the front of his pants, allowing extra room for his full stomach.

After stretching for a second, he leaned forward with a groan, and rested his elbow on the table, "I wouldn't worry too much; we haven't had a lowborn win in about 10 years. The chances that this boy is anything special are remote."

Aerick cocked his head to the side. This struck him as odd, while he did not like the idea of losing his best worker, he did not like the idea of a rigged contest either. He considered for a moment, "Ambrose, May I ask you a question?"

The general waved a hand, bidding Lord Baelin to continue with his question, "What is the purpose of this? It seems to be a waste of time. If you are just going to take a couple of nobles, why bother?"

General Moore lifted his brown in surprise; no one really asked why when it came to the choosing, they just accepted the tradition, "Well, Aerick, the military has become a means to advance your status, no one actually wants to be a soldier, anymore.

The world has been at peace for so long, people see the military as a safe and easy way to advance their social status. Years ago, the ranks were swelling, and the three did not see the need for such a large military. They don't look long term, they said that there were no wars, so we have had to reduce the number of recruits. We had also hoped to increase the quality of recruit. Anyway, we developed the games as a way to cull the recruits, without making it seem like we are discriminating by class."

Lord Baelin sat back, considering, "Well that seems reasonable, but how do you determine who wins?"

"Don't misunderstand me. We do not interfere with choosing in any way, the contest is fair. It has been our experience, however, that the lowborn have several disadvantages: poor nutrition, injuries from work, lack of experience with weapons, lack of time to train. They would need to be an exceptional individual to overcome these burdens. My experience is that there just aren't that many people like that."

Aerick was satisfied with that explanation, the contest was fair. General Moore pushed back from the table and stood, as did two knights, "Thank you for the hospitality Aerick, dinner was truly wonderful, unfortunately, the hour grows late."

Following his guest's lead Aerick stood and shook the three men's hands, "It has been my honor. Do you need to be shown to your rooms?"

Ambrose shook his head, "Thank you sir, but we can manage. Aelin sent word that our engineers have set camp and are ready to begin. With your permission, I would like to get started immediately."

Barnstable was the last stop on the northern recruitment tour. These men had been away from their homes for months and Aerick understood that they wanted to get home.

Also, the recruits from other stops were sitting idle, they needed to get to the Forge to begin training, "Of course, please feel free to start when you like."

The general nodded, "Thank you Aerick, as is customary, security will be handled by the military. Once the course is set up, we will summon the contestants and begin.

Chapter 5

Teridon returned the horse and tools just in time. The sun had slipped below the horizon just as he rode into the stable. Jakes rode up just as he finished with checking in with the stable master. Teridon ran to meet his friend, "I heard some people talking; they are setting up the course now. We should go see it."

Jakes shook his head, he knew his friend; Teridon could be his own worst enemy. Despite the joking tone, he knew his friend was itching to see it.

"See the course? You know the rules; we can't see the course before the games. If we get caught we'll be arrested."

Teridon looked down and kicked at the dirt. He wanted to see the course, badly. He was looking to his friend for validation, even a bit of permission, but Jakes was far to level headed to feed into his recklessness.

Jakes chuckled softly, he knew what Teridon was doing, they had known each other for most of their lives. Jakes started away, leading the horse, "you coming?" Teridon ran to catch up.

The two skirted along the tree line; slowly making their way towards Teridon's cabin. The glow that followed dusk was beginning to fade; they would be cloaked in darkness in minutes. That did not bother them, though, they had grown up in the forest and were used to navigating in the darkness. They made small talk for a minute or two before the conversation turned to the choosing.

"Jakes, why do you care? What does it matter if you can compete or not? You aren't leaving Barnstable."

As before, Jakes knew what his friend was doing, and if he was being honest with himself, his curiosity was piqued as well. A bit curious, however, did not mean he would be doing anything stupid.

Rash and stupid moves were Teridon's forte, not his, "I never said that, you're putting words in my mouth. I said my father doesn't want me to join the military. I am still going to compete. I told him that I'd make my decision after the Choosing. Besides, you need to focus on your game, not me. You have to win, I don't."

Teridon's response caught in his throat. There was something in the woods; he slapped Jakes on the shoulder with the back of his left hand.

Jakes jerked, seeing his friend pointing into the forest. His eyes followed Teridon's finger, he leaned forward seeing what Teridon was pointing at.

Through the darkness specks of light bobbed about the forest. There was a lot of space between trees in this section of the forest, so you can see a good way. The torches moved around, blinking out when they moved behind a tree. Jakes looked at his friend; he knew exactly what Teridon was thinking, "No!" He was anticipating Teridon's thoughts.

Teridon shrugged, his hand held wide. Despite his attempts to play coy, the corners of his mouth were turned up in a wry smile that told Jakes all he needed to know. He responded as if his friend had answered, "Don't you give me that look. You know exactly what I mean, you are going to go spy."

Teridon lowered his head, trying to hide the smile from the moon's silver glow; Jakes knew him to well. He sighed and started to walk again, Jakes falling in line to his right, "You are being such a girl. Come on, what can happen? We know these woods inside and out, they don't. Even if they saw us, they couldn't catch us."

Jakes smiled, but stated silent. He knew what a stubborn ass Teridon was when an idea was in his head. Stubborn or not, Jakes was not going to throw his future away because a friend wants to reckless with his.

"T, you know what can happen, it is far more serious than just getting caught, we would be breaking empirical law. We could go to jail!"

"You're right, let's get out of here." Teridon replied, dejectedly.

***

They arrived at the modest two room cabin that Teridon shared with his mother. It was surrounded by the small garden they kept to grow vegetables for themselves. The cabin was provided as part of their contract. They were expected to maintain the property and keep it in good repair, but they went even further. It was taken care of like they actually owned it, the walk was raked and packed with dark clay, and once spring was firmly entrenched, they would plant wild flowers along either side.

Winter had just broken, so the garden had not been turned over yet. The dead stalks of last year's crop still stood cracked, dried and white, waiting to be pulled.

Light radiated from the cabin's small window. His mother would have been home for a few hours already. As the head of the household staff, she was, typically, at work in the small hours. It had taken several years for her to work her way up, but now she drew a salary, beyond the cabin and food.

He bid Jakes goodbye, who mounted his horse and started along the road, horse shoes clicking on the stone as he rode towards Barnstable proper.

***

The heat of fireplace hit his face as soon as he walked through the door. He loved the feeling of the hot dry air on his face; the contrast to the chill that remained in the air outside felt like home. The heat was pouring out from the stone hearth at his right. It was a simple stone fireplace, built from a mix of light and dark grey fieldstone.

A black iron kettle hung off the cooking hook, inches above the fire. A stew bubbled away inside, filling the cabin with the smell of root vegetables and herbs. His mother sat at the small two person table, reading by the light of a small oil lamp, "Hi honey, have some stew, there was a welcome banquet for the recruiters today and I was able to take home some of the boar"

"That's great ma, thanks."

The heat of the fire on his face felt fantastic as he spooned the thick stew into a bowl. Even though spring was upon them, the nights were still cold, and they would be for the next month, at least.

He sat down at the table, ripping off a chunk of bread to sop up the stew. He ate quickly, not really in the mood to chat. The stew was delicious, thick and hearty loaded with the boar, along with potatoes, carrots and other vegetables, that he did not recognize, "Ma, do you mind if I go to bed early? I'm beat and I have to be up early again tomorrow."

She looked over her book to shake her head no; he left the bowl on the table and retired to the other room of the cottage. His mother had sacrificed the room so he could have privacy when he had grown into a teen.

***

Teridon tossed and turned in his simple bed, really just a sack of straw with a blanket on top. His mind churned, and the harder he tried to stop it, the harder it churned.

He had spent two years preparing for the Choosing, and now that it was days away, he could not think of anything else, including sleep.

The Choosing represented his future, he could leave Barnstable, do something of consequence. After staring at the ceiling for a time, he gave up on sleep, and went to the window, staring out over the moonlit field. He watched the moon travel across the sky, allowing his mind to wander. The moon had completed a quarter of its journey through the sky when he decided sleep was not coming, and he could not sit idle with his thoughts any longer.

It would be easy to sneak past his mother, who slept soundly on a cot in the main room. He dressed, keeping the full moon in mind while donning black pants, a dark grey shirt, and a black cloak. He opened the door of his room slowly; careful to make sure it did not creak.

He tip toed by his mother and out the front door, again making sure it did not creak. The sliver light of the full moon lit his way. He covered the short distance to the forest border quickly. Once at the tree line, it took some time for him to find the area where he saw torches earlier. He found the spot, but nothing broke up the silver light of the moon, no torches bobbed, no shadows moved, the laborers had already moved on.

He was concentrating on the forest when he heard a voice behind him, "I knew it! I knew you were going to spy! I knew you weren't going to let this go. You aren't going without me!"

Teridon turned and clasped Jake's shoulders, and the two boys took off into the woods.

***

Two boys ran through Westin Forest, trying to stay low, out of the view of any guards patrolling the area. They were breaking the first rule of choosing, contestants cannot see the course before the games.

They were taking a risk but Teridon couldn't stop himself. They weaved in and out of the trees; this section of forest was mostly hemlock, tall and straight with high canopies. Those canopies interwove and blocked sunlight from filtering to the forest floor, the result was smooth ground without much undergrowth.

This was great for moving quickly, but terrible for disguising movement. The ground was soft and pliable from the buildup of hemlock needles. The soft carpet of needles muffled their steps, allowing them to move silently.

The full moon hung high in the sky, silver light filtering through the high branches; softly lighting the entire forest. It was beautiful, but dangerous, the moon lit the forest for the guards as well.

They continued deeper into forest until they came to Wilder's creek, which considered the dividing line between the outer forest and deep forest. No one remembered how the creek was named, but it was named so long ago that the creek was now a river. Over time the creek had dug a gorge, about thirty feet deep. The water filled the bottom, leaving only a thin strip of stones on either side. The top of the gorge was a sharp cliff that dropped almost straight into the river. That sudden drop had claimed more than a few unsuspecting riders and horses.

Using the creek as a landmark, and where they saw the torches earlier, they needed to head west.

The moon continued its travel across the sky as they walked along the creek. They had yet to find the course, and they were starting to wonder if they had gone the right way. They should have come across something by now. Maybe he had misjudged the location of the torches they had seen earlier.

Even worse, maybe the torches were nothing but hunters on their way to the hunt, and they were chasing shadows that were no longer there?

Jakes gave voice to these thoughts, "Maybe we are too deep? We should head back towards the road."

Teridon agreed. They had missed something. He turned and started walking away from the creek, back towards the road, Jakes following a step behind. They walked for a few short moments before the forest broke into a small clearing, about ten paces across.

The carpet of needles was gone, the ground was freshly raked and the rich brown soil was visible, even in the moonlight. They hurried back into the cover of the trees, and began following the trail. Disappointment greeted them when the path ended at a wall of trees. The path had been cleared and raked, but it looked to be unfinished, the path was there one step and the next step was trees.

Teridon turned with a shrug, "Let's go the other way, this has to go somewhere. They wouldn't was there time and just clear a small section." Jakes nodded and started off into the darkness.

They followed the path as it wound through the forest. Staying in the trees, they kept a sharp eye out for any guards patrolling the area. The path continued like this for some time before widening into a large circular clearing.

Several smaller paths converged at the circle; while a single path, about twice the size of the smaller, lead away. The clearing was about 30 paces wide. Raked into the middle was a smaller circle, about 15 paces wide, ringed with an earthen mound. To Teridon, it looked like a wrestling ring, but he could not imagine wrestling being part of the contest.

None of the pre-contest training had anything to do with wrestling. He pondered for a brief moment before they moved off along the large path, and away from the clearing. As they walked, the path had begun sloping upwards. It was gradual at first, getting more severe as they continued. The forest, and most of the land this far north, was fairly flat, so this rise was artificial, constructed by the engineers.

They reached the top, the final steps steep enough that they had to use their hands to climb.

The incline ended at a small platform, two or three paces wide. Teridon inched up to the sharp edge. He carefully peered over the edge, fighting his fear of heights. The ramp was built with cut logs, stacked on top of each other, and then packed with mud. The rich forest soil had a good amount of clay, so became rock hard after drying out. But the engineers knew their craft, going even farther they had mixed hay with the dirt and water, the result was strong enough to support a small army.

He took a deep breath and looked down the side, the moonlight bright enough for him to see to the floor, it looked to be taller than Wilder's Gorge, and straight down. There was no obvious way down, the wall was shear and there were no ropes, ladders or handholds. Clearing the forest was one thing, but constructing this structure in such a short time was amazing.

Teridon was so busy inspecting the ramp that he did not notice the light coming down the trail.

He jumped when he felt the hand grab his foot, jerking around, he saw Jakes hanging from his foot. His friend had jumped the last couple of steps, using his leg to pull himself up.

Jakes' eyes were wide open, he grabbed Teridon's shirt, "T, let's go, now! Someone is coming!"

Snapped from his contemplation he heard a voice in the darkness, "STOP! STAY WHERE YOU ARE!"

There was no way down the shear drop behind them, so they took the only option and ran down the ramp, hoping that the guards had not reached the ramp yet. Stumbling down the steep slope, Teridon had no choice but to let momentum to carry him down the slope. He had to fight just to stay on his feet. If he fell, his flight would be short lived.

The bottom raced towards them and the light was getting larger. If they continued down the ramp, they would run headlong into the guard. They could not get caught. Making a quick decision, Teridon cut right and jumped off the side of the ramp, dropping several feet, and landing heavily before sprinting away into the forest.

Teridon looked to his left as he ran, Jakes was gone. They had gotten separated. There was no time to dwell on that mistake. He put his head down and ran, weaving in and out of the trees; trying to lose the guard, who easily kept the pace.

This wasn't one of Baelin's manor guards; they could not keep up with him. The full moon, allowed him to run at a full sprint; unfortunately it allowed the soldier to do the same. He focused on running, trying not to trip as he ran through the night.

Teridon was the best athlete in Barnstable. Only 16 years old, he was already bigger and stronger than most of the town's adults. He had very little trouble besting the in races.

He wasn't being chased by a local, this time. This man was physically fit and easily keeping up. Sticks cracked and leaves crunched as his feet pounded the ground. There were no more thoughts of stealth, no concern for his body; he just needed to get away. Every step closer the soldier got was a step closer to losing his future. The soldier was fast, so fast; he was not just keeping pace, he was closing the gap.

The dense, cold, night air made breathing difficult, and his lungs burned from the effort. Every labored breath sounded in his ears. He focused on that sound, pushing the pain to the back of his mind, and keeping his breathing as slow as possible. While he focused on breathing, a loud crack sounded into the Forrest; he has stepped on a large stick. His foot stopped on the stick and then dropped the rest of the way to the ground after it broke. His toe hit the ground first and his arm flailed wide as he stumbled. He was able to catch himself, but his momentum was gone. The soldier was only a step behind him now. He needed to change something.

Ordinarily, brute force was his advantage, but not this time. He was not going to be able to get away by running. His advantage, this time, was an intimate knowledge of the forest. With that in mind, he broke hard left, towards the river, and the gorge.

Surprised by his sudden move, the soldier tried to follow, stumbling and falling when his feet slipped on the carpet of needles. Hitting the ground in roll, the man put his hands on the ground and jumped back to his feet, but like Teridon, his momentum had been stalled.

Teridon sprinted towards the creek, not wasting the opportunity to open up space. Behind him, the soldier's heavy footfalls thumped on the soft ground as the chase began anew.

**

The river was fast approaching. He had not thought this far ahead, so there was no plan. The cliff loomed; he dropped to the ground, sliding on his hip, trying to stop his momentum before he went over the cliff. It did not work. He slid across the ground. The carpet of needles was too slick to slow him. The blackness of the cliff was coming ever closer. He had to stop his slide, somehow. He could only do one thing, rolling onto his stomach, clawing and grasping at the soft dirt, desperately trying to find purchase; what he got was handfuls of hemlock needles and dirt.

His gut lifted into his throat as he dropped, falling about 15 feet before the gorge tapered slightly towards the river. He landed feet first on the steep slope, sinking deep into the soft earth; momentum pulled him down the slope, but his feet were stuck. He fell backwards, hitting hard when his feet ripped free slope.

Chin tucked to his chest, he fell down the hill, rolling head over feet. After flipping three or four times, his momentum was dulled enough to stop rolling. His knees sunk into the slope and he slid in the loose dirt until his feet touched the rocky bottom, and he was finally able to stop. His fall had knocked debris loose; dust and pebbles cascade around him, covering his face in dust.

Still on his hands and knees, he was shaking dust from his hair when his pursuer ran off the side of the cliff. The soldier dropped until landing on the same slope he had just rolled down. The man's feet sunk into the slope and he pitched forward, starting headfirst down towards the river.

The soldier had outstanding reflexes and was able to tuck his shoulder and go into a shoulder roll. Rolling once, the man's fall stopped about ten feet from him.

Teridon ran to check on the soldier. Rolling the man over, he was breathing, but unconscious. Feeling around the man's head and finding no blood, he was satisfied that the man was not seriously injured. Dragging the soldier's limp body out of the water, he laid the man on the small stretch of rocky ground along the side of the river. He climbed out of the gorge and up onto the firm ground.

Jakes was in this situation because of his prodding, and he was determined to get his friend out of it. The fall had jarred him, and most of the running he had done was mindless; he did not know where he was.

Even worse, he had no idea which way Jakes had gone after they split up. His best guess was that he came from the right.   About to start heading that way, there was a faint scream from his left.

Teridon sprinted towards the sound. Again, there was no attempt at stealth. He was focused was on getting to the sound as fast as possible.

***

Jakes was panicked. Branches whipped his face as he ran blindly through the forest. The panic drove him, and he was not paying attention to where he was running. He should have been more aware, but that did not matter now, his sole focus was escape. With no other choice, he put his head down and ran for all he was worth. He had a significant head start, but that was quickly being eaten by his pursuer. He tried weaving around trees, but that was not helping, the guard was faster, and easily catching up. He decided that his only chance was to get back to the road and then run home.

He stopped, turned and ran directly at his pursuer. The shocked soldier tried to stop, slipping on the hemlock needles; slipping but not falling.

The guard's stumble did not give Jakes much of an advantage and the man easily caught up to him.

It was ten strides before the collar of his shirt pulled tight around his neck. The soldier had caught him. His shirt ripped, and Jakes was able to get away, but his momentum was stopped. He took one more step before the soldier wrapped his arms around his waist. He was ripped backwards and thrown to the ground like he was a doll.

Jakes screamed as his shoulder and head hit the ground. The soldier's arms will still wrapped around his waist, the man controlling him. Pushing him onto his stomach, the solider pushed his face into the ground as he wrenched his right arm behind his back.

The solider never said a word as he pulled Jakes to his feet and started to walk him towards the clearing. His wrist was locked and the soldier pushed his arm up. He was up on his tip toes, trying to take pressure off his shoulder; it did not work, pain radiated throughout his upper body. Jakes knew he was in trouble.

He had given up trying to get away, and was hoping he would be able to get out of this without being thrown in jail. The solider pushed him along; in a daze, his thoughts were consumed with his future and the pain in his shoulder.

There was no attempt to be gentle, if he did not walk fast enough, the soldier pushed up on his arm, shooting pain through his body, reminding him of who was in charge.

Suddenly, the pain in his shoulder was gone. There was a rush of air on the back of his neck as the soldier grunted. Jakes whipped around to see the soldier hit the ground.

***

Teridon saw two men in the silver moonlight. He was gaining quickly. As the distance closed, he saw Jakes being pushed along by a short, but stocky, soldier. About Jakes' height the man was thick with muscles. He didn't think about anything, he ran harder. The gap was closed, he was upon them. Taking one last step, he launched himself at the solider.

His forearm struck the man's side just above the waist, folding him around Teridon. As his full weight impacted the soldier's side; he tackled the smaller man to the ground. Teridon rolled over the soldier's back, and slid across the forest floor.

Planting his foot in the ground, he used his momentum to jump back to his feet. It was a move he used all the time, it always shocked people to see such a large man move with grace.

Jakes stood off to the side, watching the melee. Teridon pushed him, "GO!" Jakes didn't ask questions, he turned and ran into the forest.

Teridon was committed now, and Jakes needed time to get away. He dove onto the soldier's back. The man lay face down, gasping for breath. Teridon had hit him with all his weight, at a full run; he had probably broken a rib or two. Rolling the soldier over, the man's eyes were wide open; his bearded mouth was twisted in pain. If he was afraid, his face did not show it. He had to give the man credit for his fortitude. He punched down, to the right side of the soldier's temple, just behind his eye. The eyes rolled back as the man slipped into unconsciousness.

Teridon was starting to stand when the darkness exploded with a flash of bright white light. His head was whipped to the side, as he spun to the ground, landing hard on his stomach. He never saw what hit him, just felt the results.

Recovering quickly, he pushed up to his feet, dirt and needles falling back to the ground as he stood. Two more soldiers had arrived and were focused on him. Both men were taller than the man he had just dispatched, and were lithe and lean, muscles tensed, ready for action.

His mind was fuzzy and he could not open his left eye. Acting purely on instinct, he punched the closest solider. He struck the man's right cheek; the impact did not stop his momentum, which carried him closer to the soldier. He turned his arm over and struck the guard with his elbow, using his momentum to build more power. The bone of his elbow connected solidly with the man's temple, and the soldier's knees buckled.

Cocking his fist back, he was about to finish the kneeling soldier, when he felt his fist wrenched backwards. An arm looped under his armpit and slid to the back of his head, while another arm wrapped around the front of his neck.

The hand on the back of his head started to push his windpipe into the crook of the arm around the front of his neck. He was starting to feel lightheaded when his captor hissed directly into his ear, "Stop struggling or I will break your neck, hick." Foul breath assaulted Teridon, and for the first time, he felt fear.

There was no anger or threat in the man's voice; he was simply stating a fact, struggle, he would be dead. There was no doubt the man would kill him and not give it a second thought.

His intentions had been to delay the men long enough for Jakes to get away. He hoped his friend was given enough time, because he was finished. Recognizing there was no further fight to be had; Teridon raised his hands and gave up.

***

Jakes felt like his heart was going to explode. He was in good shape but had never run this hard, for this long. He needed to get away from Teridon as fast as possible, and had been running at a full sprint since leaving his friend. A branch slapped him in the face.

The forest felt like it was closing in around him. The open spaces between trees felt like they had shrunk and the trees were only inches apart. He was having trouble controlling his breathing. The panic, the run, and his nerves were making him pant. His head started to spin as he ran short of air. He felt like he was going to faint, '*I have to stop*' kept repeating in his head. He needed to find cover, so he could stop and calm himself.

Off to his left, a cluster of trees grew tightly together. He needed some semblance of cover, and this stand would have to do. He ducked into the stand of hemlocks, pushing the underbrush out of his way. The trees were spaced too far apart to provide a true hide out, but they broke up his silhouette and were the only option he had. He leaned heavily against a tree and tried to slow his breathing, and control his emotions. Breathing slowly, deliberately, pulling long breathes in through his nose, and then expelling them with longer breaths out through his mouth.

By focusing on his breath, he was able to calm himself sufficiently for his breathing to normalize. Closing his eyes, he felt the cool air entering and the hot, used, air leaving his body while his heart rate began slowing.

Once he was able to get some air, his head stopped spinning and he was able to open his eyes. Looking around, there were no lanterns, no footsteps thumped in the distance. They must be busy with Teridon. Relaxing a bit, he started moving again. Teridon had sacrificed himself to free him; he could not waste the opportunity.

Having calmed himself, he was now focused and thinking clearly, there was no more blind running. He needed to get back to the road and then get back to home so he could have an alibi.

He had no further problems leaving the forest. Once on the road, he turned towards Barnstable. The road was one of the many that crisscrossed the empire. It was part of an extensive system of stone roads that crossed the continent, connecting cities and towns. They were ancient when the empire was founded, left from a civilization that was long dead. Still in great repair; they had been maintained by every government that had come before. The roads were too great of a tactical advantage to let fall into disrepair.

They allowed troops and trade to move easily and freely without regard for weather, mud wasn't a concern when it rained, and snow was easy to clear in the winter. The road that led to Barnstable was unusual in that it didn't go anywhere. It wound to, then through, the town, past Lord Baelin's manor, into the forest, where it abruptly ended a couple of hundred yards in.

There have been so many theories presented throught the ages as to why the road went nowhere: there used to be a city in the forest, there was one on the other side of the forest, and any number of truly crazy theories. None had ever been confirmed and the most widely accepted theory was that whoever built the roads had intended to cut through the forest, but found it too much work for too little gain. The only reason to cut into the forest was lumber, but it was too far away from any of the major trade or ship building cities to make that lumber worth transporting.

***

He arrived home to find his father was already awake. This was not unusual, the forge needed to be fed around midnight so the coals were ready first thing in the morning. He moved to the back of his house and snuck in through his window. Able to get in without incident, he quickly got undressed. Suddenly exhaustion washed over him. He dropped heavily onto his bed, sleep taking him before he even settled on his feather pillow.

Chapter 6

Lord Aerick Baelin woke to frantic knocking at the bedroom door. Rubbing the sleep out of his eyes, he grabbed his robe, whipped the door open, and glared at the guard standing in the hall.

"Do you know what time it is?"

The chubby guard would not meet his lord's eyes, looking down while shuffled from side to side, "Yes sir, I am very sorry sir, but General Moore requires your presence immediately; there has been a security breach."

Aerick's eyes narrowed, security breach?

"Tell the general I will be down in 5 minutes."

He went to his wardrobe and dressed quickly. Once dressed, he hurried to meet the general. The situation was serious and needed to be dealt with. Any breaches reflected poorly on him.

***

Aerick came down the stairs to find a hectic scene. General Moore sat at the far end of the hall, Sirs Loorie and Shanin at his side. The three men were talking, holding hands in front of their faces to obscure their mouths. Several of the soldiers stood facing their commanders. The four men stood at attention while the commanders conversed.

Aerick walked swiftly towards General Moore, he needed to get control of whatever situation had presented itself.

As lord of the region, imparting judgment for crimes was his duty, not the military's. The military were merely guests, honored guests, but guests all the same. He rushed pass the line of soldiers to find the Jace boy tied to a chair. The boy's legs were tied to the thick square chair legs and his hands were tied behind his back. The boy's head had lolled to the left side, and he appeared to be unconscious.

"General Moore, what is going on here?"

General Moore started the proceedings, "Thank you for coming so quickly lord Baelin, I know the hour is late, let's begin."

Aerick rounded on the badly beaten boy. The left side of his face was swollen and bruised; his eye was swollen completely shut. His head just hung, like his neck could not support its weight.

Even more striking, however, were the four soldiers standing behind the boy. Three of the four had bruises on their faces, one was hunched over, holding his side. The boy had delivered a beating of his own.

Aerick tore his eyes away from the Jace boy, focusing on the situation at hand, "General Moore, I ask again, what is going on here? I am the lord of this region, duly appointed by the Three. The military has no jurisdiction over the enforcement of empirical law within its borders. I adjudicate crimes and dispense punishment within this region. I demand to know what happened and why I was not summoned earlier."

General Moore was genuinely surprised. A small, backwoods, lord had the guts to take an empirical general to task. He had new respect for the man, most of these 'lords' would have been far too intimidated to utter a word against him, let alone the rebuke Lord Baelin had just delivered, "My apologies lord, there was no offense intended, we were waiting for you before we began."

Aerick took a deep breath; He needed to take control of this situation. While having a healthy respect for the military and its commanders, he refused to be rolled over, "I understand general, but I will control these proceedings from here on. Now, can you explain what is going on?

General Moore nodded, any concerns he had about this man being unqualified to levy judgment were gone; the man had a spine, "Of course, Lord Baelin. And again, please accept my sincere apologies for any slight, it was unintended. Mr. Jace, along another individual, was caught on the choosing course. When security confronted them, they ran. Mr. Jace then assaulted three of my soldiers before he was finally subdued. The other individual was able to get away due to Mr. Jace's intervention, and has not been identified."

Aerick was stunned. It was unbelievable that this farm boy could take down a single soldier, let alone three.

The general continued, "We have questioned Mr. Jace, but he will not identify the other person."

Aerick did not see the point of investigating further, if the boy wanted to accept punishment, than why waste resources that were needed elsewhere, "General, it would seem that the assault was carried out by Mr. Jace.

If the other individual's only 'crime' was spying on the course, it would seem that we have the real criminal here. There seems to be no need for further investigation."

General Moore agreed wholeheartedly. This was the last stop on the recruiting circuit, and he wanted to get home. An investigation would delay things at least a day, probably more, "My thoughts exactly, Lord Baelin. If the boy wants to accept the punishment by himself, let him."

Teridon watched the scene through his good eye. His left eye was would not open at all. His head was in a fog from the beating, and he was having trouble focusing on anything. Slowly shaking his head from side to side, he tried, unsuccessfully, to clear that fog. He could only shake softly; it hurt too much to shake any harder.

Lord Baelin rounded on him, "What were you thinking?"

Teridon responded groggily, "I am sorry sir; I was just trying to see the course. I knew it was against the rules." His head still hung, hurting too much to lift.

"I don't care about that! Contestants try and see the course all the time. What would make you assault THREE SOLIDERS? DO YOU KNOW YOUR PLACE? WHAT GOT INTO YOU, IDIOT?" Spit flew and ran down Teridon's face; he had no way of wiping it off, so he just endured the humiliation as it slowly slid down his cheeks.

General Moore was standing behind the man. He clasped Lord Baelin's shoulder and leaned close, whispering into the man's ear. Teridon could not hear what was said, but whatever the general told Lord Baelin seemed to calm the rage. He backed away for a second, catching his breath.

"What are we going to do with you son?" General Moore asked, rhetorically, as he stepped up to take Lord Baelin's place.

The general was not looking for an answer, but Teridon gave him one anyway, "I am sorry sir. I knew it was against the rules to see the course, and when the soldiers saw me, I panicked. I wasn't trying to hurt anyone, things just got out of control."

General Moore cocked his head and raised his eyebrows, "Out of control? That is quite an understatement, do you not think, Mr. Jace?"

"Yes sir, I guess it is." Teridon was trying his best to show contrition. It was a new emotion for him. Lord Baelin had calmed and composed himself. The general stepped back and he moved up to face Teridon. His tone was measured, but barely hid the anger that boiled underneath, "Mr. Jace, you are within a hairs breath of losing your head. Count yourself lucky that I hold your mother in such high regard and that you have been such a good worker. As the duly appointed lord of this region, it is my duty to dispense justice. With that in mind, your punishment is as follows: you are barred from competing in the choosing, permanently. Now get out of my sight."

Teridon gasped, his future had been torn from him with those small words. There would be no military, no ranger training, nothing. He was going to be trapped in this life until he dropped dead. There was no other way for the low born to enter the military, and the military was the only way for him to get out He had no education and no real skills, he could do manual labor and that was it.

The soldiers standing behind him began yelling, protesting the decision.

Teridon lifted his heavy head, and opened his mouth. Lord Baelin cut him off, "Mr. Jace, you have your head and your mother has a job, I would think on that before your big mouth costs you even more."

His eyes hardened even further as his gaze moved up, over Teridon's head, "As for you four, I AM THE LORD OF THIS REGION! I determine the punishments levied in my territory. You four will accept my judgment, and shut your mouths."

Sir Loorie had enough. He understood his men's frustration, but the punishment was levied in accordance with empirical law, the law they swore an oath to uphold. They needed to respect Lord Baelin's sovereignty, "It took four trained soldiers to subdue a farm boy. I would shut my mouths, if I were you. Cut him loose, Lord Aerick Baelin has given his judgment."

Looking down, the lead soldier replied muttered something. Teridon couldn't hear what it was over the ringing in his ears. He had obviously taken several hits to his head. None of the soldiers moved. They stood grumbling, irate that he had gotten away with assaulting them. Teridon took note of how differently an outcome can be perceived, depending on the person's perspective. The soldiers felt that Teridon had gotten off without any punishment, while he would have rather been executed.

After giving the soldiers a moment to calm down, Sir Loorie lost his patience when they continued to ignore his order. He understood that the men were angry but he refused to tolerate insubordination.

Slamming the hall door open, he called for the guards, who were standing guard outside, "I want these four arrested for failure to follow a direct order, and insubordination."

The guards pulled shackles and moved around the soldiers. Sir Loorie continued as he cut Terindon's bonds, "You were given a direct order that you refused to follow. The punishment for insubordination is death, you four are lucky that I am taking the emotion of our current situation into account and sparing you that. But, please, keep talking, I can be persuaded to change my mind."

The soldier, who was about to speak, snapped his mouth shut as Sir Loorie left the room. Teridon was not taking his chances and ran out with the man. He wanted to get out of the manor before anyone changed their minds.

Chapter 7

Jakes woke to bright sunlight streaming through his window, into his eyes. He had barely slept last night. Concern for his friend, mixed with the excitement of the night, had kept him tossing and turning. Teridon had saved him, and he owed him a great debt. He dressed quickly and walked into the great room. His mother was working by the hearth, kneading dough to make bread for dinner. His family was considered upper class in the outlying territories, like Barnstable. They had a two-story home, and it was large enough for he, his brother, and his parents to have separate bedrooms. He tried to sneak by her, calling out when had reached the door, "Hey mom, I am going to Teridon's."

"OK, but don't be gone to long, the notice came this morning, the Choosing will start tomorrow. You need to get your last bit of training in"

He was already out the door when her response came, but he had heard her.

It was a couple of miles to the contract farmer's cottages, and there was no sense walking if he had a horse. He went to the back yard, untied the horse, and swung into the saddle, and spurred the horse to a brisk trot.

***

Jakes found his friend leaning against the right side of his house. More precisely, he assumed the pile of flesh covered in a cloak was Teridon. He couldn't see a face, the lump's head was covered in the cloak's hood.

Jakes pulled the hood back. Teridon slowly raised his head. He was shocked by his friend's appearance. His face was badly blackened from bruising, the whole left side covered by a deep purple bruise that had already began to yellow around the edges. His left eye was swollen completely shut, "What happened?"

"Did you get away?" Teridon asked. He nodded, hoping that his friend would give a bit of explanation. Teridon looked with a wry smile, "There was a bit of a scuffle." Jakes rolled his eyes as his friend continued, "I tackled the first guard so you could get away, then the other two came, the second hit me, I hit him back and the third got me from behind." Teridon's jaw must have been injured as well. His mouth was only opening half way and speaking seemed to be a painful endeavor.

Jakes saw that he winced with every labored breath. He was clearly having trouble breathing as well, "Are your ribs broken? Can you breathe?"

"I don't think my ribs are broken, but my nose is." He paused, sighing heavily, "Jakes, they got me; they pulled me in front of Lord Baelin and the military. I am permanently barred from competing in the choosing, my future is gone, I'm stuck here, I'll die here." His entire body seemed to deflate when he said that.

Jakes didn't know what to say, "I am sorry." He was not sure what his reaction should be.

Teridon shook his head, "don't be sorry, you were there because of me, and I was going to get you out of it."

He slumped back and his head fell to his chest, Jakes saw it now. Teridon's posture had nothing to do with physical pain. It was the death of his dreams that hurt him so badly.

Chapter 8

"HEY WORTHLESS!" The gravelly yell came from the other room.

'Great, Dad's home.'

He rolled onto his back and sighed deeply. His father had dragged him and his mother to this pit of a town about 2 years ago. A tailor by trade, he moved to Barnstable to set up a company that produced jackets and travel gear. He chose this forsaken area because of the booming fur trade. The quantity and quality of the furs and hides that the area produced were unmatched. Trappers were pushing deeper into the forest than ever before, and they were pulling out huge amounts of top quality stock.

His thought was that being closer to the raw materials will save him on production costs and increase his profit margins. It turned out that his father was right, but while worked out for him, the rest of the family was forced to follow.

Patrick hated this place; he missed his friends back home. Most of all, however, he hated the weather. It was constantly cold and damp. You would not know it from looking at the locals, however. They wore short sleeved tunics, while he was still bundled in thick wool cloaks.

He rolled out of his bed, falling to the wood floor with a thud. His head sagged between his outstretched arms. He took another deep breath, stalling as long as possible. After a moment, he started towards his door. Patrick was a small child, who had been bullied most of his life.

Unfortunately, the biggest of those bullies was his father. The man may have been a successful in business, but he was a miserable failure as a father. As he slowly pushed the door open, he thought, "*worthless, huh*?" Well at least that was a new insult. His father had taken to making fun of their family name, Lueless, to demean him.

The door creaked as it openend. His father stood in the front door, across the great room; short and thick, he darkened the door and cast a shadow across the floor. A dense black beard framed his square jaw and covered his thick neck. He wore a flannel shirt, cotton leggings, and one of his new spring travel cloaks.

He sneered, "Where were you?"

Patrick was confused. He wasn't supposed to be anywhere. He had been busy training for the games, "Where was I supposed to be, father?" Not wanting to anger the man further, he avoided looking directly into his eyes.

His father rolled his eyes and huffed, "You were supposed to come with me to meet with the new trapper, what were you doing, idiot."

Pat was at a loss, he didn't recall any plans, "since when?" He risked a beating by challenging his father, but he did not know what the man was talking about.

His father was exasperated. He threw his hands in the air, "Are you that bloody stupid? I told you last week."

"You told me that you might want me to meet someone, you never told me anything else." Suddenly, his father was in front of him. The man cocked his hand back and slapped him across the face. His neck head snapped around, and he almost dropped to a knee. He managed to stay standing, refused to give his tormenter the satisfaction. Fighting every instinct, he turned back to face the man.

"Are you talking back to me, you little prick?" The man's face was so close, Patrick felt the course outer strands of his father's beard scratching his face.

His father cocked his hand back again, and Patrick's resolve faded. He turned his head and looked away, "No sir, I am sorry."

His father did not back off him, "Was that so hard. What have you been doing, you useless lump?"

"I was just about to go training, sir."

His father leaned back, and had a deep, hearty, laugh, "Training for what? What could you possibly be training for?"

He looked at the floor, still not able to meet his father's eyes, "You know that I had been helping Rob training for the Choosing."

His father's laughter got even deeper and louder, "Why would he have someone like you help him? Wouldn't he want someone that could help him WIN?"

Patrick was about to reply, but thought better of it. The last thing he needed was for his father to figure out that he was not just helping Rob train, but he was training himself as well. In truth, there was nothing about the military that appealed to him.

It was, however, a way out of this hole, and away from this man. That, it turned out, was quite a motivator.

Patrick shouldered past his father, "I am going to train, I don't care what you think about it." He was practically running when reached the door.

"Get back here, boy, I am not done with you!" His father yelled at his back. He heard the command, but ignored it.

Chapter 9

Jakes tried to take Teridon's mind off last night. He wanted to give his friend something to do, "Come on, let's go train, if you can't compete, you can help me get ready." The only response was a small nod. It was not much, but Jakes hoped that Teridon started to accept his fate. He helped Teridon up, and led his friend towards Barnstable. Teridon shuffled along behind him, without saying a word.

***

The training area had been set up late last summer, when the Choosing had been first announced. Open to all perspective contestants, it had various obstacles, each with a plaque that had instructions on how to complete it. In the center was a rack of swords and a small tent, with books of the sword forms that they needed to learn.

Most of the contestants had made training their sole focus, so they were at the course for good portions of most days. Teridon did not have that luxury. He could only train during the rare moments that he was not working. He had made copies of the sword forms, practicing them with a makeshift wooden sword in the dark behind his cottage.

Jakes checked in with the attendant, grabbed a practice uniform and disappeared into the changing rooms. Called rooms, they were really just curtains hung over a wooden frame, but they gave a measure of privacy. The uniforms were utilitarian, simple white leggings and shirt, meant to put all contestants on the same level, regardless of status. Teridon looked over the training grounds, biting down on his lip in anger. He had no one to blame but himself. He knew the rules and he broke them. And, for nothing, he did not need an advantage. He easily bested his peers in most activities; he had no doubt he would have again, but he stupidly decided to push things. Admitting that to himself, however, did not make it hurt any less.

There were already several people on the course. One caught Teridon's attention, Patrick Lueless. Lueless strutted around Barnstable with his nose up and chest puffed out, like he was above Lord Baelin. He acted like he owned the town. The two despised each other. Lueless felt that Teridon was lowborn trash, and Teridon thought he was an arrogant prick.

Part of him had hoped yesterday would have forged a truce between the two; He had saved the other boy's life, after all. But, in seeing the boy, it was clear that Lueless had no intention of mending any fences, or, at the very least, just leaving Teridon alone.

"Hey Terry." Patrick greeted with fake cheeriness. He knew Teridon hated being called 'Terry', so he made sure that to always addressed him as such.

Teridon did not reply, fearing a response would get him in even more trouble. He had no doubt that Lueless was the type that would go running to his daddy should anything happen between the two.

Lueless continued taunting, "Heard you had some trouble last night. Looks like you finally got the beating you deserve. Unbelievably, it made you even uglier."

If Lueless was trying to get Teridon to explode, he would have to do better than petty insults, "That's the best you have, huh? Pathetic." He was in no mood to be played with and just wanted to be left alone with his depression.

A cold smile flashed across Lueless' face, "Pathetic, maybe, but I am going to be competing and you are going too stuck in this hole, farming someone else's land. You were born nothing, and, now, you will always be nothing. Don't worry, Terry, when I come back, I will be sure to make sure that you and your moth-" The word caught in his mouth. Teridon hit Lueless in the chest. His open palms struck Lueless just above the bottom of his rib cage, knocking the wind out of him and lifting him off the ground.

Lueless flew through the air for several feet before landing on his back, arms and legs splayed out. After sliding to a stop, Lueless tried to sit up, but Teridon had other ideas. He kicked Lueless in the center of his chest, throwing him back into the dirt. He knelt on the boy's chest with one knee.

His full weight bore down on Lueless' chest pinning him firmly to the ground. Teridon leaned over, coming nose the nose with the much smaller boy, "If you ever mention my mother again, I will beat you until you are unrecognizable. Your daddy won't be able save you, you arrogant piece of dung. Don't EVER think that you are above me. You are a spoiled little boy, and if you, somehow, manage to win, you'll find out quickly that the military won't spoil little Patty."

Teridon braced himself against Lueless' face, using it to push himself up, while pushing the boy's head into the dirt.

He turned to Jakes, who had been standing behind him, "I don't need to be around this garbage, train hard, friend, you to make sure you beat little Patty."

Chapter 10

The sun was just about to slip below the treetops. Night was fast approaching. Teridon stood among the crowd of spectators who had come to see the start of the Choosing. The crowd stood in a half moon, framing the 15 contestants lined up in front of a raised dais. The contestants were mounted, each with a soldier ready to lead the boys into the forest. The contestants had no hints of where they were going, the soldiers would lead them to the start. They were mounted so they would not be able to feel the forest underfoot, count steps, or gauge direction.

General Moore stood at the center of the dais with his arms held high, motioning for the small crowd to be quiet. It took a moment but eventually the murmurs faded away, and the general opened the choosing, "Contestants, spectators, welcome to the Choosing. This contest is the way the military selects the best and the brightest from throughout this great land. The Aragonian military is the empire's crown jewel, and these games ensure it stays that way. Five centuries ago, the empire was on the verge of collapse. Battles had been lost and the military was in shambles. It was then that the great general Martel took command. This great man had a revelation. A small force of dedicated soldiers, well trained and well armed, was more effective than a large force of conscripted soldiers. Conscripts were lazy, corrupt, and quick to run. His force of volunteers would be dedicated to the cause, forged in training and ready to fight until death or victory. With this in his mind, he gave the entire military an ultimatum, shape up or leave. His reforms are the reason for centuries of the great empire's military dominance, and led to the contest that you are participating in today. Only the best will be accepted into my military. These games will determine who among you fit that description, which among you are among the empire's best and brightest. Who among you deserve to be accepted into my great military"

He allowed his thoughts to drift for a brief second, remembering a time when those words were true. General Moore held his hand up and dropped it. The choosing had begun. The two braziers flanking the finish line sprung to life, as leather hoods were slipped over the contestant's heads. The soldiers led their charges into the woods.

Teridon watched the procession of contestants until last horse disappeared into the woods. Once they were gone, he walked away, dispersing with the rest of the crowd. The contestants would be gone for hours, and he couldn't bear to wait around.

His head was a jumble of emotions: pain, frustration, depression, anxiety. Primarily, was the sense of disappointment, of opportunity squandered. Wanting nothing more than to crawl into a hole and die, he skulked away from the field.

***

Jakes shrugged and twisted his head, trying to dislodge the frustrating hood. He couldn't see anything, and the hard leather rubbing against his ears caused enough noise that he couldn't hear anything, either. His hands were tied to the horn of the saddle, so he had to concentrate to stay upright on the horse. He had no idea how long they rode before the horse stopped and he felt his hands being untied.

Once his hands were free, the soldier spoke, "You may take the hood off, please be careful when you get down."

Jakes untied the cord and slid the hood off. He looked around, assessing his situation. Slowly spinning the horse, he looked over the small clearing. There was a fire burning in the center, giving enough light to illuminate the whole circle. Next to the fire slouched a small canvas pack. He swung his leg over the horse and dismounted. Picking up the pack, he opened the top flap to find basic survival supplies: a spade, coil of rope, short knife, wire saw, flint and oiled twine, and, finally, an oiled cloak, in case it rained.

The soldier stood next to the horse, not saying a word, allowing Jakes time to inspect the clearing. His inspection did not take long. Once done, the soldier began the instructions, "Please stop me if you have any questions. This will be your only chance to ask. Once I am done giving these instructions, you will be on your own."

He paused briefly and when Jakes did not ask any questions, he continued, "You have until sunup to complete the course. If you don't complete it, for any reason, you will be disqualified. If no one completes the course, than there will be no candidates.

The top three finishers win the guaranteed positions. However, if anyone sufficiently impresses the general, or the knights, they can offer a position as well, providing you complete the course. Do you have any questions?"

"No, thank you, sir." Jakes replied, the rules had been explained during training and were straight forward. He grabbed a stick and wrapped the end with a small length of the oiled twine. He touched the stick to the fire, which merged with the twine and the torch flared to life. The solider stood silently holding the horses' lead. The final remnants of the sun winked out, night had fallen, "begin." The soldier said as he faded into the dark.

Jakes looked around again. The clearing had been cut into the forest with no markings or voids telling him where to go. He stood in the middle of a circle with no opening.

The fire's light made it impossible for him to see outside the clearing. There was just a black wall beyond the circle of light. The clearing had been raked clean and he spun once more, hoping to find a marking somewhere; there were none. Needing to focus, he closed his eyes and took a deep, slow, breath. Teridon had always been the act first think later type, while he was much more analytical and deliberate. Once his eyes opened his mind was clear. The moon was full, and its light should have lit the forest, like the night before.

He stared into the fire for a moment, the flames dancing and his eyes began to hurt. He realized that the fire and torch were the problem, or, more specifically, the light they were throwing.

The bright light was overwhelming the dim moonlight, and was destroying his night vision. He stamped out the fire and put out the torch, the darkness consumed him. He sat down, cross-legged, so his eyes to adjust to the dark without fear of tripping. It took a few minutes, but eventually the darkness gave way to the pale silver moonlight.

He could now see past the edge of the clearing. There was a path, but a strip of trees, about ten paces across, separated it from the clearing. The fire's light had prevented him from seeing it. He gathered the pack and started down the path. He moved quickly, but carefully. The last thing he needed was to break a leg because he was careless.

Like the clearing, the trees had been cleared from the path and it was raked smooth and clean. His eyes adjusted to the dark, the moon gave plenty of light and he began jogging, comfortable moving faster along the smooth path.

After a couple of more turns he came to a wooded stockade. His head was about a third of the way up the wall, so he estimated it to be fifteen feet high. Spanning the path, a spotter positioned to the right. He grabbed the knotted rope that hung in the center and pulled himself up. Once at the top, he turned on his stomach and dropped to the ground, landing heavily in the soft ground.

He faced a couple of more minor obstacles before he arrived at a large circular clearing, the same clearing he had seen with Teridon. Sir Shanin, one of the general's assistants, stood in the middle of the clearing, "Greetings Candidate. This will be a test of your swordsmanship. You were shown a series of sword forms. You must complete the forms to my satisfaction, before you may continue." There was a rack of swords next to the man. He grabbed one and sunk it in the ground between Jake's feet.

Jakes removed it from its earthen sheath, testing the weight and balance. It was a standard empirical short sword, thick and straight, the tip was a symmetrical triangle with a fine sharp point. The balance was decent, slightly heavy at the tip, as was common with this design. Taking a deep, steadying, breath, he assumed the starting position. His feet were together, the sword held on his left hip, like it was in a scabbard. Taking a step back, he assumed ready stance, right foot back and sword held out in front. After a brief pause, he began the forms. The first form was easy, it was in the shape of an 'I', with a parry and attack at each leg of the 'I'. The military had 15 mandatory forms. An instructor had taught all perspective candidates the series last fall, when the practice course was erected. Jakes had practiced them daily since. Firmly embedded in his muscle's memory, he was able to do them smoothly and without thinking.

Despite the chill air, he was dripping sweat as he completed the final form. By far the most complex, it was intended to simulate an attack by 6 attackers, with several rolls and balance tricks. He returned to the starting position once the form was complete, his chest heaving from the effort. He took a moment to gather his wind before he handed the sword to Sir Shanin, pommel first. The knight refused the sword, "You will need that, Candidate. Your forms were impressive; you may continue." The knight handed Jakes a scabbard.

Jakes started down the wide trail that led away from the clearing. He buckled the scabbard while jogging down the path.

Flashbacks assaulted him as he started up the incline where all the trouble began the night before. His stomach turned as he thought of Teridon and his friend's sacrifice. He pushed those to the side, He needed to focus. Quickly climbing the rise, pulling himself up the last part. He looked over the edge. His eyes had completely acclimated to the dark, and he had no problem seeing how high the cliff face was. It suddenly dawned on him.

One of the biggest tests was resisting the urge to light the torch. Had he done so, his eyes would have never adjusted, and navigating the course would be impossible. Everything was just a little too long, too high or too deep to see using the limited range of a torch.

There was no obvious way down the shear wall. Pawing through the pack, he pulled out the rope and spade, using the spade to dig a hole around the top log. The log was huge; he dug down two feet before reaching the bottom. Once he hit the next log, he found a gap and fished the rope under the log. Lying in the dirt, he was barely able to get his arm around it. After tying off the rope, he let it fall, uncoiling until it hit the ground. Checking to make sure it was secure, he started down.

He squeezed the rope between his legs and feet, sliding down using his hands to control the speed of descent. He slid slowly, not wanting to risk getting out of control. A fall from this height would break bones.

He looked up, the corona of torchlight shone over the edge. The pool of ligt growing until the torch bearer appeared. He locked eyes with Lueless, who stood holding a torch and glaring down at him. How did the boy get past the forms so quickly? He wasn't in the clearing when Jakes left.

Lueless stood straddling the rope, torch burning in one hand, the glint of steel in the other, "You stood there and let that trash embarrass me. You did nothing while lowborn trash assaulted me, I am your equal, not him. I won't be embarrassed like that, not without retribution. You don't deserve to win, Pints, you don't deserve the rewards.

You stand with trash, so you deserve to be trash. You're going to be stuck in this backwater hole with your trash friend."

Lueless swung down with the sword, the torchlight running across the blade as moved. Jakes started to yell as the rope went slack. He splashed into the shallow pool of water that had collected at the base of the wall.

His left arm was over his head when he landed, and sunk into the mud. Pain exploded from his shoulder and ribs. He tried to get up but couldn't breathe. Every attempt at drawing breath met with blinding pain. At least one rib was broken, maybe more. He tried to move his arm, but the pain radiating from his shoulder was excruciating.

He lay helplessly in the water as two contestants ran past. Their boots splashed water and mud into his eyes and mouth. Lueless looked down at him a spat as he ran by, the spittle landing in the puddle beside him. He had to move. He was hurt, badly, but lying in a pool of water was not going to fix his shoulder. He was going to be in pain no matter what. Grimacing, he stood. Once upright he found that he could not lift his arm; it hung uselessly at his side, pain radiating from his shoulder in pulsating waves. He had to block it out, and push through. He took a long steadying breath and continued down the path.

He arrived at a wooden tower. The next obstacle loomed. A rope ladder hung off the platform, and light shone from the series of platforms above, giving the illusion that they were floating in the sky. Jakes stood at the bottom of the ladder, which seemed like it went up forever. He could not lift his arm over his head, how would he get up this with one arm? Pushing the self-doubt away, he flexed his hand and found that his grip was strong\; though flexing his muscles shot a jolt of pain throughout his upper body. He needed to ignore the pain and move.

Bracing himself for the coming pain, he grabbed a rung and started up; using the bad arm to steady himself as he climbed with his good arm and legs. Pain wracked his upper body as he pulled himself onto the platform. There were torches at the four corners and a small brazier in the middle, the fires softly lighting the platform. He sat to warm himself by the brazier, allowing his shoulder to rest.

He sat until the pain subsided a bit. Floating off in the distance was the light of another platform, a narrow beam connecting the two. He put on foot out on the beam and then the other.

He teetered, not being able to hold his bad arm out for balance. After pausing to catch his balance, he started moving again, as carefully as possible.

His was heart was pounding; the line between success and failure was a 4 wooden beam, barely wider than his foot. After several nerve racking moments, he stepped onto the far platform, and was able to breathe again.

From a distance the two platforms looked the same, but once he was standing on the second platform, he found it to be much larger. Still lit with torches and a brazier, the light was only in the middle, the corners were cloaked in shadow.

The second knight, Sir Loorie, stood in the middle of the platform, next to the brazier, "Hello candidate. You have done well so far, and you have proven that you can remember forms, but do you have any real skill? We will find out. Candidate, defend yourself."

A soldier emerged from the shadows to his right. He stabbed at Jakes' midsection. Despite the sudden attack, calm washed over Jakes, a product of his training. He skipped backwards and drew his sword, snapping it up, easily blocking the soldier's clumsy thrust, while he sucked his gut in. Falling into a ready stance, he felt his balance and weight. His left side was back, hiding his useless arm. The soldier pulled back and swung with an overhand chop. He was baiting Jakes, trying to get him to block the strike, and allowing the larger man to overpower him. He had fought with Teridon enough to recognize the tactic.

The best defense against a strong, aggressive, opponent was to move, and use their aggressiveness against them. Standing and going toe to toe would get him killed.

Jakes slid to the left, avoiding the strike altogether. The move surprised the soldier, who was expecting an inexperienced opponent. The man had over-committed to the strike, expecting to be chopping through a block that did not materialize. Striking nothing but air, he was pulled completely off balance and stumbled forward as the tip of his sword sunk into the wood of the platform.

Skipping to the side, the soldier fell onto the embedded sword and the pommel drove the wind out of the man. The man doubled over and then crumpled onto his side, gasping for air. Jakes' sword hovered over the man's throat. The man's teeth were clenched and he was rolling in pain, he groaned, "yield."

The knight's eyebrows raised, "Very impressive, you may continue."

Jakes stood staring off into the darkness; the light on the platform had completely ruined his night vision. The only thing he saw was a rope tied at his feet, extending into the darkness. It was the only way down, so before he had a chance to think about his arm, he wrapped the rope around his good arm and jumped. The pressure on his arm increased as he reached the bottom of the swing, the pain finally forced him to release his grip.

Dust flew as he entered the deep pile of straw under the swing. Landing feet first, he crumbled as pain shot through his body when he hit the ground underneath. Straw caved in on him, and he fought to breathe as his nose filled with dust. Coughing and wheezing, he fought through the pile, using his good arm. The mass of straw felt like he pushed through thick mud. He could not muster enough strength with his injured arm to move the straw, so he had to muddle through with his good one. It took several minutes, but he was able to push through, falling out of the straw. He coughed a few times and was finally able to get his breath.

The path was ahead was clear, and he started to move. His night vision slowly came back, and he was able to quicken his pace as it did. There were no more obstacles, and it had become a race to the finish. With no idea how long he would have to run for, he set a moderate pace, one he could maintain if it was a long run. The path wound through the forest, the moon was still high and full, and Jakes easily followed the path.

His shoulder was burning with pain as he pumped his arms, but the excitement of finishing dulled it enough to make it bearable. He allowed his mind to clear and he focused on his breathing as he ran along the path. The ground was soft, giving slightly with each footfall.

He did not know how long he had run for, but he focused again when he saw points of light dancing in the distance. Normally, he was not the vindictive type, but with every stride, the pain in his shoulder reminded him of Lueless' treachery. He fought to keep himself under control as the anger welled up from deep inside. He was not Teridon, and had no desire to risk his future for the immediate satisfaction of revenge; winning despite Lueless' cheating would do be revenge enough.

He had been maintaining an easy pace since leaving the straw, but now he had extra incentive, and broke into a hard run; no longer interested in just finish in the top three, he was going to win. Two boys were casually trotting along, not expecting anyone to be close to them. With his pace, he easily caught them. Holding to the far left side of the path, Jakes ran right by the two.

"Get back here, Pints. You're not winning." Lueless yelled as he ran past.

Something small hit him in the center of his back; Lueless had probably thrown a rock. Chuckling at the boy's pettiness, he focused on his breath, and pulling away from his competitors.

He kept the torrid pace for a while, he estimated about a mile, before slowing back down to the easy jog he had maintained earlier. Lueless was long in his dust and he could focus on finishing without burning out. He wanted to maintain some energy in case he needed a burst at the end. A halo of light outlined the treetops, dawn's glow had appeared, and time was running short. He had to finish by daybreak.

He had been running most of the night, his energy beginning to wane and adrenalin had started failing. He was starting to feel every ache, cringe at every pain. His injured ribs were tightening like a corset, and sharp pain was radiating from his shoulder with ever footfall. Breath labored and body racked with pain, he was pushing towards failure.

As he was about to fall, the trail opened. The glow from those giant braziers lit the finish line.

The finish line in sight, he felt the last rush of energy surge; he used it to push through the last part. General Moore stood just beyond the finish line. Jakes stumbled across and collapsed at his feet. He fought to catch his breath through broken ribs and the cold air. General Moore greeted him with a warm smile, "Congratulations!" He turned to the crowd and announced, "YOUR WINNER", the small crowd, which had returned to see the finish, applauding.

Lueless came running across the finish line to see the applauding crowd, General Moore standing over Jakes. He slowed and glared at the boy. Jakes slowly turned to look at him; returning that glare with a warm grin, which infuriated him.

Despite the pain and injuries, Jakes had fought through and beat Lueless, cheating and all. That was the sweetest revenge, his warm smile was genuine, the fact that it irritated Lueless was just a welcome benefit.

General Moore crouched to help Jakes to his feet. His side had completely tightened up and he was could not stand straight. The general helped him stand, "What is your name, son?"

Jakes stretched, trying to straighten up and meet his new commander, but, despite his effort, he could not, his side had completely tightened. He did manage to spit out his name, "Jacob Pints, sir."

General Moore put his arm around Jakes' shoulders, helping to support him, "Recruit Pints, welcome, you have shown yourself to have the raw abilities to be a valuable addition. It is my pleasure to offer you a position with the Aragonian Military, if you will accept." Jakes was overcome, it finally hit him that he had won and would be joining the military. For a brief moment, he forgot the pain, "It will be my honor, sir." He never even gave his father's request a second thought.

General Moore narrowed his eyes, noticing that Jakes' arm was hanging, "What happened to your arm son?"

Jakes looked over at Lueless and glared, before turning back to the general, "I slipped sir."

Assessing the injury, "Go see the company doctor, Recruit, Get that taken care of. I don't think anything is broken, but you definitely your shoulder reset. I doubt there is much they can do for your ribs, unfortunately."

"Thank you sir, I will go right away." Jakes walked away with a spring in his step, as much as he could muster. But he could not help his emotions; he had beaten the game and that cheating prick. He was ecstatic.

General Moore waved Aelin over, "make sure that the boys are ready to leave tomorrow. Also, please gather Sirs Loorie and Shanin. Then send them to me." The protocol officer nodded and ran off towards the woods to collect the knights from their posts.

Chapter 11

A large lump was leaned against the platform at the finish, covered in a traveling cloak. Jakes did not need to ask who it was. Déjà vu answered the question before it was asked. He ripped the cloak; Teridon was under it, fast asleep.

He gently shook his friend's shoulder, beginning the agonizingly slow process of waking his friend. Teridon cracked his neck, uncoiled his body, and stood, stretching his hands over his head and rising up onto his toes to stretch his legs. His eyes were half open, voice heavy with sleep, "what happened? Is it over?"

Jakes' face lit up, huge smile plastered on his face, "I won! And, even better, I beat Lueless too!"

The same giant smile flashed across Teridon's face. Then, he saw Jakes' arm hanging limply at his side. The smile vanished and Teridon's jaw clenched, any trace of happiness left his face, "what happened?"

Jakes tried to relay the story calmly, knowing his friend's temper, he did not want this to escalate, "Lueless cut a rope that I was climbing down, I fell 15 or 20 feet off that ramp from the other night. He tried to handicap me, but it didn't work. I still beat him."
Rage flared in Teridon's eyes, Jakes quickly tried to calm his friend, "don't! Don't cause any more trouble for yourself. I won; he cheated and lost, what could be better?" He knew Jakes was right, Lueless will get his someday.

***

The two friends split up. Jakes headed towards the companies' doctor, while Teridon walked home, exhausted and needing sleep. His small nap had not satisfied his needs. Trudging along the road, each footfall was heavier than the last. Weaving as he walked, he was unsure if it was the exhaustion, depression, or a combination of both, that was affecting his equilibrium.

He was too lost in his thoughts to care. This was the end. His future had forked from Jakes' and there was nothing he could do about it. Teridon's hood was pulled tight around his head, the sun was out and the day was starting to heat up, but he did not care, he wanted to hide, and his hood was the only cover he had right now.

A couple of horses passed at a gallop, he could not care less who was riding them, and he never even looked up. Sunlight was filtering through the treetops, casting shadows on the gray road. Head heavy, he let iut hang and stared at the road, shadows and light alternated as he walked along. The sunlight coming from the side hurt his eyes, so he pulled his hood tighter and lower.

As he did, his hand brushed his bruised face. The resulting sting reminded him of his poor choices. Over the years he had heard so many clichés that would seem to apply to this situation: tomorrow is a new day; if it doesn't kill, it hardens you; never stop moving forward, there is always light at the end of the tunnel. He was trying to think of one that would help him feel better, but drew a blank. It may be a new day, but it sure didn't feel like it was a new start.

***

The Doctor latched the wooden mechanism around Jake's arm, "grab the bar. This is going to be painful, but don't let go until I say, if you do we will have to start over."

The mechanism was a box, open on two sides; about three feet long and had several leather straps along the length. It was attached to a table and had a long corkscrew that ended with the metal bar. He sat on a low stool; his arm was forced out straight, directly in front of him. The doctor's assistant, a boy who looked about 14, moved to behind him, and wrapped his arms around Jakes' shoulders.

Jakes took a deep breath and grasped the bar. The doctor nodded to the assistant, and the boy's grip tightened around his shoulders. The doctor cranked the mechanism with a sudden movement, wrenching Jakes' arm and pulling it out.

Pain shot through his upper body as the doctor cranked, again using a fast, jerking, movement. Jakes screamed, the doctor cranked again, his arm was pulled farther away from his body while the assistant was pulling backwards, away from the device. One last crank and his shoulder popped then fell back into place. The doctor reversed the crank, releasing the tension, and the pain slowly subsided.

The doctor started to unbuckle the mechanism, while giving instructions, "You will feel better today, but the pain will return tomorrow, probably worse. Your arm needs to be immobile for a few days, until the swelling subsides. After that, you need to take it easy."

He took out a length of cloth and tied it around Jake's neck, a pouch hung by his chest, "That is a sling; it will take the weight of your arm off the shoulder. You have to rest the joint."

Jakes headed home after leaving the Doctor. He was heading for the real pain, telling his father that he was joining the military, not running the smithy. His father was going to be furious. He walked slowly, trying to stretch the trip home for as long possible. His father was not home, he let out a long sigh of relief. Every last bit of his energy was drained, he dropped heavily to his bed, and sleep came quickly.

***

A knock on the door snapped him awake, how long had he been sleeping? He watched the door swing open through heavy eyes. His father walked into the room, "Hello son, I heard about your performance and it was impressive. I don't know why you bothered competing, but that's your choice, I suppose."

His head was still fogged with exhaustion. He took a second to gather his thoughts. This subject needed to be handled delicately, "Father, there is no easy way to say this, so I am just going to say it. I have decided to join the military.

I know that turning the shop over to me is important to you, but I will never have this chance again. I needed to seize it."

He was expecting a backhand from his father. He cringed, but no slap came, there was no response at all. He continued with a little more confidence, "I am afraid that if I don't I will regret it for the rest of my life. Father, How can I run the business if I am bitter towards it?"

He had assumed his father was going to be furious. But, that fury that never came. His father sat down on the bed, looking defeated but not angry, "This is no shock, son. Once I heard about your performance, I knew you were leaving. If I am being honest with myself, I cannot blame you.

The life of a small town blacksmith pales when compared to an officer in the military. You are wise when you say that you cannot run a business if you are bitter towards it. Son, you have my blessing, with one caveat."

"What's that father?"

"When your commission is completed, you will come back here, and take over the business."

Jakes tried to be honest, even if lying would make things easier. One can never know what the future held, so he wouldn't completely dismiss coming back, but he could not commit either, "I promise I will consider it dad."

His father nodded, appearing to respect his honesty, "I guess I can't ask for more than that. Good luck son."

"Thank you, father!" Jakes was overcome with emotion; his father had just taken his last doubt away. He was going to be an officer in the Aragonian Military, and he would do so with his father's blessing.

Chapter 12

Teridon's breath caught in his throat when he arrived home and saw the horses tied up outside the cottage. Panic welled up from his gut, Lord Baelin had changed his mind; they were here to arrest him. His instincts screamed for him to run, but he just didn't have the will anymore, his shoulders slumped and he continued up the walk. Not wanting to make things worse by showing disrespect, he slid the hood off his head and let it fall around his neck.

Not wanting to let these men see a beaten, broken man, he stood straighter, pulled his shoulders back, stopped shuffling his feet, and began striding with purpose again. His stomach knotted as the front door swung open, he suddenly began doubting this decision. But, his choice was made, there was no running now; though, it took every ounce of will to keep walking and ignore the voice in his head screaming, '*get away, get away, RUN YOU FOOL.*'

The back of his jaw tightened as one of General Moore's knights walked out of the cottage. Sir Nidan Loorie stopped to face him, and he braced himself, preparing to be arrested. Standing face to face with Teridon, Sir Loorie leaned close and examined the bruise on Teridon's face, letting out a low whistle, "Are you Teridon Jace?"

Teridon looked down to meet the shorter knight's gaze, determined to show the knight he was physically beaten but not broken. Teridon grimaced as the knight traced along the border of the bruise, along his chin, "Let me ask you a question, Mr. Jace. Why did were you so upset when Lord Baelin banned you from the choosing?"

Teridon lifted an eyebrow, what a stupid question, "Why wouldn't I be? I had trained for months and I wanted to run."

Sir Loorie shook his head, "That's not what I was asking, son, let me be more specific; why did you want to join the military?"

"I wanted to be a soldier sir; joining the military was my dream. For most, it is a means to an end, but I actually wanted to be a soldier. I wanted to be a ranger. I had worked so hard for it, but had it snatched away because I was stupid."

Sir Loorie smiled, a wide hearty smile that lit up the man's face, "That was the answer I wanted to hear. I am going to be blunt; almost no one joins the military to be a soldier anymore.

People join thinking that military duty is prancing around with pretty clothes, playing with swords and getting women. That attitude does not forge men or breed true soldiers, it breeds, soft, undisciplined boys. Those soft boys end up serving in situations that require hard men. Our military has suffered, greatly, because of this attitude. There is going to come a time that we will need to actually fight a war, and that if things continue, that war will be short lived."

Why was the man telling him all this? Did it excite him to waive Teridon's failure before him? Make him twist in the wind before he arrested him?

'Just arrest me and get it over with, you prick.'

"You broke the law, son." Teridon braced himself, here it comes, "But, while doing so, it took three trained soldiers to subdue you, and only after giving those three all they could handle. You have no formal training, yet you were able to take down three trained veterans. You have a natural aptitude for the fight, son, I can see it in the way you move. Your attitude is what the military is missing." Hope flooded into Teridon, was Sir Loorie offering him a position?

"I fought for you, boy. I tried to get a position for you, but General Moore is shortsighted and would rather play wet nurse to a bunch of pampered nobles than to be the hammer that forges true soldiers."

Teridon's hopes cratered, the brief respite from his self-loathing was over. His actions of the other night would haunt him for the rest of his life.

"Unfortunately, Mr. Jace, Lord Baelin's sentence will stand. You have been banned from the choosing, which means you are banned from the military. Still, I think it's disgusting to see talent wasted, especially given the dreck that we have recruited, so I come to you with a proposal, become my squire. This is not an easy way out, mind you; you will have training every bit as hard as your peers; the work of a squire will be on top of your schooling and martial training.

I have already asked your mother, and she has given her blessing. Please, think on it; if you want to accept, please meet me at the muster grounds at sun up tomorrow morning. If you are not there, I will assume you have declined; the offer will not be extended again."

Sir Loorie mounted his horse and spurred it down the road at a gallop the two other riders matching the knights pace. Teridon stood in a cloud of dust, stunned but exhausted. The range of emotions that the last several minutes had dragged him through had sapped the last of his strength. His mother ran up, she had tears welling in the corners of her eyes; he collapsed into her arms. She took a step back, he outweighed her by a good portion and she was barely able to hold him up. "What happened to you?" she lightly touched his face.

Before he could answer, she did, "It's OK, Sir Loorie explained what happened, I understand. You have to go; I will not have you stay here for me."

"Thank you." was all Teridon could say before walking into the house and collapsing onto his bed. His mother sat at the kitchen table and began to cry. Not tears of sadness but tears of joy, her son was going to be something.

Chapter 13

Teridon was already waiting when Sir Loorie arrived at the muster grounds, a huge field just outside of Barnstable proper. The engineers and recruits were mulling around, making final preparations before they left for the empirical capital, Capuamundi. Sir Loorie stood across the field giving orders to several people loading a wagon. Not wanting to give the man an opportunity to change his mind, he ran, "Sir Loorie, it would be my honor to squire for you, I cannot thank you enough for this opportunity, sir, and I promise that you will not regret this."

The knight was seemed genuinely pleased, "Excellent! There is no better time to start than now. My equipment is in the wagon behind me, please make sure it is packed and secured. You will be riding alongside our stage."

"Yes sir!" Teridon ran over to the wagon and inspected the bindings: he pulled on the thick hemp ropes, they were taught; he inspected the tie down points, they were secure; He inspected the axle and wheels, the bearings were greased and there was no visible damage; everything appeared to be in order. Satisfied with his inspection, Teridon pulled the oiled canvas tarp over the load and secured it at the four corners, then ran back to Sir Loorie, who stood next to the general's black stage.

A small, odd looking, animal stood grazing next to the stage. It appeared to be a horse, but it had short, fat, legs; curly hair, and was longer than it was tall. He was unsure what to make of it. It did have a saddle, so it was meant to be ridden.

"What is that?"

Sir Loorie absently replied without turning, "It is a horse." He immediately regretted his flippant response. The boy probably never had seen an ambler. Most country folk could not afford one horse, forgetting about the luxury of two, "It is an ambler, my boy. It is bred for long distance riding, just as sure as a charger is bred for battle. The breed has a fourth gait, ambling, that makes long distance riding much more comfortable. Plus, a war horse is far too valuable to exhaust, so we don't use them for transportation. Anyway, I will be inside the stage and you will be riding alongside, so this horse is for your comfort."

"Yes sir. Thank you."Since Teridon would be riding the animal, he started checking it like any other horse, making sure the girth was tight, the shoes were secure and the bridal was properly fastened. Teridon finished his checks when Jakes came up, "Hi T, did you come to see us of?"

"No, Sir Loorie offered me a squire position. I accepted this morning! He was impressed with the way I fought and thought that I should have been given a chance. He couldn't convince Baelin or the general to loosen the sentence, so he did the only thing he could, and offered me a job squiring for him."

Jakes was swaying back and forth like he did when he was excited, "That is incredible! I can't believe that we are going together, after all."

"Not quite, I will be working and training on Sir Loorie's estate. I'm not sure if I will be able to get out to the Forge. It's all up to Sir Loorie."

That did nothing to squelch his friend's excitement, "This is incredible. I am sure we will see each other."

They were shaking hands when cold water was dumped on them. Lueless rode up, mounted on a striking black and white speckled stallion. He did not acknowledge Teridon, speaking past him and directly to Jakes, "We are about to move out, Pints. The commanders want us back to the wagons."

Lueless could not resist a jab at Teridon, "Here to clean up after we leave, Terry? One of the general's draft horses took a giant shit, I suggest you start there. Hurry, before the pile starts to harden."

Nothing Lueless could say would get him to risk his new position, "I am here on behalf of Sir Loorie, Patrick. Maybe you know him? He is one of your commanders. I am a member of his staff, and acting under his order." He kept a calm, even, tone, not wanting to escalate the situation.

Lueless laughed, "You weaseled your way in, huh? Well whether a servant for a knight, or servant for a minor country lord, it doesn't matter, you are still a servant. So go get me a drink of water, boy."

Jakes tensed, ready to grab Teridon. To his surprise, however, Teridon just turned and walked away. It took about an hour for the entire company to form up.

Once the general was satisfied everything was ready, the column started out, moving with fits and starts.

Teridon mounted the odd little horse, his feet were barley off the ground, but Sir Loorie was right, it was extremely comfortable to ride. It was not fast, but it was extremely smooth, just as Sir Loorie had promised.

Barnstable had been the last stop on the recruiting circuit, so the column would be heading to Aragonian military's training headquarters, the Forge. Sir Loorie's little portion of the column, however, would be heading to the knight's estate, outside of the capital city, Capuamundi.

Chapter 14

The first days out of Barnstable were filled with excitement. Teridon had expected squiring would be hard work, but he was used to that. What he had not known, however, was how much he needed to learn: he had never actually fed or watered a horse, had never sharpened a sword, never had to polish and oil armor, among other things. He had to learn all of these skills, and fast. They were all duties he was expected to perform. In addition, he was expected to set up Sir Loorie's camp at night and pack it up in the morning. Typically, he was up before Sir Loorie and to sleep long after. Still, it was amazing to be out of the prison that was Barnstable.

***

The sun was well past its zenith, on the third day out from Barnstable, when column ground to a halt for their afternoon rest. The break gave the soldiers a chance to stretch their legs and water the horses. As soon as the column stopped, Teridon jumped off his horse and ran to the supply wagon, grabbing the folded travel bench. He unfolded the bench in front of the stage door, pushing it into the ground, then placing a water skin and beef jerky on the bench. Whenever the column stopped, he was expected to make sure that Sir Loorie was comfortable before taking care of his own needs.

The door of the black lacquered stage opened, followed by the general and two knights. Sir Loorie waved one of the staff squires ran over. The knight leaned in and whispered something to the boy, who ran off.

Sir Loorie walked over to a supply wagon, and pulled two wooden training swords out of it, and waived him over, "I promised that you would be more than just a squire, and you would be given proper schooling as well as a soldier's training. Before we begin, though, I need to see your skills. I know you are big and strong, but not much else."

He flipped the sword to Teridon, who made a clumsy attempt to catch it. His hands clapped together just after the sword fell through them. The sword hit the ground and bounced, the hardwood making high pitched cracking sounds as it bounced from tip to hilt and back off of the stone road surface.

Sir Loorie rolled his eyes when Teridon took his eyes of him, and bent to pick up the sword, '*Have I made a mistake? Had the boy had just gotten lucky that night?*' The boy seemed to be an uncoordinated mess right now.

'*Too late now*' he thought. He attacked with a simple overhead swing. Teridon picked up the sword and raised it just in time to block the strike, but he paid a price.

Holding the sword tightly and parallel to the ground, he bore the full brunt of the strike's impact. Vibrations flowed through the sword and up his arms. His hands went number and it was all he could do just hold on the 'blade'. Teridon flexed his hands, trying to get feeling back into them.

The knight advanced on him, faking low with a short thrust. Teridon completely fell for the feint, stabbing to the knight's undefended face. Sir Loorie bobbed his head, easily avoiding the clumsy stab. The knight slid inside the Teridon's outstretched arm, throwing a short punch his ribs. He pulled his elbow in tight to his ribs in response. Sir Loorie kept moving closer. He drove his elbow into the center of Teridon's back, using his weight to put more power behind it. The force drove the boy to one knee. Sir Loorie moved to finish him, sliding behind his kneeling form.

Throwing the sword away, Teridon rolled forward; barely avoiding the knight's thrust at the back of his neck. He rolled over, looped his leg behind Sir Loorie's knees and kicked across the front of the man's hips with his other leg. He flipped his hips over as he rolled with the knight. Sir Loorie doubled over, while Teridon pushed up for more leverage. His weight, combined with the leverage, slammed the knight to the ground. Continuing his roll, Teridon mounted the man with a cocked fist.

Sir Loorie held his hands to the side, "I Yield! Well, you certainly can fight with your hands, but have you ever fought with a sword? Your technique was rudimentary, at best, and you made very basic errors, starting with trying to catching it by the blade and looking down to pick the weapon up."

Teridon stood and helped Sir Loorie to his feet. He looked away, not wanting to see the wealthy knight's judgment as he responded, "No sir, we could never afford one. I used a machete to practice for the choosing, but only the forms, I never fought anyone."

Sir Loorie's eyes softened, his expression showing concern, "Are you embarrassed, son?"

Teridon responded with a slight nod, embarrassment was probably written across his face. There was no need to call further attention to it. The knight grasped his shoulders and looked straight into Teridon's eyes, gravity in his voice, "Don't be, don't ever be embarrassed by humble roots, embrace them, use them. You may feel embarrassed, you may want to hide them, I am sure you were teased by the rich kids, made to feel less than them. But, unlike them, your roots are strong, resilient. Those kids have never struggled. They've been coddled and waited on their whole lives. Their roots are built on a foundation of mud. They are a tree that can be uprooted by a small wind. You, on the other hand, have already weathered many storms. Your roots deep and strong, those roots will carry you through future storms. And make no mistake, my boy, there will be future storms. Think on that son. I think that's enough for today."

"Yes sir!" Teridon had never thought of things like that, he loved the tree analogy. He could barely contain his excitement. Sir Loorie was going to keep his promise and train him. Also, for the first time in his life, he was not embarrassed about his station in life, all because of the knight's speech. He was ready to work hard and change it, but would never again hide from it. He wanted to tell Jakes what had happened but that was impossible.

The recruits were in the back of the procession, and were not allowed to speak with anyone outside of their ranks. Instead, he redoubled his efforts at his own duties. Sir Loorie returned to the stage while Teridon finished watering his horse, then cleaned up after the knight. He was putting the bench back in the wagon when General Moore returned from checking on the recruits. He gave the signal for the company to move, and then disappeared inside the stage, slamming the door behind him. Teridon raced to his horse, as the column started moving again.

Chapter 15

Dark, angry, clouds loomed in the distance. Thier tall, anvil shaped, tops flashed with light and thunder clapped faintly in the distance. The company was heading towards nasty weather. The recruits rode in covered wagons, separate from the rest of the train. About forty recruits were spread through 10 cramped, but reasonably comfortable, wagons. If they did hit weather, they could to close the side shutters, which would keep the wagons, mostly, dry. Jakes shared a wagon with his fellow Barnstable recruits, Lueless and Robert Marve. Rob was the third recruit from Barnstable, and was Lueless' only friend in the town. The boy was friendly enough, and Jakes never could figure out why he was friends with Lueless, but he was, and he didn't hold it against him. Thunder cracked louder, sounding like it was overhead. There was no longer any question; they were going to roll into the heart of that storm. It was not surprising, storms were frequent in the spring and, up until now, and the weather had been benign.

Jakes and Rob sat in their bunks, which doubled as benches during the day. They were making small talk while Lueless kept to himself. The two talked of what they were going to do in the military, school, growing up in Barnstable, what they wanted to do in the future, anything to pass the time. Lueless, however, complained, when he bothered to speak at all.

The wagon shuddered as it stopped for the afternoon break. Jakes and Rob got out of the wagon to tend the horses. They had been given protocol books to study when they were moving, and they were expected to tend to their wagon and horses when stopped for breaks. Then, when they stopped for the night, they had to set up camp and cook their own food.

Jakes tended the horses, while Rob inspected the wagon. Lueless, as usual, stayed in the wagon, the work was beneath him.

A light rain began falling, and they started to rush to finish before the storm really hit. Jakes watered and fed the horses while Rob fetched the driver's rain gear from the supply wagon.

The wagon still needed to be inspected and they needed help or they would not get it done before the torrent was upon them. Rob had enough; he ripped the wagon door open, "are you planning on helping? Or are you going to sit on your ass while we get soaked?"

Lueless was reading, he did not bother to put the book down, "Help with what?" Rob did not have time or patience to play Lueless' games, "I need to get the driver's rain gear. I don't have time to inspect the wagon. Get off your ass and help."
Lueless threw the book, "fine, whatever."

Rob ran off the get the driver's rain gear, leaving Lueless to do the inspection. Rob handed the oiled cloak up to the driver just in time for the skies to open up. He ran to back to the shelter of the wagon, slamming the door as sheets of rain began to fall. The wagon groaned as it lurched into motion. Rain hammered on the wagon's wooden roof. They settled onto their bunks to read about the fascinating subject of Aragonian Military protocol, they needed to pass a few hours until stopping for the night. The roads made travel in this weather passible, there was no worry about mud and they drained well because of a slight crown in the road's surface.

Travel time was slow and boring. The books they were studying did not help the time go any faster. Lueless, as was his custom, used the large book to shade his eyes as he engaged in his favorite activity, napping. The rain had calmed from a torrent, settling into a steady drumbeat on the wagon's roof. Jakes was trying to read but between the rhythm of the rain, the slight rocking of the wagon and the dryness of the book, He found himself getting lulled to sleep.

His eyes were heavy, and he leaned against the wall, concentrating on the vibrations of the road and the sound of the rain, he began to fall asleep.

Those eyes snapped open. There was a strange creaking, followed by a thump. He looked at Rob,

"What was that?"

Rob was looking around, he heard it as well. He shook his head and gave him a shrug, not knowing what it was either. Jakes leaned back against the wall. Suddenly, the wagon lurched to the right and ground to a stop. He was thrown across the wagon, into Lueless' lap.

A terrible screech vibrated around them, the metal axe scraping on the stone road sent chills down his spine. He looked out the window; the front wheel was rolling across the road. He stared as the wheel slowed and fell over.

Jakes turned on Lueless, "I thought you checked the wagon."

"I did!" Lueless snapped back, though he did not make eye contact with either of them.

"YOU LYING SACK!" Jakes yelled as he dove across the wagon. Rob grabbed him as he did, pulling him back before he was able to grab Lueless.

"Jakes, stop! This isn't helping, we need to get this repaired, and he isn't worth getting expelled."

Jakes gathered himself, "you're right, we'll deal with you later."

He pulled on his cloak and left the wagon, still trying to calm himself. He silently thanked Rob for intervening. Fights between candidates were forbidden and were grounds for dismissal. Lueless rolled his eyes and lay back down. If he cared about Jakes' anger, he gave no sign of it.

***

Jakes, and Rob, found the driver already working on the wheel. They had gotten lucky, the wheel was remained intact. The bearing had failed and needed to be repacked and repaired. It was a basic repair, had they needed to rebuild the wheel, they would have fallen a couple of hours behind, at a minimum.

The wheel was flat on the ground, and the driver was already working on repacking the bearing with grease.

A repair wagon had stopped behind them. The driver asked Jakes to get an apparatus from it. The driver had called it a jack. It was large hardwood block with a long, thick, wooden corkscrew sticking out of the top. The two boys set the jack up under the axle and started to spin it until the weight of the wagon was on it.

Once the jack bore the wagon's weight, it took all their strength to raise the massive wagon. Jakes and Rob stood opposite each other, each holding a long metal handle. They pushed with all they had to get the jack to spin. After several turns of the crank, the wagon was high enough that the wheel could be reattached. Once the wheel was on, the driver hammered a long iron pin into the axle, securing it again.

They lowered the jack, holding their breath as the wagon's weight transferred back onto the wheel and repaired hub. Once the driver was satisfied with the repair, he thanked them and climbed back into his seat. Snapping the reigns, the two draft horses started away. Both Jakes and Rob returned to the wagon wet and angry. Lueless was inside, napping.

***

The column traveled along the Ring Road, which wound all the way around the world's largest lake, Lake Nemi, passing several cities on its journey around the massive body of water. The most important city along the Ring Road, and in the empire, was the Empirical capital, Capuamundi. Teridon saw the city for the first time just after sun up. The city was built on a solitary hill and was surrounded by a flat plane on three sides and the lake on the fourth. It was easily visible across the corner of the lake, even though they were miles away. They would not actually arrive at the city until tomorrow, and that was if the moved quickly.

Teridon had never been outside Barnstable and could not take his eyes off the huge city. As the procession wound towards the city more and more details revealed themselves, and he was in awe. The hill was tall and fat, with a perfectly flat summit. The city began, millennia ago, as a fortress built on the summit. It had spilled down the hill as it grew, engulfing it as moved down.

The focal point of the summit, especially from a distance, were the two large spires of the Kethi-Draal, the Aragonian Empire's seat of government and the only building that still stood from the original fortress. They continued along the ring road. As they rounded the lake, the sun's reflection off the top of the spires seemed to follow him. It was like the shaft of light was aimed right at him, and someone was moving it to keep it there.

***

It was well past the midday break when Sir Lorrie's small portion of the Column broke away. They turned at an intersection while the rest continued towards the city, though they would only pass it on the way to the Forge.

Once they separated from the smells and sounds of the column, Teridon was able to feel the warm gentle breeze as it traveled across the slightly rolling plain.

The smell of wildflowers wafted on that breeze, reminding him how different the climate was, away from Barnstable. He was much further south; spring came to the area long before the northern territories.

They followed the small road away from the intersection, moving away from Capuamundi. Teridon lingered behind the wagons and attendants, taking in the sights, sounds, and smells of his new home.

***

Dusk had almost turned to twilight when it rounded the last hill and Teridon saw the estate. He had been expecting something like Lord Baelin's, which was the largest home he had ever seen, but Sir Loorie's home made Lord Baelin's look like it was the little cabin that Teridon had grown up in. It was built, primarily, out of light grey stone, and was at least twice the size of Lord Baelin's manor. The only wood used was for the window sashes, the doors, and decoration. Teridon was amazed by the building's large windows. The buildings up north had small windows, if any at all. They obviously were not as concerned with winter in the south. This building would have been impossible to heat in a northern winter.

As he continued towards the manor, farm fields stretched out on either side, continuing off farther than he could see. The grounds were breathtaking, even at dusk. The fields were perfectly laid out, and they had enough land to use crop rotation, there were fields that were not being worked, there were fields growing peas and there were fields growing staple crops. The field unworked field was allowed to lie fallow so it could replenish its nutrient.

It was the most modern farming technique in use, but Teridon had only heard about it. In Barnstable, fields were cut out of the woods and there were not enough farmland to allow any fields to lay fallow, all land needed to be producing or people would starve.

It struck him, and not for the first time, how different the land was in the south. The surrounding terrain was, primarily, rolling grass lands, and there were very few trees. This was a stark contrast to Barnstable, which was cut out of the world's largest forest. The small procession rounded an immaculately manicured circular green, stopping in front of the manor house. They were greeted by stable boys and servants, who tended the horses and began unloading the wagons.

Sir Loorie chuckled off to his side, "Close your mouth, Son, follow me." Doing as he was bid, Teridon followed him into the house.

They were greeted in the foyer by an older, but still beautiful, woman and boy, who looked to be about Teridon's age. Sir Loorie moved to stand next to the tall blonde woman. His chest was out his and his chin was high, he was obviously proud of his home and family, "Allow me to present my wife, Elizabeth Loorie."

Teridon bowed in greeting. As was custom when meeting someone of higher station, he made sure to avert his eyes. Sir Loorie moved and put his hand around the boy's shoulder, "This is my son, Krystoph."

As Krystoph and Teridon were of similar ages, a more familiar greeting was customary. Krystoph held out his hand, "Please, call me Krys."
Teridon firmly grasped the outstretched hand with a smile, "Teridon, I am so happy be here and happy to meet you, Krys."

Krys was several inches shorter than Teridon and significantly smaller in stature, with a doughy physic. His soft face and double chin made him look several years younger than Teridon, despite being a year older. He wore a short sword at his hip, but did not wear it comfortably. He held his arm away from the sword, looking if he was afraid to even touch the weapon. From the awkward way he carried the sword to his physic, pale skin and soft hands, Teridon guessed he was an academic not a soldier.

Introductions completed, Sir Loorie spoke again, "Krys, please show Teridon the house and grounds, and then get him set up in one of the guest bedrooms. Make sure he has clothes, boots and anything else he came lacking."

"Yes sir." Krys waved Teridon along, and left the foyer.

Teridon followed him up the large central staircase. The landing at the top of the stair overlooked the foyer, and hallways extended off to the left and right. Dark wooden doors broke up the white stucco walls, on both sides of both halls.

Krys led him to the end of the right hall, motioning to the door at the end, "Here's your room, get unpacked, Tomorrow we'll get started. Make me a list of things you need, I'll gather them tomorrow."

Continuing the trend of the day, Teridon was at a loss for words, he nodded dumbly in response. The room was the same size as his entire cottage in Barnstable.

An oak writing desk stood on the far wall and a large wardrobe standing next to it. Both were stained the same dark color as the door.

A wash basin, chamber pot, and a mirror were off to his right; to his left was the bed, a real bed, with a feather mattress. Anxious to try a real bed, he washed and went to sleep, choosing to sleep naked so he could feel the soft cotton bedding on his skin.

Chapter 16

The company arrived at Fort Martel, the Aragonian military's training compound. The fort was named after the founder of the modern Aragonian military, the great general, Charles Martel. Very few people knew the fort's real name, however, it was known throughout the empire by its nickname, the Forge; a play on the symbol of the military, the hammer. The wagons were queued up at the fort's gate, the candidates were being checked in, one wagon at a time. A pattern began, wait a few minutes, inch forward, wait some more, move again, wait, move, wait.

The three boys from Barnstable were in one of the last wagons in line, so there was nothing for them to do but wait their turn. Jakes' stomach was knotted with anxiety and anticipation. Anxiety always rose from the unknown, and there was nothing more unknown that what waited behind that tall stockade fence with the sharpened tips. The wait was not helping, either, it gave him time to think, and in this case, thinking was a detriment. He tried to focus on anything but the waiting, there was a nice breeze, the wildflowers had begun to bloom, and it was warm, a perfect spring day. But, none of that took his mind of what lay ahead.

Every time he tried to think about something else, his thoughts immediately shifted back to the unknown. What would the training entail? Would he be a good soldier? Had he made the right choice leaving Barnstable and giving up the smithy? The wait allowed his thoughts to wander and his anxiety began to peak.

About ten feet tall, the sharpened tips of the stockade loomed over them as they moved towards the wall, one wagon length at a time. The wicked tips were intended to keep the recruits in, not repel attack. The fort was located in the heart of the empire, and the chances of attack were remote, if any at all.

***

They waited another hour, or so, before their wagon rolled through the gate. Up close, they were able to see that it was actually two gates. The outer gate was two large wooden doors that were swung open to either side of the road. The inner gate looked like the same two doors, but they swung into the fort. They rolled inside, stopping at closed inner gate.

The outer gate slamming shut behind them, it did not make much noise, but the doors sealing shut vibrated the wagon.A clerk entered the carriage, carrying a large, leather bound, book, "Names."

"Jacob Pints."

The clerk flipped through the book, until he found Jake's name. Nodding, he looked at Lueless.

Amazingly, Lueless was able to reply without sneering, "Patrick Lueless." Again, the clerk leafed through the book, nodding after he found Lueless' name. He turned to Rob.

"Robert Marve, sir."

Finding Rob in the book, he gave them their assignment, "You will be in assigned to Sergeant Hilgley, 12th training regimen." The clerk just exited the carriage and the wagon started to move again. That was it. There was no pomp, no flair.

***

The wagon creaked and groaned as it stopped in front of the purser's hall. Jakes was staring out of the shutters, taking it all in, when the wagon's door was ripped open, and their commander entered, his heavy footfalls vibrated the benches. Sargent Hilgley was adorned in dress black leather armor with black pants, bracers, and greaves; a silver cape hung from his shoulders. The black leather was offset by polished metal buckles. The sword that hung at his side was not the standard military short sword; it was a four foot long hand and a half sword.

"MOVE"

His beard was down to his chest, and the curly hairs were thick enough that the bottom moved with his mouth when he was yelling. The man was intimidating; enough that even Lueless to move with purpose.

He actually ran out of the wagon. Outside the wagon, Jakes and Rob stood at attention, waiting for orders. Lueless, however, had not studied the protocol books. He tried to follow the other boys' lead but could not emulate their movements with any great accuracy. His feet were apart, his salute was sloppy, and his posture was terrible.

"Go inside and get outfitted!" Sargent Hilgley ordered as he stomped out of the wagon.

Jakes and Rob turned on their heels, and marched towards the pursuer's hall. Lueless started to move, but never finished turning. His head snapped while he was thrown to the ground. He rolled over, looking up at Sargent Hilgley straddling him,

"Recruit, why are you disrespecting me?"

Lueless was terrified, the gravity of the situation finally hitting him. He stammered, "I am not disrespecting you."

This response used up what little patience the Sargent had, "YOU ARE NOT, WHAT?"

For the first time, Lueless realized that this was not Barnstable, he was not the bully anymore, "I... I am not disrespecting you, sir?"

That answer seemed to set the Sargent off. The man's eyes were already ice, but they seemed to get even harder, "BULLSHIT! YOU BETTER STRAIGHTEN YOURSELF OUT, PUNK. YOU DO EXACTLY WHAT I SAY AND YOU BETTER DO IT BEFORE I AM DONE SAYING IT. IF DON'T IT WILL BE MY FOOT THAT BOOTS YOUR ASS OUT OF MY COMPANY. YOU MAY HAVE BEEN HOT SHIT IN THAT HOVEL YOU CAME FROM, BUT YOU ARE NOTHING NOW." The man was hard, and not bluffing, "DID YOU HEAR ME? ARE YOU DEAF? MOVE!"

Patrick did not even bother to wipe the dirt off his clothes before running inside.

Dust fell off of Lueless as he ran into the hall. Jakes was going to ask what happened, but Lueless' glare stopped him. It was pretty clear what happened.

They were measured and given their uniforms, sword and boots. Sargent Hilgley was waiting for them at the back door. Once the three were ready, he rounded on them, "Get that gear above your heads! Get moving, run that gear to your barracks!"

The sergeant jogged next to them. He easily kept the pace as they ran along the rows of raised barracks. Following orders, they raised their supplies above their heads, and started running, even Lueless kept the pace. It had been all of an hour, and the glamour of military service had already faded. Military service was not glamorous, it was hard, and it was dirty.

***

In the following days and weeks a routine formed. They were up before the sun for a morning run.

After the run was weapons and combat training. The afternoon was military philosophy and tactics. After dinner, they were expected to clean and maintain their equipment. By the time they were allowed sleep, it came easily. Surprisingly, Lueless did not whine or complain, sometimes, he even pulled his weight.

Their duties were tedious, but they were constantly busy, so the days passed quickly. One day bled into another as their routine ground on, with nothing unusual to mark a specific day or break the tedium. That was, until Lueless' bed was found empty.

Chapter 17

Patrick had enough. He could not stand being screamed at and constantly demeaned; this life was not for him. He would have stayed home if he wanted to be treated like this. He had made the decision to go leave about a week ago, but waited until he had the full moon to light his way. Tonight, the moon was finally full, he would be able to move without a torch or lantern. Packing up what he could fit into his travel bag, he snuck out of the barracks.

He had been scouting the fort over the last several nights. The main gates were guarded at all times, but the rest of the fort was only lightly guarded. There were smaller gates throughout the fort. These gates were basically doors in the stockade, and were not guarded because they were locked at all times. Over the past week, he had tested each of them. He had found one, in the back corner, that had worn to the point that a hard pull could open it. The gates were meant for foot patrols, and were small enough that they could be opened without much notice, perfect for his escape.

Patrick stood in front of the gate, and took a deep breath, this was his last chance to change his mind; once he opens this door, he is a deserter; his life would be forfeit, the punishment for desertion is death. He did not need to think hard, he braced himself and pulled, the latch snapped open with little resistance; he was now a deserter. Moving quickly, he stayed close to the wall, which gave him some cover as he headed towards the stable. The fort was too far away from anywhere to leave on foot, so he needed a horse.

There was no staff on duty at night, so the stables stood dark. The guard did patrol them periodically, so he had to act quickly; he had to get out before a patrol came by. The door to the tack shed was unlocked, as usual. He grabbed a bridle and saddle, and then went to get a horse. The stables were through the back door of the tack shed. He took the first horse, not caring what it looked like. It was transportation and nothing more. Once the saddle and bridle were secure, he walked the horse out of the stable and closed the gate behind him. To Patrick, closing the gate symbolized the closing of his life in the military. Swinging into the saddle, he spurred the horse towards Capuamundi.

Chapter 18

They ran through the barracks, looking for any clues. Lueless was gone, along with most of his belongings. They looked through the tiny room one more time, but there was no sign of him. There was no other option; they needed to tell Sargent Hilgley. He had probably snuck off to one of the brothels, which dotted the countryside around the Forge, and fell asleep. Visiting the brothels was frowned upon, but it happened.

Ultimately, the why did not matter, Lueless was not here, and the sergeant needed to know, "Rob, I'll go find Sargent Hilgley. You keep looking for him."

As he did every morning, Sargent Hilgley stood on the parade grounds, waiting for the company to form up. While a fair man, he was not a friendly figure. The man would not be happy, and the company would pay the price for Lueless' selfishness, but what else was new.

"Sir!" Jakes snapped to attention in front of the sergeant, right hand held to his brow in a salute.

Sargent Hilgley's eyes narrowed, "Pints, what can I do for you? Is your company planning on joining you? Or, do I have to go get them?"

Jakes swallowed hard, "Sir, recruit Lueless is gone, sir." Jake's nerves were getting the better of him. He tried to stand still, but found himself swaying.

Anger flashed across the Sargent's eyes as his face hardened, which Jakes would not have thought possible, "gone? Explain yourself, Pints. Is this a joke?"

Jakes felt like he was melting under the glare of his commanding officer, "Yes sir, and no sir, it is no joke. Most of his belongings are gone, along with his travel pack. His bed was messed and appeared slept in, but it was cold. We tried to find clues or a note, but there were none."

The Sargent bit his lip, drawing blood in anger. He pushed past Jakes, and broke into a run towards the barracks. Sargent Hilgley slammed the front door open, and stomped to Lueless's bed as the door vibrated behind him. He paused for a heartbeat before grabbing the bed and flipping it over. The platform flew and landed, askew, on the bed next to it, before slowly sliding and falling to the floor. There was nothing under it. The Sargent turned and opened Lueless' foot locker, dumping the contents out.

There was a straight razor, some soap, a couple of glass beads, some pins, an old, ripped, cloak and Lueless' spare boots. Kicking through the junk that fell out, he found no clues. The sergeant left the barracks and raised the alarm, "DESERTER!!!" The camp exploded into action. Guards climbed the ladders to the top of the walls, as Jakes, Rob, and the rest of their company started to search the yard around the barracks.

Sargent Hilgley went back to the parade grounds to direct the search. He had tried to get the boy to shape up, but, ultimately, he had failed. The boy was weak, and he had no business in the military. Still, he took the failure personally. Boys, like Lueless, hid from their failures, men did not.

He stood in the center of the grounds, as the stable master approached, the man one of the few civilian employees at the Forge. A trusted member of the staff, he had been working there for as long as anyone could remember. The man approached with his head down and hat in hand.

The small man did not meet the Sargent's glare as he began, "one of the horses is missing, sir."

Sargent Hilgley spoke softly, not wanting to berate an old man, "please explain, how someone could sneak a horse out?"

The man still did not meet the sergeant's eyes, "I wish I knew sir, there was nothing out of the ordinary last night, the gate was locked when I got up, we were just short a horse. I hadn't even though to count until the alarm was raised. I am so sorry sir, I am here to resign my position."

Sargent Hilgley clapped the man on the shoulder, "Nonsense man! I don't think you had anything to do with this. The boy had decided to desert, he was going to get out whether you saw it or not."

The stable master's shoulders dropped and he started to breathe normally again, "the tracks leading away from the corral appear that he was heading towards Capuamundi."

The Sargent eased the man's nerves, "I am sorry you were dragged into his, but if you see anything further, please let me know."

That sealed it, the boy had deserted, a crime punishable by death. First, the coward needed to be caught which will be a problem with the mass of humanity that lived in the capital.

The best that could be done, now, was issue a death warrant and hope the boy turns up. When he did, Sargent Hilgley would swing the headsman's axe himself.

Chapter 19

A slender boy, closer to a man, was an anonymous part of the crowd that filtered through Capuamundi's north gate. A guard looked the young man over. The boy looked like he had a little bit of money and an education, so he waved the kid through.

Patrick Lueless was finally free, free of the military, free of his father, free of his past, and he was terrified. As much as he hated his past, the certainty of it provided a kind of comfort. The freedom his present offered was anything but certain. He had never been to the city before, so he had no idea where to go. Not that it mattered; the rush of the crowd took control. The wave of people pushed and pulled, bumped and dragged; he was forced past the gatehouse, and through the gate. His pulse raced, the loss of control was terrifying. He needed to get away from the narrow gate. The crowd pushed him along until he was clear of the gate and the road opened up. The crowd spat him out, and he ran away from the gate and crowd, up the hill.

Capuamundi's streets were laid out in a grid. Four main roads ran from the bottom of the hill to the summit, connecting the upper and lower gates. Cross streets wrapped around the hill, connecting the main roads. A small square stood at the intersections, where the cross streets met the main roads.

Patrick had made a bit of money selling the horse. It was not much, but it would get him a few nights at an inn. He could be comfortable while he got his feet under him. He was about to enter the first inn when fate intervened. There was a commotion in the nearest square. He wandered over to see a man standing on a bench, yelling at passersby. While most just ignored the ranting, he stood transfixed by the spectacle.

"What are you?" the speaker asked the crowd, "I'll tell you what you are. You are SLAVES!"

The crowd paid the man no head, and continued to go about their days with nothing more than a glance. Patrick, however, found himself drawn in and slowly moving across the square. "You walk to and fro, going about your days, thinking you are free, BUT YOU ARE NOT! You are slaves to the three. They take everything from you, leaving nothing but crumbs for the people that earn it.

They steal everything from you, giving you nothing in return. OH! They tell you they provide you freedom, they tell you they provide you law. They tell you they protect your property. They tell you they provide the banks that allow you to borrow money. But these are lies. You become a slave to the property they let you have, and to the money they lend. Their money is a drug, the delivery system is the economy, and the addicts are YOU!"

Try as he may, Patrick could not take his eyes of the man. Tall, with a thin face he had piercing blue eyes; so blue they did not look real. Framing that thin face was a closely shaved beard, and long black hair that hung over his shoulder. The man took a deep breath and was about to resume speaking when the city guard marched into the square. The leader, a captain, jumped onto the bench and spoke to the robed man.

The robed man pushed the captain away, "NO I WILL NOT BE SILENT!"

The captain pulled a club out from his belt. He took a wide swing and struck the man behind the knee, buckling it. The man fell off the bench, landing hard on the stone road. The Captain jumped off the bench and swung the club again, a huge overhand strike connected with the prone man's ribs, then another that connected with his face. The guards surrounded the man, and the man looked around, then raised his hands in Surrender.

Patrick was horrified, what had this man done? He had only been speaking his mind, why would he be beaten bloody and arrested for that? Capuamundi was supposed to be a free town, where people could speak freely.

He stood by as the man was roughly pulled to his knees. A guard wrenched the man's arms behind his back and secured them in iron shackles.

***

He grunted as pain radiated from his shoulders, they were not even trying to spare his joints. Through the pain, and out of the corner of his eye, he saw that teenager inching closer. The goal of his speech was to instigate the guard, and have a crowd watch him be beaten and arrested. He found it the best way to turn people to his side. The sympathy these beatings engendered softened people to his message.

While he had been speaking, he saw that a teenage boy was on the hook, and that boy was moving towards him now.

The guards threw him in the paddy wagon, which was waiting outside the square. He pulled himself onto the bench, and slumped against the bars as the driver started the wagon moving. His ribs were badly bruised and blood leaked out of his mouth, tracing down his chin. Taking the beating may serve a purpose, but it did not make it any less painful.

The driver released the brake and eased the paddy wagon into motion. Patrick ran up and jumped up onto the back step. The driver was obviously not expecting trouble, the wagon was unguarded, and the driver stood on the front, ringing a bell, focused on getting the wagon through the crowd. He never even gave the prisoner a passing glance.

The bloodied prisoner turned to Patrick, mouthing 'help'. After what the guard did to him in the street, with eyes watching, he could only imagine what it would be like behind closed doors. This may be the only chance to get the man out. If he did not, the man may never walk out. He pulled on the lock hanging off the door's latch, '*how can I open this?*' He had no idea how to pick a lock. The man seemed to read his mind, and slid down the bench.

Once up against the bars, he whispered, "There's a master key in my pocket."

Patrick fished around in the robe's deep pocket, finding a skeleton key resting on the bottom. These keys were the reason that the clasp style locks were no longer used, a skeleton key was able to open most of them. The modern tumbler locks could still be picked, but it took great skill and there were no universal keys. Luckily, the guard had not updated the locks on the wagons. He turned the key and was surprised when the lock actually dropped open.

The robed man jumped out of the carriage, and they ran away from the wagon, into the sanctuary of a small ally. Patrick used the key to unlock the clasp lock that hung off the side of the man's shackles. Hands free, the man grabbed him and dragged him into the crowd.

They pushed through the crowd, putting distance between them and the wagon. It would not be long before the driver looked behind him and raised an alarm. Patrick did not even think to question where they were going, following the man just felt right.

His lungs were burning from the run up Capuamundi's hill. It was not particularly steep, but it was long and any running up any hill was taxing.

Finally, they turned into an ally. There did not seem anything special about it, but they ran to the end, stopping in front of a plain brick wall. Patrick leaned heavily against the wall, panting to catch his breath.

"Who are you? What is your name?"

The man was pulling up a metal grate at the bottom of the wall, "I don't believe in keeping our given names. I believe what is really important is the work we do. So, please call me Preacher." The man climbed down into the hole that was revealed when the grate was moved, "are you coming?"

End Part 1

Part Two

Chapter 20

Teridon stood in a relaxed stance, with his weight evenly distributed between his feet; feeling rooted to the ground. He looked to his left and right, checking the five men that encircled him. The man behind him may think he had been forgotten, but he could hear the man's feet shuffling on the hard ground, and he felt the man's presence.

He was shirtless, wearing only thin woolen leggings. Now almost 21, the past five years had seen him grow to well over six feet tall and become thick with muscle. The sun shone off his clean shaven head, his hands were loosely in front of his face. A small nod, and the five men attacked. An onlooker would have seen chaos, but he was a skilled fighter; to him, his attackers moved like they were in water. The first attack came from his right, a straight punch at his head, not bothering to move, he casually directed the strike past his face, using the punch's inertia to control the attacker. He allowed the attacker to come into his body, driving his thumb up the man's side. The punching arm went limp when struck a small pressure point in the armpit. He snapped the attacker into the man coming from the left side. Both men tumbled to the ground, landing in a heap.

Turning his attention to the attacker in front, Teridon shifted his weight, snapping a quick kick to the center of the man's chest, driving through the man. The attacker doubled over and dropped to his knees, gulping and wheezing, desperate for breath that was not coming. He felt the final two men closing from behind, their heavy footsteps vibrating as they ran towards him. He dove forward, tucking into a roll and coming up facing the final two men. They attacked at the same time, one man punching while the other tried to tackle him. He blocked the punch and spun to the outside of the puncher's arm, using him as a shield from the tackler. The tackler was wholly committed and he ran by, stumbling, then falling face first into the dirt.

One out of the way, Teridon drove his elbow into the punchers ribs, doubling him over, then dropped an elbow into the center of the man's back, dropping him onto the tackler.

Groans overlapped each other as the five men untangled. Teridon loved martial arts. He had trained for so long that he was able to just react, there was no thought required.

This was a stark contrast to his school work. He took the same military history and philosophy classes that he would have taken if he went to the Forge.

Sir Loorie insisted that if he wanted to train like a soldier, than he had to train in all aspects, not just the fun parts.

The knight had not known, however, that Teridon was mostly illiterate when he had come into service, so he literally started from scratch when his schooling began, learning to read and write. He worked until the small hours of the night for the first few years, but his hard work had paid off; not only was he now literate, he had even had begun to enjoy reading; as long as could there was time to exercise his boredom out on some poor sparing partners.

"One of these days, we are going to get you." Ian said.

He merely replied with a smile as he wiped the dust from his sweat-covered chest, both men knew it was bluster. A servant ran up, "The lord has returned!"

Teridon grabbed his shirt and ran to greet his patron.

***

Sir Loorie had planned on retiring after the last recruiting tour, but his experience, name, and reputation were too valuable to let him fade away into retirement. After a month or so at his estate, he had been offered a position as a military advisor to the King, one of the empire's three sovereigns. The job kept him in the capital for weeks at a time, and he was returning from his longest stretch away yet, over two months.

Sir Loorie stretched tall as he exited the stage. He waved in greeting when Teridon ran out from the side of the house. The reason for was kept a closely guarded secret, not even his family knew why he had been gone for so long.

Sir Loorie greeted Teridon warmly, clapping his shoulders as he teased, "I saw you practicing as a rolled up the road. I bought you those beautiful weapons, but you refuse to use them."

Teridon laughed, "I use them, but I need to practice empty handed as well. Too many use the sword as a crutch and forget how easy it is to get disarmed, especially in the chaos of true battle. I want to be able to defend myself, armed or no."

He was always shocked that someone so young, and with his background, would show so much maturity.

Thinking back to the night he gave the boy a second change, he had to sigh. There were a great many soldiers that could learn from the boy's work ethic. He would have been an amazing soldier; he was thankful that he looked past a youthful indiscretion. Even more, he was proud of the progress the young man had made.

Teridon's tireless work had paid off, he had molded himself into one of the best fighters in the empire. He was offered prizefights and security details on a regular basis, but he turned them all down; he owed Sir Loorie his life, and was fiercely loyal to the man.

The boy had become such a good fighter that he had begun developing his own style. Finding the traditional shield and short sword far too limiting, he used a bastard sword as his main offensive weapon. He held a main-gauche in his off hand, laid down along his forearm. It was a dagger of his own design, the pommel was one-sided, so it could lay flat on his arm, and the other side extended out with a small, sharpened, hook, that he used to disarm his opponent or tear flesh. The blade's spine was extra wide to disperse the force of a blow, as it was primarily used for defense.

Sir Loorie's eyes hardened, "I wish I had more time for pleasantries, but I need to speak with you. Get cleaned up and meet me in my study."

***

Teridon filled the porcelain washbasin from the pitcher of warm water that sat on the floor next to it. Training always left him covered a patina of dirt and sweat; he dunked a course washcloth into the basin and began to peel that layer off. The cloth turned from white to black as he moved down his muscled chest, the perfumed water in the basin darkening with every dunk of the cloth. Once cleaned, he pulled on a fresh shirt, and rushed off to Sir Loorie's study.

***

He pushed the heavy, oversized, door open with a creak. Krys had gotten here first, and stood idly chatting with his father. Sir Loorie gestured for both boys to sit; they did as instructed, sinking into the plush chairs facing the knight's huge oak and stone desk, which was longer than the knight, was tall.

Sir Loorie stood in front of them, leaning on the edge of the black stone desktop. The knight's easy smile had been replaced by a hard, tight, jaw and eyes like ice.

"There is no simple way to explain what has been happening in Capuamundi, so I will just be out with it. You both know that I have been spending more and more time in the capital. Well, I can finally tell you why, the king is retiring, and the nobility, and military, were polled last month. Well, after the results were counted, I have been elected to be the next King."

Both boys lit up with excitement. They were young, they did not understand. This required tact, he did not want to frighten them, "Unfortunately, I do not know what to make of the election. It is unusual, I did not ask for the nomination and I have no idea who nominated me."

The customary election process was that a candidate puts themselves forward, once the field was full, the names were distributed throughout the empire.Once distributed, their constituents vote, the nobility and military for the King; the middle and lower classes for the Pauper, and everyone voted for the Advocate. After the vote, they are confirmed by the other two. Sir Loorie's name had been put forward by an unknown party, and he was elected based on his fame alone.

Teridon leaned forward, eyes wide, "Is that even legal?"

Sir Loorie shrugged, "Yes, it's not the usual way to nominate a candidate, but it is legitimate. Usually, people put forward like this never get traction outside of a village, or at most a province. When I first heard about this, I had assumed the same would happen here. But, my name carries more weight than I thought."

Krys stared unblinking, "are you going to accept?"

"Yes, yes I am. It would not be proper for me to turn it down. It is my duty, whether I asked for it or not. Alexander, the current King, steps down tomorrow. I will meet with the other two next week and will be sworn in the next day. I just wanted to give you boys an idea of what was happening. I'll try and keep you updated if I learn anything else"

The two boys stood, and turned to leave. Sir Loorie grabbed Teridon's arm as he followed Krys towards the door, "Please, Teridon, sit, there is something we need to Discuss."

Krys turned, "do I need to hear this?"

"No, son, I need to speak with Teridon about his future, I'll catch up with you later, we need to speak as well. Things will change around here, whether for better or worse remains to be seen."

Krys shrugged his shoulders and left.

Sir Loorie took Krys' place in the plush chair, "Please, Teridon, sit back down."

He tentatively took the seat again. His place in the household had been at the knight's pleasure and his heart thumped, assuming that had come to an end.

"I need you to come with me. I want to appoint you my head of security. This whole thing stinks. My gut is screaming that there is going to be trouble. I need someone I can trust to watch my back, and who will have no problem defending it."

Much like five years ago, when Sir Loorie gave him a second chance at life, Teridon was dumbstruck. He took a moment to gather his thoughts, "I am honored, sir, beyond honored, but, I'm not qualified for something so important. There are far better choices, men with actual experience."

Sir Loorie smiled, warmly, his eyes softening, "Nonsense, listen, I understand that you are green, but you have a military mind, and you are a gifted fighter. Most importantly, though, I have no doubts about where your loyalty lies. I am about to wade into a cesspool of intrigue and betrayal; loyalty is going to be far more valuable than experience."

Teridon slumped back into the chair, considering. He was not sure if he could do the job, but Sir Loorie obviously had faith in him, and that was enough, "it would be my honor sir."

Clapping Teridon on the shoulder, he beamed, "thank you son, you have no idea how much this means to me. You will be amazing, you'll see. Prepare yourself; you will leave within the week."

Chapter 21

Teridon moved along the small column, making sure the furniture, clothing and various other goods, were stowed, secured, and ready to move. The sun had just broken over the horizon and, other than some stray whips of clouds; the sky was a clear deep blue. Rain was not going to be an issue today, so the ten wagons could remain untapped. Once satisfied everything was secure and ready, he gave the order to move.

The drivers cracked the reigns, while barking commands at their horses, and the small procession started moving to meet Sir Loorie, who was already in Capuamundi.

Climbing up onto his speckled chestnut mare, he rode to the front, setting an easy trot to pace the train. They would get to the capital this afternoon, and, if everything went to plan, the wagons would be unloaded by nightfall.

Even though he had been to Capuamundi numerous times over the past few years, going into the city still excited him. Today was doubly exciting; he was going into the old city for the first time. People could not just walk into the old city, and until know, he had never needed to go there. Today, he finally did.

***

It was late afternoon when the train rolled through the yawning maw that was the city's western gate. The door was raised and lowered by complex machinery that was sunk into gate's walls and operated from a secure room on top of the wall. If the city was attacked, the gates could be dropped into place, crushing anyone under them. Most importantly, if everything went to pot, the gate can be secured by a single person.

Sharpened triangular teeth, almost as tall as a man, hung from the bottom of the gate ready to cut through any attackers caught under the gate as it drooped from its pocket inside the stone bulwark.

They rolled through the gate, those teeth looming just overhead as they entered the sally port, a kill zone between the two gates. The sides were solid rock, with murder holes cut into them and galleries along the top, any men trapped inside would be decimated in minutes. The inner gate was a mesh of large round steel bars, and the bottom had the same sharpened teeth as the outer door.

As with the outer, it also dropped into place. The mesh would allow defenders to attack the invaders, trapped inside. These gates, along with tall thick walls, were the key to the city's defense and were the model for defensive fortifications throughout the empire.

Teridon stopped just before the inner gate, and fished a thick scroll from his saddlebag. One of the guards approached and grabbed the scroll without saying a word. He unrolled it, gave it a cursory inspection, and then waived him on without saying a word.

The column jerked into motion again, they followed him through the inner gate, than rumbled up the hill, towards the old city. Teridon was trying to stay focused, but he had seen this part of the city many times, and it was a fight to stay engaged.

Looking around, he caught sight of a woman in the crowd, she was beautiful, he spun to get a better look, but the crowd had already swallowed her up. He tried to remember her face, tanned skin, and shimmering black hair, in the extremely unlikely event they crossed paths again.

Yelling drew his attention forward again, and he had to yank the reins hard to keep from running over a group of women that were on the side of the road. He waived in apology and focused forward.

The road flattened out as they neared top of the hill and the upper wall. This wall was much smaller, no more than ten feet. It was one of the structures left from the original fort, built to protect a much less important location that stood in a much more defensible position.

Capuamundi had not always been the capital of the empire. In fact, was not always a single city. It began as two separate entities, Fort Mundi, on the hill, protected the area's center of trade, Port Mundi.

Even though it was inland, the port was, and still is, the world's largest. The city's location on the deep lake, and the four great rivers that fed it, made it just as accessible to trade as any ocean port.

Unlike those ocean ports, however, the city did not have the harsh winter of the north, or the great storms that plagued the south, especially in late summer. A sheltered port, benign weather, and central location inside the empire had made the city the heart that pumped trade throughout the empire, and the world.

The port's trade produced fabulous wealth, and its power had grown along with that wealth. People flocked to the burgeoning city, settling on hill, around the fort, and around the port. With the explosive growth, it did not take very long for the two cities to collide on narrow plain that separated them. Once they did, it made sense to merge them into a single great city, and it was named Capuamundi. Combining the two governments had cut the expenses, kept taxes low, and allowed the city's wealth and import to accelerate. Even with that growth, the city was a trade center, but did not have any government functions. That changed when empire's original capital city was sacked and destroyed. Wanting a more defensible location, Selumin Aragon chose to move the capital inland. Already the country's financial center, Capuamundi was the obvious choice. He converted the fort to his residence, fortified the lower city, and built the Kethi Draal.

Most historians point to this as the start of the true Aragonian Empire. Though the territory had borne the name prior, it was not until Selumin's vision was joined with Capuamundi's riches, that a small, inconsequential, country began growing into the greatest empire on the planet.

Teridon approached that ancient fort wall at the head of his train. The gates were closed, lest the impression be given that ordinary citizens were welcome inside. These gates were simple, just stout wooden doors.

They were meant for keeping people out, not armies. As before Teridon rode to speak with the guard. This guard's eyes were steel, his square jaw taught, the man was serious, there would be no cursory inspection this time.

The guard stepped up to meet him, "Name, sponsor, and purpose of entry."

"Teridon Jace, sponsored by Sir Nidan Loorie, these are his effects."

"Give me your patience."

Teridon handed the scroll to the guard, as he did at the base of the hill. The patience has the Loorie family crest and purpose of visit, along with a list of the individuals who would be entering. A patience was the only way into the old city, unless you lived there, or were a member of the government and worked inside. Anyone who needed to petition the Three needed to meet with their local lord first; they would issue the patience allowing entry.

The guard took the scroll and disappeared into a door in the wall. They were going to compare the sigil on the patience to the book of nobility. The book had a picture of every noble sigil in the empire along with a description of the house. It was published every five years by the Three and was used to authenticate documents throughout the empire. The guard was inside the wall for a few moments, then came back out and handed the paperwork to him, while ordering the door opened with a wave.

Inside, it was like they had arrived in a different city. Gone were the crowded streets of the lower city, the crushing throngs of humanity had been replaced by sporadic groups of two or three strolling casually along the dark cobbled streets. The houses were large, stone affairs. Ornate, they were decorated with rich wood and black iron, some even gold accents. The green lawns and lush gardens gave the upper city a pleasant smell, a stark contrast to the dank lower city.

The Kethi-Draal and towers of the Three loomed over the much shorter homes, dominating the view. He rode up ahead, his excitement was too much to contain.
The ornate homes fell away and the road opened into the Crier's Square. The large flat area was paved with large granite stones, blackened with age, but were still spotted here and there with the original light grey. The stone's sharp edges and fine fitment had been weathered away so they now had rounded graceful edges, making for a rough ride in the wagons.

The Kethi-Draal stood off to his right; this was the first time he saw the building up close, and it was spectacular. Its twin, gold capped, spires, and were even more beautiful than he though they would be. The flying buttresses, running along the sides of the building, were amazing. It was one of the empire's largest buildings and it remained engineering marvel despite being built millennia before.

The design has been the inspiration for all large buildings since, and it had served as the seat of government since Sulemin built it. The building housed the Hall of the Three and the Hall of the Council. The council was the representative body of the people. It met every two years, providing the three with information and suggestions based on the circumstances throughout the empire.

The representatives were elected by each of the empire's regions, currently fifty two in number, and each representative served for one session.

It had been set up after a popular uprising, as a way to placate the masses, to show they had a hand in governance of the empire. It was all a show, however, it held no real power.

Teridon continued into square, the Crier's rise stood directly across the square, backed up to the wall, and halfway between the towers and the Kethi Draal. The large stone rise looked natural, a giant granite slap that had been flattened for use as a stage. It was named for the criers who used to stand and give their daily reports to the fort's citizens; now, it was used for political speeches and sporadic events.

He turned left, towards the towers of the King, The pauper, and the Advocate. The three towers were identical, five floors tall, much shorter than the Kethi Draal's spires. The bottom two floors were square and the round tower rising from the center of that square base. They were constructed of dark stone, and capped with black slate roofs. The roof had a large chimney protruding through the center; the common central stack poured smoke into the early evening sky, the kitchen's fires were going full flame getting supper ready. He had to remind himself that he was there to do a job, not gawk at buildings.

He pulled the reigns toward the towers and cantered up to see that the wagons had parked in front of the tower and attendants were already climbing about them, unloading the contents. He dismounted in front of the tower and pushed the thick black door open, his hand sliding over the polished wood before slowly stepping into to the large foyer. His boots clicked on the polished marble floor as he walked over the blue hammer and the gold crown embossed in the stark white floor, the symbols of the office and the empire.

Despite his past few years on Sir Loorie's estate, he was still a simple farm boy at heart, so he allowed himself some time to wander about the tower, taking in the splendor. The interior was much larger than it appeared from the outside. The first floor was for the business of the King, with receiving rooms, offices for staff, kitchens and the formal dining area and ball room. The second floor was the residence; household rooms; rooms for entertaining personal guests; play areas for children; the private dining room, and a private kitchen.

The third floor had only one room, the library. Pushing through the double doors, he walked into the huge circular room.

It was completely open, save for the chimney in the middle. The walls were lined floor to ceiling with dark wooden shelves; the top shelves were only accessible using the tall ladders that rolled along each set of shelves.

The center of the room was a great stonework cube, the chimneys from the kitchens and lower floors ran through it. In each of the sides of the cube gaped a great fireplace, heating an lighting the room. Large chairs and several desks surrounded the center, each desk dimly lit by oil lamps. If the room had any windows, they were covered by shelves and books.

Sir Loorie reclined in front of the fire off to his right, the dim orange light of the fire flickering about his face. He looked up from his book and motioned Teridon over. "Welcome to your new home. Please, investigate the tower; you need to know it like it is the forest back in Barnstable. Take some time to get a lay of the city; you need to know that just as well."

Teridon sat lightly next to the old knight, and he could see the detail of the man's face. His eyes were sunken, dark circles sagging under them. He looked completely spent, like he had not eaten or slept in days.

"Yes sir, I will. Sir, may I speak freely?"

"Of course, son, speak your mind."

"You look terrible. You need food, or sleep, maybe both, but you need something."

The knight slumped back into the chair, book falling into his lap, "I know, my boy, I know; thanks for the concern. Unfortunately, sleep has been a precious commodity of late. My dreams have been... strange. The stress must be getting to me."

"If I may, maybe you should spend these last couple of days at your estate, sir. It may help you get some sleep before the real stress begins."

"That's a great idea. I think I am going to do just that."

***

Teridon spent the rest of the day walking throughout the tower, trying to learn every nook and cranny. He had already seen the lower floors, so he started at the top and worked his way down. The tower was a security nightmare. There were bare windows on the ground floor, doors with no guards, people coming and going all day, all those were fairly simple to fixes, but the basement was no such thing.

If looking at the front of the tower, the basement was below ground, but the ground fell away as one rounded the tower, and the lower grade meant that the basement was exposed in the rear, opening to the servant's quarters behind the tower. There were four separate entrances, all invisible from the square.

If the doors were breached, defending the tower would be impossible; any guard would be overwhelmed by a flood of attackers. Something would have to be done about it. He had one other real problem; there was no way to evacuate the upper floors. If there was a fire, it would rush upwards, using the tower like a chimney. Anyone in the upper floors would be trapped, the only way out jumping to the ground, five floors below.

Chapter 22

Damon Maxk sat at a large wooden desk, surrounded by tilted stacks of paper. Any moment, one of those stacks could let go and bury the old man under an avalanche of paper. As cities go, Capuamundi was fairly safe. The city guard did an admirable job policing it, but anytime there was such a concentration of people, some level of crime was going to follow, it was inevitable. As the Pauper, he was elected representative of the lower and middle classes, giving them a voice equal to the nobility. It was a duty he took extremely seriously. While he represented the entire empire, he had grown up in Capuamund's lower wards, and he made sure that he kept an eye turned to those wards. It kept him connected to the people he represented.

He passed his free time searching through the guard's reports, trying to see developing patterns, proactive actions were always more effective than reactive ones. It was a habit that started during his time as an alderman in the lower city. Now, he was a member of the three, he had to oversee an empire, not command the city guard. That said, he spoke with the guard commanders on a regular basis, but did not meddle in their affairs, usually.

"Still looking over those damn reports? You have never been able to step out of the alderman's shoes." The advocate teased as he walked into the room.

Damon replied with a faint smile, "Maybe."

The other man laughed, "No maybe about it."

"It keeps me grounded and it connects me to the people I serve. Plus, it helps me remember my roots and never forget that I was a commoner once. Unfortunately, business looms, have we heard the results of the voting?"

The advocate laid a scroll down on the desk. The Pauper tentatively picked it up, then, after a heartbeat's pause, unrolled it, revealing the results of the empirical polling, Nidan Loorie.

He had been concerned since Sir Nidan Loorie's name was put forward, and now he was terrified. Having someone so well known, and so closely tied to the military, was very worrying. Why had the man put his name forward? What was the man playing at?

Was he intending a coup? If he decided that he wanted to destroy the three and consolidate power into a single emperor again, he would have the muscle to do so. The advocate saw the tension on the other man's face, "Be at peace, my friend; Nidan Loorie is a good man, and all reports tell me that he did not put his name forward; he was nominated by an outside party. They further tell me that he accepts the position with great reluctance. While no one can tell the future, I see nothing that indicates the man is planning anything untoward."

While appreciated, the advocate's attempt to ease his mind did not work, "We shall see if he remains such a good man after his taste of power."

"Power? You have always been such a worrier; he is the head of one of the empire's oldest noble houses, and a decorated military officer. The man knows power; he's had it his whole life."

"People follow him because of his wealth, or because of they had to, but that is not power, having the might and wealth of the empire at your beckon call, that is power, so, like i said, we will see if he remains a good man after a taste of power."

Sir Loorie was a well-known, and well loved, member of the military. The man was retired, but the old knight had extremely powerful friends, both in the military and within the nobility, and those friends would huge problem if the man decided to seize power. Still, the election was legal and had been confirmed by the territorial governors. The two men turned as a short man, looking to be about thirty, walked into the office. He had a slight build, with fair skin. It did not look like he got out much. He had no apparent scars, and his hands looked soft, with no calluses or cracks. He was not a solider or laborer, he was an academic, spending days with his head in books.

The man wore a blue, loose fitting scholar's robe that shows he came from some money, dying was expensive and blue was the most expensive color.

"Have you met my new assistant?" Damon asked. The advocate shook his head no. "This is Rosi Starling; he has just graduated from university. He is one of the finest students ever to come out of my ward. I offered him the position before he had graduated, and to my great pleasure, he accepted." Damon positively glowed as he spoke about the man, his pride worn all over his face.

The advocate nodded, "Pleasure to meet you, son."

"The pleasure is mine, Sir. Sirs, I am here to discuss the schedule, Sir Loorie will be coming for confirmation at eight tomorrow morning. If I need to reschedule, I need to do so tonight."

"No, eight will be fine, thank you Rosi."

The Pauper took a deep breath and sunk back into his chair. He was able to stay ahead of everyone else by paying attention to the patterns in life. Unfortunately, there were no patterns in what he was seeing; it was nothing but a muddled mess, and that made him very nervous.

Chapter 23

Teridon stood in the courtyard. He had explained his security concerns to Sir Loorie. The knight had gone back to his estate to relax for a few days, and had left Teridon in charge. Sir Loorie had concurred with Teridon's concerns and had given him permission to get his security upgrades started. Looking over his list one more time, he went to the basement.

A thick old man was barking commands at the laborers that were emptying the dimly lit basement. They were moving the last remnants of the prior tenant out. The man's chin blended with his wide shoulders and his large pot belly that was, probably, rock hard. He had worked his way from a mason's apprentice up to a grand master, but those years of manual labor had hunched and hardened him. From there, he had been hired to oversee the maintenance crews that took care of the capital area; that included the towers, the square itself, and the Kethi Draal. He was extremely good at his job, but was not the friendliest sort.

Teridon tapped the man on the shoulder, "may I speak with you?"

"Sure, what can I do for you, kid?" He replied without turning.

"I am Sir Loorie's head of security..."

Scott cut him off with a laugh, "Wow, someone really thinks a lot of himself. Head of security? What are you, twenty? Run along, kid, stop wasting my time." He went back to supervising the work.

Teridon ground his teeth. He had not been dismissed like that since Barnstable, and he fought to keep his quickly rising rage in check. He had spent his life as little more than a servant in Barnstable, and after watching his mother being dismissed, looked past, and disrespected his whole life, he did take it very well. He responded with a hiss, "Excuse me."

The man did not even turn around, "What? I don't have time to play with a little boy who thinks he is a big shot. Learn your place, boy, and leave me alone."

Teridon had enough; he rounded on the shorter man, fighting the urge to grab the man's fat throat and throttle him, "Sir, I am here on behalf of Sir Nidan Loorie. You do know him? Yes? I am his head of security, whether you believe it or not.

I understand that I am young, but that does not change my position, or blunt the disrespect you show me. I have identified several areas of this tower that make securing it difficult, if not impossible. I will need them corrected before I will allow my patron to reside here."

Scott dropped all semblance of decorum, he rolled his eyes, his voice dripped with disgust, "What are you babbling about, kid? Your boss ain't the first to live in this tower. You think you are the first to go through the tower? Well, you ain't. Better MEN than you have lived here, and no one else ever had problem securing the tower!"

The clear emphasis on the word man enraged him. It was taking every ounce of his will to keep his anger in check. His forehead throbbed as his blood pressure spiked, "I am going to give you one last chance." He took the list of items and slammed it into the chest of the man. Years of hard work had kept the old man strong; even so, he could not stand the force of Teridon's anger. Stumbling backwards, he tripped and landed heavily on top of a crate.

Teridon stepped forward and loomed over the sitting man, waiting for him to say something else. Scott sized Teridon up for a moment before slowly taking the list.

"If these changes are not started by tomorrow morning, you will NEVER walk into this tower again." The man started to respond. Teridon cut him off, "Do not say another word." he hissed and stomped out of the basement.

***

Teridon was in his room when the metallic ting of hammers striking chisels began echoing through the tower. Suddenly curious, he rose and wound down the four flights of stairs to the courtyard below. As soon as he exited the tower, Scott lumbered up to him, "I am sorry for the misunderstanding earlier, sir."

Teridon's anger had cooled significantly since their confrontation, "Don't worry about it, I am sorry for losing my temper. We are all under a lot of pressure because of the short time frame, and I am far from a sir, my name is Teridon."

Teridon held his hand out, a hand that Scott accepted with an iron grip, "Scott. Come on; let me show you what we are doing. I decided to use steel bars, instead of iron, they are stronger, wont rust, and will be easier to anchor. The anchor points can be thinner, so we can sink them farther into the wall.

We'll chisel out some of the mortar and slide the anchor points into the void between stone. We'll then fill the void with mortar, embedding the anchor points. When it dries, it will be like it is part of the wall. The bars will be at full strength in a few days."

Teridon was impressed. He lifted the steel latticework, inspecting the bars that would protect his charge, "How strong is full strength."

"Strong enough that they cannot be pulled off by a horse. Now, hook a few draft horses up and pull, then the bars may fail, but the anchor points would not."

"Perfect, now, about the rest of the list."

"I have workman blocking up the basement entrances as we speak. When they are done, we will build a new single entrance, complete with a security vestibule. There will be two small slits, so that whoever is inside can be easily dispatched, if necessary. Also, there will be a lever system, which I designed, so the door can be closed and locked without entering the vestibule or leaving the tower. Once locked in, there is no way out."

Teridon was pleased, despite their rocky start, everything was moving nicely now. He had to give Scott credit; the man was very efficient at his job, "When will the work be completed?"

"The vestibule will be completed later this week. I thought through the evacuation problem. The best solution I could come up with was a climbing rope in each room. A cleat will been installed below the windows and if escape is necessary, there is a box below each window with a rope that can be thrown out the window."

"Thank you for your hard work, Scott, it has been much appreciated. Please, pass that on to your workers as well."

Scott shook his hand again, "You are welcome, son. And, I will."

***

"STOP, YOU AT THE TOWER! YOU CAN NOT BE HERE!"

Teridon was casually walking around the base of the tower, inspecting the work. He jerked around to see what the commotion was; smiling broadly when he saw Jakes astride a dark brown stallion and wearing the colors of a city guard commander, blood red doublet over a bright white shirt, a matching red cape flowed behind him as he rode.

It had been four long years since he had last saw his friend.

Jakes cantered up, looking askance at Teridon, "I kept hearing about this boy who has got in in his head that he is the head of a Knight's security detail. It was so unbelievable that I just had to go investigate." He burst out laughing as he jumped off the horse. Teridon shared in the hearty laugh, "What have you been doing? Aren't you wearing the wrong uniform?"

Jakes' eyes shot wide, he looked back and forth, then dismounted, "OH MY! You're right. This is the wrong uniform. Do you think I am going to be in trouble? What have you been eating T, you are even bigger than I remember."

Teridon accepted his friend's compliment awkwardly, as he always did. His bravado was largely a front, and he was never comfortable when people told him good things.

"I have been training on Sir Loorie's estate, I was a squire, but I wasn't very good at it, so he decided to put me to work doing something I am good at. When he found out he was elected King, he needed someone to watch his back, and he asked me. How have you been, why aren't you in the army anymore?"

"Wow, good for you, friend! I'm still in the army, but I asked to be transferred. The guard is a civilian organization but they rely on the military to fill the command positions.

Civilians don't have the experience to command a force the size of this city's guard. They were asking for volunteers to fill a couple of open positions, I was married, and didn't want to be away from my wife for years at a time. So I volunteered, and here I am."

Jakes really skipped over a major part of that story, "You are married!?"

Jakes was suddenly beaming, "Yes, it will be two years in a couple of months. Maybe you can meet Nydelis someday. Though I am not sure I trust you around her."

Teridon responded to the jab by punching him playfully in the shoulder. He wished that they spend more time catching up, but he had so much to do, "I am sorry I don't have more time, but the work is unending and the preparations are not yet done. Sir Loorie will be returning later this week and I need to finish before he does."

"I understand, call on me soon."

Even with the stress, seeing Jakes lifted his spirits, "I will, let's go to dinner. We have four years to catch each other up on."

Jakes mounted his horse, "That sounds great; we will do it soon, Goodbye friend," cape flying behind as he trotted away.

Teridon got back to work, stepping a bit lighter, he had a friend in this town, and that was a welcome turn of events.

Chapter 24

Nidan Loorie had spent the last week relaxing at his estate while Teridon was doing the heavy lifting in Capuamundi. His leisure time was over, however; he needed to finish preparations at home before he returned to the capital. The first order of business was pushing his, plentiful, doubts aside and officially installing Krys as regent. He had paid for the best tutors, and his son had been an outstanding student, but school and life were very different. Krys never had the responsibilities of a household to worry about. Unfortunately, he had no choice, once sworn in, he would no longer be Sir Nidan Loorie; he would be the King, and he would be living in Capuamundi. In his stead, Krys will serve as head of household until Sir Loorie stepped down or died.

Krys entered the room, breaking his contemplative fugue, "Hello father."

"Hello son, please, sit, there are important matters we need to discuss."

Krys sat in the same chair he had weeks before, when his father told him about the election. He sat lightly, his mother had prepared him for the conversation and he was ready, excited for the opportunity.

"Son, you know what has been going on. I know you have been feeling like events are passing you by, but that is because your role in this begins today."

Krys followed along, nodding intently, playing the part of dutiful son. His father continued, "You will be named regent this afternoon. Once I am named King, you will be the head of this household. You are my only son and heir, you will be the Regent until I die or I return."

He tried to contain his excitement, while overwhelmed, he felt ready, "I understand father, what do I need to do?"

"Nothing, right now, there will be a short ceremony this afternoon. As far as the actual day to day duties, I am sure you will do fine, your mother will be an invaluable resource and your education will serve you well.

That is not what I wanted to talk to you about, however. Son, I have worked, long and hard, to make this a home for all our staff. It has been my intention that members of this staff would be treated as family and that they would stay in our employ because this is a good place to work, not because they need a job.

I would expect that you continue this attitude. Don't let the sudden power go to your head, son. You are responsible for the staff; it is easy to forget that these are real people with real lives and every decision you make affects them. They count on you, do not ever forget that or take it for granted."

"I understand father."

He was still trying to play the role of dutiful son but it grew more difficult with every passing word. His father was a good man, but far too soft. The staff had no fear of him, they walked around like they were part of the family.

A smile creased the corners of his father's lips, "You will do great, son. If you learned anything from me, let it be this, treat people like you wish to be treated."

"I will try my best to remember that advice, father."

"I know you will, come, follow me."

***

They rounded the corner and the hallway opened to the great entry foyer. His mother stood waiting between the great curved staircases. She grabbed him and pulled him into a huge hug, "Krys, you will be amazing. I am so excited for you."

"Thank you, Mother."

The ceremony would actually take place on the home's front steps, with the staff witnessing the transfer. He pulled himself away from her embrace and she grabbed his hands one last time, "You will do great, honey."

By everything right, she should be regent, but the Loorie's were a noble family; succession was governed by empirical law. A female could only become the head of a noble house if there was no male heir, or if the male heir was feeble minded.

"Thank you mother; father, I am ready to begin."

Nidan threw open the double doors. The staff of about 30 people was gathered around the base of the stairs. They were casually chatting amongst themselves. Rumors had spread about why they were gathered, though it did not seem to concern them much.

Krys stayed back in the darkness of the foyer as his father stepped out of the foyer and onto the top step. He held his hands high, to get the staff's attention.

The conversations slowly stopped as they turned to look at their lord. Krys shook his head, the conversations should have really stopped immediately, but the staff did not respect his father.

"This will not take long, but I have an announcement. As you may have heard, I have been elected to the Council of the Three, and I will be leaving for Capuamundi shortly. As of today, my son, Krystobal Loorie, has been appointed regent. He will serve as such until such time that I return or my death. He speaks with my voice, and acts with my blessing. Krystobal, do you accept this position, and promise to serve honorably until such time that I return or die?"

"I do, father. It is my honor."

"Then, I appoint you Regent of House Loorie and the lands under its control."

The staff responded to the announcement with soft, polite, applause. Sir Loorie was a pleasure to work for, and paid well, but many of the senior staff had been through these transitions before. The progeny is rarely the equal of the progenitor.

Chapter 25

Teridon had been working nonstop since arriving in Capuamundi. For these last two weeks, sleep has been nothing a fond memory, but it would be over when Sir Loorie arrived later this morning. He was supposed to have arrived early this morning, but a runner had come just after dawn with the message that he would be delayed a few hours.

He used the delay to do a final inspection of the tower, making sure everything was ready to receive the new King. Walking next to Scott, they started in the basement, where the unnecessary entrances had been blocked off, and the servants would be funneled through a single, defensible, entrance. Then they went up to the square, to look at the steel bars, imbedded into the window openings. Teridon absently pulled on the bars. Scott chuckled at his back when they did not budge.

"You're big, but a horse couldn't break those bars."

He shared the man's laugh, he hadn't even thought about what he was doing before pulling on the bars, but they obviously would not move.

"Well, it seems your reputation is well earned. The work is everything I asked for."

Scott laughed harder, his belly shaking as he did.

"And, what reputation would that be?"

"A cantankerous old coot that is impossible to deal with, but happens to be the finest mason in the southern empire. It was a rocky start, but your men did fine work."

Laughing even harder, the man clapped him on the shoulder

"Thank you; it's why they keep me around. But, you're wrong about me, I am the best mason in the whole empire.

"Oh, then please accept my apologies." Teridon bowed deeply.

"Are you Teridon Jace?"

Teridon straightened to find a short, slight, man standing in front of him, "I am, and you are?"

The man bent with hands on his spindly knees, panting from the short run, "Rosi Starling, Damon Maxk's assistant. I need to speak with you."

"Oh yeah, that's right, please, come on inside."

He held out his hand, and Rosi grasped it with a hand that reminded him of a dead fish, clammy and limp. They walked into the foyer, and Teridon directed Mr. Starling to the small sitting room off to the side, "Please, Mr. Starling, sit. Can I offer you something to eat? Some wine?"

The room was small, meant for brief meetings, there were two indigo sofas facing each other, the dark wood accents on the handles standing out against the white marble floor. Rosi sat, lightly, crossing his legs at the knee, "No, but thank you, I just wanted to make sure that the schedule for the next few days was clear, it will be busy, so best get any questions out of the way now."

Teridon dropped heavily onto an sofa, its frame creaking from the force of his bulk. He leaned forward and poured a cup of water from the pitcher that sat on the dark wooden table between them, "I think so; once the confirmation is complete, the three will move to the Crier's rise, where the ceremony will take place; Once complete, they will be present Sir Loorie with the gifts of his office. After that, we will retire to the king's tower for the banquet."

Rosi raised an eyebrow in suprise, he expected that he would have to walk this oversize dolt through everything. He was truly shocked the lout would bother to read the itinerary, "It sounds like you have a good handle on the situation, any questions?"

"What are the security plans? All three of them will be in one place, and surrounded by dense crowds. It doesn't take much imagination to see the problems with that situation."

Rosi nodded in agreement, "It is of great concern to us as well. The city guard will be present throughout the ceremony, and the entrances to the old city will be tightly controlled. They will be prepared to act if anything should happen."

"I mean no offense, but, that's not enough. If anyone wants to assassinate one of them, they would be dead by the time a guard gets there. I insist on accompanying Sir Loorie, the whole time."

"Of course. Now, I have a question for you; when is Master Loorie planning on arriving? He has already missed the morning meeting. It is my understanding that this is unusual."

"Your understanding is correct; he is a very punctual person. A runner came early this morning. He had a late start because some business needed to be concluded. Unfortunately, I don't know anything further."

Rosi stood, Teridon rising with him. Teridon held his hand out. Rosi accepted the gesture and Teridon's hand engulfed his. The huge man's strong hand a stark contrast to his limp grip and sweaty palm, "I understand. I will await your lord's arrival in the Pauper's tower, if you could please send him to the hall when he is ready. It was a pleasure to finally meet you; I trust you will have a good day."

"Thank you, I will send him as soon as I can."

***

Teridon looked through the swirls of the thick lead glass window in his bedroom to see his Sir Loorie's stage rolling into the tower's circular drive. He let out a long sigh of relief before running to meet it. It was a little past high noon, and he was already very late.

He opened the stage door to find Sir Loorie sleeping inside. The knight always fell asleep while riding inside a stage, not that Teridon could blame him, the rocking always put him to sleep as well. He stepped into the coach, and shook sir Loorie awake.

The man awoke with a start, his breathing was quick and shallow; his clothes were a mess and his hair looked like it had not been brushed in a week.

"Sir, are you OK? What is the matter?"

The man's eyes were heavy with sleep, as was his voice, "What are you talking about? I'm fine."

Teridon didn't believe him. He was an old solider, nothing was ever 'wrong', "I'm sorry, sir, but, you look terrible."

The knight slowly shook his head, trying to get the sleep out of it, "Sorry son, I must have been having a dream."

He still did not believe the man, but there was no time to dig deeper; they were already very late, "That's fine. I am sorry to push business, so close to your arrival, but the other two are expecting you sir, you are already very late."

He rubbed the last bit of sleep from his eyes, "I know. I need to get cleaned up first. I'll be as quick as I can."

Sir Loorie exited his stage and disappearing within the tower. Teridon shook his head, he did not know what the knight had dreamt about, but whatever it was had left the knight shaken and pale.

***

Sir Loorie wound up the tower's stair, each heavy step echoing off the stone of the narrow stairway. His muscles were sore, and his legs felt like someone had added weight to his boots. He usually had his best sleep while being rocked by the stage, but he today, he felt like it had sapped his energy, not refreshed it.

He had been plagued by strange dreams had plagued since the election, and sleep had been a rare, but precious, commodity, no matter where he tried to get it. Teridon was right; the stress was getting to him.

His boot landed on the top step, the five flights feeling like one hundred. He tried to shake away the feeling of dread as the door creaked open and he entered a room that was identical to the one in his dreams. The white velvet comforter was tightly tucked around the mattress of large oak bed that sat to his right, a hunting scene carved in the headboard. The same white chairs sat in the sitting area straight ahead, even the same book sat on the small table between them. It was Sir Loorie's favorite. Thebook was a true story; it is the recounting of a small kingdom successfully defending itself from an aggressor that was larger and far more powerful. Both kingdoms had been lost to time, however, so there was nothing left of the two, save for this book. He would read it from time to time, to remind himself that war was not just power and numbers, strategy and dedication were just as important, if not more so.

He stood in the center of the room, taking deep breaths through his nose, letting them out in a long slow streams through his nose, '*they are dreams, toughen up, this is reality.*'

The boy was right, this was all stress, but time was short, he would have to worry about his insanity later. After peeling his shirt off, he tested the water in the large stone wash basin, it was very hot, like he preferred. Using course pumice soap, he washed the sweat and grime from his arms, face, and chest. He was still trying to calm himself as he wet his hair and brushed it back.

He took a towel from under the basin and pushed the soft cotton against his face. Things always felt better after cleaning the grime of the road off.

Lifting his head from the towel's soft pile, he slowly turned to the abomination that hung in his wardrobe. The uniforms of the three were traditional affairs, modified slightly over the centuries. The King's uniform was absurd, it appeared to have been designed for a fool, not a King, but it was the uniform. He pulled the tight black pants on, squatting, trying, unsuccessfully, to stretch the stiff cotton out.

He finally resigned himself to the fact that his nether regions would be compacted, and he pulled on a light white cotton shirt, tucking the tails into the tights. Then, he groaned as he held up the ugliest jacket he had ever seen. It was gaudy, blood red with gold piping, toggles, and collar. There was no lapel, the jacket completely wrapped around his torso, fastening along his left side. He slid it on, pulling it around his body, and then buckled the toggles.

He closed the wardrobe's door, and groaned, even louder, when his reflection appeared in the floor-standing mirror behind the door, he looked ridiculous. He sighed deeply, questioning, and not for the first time, his choice to accept the nomination.

He stared at himself for another second, trying to get used to the ridiculous uniform. He did allow himself a moment of mirth, chuckling as he imagined picking up some fruit and juggling. He was so focused on how he looked, that he had almost forgotten about what the outfit meant. The knock on the door reminded him,"Come in."

The door swung open, and a servant sheepishly peeked in, "My lord, the Advocate and Pauper have arrived." The servant said, meekly, without meeting the knight's eyes. He had been so late that it was just easier to have the other two come to him.

"Thank you son, please seat them in the library and provide them whatever drink they would like. I will be down directly."

"Yes Sir."

Sir Loorie sat and pulled on the knee high boots, which he rolled back over so they actually sat around his upper calf. He walked around a bit, finding that he actually liked the boots; they were well made, thick leather and were very comfortable with thick, but flexible soles. '*Well, there is something.*' Now dressed, he could not delay any more. He left the room to meet his colleagues.

***

The other two men were seated in front of one of the library's great fireplaces, casually speaking with each other as they sipped pewter goblets. They appeared to be in good spirits, with none of the tension that Sir Loorie had expected.

"Good day gentlemen."

The two stood, they wore simple clothing, he had to get clarification on the times when the uniform was required, the less he was in it, the better.

"Good Day" they replied, in unison

He offered his hand to the closer of the two, "Nidan Loorie."

The smaller man took his hand, "Damon Maxk."

He reached out to the other man, who also took his hand, "William Michell."

"Please, sit." Sir Loorie motioned towards the chairs. The two sat back down around the low marble table.

As host, Sir Loorie made sure his guests were comfortable, topping their goblets with wine before filling his own. Hooking his two fingers around the stem of his own goblet, he sat in his own chair, taking a deep pull of the refreshing chilled white, then sinking back into the soft velvet cushions and crossing one leg over the other. Taking a moment to feel the cool liquid slide down his throat, he smiled at the men; it was time to begin, "it is a pleasure to meet you gentlemen. I am sorry for my tardiness, I was unavoidably delayed. Unfortunately, there were a lot of loose ends that needed to be tied."

Damon took the lead, "That is quite alright, we certainly understand. Unfortunately, time is short, so we do need to get to business."

Sir Loorie nodded in agreement, motioning for the man to continue.

"I am going to be blunt, I, we, are deeply concerned with your election. The King needs to put the needs of others above his own, or, in your case, the needs of his friends. Our fear is that your dedication to the military will see you playing favorites.

Also, your association with the military gives you power that the two of us have no hope of matching, you will be holding the Sword of Shebalb above our heads. In short, there is a reason having former military leaders on the council is highly unusual."

Nidan was not sure if he should be angry at the man for questioning his integrity, because the man questioned his service, or maybe both.

"I understand your concerns, and stipulate that they're valid, I can assure you that this was not a position that I asked for, I did not campaign for, and I surely am not here to usurp anyone's authority. The only reasons I accepted the election and took the position are respect for the office and respect for the two of you. As for my standing within the military, I have none. I have been retired for several years, and I was the last of my generation of commanders. I highly doubt that anyone in the military is going to be looking to me for any special favors, outside of the usual requests."

William spoke for the first time, "Tell me sir, do you know who nominated you?"

"No, sir, I do not, though it is information I would like to have. I had my security detail do a cursory investigation, but they were not able to glean any information in the short time they had."

William shook his head in frustration, his investigation turned up the same thing, and there just was not enough time to do a thorough investigation. It did hearten him that the events seemed to trouble the knight as much as they did him. When he had time, he would need to look into the unseen force at work, but that was another matter, for another day, "You say that you are not here to usurp our positions, and I want to believe, but, tell me, what are your plans for the position, sir?"

He took a moment to answer; he had not thought about it and he wanted to give a thoughtful response, "My intention is to continue the work of the prior king, to make sure that our military remains strong, but only in strategically appropriate areas, eliminate wasteful expenditures, and above all, to ensure that the kingdom remains safe and secure. In addition, as the voice of the nobility, I will promote charity among the upper class and be a fair arbiter of disputes between nobles and commoners."

The Pauper put his goblet down, the metal scraping on the stone table as he leaning over the table with his chest was puffed out, "Allow me to explain the way of things. The King is expected to provide money to distribute to my constituents.

You do not 'request' charity, you demand it. My constituents expect certain things from this council, and I expect that those expectations are paid for on the backs of your constituents. They can afford it, after all, they have the money."

'*Well that certainly is blunt*' Sir Loorie thought; he could not let that aggression go unanswered, "With respect, sir, if moneys are demanded, than how can it be charity?"

The man smirked, "Call it what you like, sir, but it is one of the duties of the station. Tribute must be paid, and it is your duty to collect. Never forget, the nobility exists because my constituents allow it. They outnumber yours by a factor of ten, at least. Should the tribute cease its flow, I am not sure what would happen."

Sir Loorie fought his temper. The man was threatening him, and not subtly. It was now clear why the man was uncomfortable with a military man on the council.

These two men were used to coddled noblemen, looking to get along with everyone and not cause trouble. Sir Loorie, however, was a seasoned veteran; they were going to be in for quite a time if they thought they were going to intimidate him into submission.

He met Damon's gaze with a wide smile, "Thank you for the correction sir; I do beg your pardon, I am so very new to politics. I fear that I may need a strong mentor, such as you, to walk me through the fetid swamp into which I am wading. I am just a simple soldier; without guidance who can know what silly mistakes I may make; I will just be blindly swinging my sword. You never know who could get hurt when that starts happening."

Damon leaned back, the threat in Sir Loorie's retort was hidden much deeper than his, but it was there, none the less. The man was a fighter and he would need to be careful. He had to admit, he was impressed at the knight's natural political aptitude. The man was no simple soldier. They were going rethink their entire strategy.

Satisfied that the other two men knew that he would push back against any future threats, he ended the meeting, "Will there be anything else, gentlemen?"

"No Nidan, we shall see you in two hours."

Sir Loorie took a deep swallow of the wine as the two men left. It was just what he needed to take the edge of the day off.

"Teridon!" The boy peeked inside the door from his post on the landing.

"Begin the final preparations."

"Yes sir!" The boy left, slamming the door behind him. Nidan cringed at the reverberating boom, why does that boy need to slam every door he touches?

Chapter 26

The low, somber, tone of the Kethi Draal's bells rang out over the city. The new king had been chosen. Everyone in the city knew what three short tones followed by a long one meant, a swearing ceremony would be held today. People were already heading up the hill when the long tone stopped. According to empirical law, the public must witness the ceremony when a new member of the Three took the oath of office. But, more important to the denizens of the lower city, the swearing was one of the two times that gates of the old city opened to them, the other was to view the body of one of the three after death.

Though open, entrance was limited to the first one thousand new city residents. The city would be abuzz tonight, a member of the three is sworn in so infrequently, it is cause for great celebration throughout the empire, but more so in the city itself.

The city guard had been warned prior to the bell ringing, and they were ready for the rush of humanity. A mounted watch commander was posted at each gate. Pens had been erected to narrow the gates, allowing only one man through at a time.

Jakes rode up and down the line of people queued up at the West Gate, scanning the crowd as he rode. He was not able to note anything that stuck out or looked strange. For the most part, the crowd was respectful and obedient. He had expected chaos, so he was pleasantly surprised at how smoothly the whole process was going. The last swearing ceremony was about 10 years ago, so he only stories to go by, but according to senior guardsman it had ended in citywide riots.

People rushed the gates when admissions were cut off, and refused to go back down the hill when the ceremony ended. The guard turned to force, and the riot ensued, resulting in multiple deaths and hundreds of injuries.

Something caught his eye as he rode up the line, a familiar face in the crowd, a smaller man, about his own age. After a double take, the face was gone; he must have been seeing things. Anytime there is this many people in one place, you are bound to see someone that looked familiar. He refocused, and kept the people moving.

***

The sun was slightly past its zenith when a single long tone sounded, then hung in the air over the city. The quota had been filled, and ceremony was imminent.

The guards fanned out around the lines, beginning the long process of breaking up the crowd. With the action, no one took particular notice of the last couple of people through the gate. Why would they? The two were wholly unremarkable.

Patrick Lueless usually did not question Preacher, but he could not see any good coming from this venture. They were walking into the teeth of the nobility, and the city guard would be at their most vigilant. While he did want to see who their new enemy would be, the risks seemed to outweigh any possible gains. The last adversary was a doddering old fool and he hoped the new King had the same, admirable, quality, and allow their activities to continue unmolested. Unfortunately, none of that would be revealed today, only time would tell that tale.

***

Jakes reached into his horse's saddle bag and pulled out a large cone, made of thin rolled metal, and open at both ends. The guard used these to amplify their voices, making crowd control easier.

Raising the cone, he pressed the leather mouthpiece against his lips, "THANK YOU FOR YOUR PATIENCE, BUT ADMISSION IS CLOSED. PLEASE DISPERSE; THE BELLS WILL RING AGAIN WHEN THE SWEARING IS COMPLETED. PLEASE REMAIN CALM AND MOVE SLOWLY DOWN THE HILL." Jakes rode back and forth, yelling orders as he moved along the line.

Save for some minor grumbling, the crowd did not put up a fight, and dispersed. All told, Jakes was very pleasantly surprised at how smoothly the whole operation had gone.

Chapter 27

Nidan Loorie felt positively ridiculous as attendants ran about putting the final touches on the preparations. A tailor stood behind him taking measurements. The coat he was currently wearing had been made big, so it could fit most people, since there was no time to get the new on tailored prior to the ceremony, the tailor had used pins and cord to give the coat a reasonable fit, but it was no substitute for actual tailoring. A better fit might help, but it would not solve the gaudy color scheme or outdated style, he couldn't help himself, "Can I make any changes made to the coat? Is there any way that you can work the.... ugly out of it?"

The tailor chuckled, "Every time I fit one of these, that's the first question asked. Unfortunately, no you can't, I am only allowed to tailor the coat, not change it"

"Lovely. Why is it so ugly?" More than a hint of sarcasm in his words.

"It is ugly now." The tailor chided lightly, "But, it was the height of style when it was first designed. It represents the style at the time of the last emperor; when the three first came to be. The uniforms you three wear are meant to reinforce the idea that the power of the singular emperor had been broken up, and transferred to three men."

Nidan rolled his eyes, and the sarcasm dripped from his words, now, "Thanks for the history lesson." The Tailor did not respond.

He immediately felt guilty for snapping at the man, he tried to treat everyone, regardless of station, with respect, "I am sorry. I shouldn't have said that, I think the stress getting to me."

The Tailor smiled in thanks, "Don't concern yourself with me sir, you have much more important things happening today, I would keep your mind on those. They are what's important." The tailor scribbled some more numbers on his paper, "I think I have all I need, enjoy the day sir, I have seen several of these, and the hard work begins after the swearing. Too many people in your position forget that, and, if I may be forward, you are a good man, not many nobles care how they treat the staff. That quality, above all, will endear you to the masses. Never forget it, and never lose it."

"Wise advice, and thank you."

***

Teridon was inspecting his final preparations for the third, or was it fourth, time. This was going to be his first true test. He was being so careful, that it teetered on paranoia. He may still fail, but it would not be because he lacked preparation or effort. Wooden barriers had been erected between the tower and Crier's rise. He paced the path those barriers created, surveying the crowd.

His height wasn't helping; he could only see a few rows into the crowd. Needing to get a better view, he climbed onto the rise. From the higher vantage, there was nothing that concerned him. The crowd was tightly packed, but looked to be in good spirits.

He looked deeper into the crowd, looking for Jakes, as a commander, it seemed logical that he would be working the ceremony. After a brief search, he spotted his friend patrolling the back of the crowd astride a massive back horse. He jumped off the platform and waded into the crowd. It took some work to get through the crowd, he was moving against the current. After several minutes he emerged, "Hey! Jakes!"

Jakes looked around, he had heard the call, but he did not know where the voice had come from. His face softened when he saw who called out, "T!" His eyes quickly returned to the crowd.

As much as Teridon enjoyed seeing his old friend, he was focused on work today, "What are the plans?"

"We have guardsman in the crowd, both in and out of uniform; we have mounted officers around the outside of the crowd. If anything breaks out, the footmen will signal the mounted patrols, and we'll break it up with all of the necessary force."

As Mr. Starling had told him earlier, the guard had a heavy presence, and seemed to have everything under control.

Jakes saw the look on his friend's face, "Teridon! We do know what we are doing; these things have happened, a couple of times, before." Jakes laughed.

Teridon returned the laugh; Jakes was right, the guard was more than capable. With his mind at ease, he could focus on keeping Sir Loorie safe, the city guard would take care of the rest, "I will be with Sir Loorie, if anything happens, I may need-"

Jakes cut his friend off, "I'll come pick your sorry behind up."

Teridon smiled, he knew Jakes would be there if anything happened. If there was one person he could count on, it was his old friend.

Chapter 28

The sun was high in the afternoon sky, the day was warm day, but not hot, faint wisps of clouds were scattered across the sky, the only things breaking up the field of blue, in short, the weather was perfect.

Teridon stood in darkness of the tower's entrance, using the mudroom as a makeshift dressing room. He slid his boiled leather armor over his head, buckling the straps on his left side, slipped leather bracers over his arms and leather grieves over his calves, fastening them with more leather buckles. The bracers and grieves had short, fat, and sharpened metal pyramids, meant for tearing skin in close quarter's combat. Leather armor was not usually his first choice, but it allowed him a significantly better range of motion than his usual steel plate and mail. If any trouble broke out today, speed and flexibility will be vital. Once his armor was in place, he draped a blood red cape over his shoulders, using the the golden buckles, emblazoned with the family crest, that Sir Loorie had given him, to fasten the cape on his upper chest. Finally, he buckled his sword belt, pulled it tight around his waist, and looped the excess through the belt so it hung down along his right leg, almost touching his knee.

His bastard sword hung on his left side and the main gauche was secured straight across his back, hidden under the cape. He looked at his dark steel helm for a moment before casting it aside, choosing peripheral vision over defense.

He felt a presence behind him, turning to find Sir Loorie standing behind him. Despite his best effort, He could not suppress a snicker, "WHAT, are you wearing sir?"

The response was nothing but a withering look, and he took the hint, getting back to business, "The signal should be coming any time, sir, I will be behind you with my hand on your belt. If there is trouble, let me lead you, I'll direct you to a safe exit." He let the other side of that statement go unsaid. With the size of the crowd packed into the square, there may not be a safe exit.

"I understand and, thank you." He smiled and clasped Teridon on the shoulder. The bell rang again, another single long tone, and the door opened, flooding the dark vestibule with sunlight.

The light stung Teridon's eyes, at first, but, after a few seconds, his eyes to adjusted to the blinding light. Once he had his sight back, he tapped Sir Loorie on the shoulder, and they started out the door. The crowd erupted when Sir Loorie exited the tower, applause washing over them as they left the safety, and quiet, of the tower. He tried to block out his nerves and focus on the task, but self-doubt constantly reared its head, he kept chanting in his head, *'focus, focus, focus.'* The barriers remained in place and the way to the Crier's Rise was clear. The other two were already waiting on the dais.

Teridon allowed Sir Loorie to set a confident, but not rushed, pace. He fell in right behind the knight. A full head taller, he slowly scanned the crowd. His left hand was under his cape, fingering the handle of his dagger. Keeping a hand on his sword would be too aggressive, the dagger allowed him to be prepared, but not overtly threatening. He was there to protect his charge, not inflame the crowd. Sir Loorie kept the steady pace, still not rushing, but moving with purpose. He allowed the crowd to see him, but did not slow. Teridon's heart pounded as he watched the cheering crowd. He could not see more than a few rows back, but the crowd seemed to be well behaved.

Sir Loorie took a long moment at the base of the stone dais. Once ready, he started up the five stone stairs to the Crier's Rise.

Teridon led, and then took a place at the right rear corner. From his vantage he could see all the way to the rear of the crowd. Mounted guardsmen rode along there, keeping an eye on the crowd from behind. He still saw nothing concerning, and the crowd's good spirits continued. The cheers reached their crescendo when Sir Loorie ascended the last step and onto the stone stage.

Rosi ran about the rise, trying to get everyone into place, which took some time, there were three men, Rosi, Teridon, a dozen representatives invited from around the empire, and an additional dozen representatives from Capuamundi itself. He pushed here, pulled there, until everyone was in place. Once he was satisfied, he nodded to the Advocate.

At the signal, the Advocate stepped forward and began, "Welcome, I am the advocate, arbiter of disputes between The Pauper and The King. I am tasked with ensuring that the government is equitable and accessible to all. I am also tasked with ensuring that no decision is made lightly and that the Pauper and King properly consider all sides before rendering any decisions; no matter how grave, or trivial, those decisions may be."

The man stepped back while the Pauper stepped forward, "I am the Pauper, representative of the people. I give a voice to the people that do not have one, and I am tasked with ensuring that people have someone to represent despite their status. I speak for them in a voice that holds the same weight as the nobility's. I am also tasked with ensuring dealings between common people and the nobility are fair and equitable."

The pauper stepped back and the advocate returned to the front of the stage, "Who comes forward?" he turned to Sir Loorie, who stepped up to the front of the stage, and stood beside the Advocate, "I am Nidan Loorie, I have been duly elected serve as the King. I will be tasked with representing the nobility, and to do so without pomp, without arrogance. I will speak in a voice that carries the same weight as the empire's common citizenry. I will not be held above the people and the people will not be held above me.

Together, it is our duty to ensure that all peoples in the empire have an equal voice in the government and that the government decisions are well considered and equitable."

The Advocate faced him, "Please, place your right hand to your left breast, and grasp Sulemin's scepter. The scepter is the symbol of the compact of the three, the symbol of one all-powerful monarch broken into three parts.

Nidan Loorie, have you been duly elected by the empire's nobility, with no force or ultimatums used, and with no promises given or payments expected?"

"I have."

"Sulemin Argon founded the Aragonian Empire. In doing so, he started a line of rulers that stood unbroken until Telemin the Wise, in his great wisdom, stepped away from the throne and gave his power to three representatives of the people."

Sir Loorie grabbed the scepter.

Teridon was still focused on the crowd and tensed when, off to his left, the crowd started pushing forward, sliding the wooden barriers forward, but just slightly. It appeared to be nothing more than an over excited crowd, but he continued monitoring them.

The advocate continued, "Do you, Nidan Loorie, swear to hold the laws of the empire sacrosanct."

"I do."

"Do you, Nidan Loorie, swear to place those laws above your own self-interests or the interests of any of your prior friends and associates?"

"I do."

"Do you, Nidan Loorie, swear to hold the other two members of the council at the same level as yourself and to abide by the decisions arrived to by this council."

"I do."

"Do you, Nidan Loorie, swear to leave behind the trappings and responsibilities of your prior offices?"

"I do."

"Do you, Nidan Loorie, swear to carry out the duties of this office to the best of your abilities?"

"I do."

"Then, Nidan Loorie, by the laws of the Aragonian Empire, You are now The King, a member of the three, holding one part of the power of the last emperor."

Sir Lorrie nodded solemnly, "I accept this burden and bear it willingly, on behalf of the people I represent and the empire we govern."

The advocate turned to the crowd, "You have all witnessed the oaths that this man has taken and can attest that they were taken freely and without reservation. You have now witnessed the transfer of power to the new King. Thank you for your witness, this ceremony is concluded."

The pauper came up to the front and stood next to the other two. The Advocate split the scepter back into its three pieces, handing the top to the King and the bottom to the Pauper. These were the tokens of their office, and the only time they were joined was during the swearing.

The bell rang again, this time the full quartet of the tower bells rang a out, the tones ringing high to low, over and over, the sound was uplifting and captured the joy of the day, especially in contrast to the somber tones of the single large bell that started the ceremony. The music told the city that the ceremony was over, and there was a new King.

The crowd was applauding, then Sir Loorie turned and waved, and the crowd broke into an absolutely frenzy, yelling, cheering, but it was all good natured, despite the excitement, the crowd seemed to be there to cheer the knight.

Below, the crowd started to push against the wooden barriers, sliding them inward and narrowing the path a bit. The crowd was starting to churn; the wall of people starting to push harder against the barriers. Teridon moved behind Sir Loorie, standing over his left shoulder. He grasped the knight's belt, as before. They descended the stairs, and then started along the narrowing pathway.

He could touch both barriers with his outstretched arms. Pushing tight to Sir Loorie, he tried to get him to move faster, but the knight subtly pushed back, setting the same easy pace as the walk up. He allowed the pace, but did not like it.

The crowd pushed harder, sliding the barrier even closer. Suddenly, the good natured crowd seemed to be on edge, the joyful yelling now interspersed with grunts and angry shouts. People in crowds fed of each other and it would not take much for the situation to turn ugly.

The crush of people put Teridon on a knife's edge. He walked with his hand was wrapped tightly around the handle of his dagger, no longer trying to hide it. While he wished Sir Loorie would take his cue and move faster, he was ready to respond to any threat with overwhelming force.

Chapter 29

Preacher stood a few rows back from the barricade, watching and waiting. Patrick stood in front of him and could feel the man's quickening breath on the back of his neck, the hot vapor revealing the rage boiling beneath the serene mask. Preacher spoke directly into his ear, voice heavy with malice, "Look at these sheep, so excited to see their new tyrant. He lives on the backs of these people, and these pathetic wretches bow and scrape for the pleasure of providing a lifestyle far better than their own. He pisses on their heads as they kiss his feet."

While distracting Patrick with his speech, Preacher began subtly moving forward, pushing the boy along as he did. The crowd was pushing forward as well; he just made sure that they moved slightly faster than the rest of the crowd.

Preacher continued his push forward, "Have they no idea that they cheer for the boot that hovers over their throats? It could drop and crush them at any time, and it would do it without a shred of remorse. How can they not see that? Are they stupid? Naïve? blind? These three leaches sit in their towers, dictating how these people live their lives. They sink their hooks into the people, sucking whatever they need to maintain their lifestyles, while they leave scraps for the people that actually supply it. And these people are stupid enough to thank them for those scraps. The three create an illusion of freedom, an illusion of choice, but no matter how convincing the illusion, it is still just an illusion. They have that figured out. If you give the illusion that people are free, if you give the illusion that people make their own choices, then your tyranny will not be questioned. As long as the boot over their necks is hidden they will not demand it removed.

Throughout his ranting, Preacher continued to push his protégé towards the barricades. Patrick's life was changed when he freed Preacher from that paddy wagon. He was able let go of the anger that had raged within him, but when the anger dissipated, it left a void. Following Preacher had filled that void with purpose, and gave meaning to his previously empty life. He was now dedicated to helping Preacher spread his ideology, and helping to build a revolution. Preacher spoke, often, about that void and how people longed to have it filled.

When the man spoke the world melted away. Unfortunately, for him, Preacher knew the effect he had, and had no issue with using it.

He was focused on Preacher's speech, making sure that he absorbed the words, he was so focused that he did not notice that he was standing next to the barricades.

"Look at your oppressor, my son." Preacher pointed at Sir Loorie as he walked towards them. Patrick's breath caught as he saw who was behind the knight. Teridon! He had wormed his way into guard duty. Did the knight know he was being guarded by low born trash? Probably not. Someone of his stature would never choose to be guarded by some stupid country farmer.

Despite leaving his past behind him, the hatred for Teridon ran so deep that it could never be forgotten, or ignored as it came rushing back. He glared as the laborer arrogantly sauntered behind the King, acting like this was somewhere he actually belonged. He was so focused on Teridon, that he jumped when Preacher spoke again,

"Are you ready to do some acting, boy?"

He looked around, confused, 'What are you talking about? Act at what?'

They continued watching the new King came closer, waving as he strode along the pathway. He moved slowly, shaking hands where he could, playing at being one of the people. Patrick knew the truth; Preacher had explained it so well. This man did not care about anything but power. He was close now; it would only be a few more steps before he was even with Patrick.

Suddenly, Preacher jerked him around, and screamed, "PICKPOCKET!" Then threw him away. Patrick stumbled into the barricade. He caught himself against the timber, which slid a bit but held. Frozen in terror, he hung onto the barricade, gawking at Preacher through wide, terrified eyes.

Preacher's face was hard as iron as he cocked back his right arm back and swung at him. The clumsy punch missed him badly, flying over his head; it struck the man standing beside him in the shoulder.

Patrick had always been a coward, and time had not changed that, so when the man spun on him, he did what he usually did when confronted, run.

Pushing off the barricade, he ran, headlong into a wall of people, there was nowhere to go, the crowd was too thick. He pushing right, then left, the crowd started closing in as he desperately tried to find Preacher in the crowd.

A short, rotund, man, moved aside and Preacher appeared; engaged in a shoving match with a large bearded man. Preacher shoved the man, who fell back into another man. That man pushed the man back towards Preacher, who stepped to the side, allowing the man to run by, hit the barrier and flip over it. Patrick felt like the crowd was crushing him, and things were about to spiral out of control. Every fiber of him screamed to get away, but he was trapped, the wall of humanity held him just as surely as walls of rock and bars of iron. His heart raced, and he hyperventilated as sweat poured off his forehead. He was being pushed to and fro, the crowd dictated where he went.

***

Sir Loorie walked along the pathway, Teridon moving in unison as he followed, the knight again setting the pace. With Teridon watching the crowd, Sir Loorie was able to concentrate on greeting, and thanking, the gathered throng. As before, he used the back of the knight's belt to direct the man, though his grip was much tighter this time. He was ready to rip the man out of trouble. They were about half way along the path when that trouble found them.

It started with a scuffle to his left, someone screamed about a pickpocket. His grip on the knight tightened and he was getting ready to pull him to the far side of the walk when someone flipped over the barrier. The man landed flat on his back, directly in front of Sir Loorie.

"GO!" Teridon pushed the knight away, pulled his dagger and dropped a knee onto the center of the prone man's chest.

The man screamed, punching Teridon's leg. The punches stopped when the tip of Teridon's dagger dug into the side of his neck, the warm trickle of blood convincing him to be still. Given the situation, the crowd, and the scuffle, he was not about to take any risks by playing with the man, "If you move, you die." He growled.

Teridon did not need to look down, he felt the man under his knee, instead, he started at the knight as he quickly walked towards the tower.

He did not look at anywhere else until the tower door swung shut behind Sir Loorie. Once sure his charge was safe, he sheathed the dagger and stood, letting the man off the ground. He took the opportunity to run back into the crowd.

Teridon watched the man push his way through. As he scanned over the people, he saw a man staring back at him. Teridon jumped the barricade, trying to grab the man, but before he could, the crowd swallowed the man up and he was gone.

***

Preacher kicked the ground. All his plans for the day had failed, miserably. The fight between the boy and himself was supposed to start a riot. Using the chaos, he was going to get close to the King and kill him. Unfortunately, the crowd was cowed by that boy's knife at the throat of a fellow sheep. He had to give the knight credit; he would not be easily intimidated. It is a credit to his service. He also surrounded himself with people willing to die for him.

The day was not a complete loss. He had been able to observe the relationship between the knight and that boy. The knight trusted the boy, and the boy was very dangerous. He knew how to handle that blade, and, by all appearances, his loyalty was unflinching. He would have to be dealt with before they would be able to get to the new King.

Sir Loorie stood waited inside the tower door when Teridon slammed the door shut, the crowd noise flooding in was replaced by the echo of the door slamming. The echo hung in air for a moment, then silence. The stone walls and stout wooden door buttressed them from the chaos outside. Now safe inside the tower, Teridon collapsed against the wall. His energy was spent from the combination of excitement and exertion. Slumped against the cool stone, he let out a long, dejected, sigh, "that went well," sarcasm heavy in his voice. He was a failure. His first security detail ended with his charge running from a small riot, and a dagger to the throat of a man who was pushed from the fray. This charade needed to end before Sir Loorie was hurt, or worse.

"Sir, I told you that I don't have the experience to do this. I'll leave tomorrow, and save you the trouble of letting me go."

"Nonsense! Teridon, if you think that you can protect me from all danger, at all times, then perhaps you are correct, I should find a new man. There has to be someone in this empire that can do the impossible. Listen, son, you set up the situation as best you could.

When the trouble started, you neutralized the threat immediately, and I stand before you without a scratch. To me, that is a rousing success. Your instincts are keen, you need to continue to develop them, and, most importantly, continue listening to them."

He appreciated Sir Loorie's attempt to make him feel better, but it did not alleviate his self-doubt. That said, his steps were a little bit lighter after their conversation.

He followed a few steps behind Sir Loorie as they walked deeper into the tower. The knight doffed that ridiculous coat as they walked, "Well, it's done. I am officially a member of the government; who has cursed me with this fate? Anyway, when I was meeting with the other two; Maxk, that little prick, made some pretty blatant threats. We are going to have to watch him. If he has any intention of moving against me, I need to be ready."

Was the Pauper behind the trouble in the courtyard?

"Would you like to put someone on him?"

"Already cultivating spies, are we?"

"No sir, that would be wrong, I merely have friends who provide me with information, from time to time."

Sir Loorie burst out laughing, "Of course, my boy, I would never suggest otherwise, but, no, just keep an eye out. Let me know if those 'friends' tell you anything."

"Understood, sir, I will do just that."

***

Teridon's day should have been done, but he could not stop thinking about what happened. He needed to know more. Until he saw the man staring at him from the crowd, he had been willing to attribute the scuffle to the crowd of people jostling for position along the walk. He had doubt about the evil intent in those piercing blue eyes, and it was no accident that it happened in front of Sir Loorie.

He went outside, and was impressed at how quickly the guard cleared the square. It was empty, save for a few stragglers milling about, taking advantage of the rare opportunity to see the old city, but the guard was in process of corralling.

He walked toward the Crier's Rise, unsure of what he was really looking for. The man's striking face was burned into his memory, a thin, almost gaunt face that narrowed sharply at his chin, sharp nose, and long inky black hair.

Unfortunately, that did nothing to identify the man. The man's body also stood out, it was larger, almost heavyset, a stark contrast to the giant face.

The man also wore a dark brown robe, but he did not spend much time thinking about something so easily changed. He needed to take the knight's advice and trust his instincts.

Teridon strolled around the square, looking over the stragglers as the guard prodded them out of the square. Maybe the man stayed behind to see the results of his actions. He grasped at straws, but doing something, even if futile, took his mind away from today's failure. Kicking at the worn cobbles, he moved trash left over from the ceremony with his boot. He wasn't sure what he was looking for, but looking felt right.

Cleaning crews had already begun their work about the square. One crew was disassembling the barriers, another swept the rise, and several others were using straw push brooms to sweep the square. They pushed towards area were the fight happened.

The boss walked from crew to crew, checking on progress. Teridon caught up to the man as he walked from the rise, "Excuse me foreman."

"Hello sir, what can I do for you?"

"Do you have to clean this area first? I would like to look through some of this mess."

The crew boss looked like he wanted to run, and would not meet Teridon's eyes. Laborers did not like being spoken to by members of the upper city, it rarely ended well for them, "No sir, but this is the bulk of the mess. We could move to the other end of the square and work our way back to this area, but the square needs to be clean before sundown."

"Thank you chief, and I understand, that will be more time than I need."

Still using his boot, he kicked through the scraps of paper and food leavings. It was an hour before something caught his eye. Squatting down, Teridon picked up a torn piece of dark brown fabric, revealing a gold pendant underneath. He ran the fabric between his thumb and forefinger, feeling the fine, soft, threads. The quality was quite good, whoever owned it had money.

The pendant, however, was much more interesting, he flipped it a couple of times. It was gold, but of very low quality; the casting marks were still visible and the surface was pitted with the impurities already corroding, turning the pits green and brown.

The design was a five pointed star with a small ruby in the middle. He was not familiar with the symbol. Someone would know what it was; he wrapped the necklace in the fabric, put it in his pocket and started back to the tower, signaling to the boss as he did.

Chapter 30

Unknown to most residents, the hill under Capuamundi had not always been the fat hill they saw now, the slope used to be much more severe. Over the interceding millennia, the city was destroyed and had been rebuilt several times, the ruins of the old serving as the foundation for the new. Each new iteration of the city was larger and the hill fatter, the slope lesser. It also led to forgotten places, places where the old buildings survived, and, covered by the construction above, allowed one to live away from the prying eyes above.

Preacher and his flock lived in one of these forgotten pockets under the city. The occupied the first three floors of an ancient tenement. A dwelling of the lower classes, the apartments were nothing but two tiny rooms. There were no privies; the occupants would have used chamber pots, contributing to foul and unsanitary conditions. This little hole was a window into the Capuamundi of old. It was not so different from the slums around the city's modern Harbor District. Buildings with cramped, smelly rooms, and small shops occupied by people who thought their little businesses freed them from the bonds of poverty. The truth was, they lived at the grace of both the mob and the government. Either entity could destroy them, if they were so inclined.

Patrick had always been curious about how Preacher had found these ruins. The way in was so convoluted. The only entrance was through a void at the base of a wall at the end of a nondescript ally off Mary street, about halfway between the east and north roads. Even knowing where the ally was did not make finding the entrance easy. It was under a metal grate, where a drainage pit had been worn away by years of weather, creating a hole to the underground.

Had a person not known what was below, it would have looked no different from the thousands of other drainage pits dotting the city. The hole led to a ledge, which followed the contour of the hill. Moving up the hill, slightly, there were hand holds cut into the piling, creating a ladder down to the old street, about 25 feet below. They were recessed into the pilling, and invisible from above. If someone did manage to stumble across the pit, then the ledge, they would see no way to get down from there. All told, the area was a very safe, and fairly comfortable, location to operate out of.

***

Patrick sat cross-legged on the floor of his room, thinking. Preacher had been more of a father to him than his own father had, but he had just tried to kill him. Stealing from a noble was punishable by death, and the man had accused him of being a pickpocket while they were in the upper city. He could have been under the headsman's axe by tomorrow morning. Tears trickled out of the corners of his eyes; he had just found out that his life meant nothing to the most important person in his life. If he wanted him dead, he would be dead. Sniffing loudly, he fought to hold back the flood of tears. He was disgusted by his weakness, but he was not surprised.

He had followed Preacher for almost five years, and until today, he had followed blindly, never questioning. This afternoon shook him to his core; for the first time, he questioned what he had gotten himself into, and what Preacher's real intentions were. His stomach churned, and he felt like he was going to shit his pants. Wrapping his arms around his stomach, he curled into a tight ball, rocking back and forth.

Chapter 31

"Bix!"

She shot up in response to her father yelling from downstairs. Why was she on the floor? The last thing she remember was the ringing in her ears, those crazy golden sparks flashing around the room, then the room distorted, spun, and went black. She ran over to the mirror, her eyes were the same deep blue that they always were. Had she imagined the whole thing?

"BISICARA! Get down here, now!"

After taking a moment to be sure nothing was amiss, she tore herself away from the mirror. Her father was an old sailor, and not particularly patient. He had spent most of his life working the trade routes along the Lake Nemi. The great lake was really an inland sea. Sailors that worked the lake were away from their families for months at a time. Last year, he decided that it was time to retire, and be a father to his daughter and husband to his wife. He purchased a building just up the hill from the Harbor district, and opened a business. They lived in the apartment upstairs, saving money on rent, which allowed them to concentrate on building the business.

She ran downstairs, through the store, finding him in rooting through boxes in the back room. She tapped him on the back, he responded without looking away from the box.

"I told you to unpack these boxes. You know I need to get an accurate inventory before I leave next week. Bix, this is the last trip north before winter. If I don't get the numbers right, we'll have a repeat of last year! We can't run out of stock this winter."

The family business was importing raw materials. Using the network of contacts built over the years of working the lake, her father would purchase fabrics the mills in the east, furs and leather from the north, and metals from the mines along the Heshian border in the south. Once brought into the city, he would wholesale raw materials to the city's artisans. Last winter was their first in business and they barely survived. They had not anticipated the spike in demand for northern furs, or the huge drop in leather demand.

They were sold out of fur by the second month of winter, and it took all season to get through the stock of leather. They could not to let that happen again this year, and er father was putting tremendous pressure on himself to get the counts right.

"I am sorry father. I forgot. I promise, I'll take care of it tonight."

He turned around, the exhaustion written all over his face, the creases around his eyes seemed deeper, the soft eyes sunken and his mouth wearing, what seed to be, a permanent frown.

"Bisicara, this business feeds our family. I need you and your mother to pitch in, or it can't work. If I ask you to do something, it needs to be done. I don't give you work for the sake of work. I give it to you because it needs to get done; especially with winter approaching." The exasperation was thick in his voice; she could be so hardheaded and forgetful.

"Yes father, I will get it done." She replied looking at her shoes.

The years had seen Bisicara grow from a gangly, awkward, teen into a stunning woman. Her tall body now fit her long slender limbs, her mesmerizing eyes really stood out against her pale skin. Suitors lined up, but she had turned them all away. She held the obligation to her family above such matters. While her father appreciated her dedication, he secretly worried that she was going to miss her opportunity to marry. She was 21, an age that saw most women betrothed, or at least on their way to it. His beautiful daughter could end up stuck here, running a store, all because of his stupid choices.

"Bix, we leave next week, are you ready for this?"

She threw her hands wide, feigning exasperation, "Father, you have asked me a hundred times, I am ready. You will only be gone for a couple of weeks, and I've ran the store before. Everything will be fine, stop worrying."

She had run the store before, but not for this long, and never without him close by. She was capable of handling the store, but that did not stop him from worrying. He was her father; he would not be living up to that title if he didn't worry.

"Hey Bix" someone called from behind. She turned, Ellen stood in the doorway.

"Can I go out with Ellen, Father?"

Her father just shook his head, "Sure, as long as these are unpacked tonight."

She ran over, kissed him on the cheek, and thanked him before running out the door.

Chapter 32

It took some time, but Patrick had finally been able to uncurl from the ball. He sat with his head between his knees, lost in thought. His head jerked up when the creek of a door broke tore through the dead silence of the underground. He jumped up, and ran down the two flights of stairs, barely touching them. Clearing the last step, he found himself standing face to chest with Preacher. All of the pain that Preacher's betrayal caused exploded out of him, "WHAT WAS THAT?" He pushed the man, who took a small step back.

If Preacher was surprised or flustered by his aggression, he did not show it. He responded smoothly, "I am sorry son, but I needed your reactions to be genuine."

"You could have started a riot! You could have killed us!" Preacher's response was a wrinkled brow and head cocked slightly to the left.

'*That had was your plan all along, you wanted the chaos, you wanted the riot.*'

Preacher saw the boy's face change as he figured out the plan, "ah, enlightenment dawns."

"But, why? What were you trying to do?"

"I am sorry, my son. I know my answer will not placate you, but the truth is, I am not ready to tell anyone my plans, there is more work that needs to be done before I will risk loose lips. It is not that I don't trust you, son, but it is that I don't trust others. I am sorry that I did not tell you what I was planning before I acted. In the future, I will promise you better communication. Unfortunately, I cannot promise more."

Patrick's rage still burned white hot, "That isn't good enough! I have been following you for five years, and I have NEVER questioned you. I have believed in you, and now you can't trust me? I don't care what you say, if you don't tell me, you don't trust me!"

Preacher dropped him to his knee with an open hand slap. His hand shot to his left cheek as the heat rose, and tears began to flow again. He was rubbing his cheek when Preacher grabbed the lapel of his shirt and yanked him onto his feet, then his toes, bringing them face to face. Preacher was breathing fast; his breath was hot, moist and putrid, smelling like death. Patrick cringed at the odor, and felt like retching at the moisture that clung to his face.

Preacher's eyes were open wide and bright white, his rage had been unleashed, "You sniveling, ungrateful, little worm. How DARE you make demands of me? I saved you from the gutter, I gave your life purpose, I have given you a family when you had none. Despite all that, all I have given, you DARE question ME? WHO ARE YOU TO QUESTION? YOU ARE NOTHING; you exist because I allow it. Go, get out of my sight. If I need you, I will come for you. Until then, SHUT YOUR PATHETIC MOUTH!"

He threw Patrick away like he was a sack of trash. He struck the wall with a sick thud. Preacher took a step back and watched him slide down the wall. He landed and slowly curled back into the ball, losing the fight with his tears, which now flowed freely.

Preacher crouched down next to the boy, fighting his disgust. He despised weakness, and could not think of anything weaker than the pathetic lump quivering at his feet. Still, he needed the boy, and his loyalty. If he had a talent, it was an ability to read people, to intuitively know how they needed to be approached. With Patrick, screaming was clearly not the way to reach him. Changing tactics, he went back to being the father figure that the boy craved. Reaching out and gently grabbed the Patrick's hand.

"I am sorry, today was a failure; I took my frustrations out on you, my son. That was wrong, you deserve better from me. You have been my most devout follower, unflinchingly loyal. This was a poor way to pay that loyalty back."

Patrick rolled to face him, his red, swollen, eyes meeting Preacher's cold, hard ones. It took some effort, but he managed to stop crying, though he continued to sniffle which was more pathetic. Preacher wanted nothing more than to wind up and smack him even harder, but he had to control his emotions.

If he allowed his rage to slip out again, he risked giving Patrick another reason to pull back. Instead of the fist he wanted to offer, he offered the boy a hand and helped him up.

Preacher tried to tread a fine line, to explain what had happened, but not give too much away, the movement's plans were his, and his alone, "You are right, it was my intention to start a riot, but it was not my intention to hurt you. I would have gotten you out of the fray. I did not want to hurt anyone; just to stir up some chaos."

This was all a lie, of course, he did not care if anyone got hurt, and, in fact, he had been counting on it. While he would rather no one loyal to him was hurt, if they were, it's a price he would happily pay.

Until now, Preacher thought that Patrick was fully behind the movement, but after today, it was clear that he still needed more indoctrination. Patrick's loyalty, like every member of the group, needed to be unflinching and unquestioning. Today had scared the boy enough to start asking questions. It was a rare miscalculation. One that he would not repeat, "Patrick, I need you. You are the only person in this forsaken city that I trust. I cannot tell you all of the plans, but know that they are audacious, even I question if they are doable. If they come to fruition, they will change the empire. You, Patrick, have a huge part to play. It may not feel that way, but without you, the plan will fail."

Pride swelled within his chest. Somehow, some way, Preacher always knew how to placate him, how to sooth even his deepest wounds. The fact was, Preacher had fallen back on his most reliable tactic, flattery. Patrick did not want to risk the man's anger, but his curiosity was piqued, "Can you tell me what the next step is?"

Preacher's eyes softened, his lapdog was begging for a treat, "Yes, though the plans changed today, the original intention was to test the new King's mettle. He is a former military man, but that can mean anything. I had not counted on the dog, however."

Preacher saw the quizzical expression, *'the idiot missed the metaphor.'*

"I am talking about the man that broke up the scuffle, the kings attack dog."

"Teridon."

Preacher's head snapped up, "What?"

Preacher would not know who that farm boy was, and Patrick jumped at the chance impress, "The boy is Teridon Jace, from Barnstable. I knew him when I lived there, and I hated him. I had no idea that he was here, and I surely don't know what his role with the King is. I haven't even thought of the trash since leaving that hole."

Preacher sat down, crossed his legs with elbows rested on his knees and chin in his hands, "Tell me more about this 'Teridon Jace'."

Truth to tell, he really did not know much, there was no reason to know anything about servants, "Well, he was a contract farmer for Lord Aerick Baelin, the lord of Barnstable and Westin Forest. He lived with his mother, who worked as part of Lord Baelin's household staff. He didn't go to school, just worked on the farm. His best friend entered the military with me, and the last I saw him, he was talking about trying to become a squire, though I don't know if he was able to."

Preacher held his hand up to stop him, "While that is all interesting, I need to know more about the boy's personality, and what we can do to exploit it."

"Ok, he was a hot head, and very easy to push into a fight. He didn't like being made fun of, and don't dare bring up his poverty, social status, or make fun of his mother. Those were his sore nerves. Want to get him to fight? Tease him about those. He was arrogant, yet at the same time, insecure. Given what we saw today, I would guess the arrogance has taken hold over the insecurity. He could not afford weapons, so he learned to fight with his hands. Rumor was that he was deadly with his hands."

Preacher's hands were folded in his lap, he looked to be enthralled, "Arrogant, violent and stupid, he seems the ideal candidate for military service, why didn't he go?"

Patrick had completely forgotten about the troubles earlier, "He wanted to, he got caught looking at the choosing course, then took out 3 soldiers before they could catch him. He was banned from the contest, permanently."

"Thank you, son, you have been very, very, helpful."

He couldn't imagine how that small bit of information helped, but he was proud to have given it. It angered him, though, that the stupid oaf was in such an important position. He wasn't sure what lies Teridon told the knight, but the man needed to know that a glorified servant protected him.

Preacher uncurled from his sitting position and stood, looming over him with an icy glare, "We need to separate dog from master. The knight has nerves expected of a veteran, and the confidence that comes from that beast backing him up. With that man at his back, there is not much that will shake him."

Patrick had managed to pull himself up and was leaning against the stone wall for support. He was not following the logic, "Why focus on the King if he is the hardest to get too. Why not go after the advocate or pauper, wouldn't they have the same affect, and be easier prey?"

'FINALLY! The boy starts to think.' Preacher had been waiting for some evidence that his brain actually functioned, "I like what you are thinking, and we will be going after them in time. Unfortunately, I can't give any more details right now, plans within plans, my boy." Preacher smiled, hoping Patrick was placated.

"No more surprises?"

"Not like that." Preacher said, glad the boy did not question that noncommittal answer.

Chapter 33

"I need you at your best, my boy. Have the night, go get dinner, go get a girl, go do something, ANYTHING, besides work."

Sir Loorie was worried about burning him out. After a bit of consternation, Teridon relented, and accepted the night off. He had been so lost in his work that he did not realize how badly he needed a break, but now that the pressure was lifted for a night, he realized just how spent he was.

***

Teridon left the old city, heading down the hill to have dinner with Jakes. They had talked about it a few times, and tonight was the first time they had been able to get together. The two weeks since Sir Loorie was confirmed had been a whirlwind, but things were starting to settle down, as the King acclimated into his new life.

'Down the hill' was upper city slang for going to the old city. While not particularly creative, it was accurate, and, over the years, it had stuck. He was off duty for the first time in weeks, and he allowed his mind to wander as he passed through the gate, and began his descent. He chuckled; he only had lived in the new city for three weeks and was already talking like a noble.

He was headed for the Poisoned Monk, a tavern near Jakes' home. His steps were light, he felt twenty pounds lighter, and without the armor that he had worn for the past week, he probably was. His light white shirt hung loosely over brown cotton trousers. Light and cool, the outfit was about as far away from his hardened leather armor and thick cotton jupion as one could be. While comfortable, his loose fitting clothes clashed with the tight, well-tailored, clothing that was currently in style, not that he cared.

In Capuamundi, only the city guard was allowed to openly carry weapons. Now a government official, he had received dispensation from the guard to carry, but walking about the new city with swords hanging from his belt would have attracted unwanted attention. Instead, he chose to keep a low profile, small knives tucked into the each boot would be his answer if trouble came calling, while not his sword, they are better than nothing.

There was a sharp chill in tonight's air; summer was waning as the season slipped into fall. In Barnstable, the leaves would already have begun changing colors. Teridon pulled a light knit cap low onto his bald head as he walked down the East road. It was a few more streets before he saw the shingle over the door with a fat man lying down with X's for eyes its tongue hanging out, and a broken bottle lying next to it, The Poisoned Monk.

The dun of a busy tavern wafting out of the door, which was propped open with an old wooden chair. It was surprising, for being one of the most popular taverns in this section of the city; the Poisoned Monk was located in a small storefront. The surprise left when he walked inside, which was much bigger than it looked from the street. To his right stood a large oaken bar that ran the entire length of the tavern. The top of the bar had been finished with thick shellac making it shine under the light of the oil fired chandeliers, hanging throughout the bar. To his left, there were rows of long tables, with benches running down either side of each table. The tables were about half full, the late night crowd had just starting to filter in as the dinner crowd left. The tavern continued back and opened to a large dance hall with a stage in the far right corner. The hall was larger than the main room and was to the left of the dining room, going behind the stores that shared the tavern's building. He did not recognize the song that the fiddler onstage was playing, but it was upbeat and there were several people dancing in the hall. The atmosphere was relaxed, just what he needed.

After walking the bar, he turned back towards the door, and he saw Jakes waving him over. There were five rows of tables and Jakes was set up at the rearmost corner, next to the front wall.

"Hi, friend, you look terrible."

Teridon fell onto the wood bench, slumping onto the table; relaxing for the first time in weeks, and it felt fantastic, "Exhausted... It has been a crazy couple of weeks."

He waved bar maid coming over, a pretty girl with black hair tied back into a pony tail. Her round friendly face had an easy smile. He met her sparkling brown eyes as she came over.

"Can I get you boys something?"

"Two tankards of ale. What are you serving for dinner?" Teridon asked

"Venison stew, with bread that was baked this morning and butter that was churned in our own kitchen."

"Sounds wonderful," Teridon replied with a smile as he held her held her gaze, "each of us will have an order of the stew and bring extra bread, if you wouldn't mind."

She let out a soft giggle as she left with their order. He turned back to Jakes, who was just staring at him.

"You are unbelievable! Not here for a moment and already giving a serving girl fits. Nothing has changed."

Teridon had always been better with women than he was; even as a boy he was able to speak with them easily. He always got tongue tied.

"I was just ordering, I don't know what you are talking about."

"Sure you were." Jakes teased, Teridon replying with a crooked smile.

"Tell me about the past couple of years." Teridon changed the subject.

"What to tell? We got to the Forge and Lueless lasted a couple of weeks before he went AWOL."

Teridon responded to that with a hearty chuckle, "I knew that pansy wouldn't last."

"Rob and I completed basic, with honors, and I went into the field. I was assigned to the 3rd infantry division, and was stationed on the border with Concordia."

Concordia was one of the few legitimate enemies of the Aragonian Empire left in the world, and it was the only border that still saw any action, thought even that was limited to small skirmishes.

"I served there for two years before I met my wife, Nydelis. Once she was pregnant, I decided that I needed more stability. Capuamundi was recruiting, so I put in for the commission. I moved here about 2 years ago, and have been a commander since. My boy is going to be three soon"

"What's his name?"

"Terry."

Teridon beamed, "I am honored, my friend, truly honored."

Jakes leaned forward, "The only reason I am here is because you saved me that night. You sacrificed your future to save mine. It was my honor to give him a name with such meaning."

"You were only there because of my prodding, if it wasn't for me, you wouldn't have needed saving. There was no way I was going to let you get caught because of something I pushed you into"

Jakes was lightly shaking his head, "If I didn't want to go, I wouldn't have been there. You pushed, true, but I am no shrinking violet, if I didn't want to go, I would have pushed back. Still, you were there for me, and I will never forget it"

"Thank you, my friend."

The thanks was sincere, Jakes saying that had lifted a burden he had been carrying since that night, a night that seemed to have happened a million years ago.

"So, commander in the city watch huh? Do you miss military work?" "Well, technically, I still am in the military, but as to being in the field, not a chance. Once I got out of basic training, I found, quickly, that the military is painfully boring. All of the delusions of grandeur that we had were just that, delusions. The bulk of our day was drilling for a war that was not coming while guarding a border that no one tried to cross. Now, I get to actually do real work and my family is a just a street or two away. How about you? What is your story?"

"I squired for Sir Looire after leaving Barnstable, though the last two have been more military training than squiring. My plans were to continue working for Sir Loorie until he finished his work with the government. Once released, accept a long standing offer with the fighters' guild. All that changed when he was elected. He had wanted me to be in charge of his security, and since I owe the man everything I have, I couldn't say no. What happened to Rob? Did he go to the field with you?"

"For a while, but he was as bored with the grind as I was. He was single, had no ties, so he petitioned to become a ranger, he was accepted shortly before I left. I haven't spoken with him since."

"That's great!" Teridon replied, a little bit of jealousy seeping in. "What can you tell me about the city? You have to have your finger on the pulse, far more than I do."

"Well, for it being the size that it is, this city is actually fairly well behaved. Still, there is a bad element in every city, and we are no different, but there is no organized crime and the crime rate is fairly low. Even the slums near the harbor don't have any regular problems, thought they have more crime than the rest of the city.

There are also cults springing up now and again, trying to push people into one religion or another. They tend to be our messiest assignments because you are dealing with zealots."

"I cannot believe, after the great proclamation, people are still trying to push that superstitious nonsense, what is the attraction."

"I have no idea" Jakes said as the food and drinks were served.

Taking a long pull Teridon asked, "Any of these cults a problem?"

"No, most of the time the people they are preaching to are more annoyed than anything else, the ones that do get traction are put down relatively quickly, though rarely quietly."

Teridon leaned back, pitching the tankard up, emptying the large ceramic mug. He had not had a good drink in months and it tasted phenomenal, it was cool, with a nice hearty honey flavor to it. He took a moment to savor the ale before he lowered the tankard and looked for the serving girl. She was nowhere to be found. It was early and they only had two girls working, so he decided to walk up to the bar. He slammed the large mug on the bar and held a finger up, signaling the barkeep.

After filling another patron's mug, she began working her way down the bar. He relaxed with his elbows on the bar; looking at himself in the mirror behind the bar. He was deep in his own head when someone knocked into his back. He swung around, coming face to face with a blonde man. Taller than most, the man was still smaller, in both height and weight, than Teridon. He looked down at a soft face; a tightly trimmed beard framed that round face, accenting the chubby chin. Teridon studied the man, had he seen him before? Not that he could recall. He shot the man a glare and turned back to the bar.

The man pushed closer with his chest puffed out, but careful not to touch him. Capuamundi's laws were clear, in mutual combat, the person who struck first was considered the aggressor, and would be the one arrested.

"Look everyone!" the man tried to address the crowd, but his voice was completely drowned out by the tavern's noise, "We have a celebrity in our midst. He has come out of his master's ivory tower to mingle with us, the little people."

Talk of a celebrity caught people's attention, and the crowd slowly started to gather. He felt a hand on his shoulder, and out of the corner of his eye he saw Jakes. He held a hand up, stopping his friend. He appreciated the support, but there would be no fight, he was not about to get himself arrested for a drunk.

Trusting him Jakes took the cue, and went back to the table, while keeping a sharp eye on Teridon. The blonde man saw the crowd gather and his rant gained steam, and volume, "It is the New King's Attack dog! Is your master going to be alright without you, dog? Is he going to be ok if his dog gets lost on the way home?"

Teridon shook his head and turned away, waving for the barkeep to fill his mug. If this man was trying to get a rise out of him, these petty insults were a pathetic way to go about it. His indifference did nothing to slow the man down, who pushed even closer,"What, dog, can't be bothered with me? Did your master tell you not to sully his name by talking to us poor wretches? You should remember where you come from, you were born poor, but now you refuse to even acknowledge us."

He turned and leaned forward, coming nose to nose with the blonde man, "I don't know who you are, and I don't care. Whatever game you are playing at, I'd stop it while you are still able to walk out of this bar. If you are really looking to start a fight, than by all means, take a swing. If not, shut your mouth and move out of my way. I want to get back to my food."

He flipped a gold coin at the barkeeper, picked up the mug, and made a show of taking a long pull, giving the man a chance to do something. The man made no move. He laughed as he pushed passed the man, "I thought as much, all talk, now get out of my way."

As Teridon was walking by the man, his focus shifted to the group of men surrounding them. He was not sure if they had come with the man or if they were just gawkers, but he chose to err on the side of caution. He leaned back, and took another pull from the mug. Using the back of his hand to wipe the head of his lips, he allowed his body to subtly shift into a fighting stance.

Jakes saw what was going on and hurried over. He slid behind Teridon, and whispered into his friend's ear, "Let's get out of here."

Teridon slammed the empty mug on the bar, "good idea." He started to back towards the door. He was representing Sir Loorie, and he took that seriously. He was not going to allow this to escalate. The group of men stared at them as they exited, but made no moves towards them.

***

"I need to know who that was and what he wants."

"T, I am sure it was just some drunk that saw you at the ceremony. It's not a big deal, but I am going to get the watch anyway. I will be back in a few minutes. Be careful."

Jakes ran off, the night swallowing him up. The street was lined by oil lamps, but the meager light they threw could not light more than a small pool around each lamp. Teridon squatted and slid a knife out of his boot, never taking his eyes off the tavern's storefront. He tucked the small dirk into the back of his belt, letting his shirt fall loosely over it. Jakes could assume tonight was a coincidence, but between the fracas at the ceremony and tonight, he chose not to take any chances. He stepped back into the shadows and waited, determined to find out who this man was and why he singled him out.

***

Jakes ran the short distance to a small wooden building. He walked into the dark guardhouse a bit confused, all city guard houses were supposed to be manned at all times. Captains only left their post in extreme emergencies.

Not jumping to conclusions, he lit an oil lamp, and walked over to the slant top desk along the wall. He flipped through the last couple of pages of the arrest and incident ledger, then slammed the huge book shut.

There was nothing entered in it that would justify leaving a post unmanned. This captain better have a good reason for leaving his post, or he would have the man's rank. That was a matter for later however, Teridon needed him now, and he needed weapons.

Reaching under the desk, he felt along the floor until finding a small metal ring. Dirt slid off the trapdoor as he pulled it up. The cloud of slowly cleared to revel a weapons cache, like the one that was hidden in every guardhouse. He had come out tonight unarmed. It was a mistake he was about to rectify. Reaching into the shallow pit, he grabbed a short sword and a small shield.

Both were low quality, standard, military issue. Still, they were better than nothing. Now armed, he ran back to the Poisoned Monk and Teridon.

Chapter 34

Teridon stood in the shadows, his eyes fixed on the tavern's front door. His cloak was pulled tight to cover his white shirt. The small niche he had found gave him deep shadows to hide in. Pressed against the wall, he made himself as small as possible, trying to maximize the cloak of darkness. He only waited a few moments before a shaft of light appeared from the side of the tavern. Five men walked out of the side door, with the blonde man in tow. A smile crept across his face. It had been too long since he had a good brawl.

Teridon stayed patient and just watched, trying to get a feel for the group's dynamic. The blonde man was the leader, there was no doubt, he pointed angrily in several directions, yelling orders at the other men. They fanned out in the directions that he pointed.

After giving his orders, the blonde man started to walk along the main street, towards Teridon's niche. The coward was looking along the street, staying in the light. He looked to be risking himself, while not putting himself in any real danger. He was letting his underlings take all the risk, letting them inspect the dark areas, where, he thought, the danger lay.

Teridon watched the blonde man work his way towards him. The man was sloppy and lazy, a bad combination. He wandered along the street, not actually searching anything, just putting on a show for his minions, trying to show that he was putting himself in danger as well. There was no way for him to see anything in the shadows that bracketed the small pools of light given off by the street lamps. Because he was not actually looking, the man strolled right by Teridon, who stood, still as a statue, in the safety of his little niche.

Teridon smiled, this man was stupid, lazy, and arrogant. Soon, he will add dead to that list.Once the man past him, Teridon ran out of shadows and drove his shoulder into the man's upper back. He wrapped his arms around the man's waist, driving him to the ground, landing with his full weight on the man's upper back. A soft groan was all the man could muster when Teridon's bulk crushed his chest. He growled and drove a knee into the man's side while grinding his face into the cobbles.

"You want to die, don't you? I don't know who you are, but you're going to get your wish." Malice dripped from every word as he drove another knee into the man's side, then a third before pinning his knee into the center of the man's back. He took the dagger from his belt, and held it against the base of the man's neck, a trickle of blood bubbled around the blade's tip.

Chapter 35

Sir Loorie sat in his study, leafing through the reports that had been delivered early this morning. They were the daily reports from the military units throughout the world. Parchment was stacked everywhere in his small office, on his desk, on the floor, in, and on, the book shelves along the wall. The piles were not getting any smaller either, new reports were added to the mess every morning.

The King serves as high commander of the military, so he needed to know the status of every legion throughout the empire, and the assets throughout the world. In addition, he was also privy to the network of spies that the military had cultivated throughout the years. Those reports were sealed in metal tubes and locked inside the oak armoire to the right of the room's door.

He was not worried about them now, this morning he was looking for one report in particular, from the fifth legion. The fifth was stationed on the Hesian border, along empire's southeastern edge. The two countries were actually separated by the crags, a mountain range filled with tall, severe peaks. Only a handful of passes to gave passage through and the tallest peaks were so high that snow covered them all year long.

Hesh was geographically the most secure nation in the world, bordered on one side by the Crags and on the other side by the great south sea. Even more than the geography, however, Hesh had remained a sovereign country because it was such a reliable trading partner. They were the largest consumer of Arogonian steel, which was the best in the world. They paid for that steel with gold, which Hesh had in abundance. The country had the world's richest, and deepest, gold mines. The two kingdoms had formed a symbiosis of trade, the empire needed gold and Hesh needed steel.

From time to time, some politician petitions the three for an invasion of Hesh, but it was just sabre rattling. Hesh did not have much of a military, true, but, the harsh terrain of the Crags would take any advantage the larger, better equipped, Aragonian military had. The Empire's military was built for fighting on a field of battle, not narrow mountain passes. Hesh's, on the other hand, was built primarily to defend those passes. According to recent reports, some cult had gained significant traction in Hostium, the Hessian capital city.

The empirical assets in the country confirmed these reports; the Gold Lords were having trouble putting the insurrection down. The last report was from the day after he took office, and since, nothing but silence. The flow of information had stopped completely. This was worrying on many levels, but mostly because without Hesh's gold and a market for Aragonian hard goods, the economy would be on fragile footing.

He finally found the report, at the bottom of a large stack on the floor behind his desk. Careful not to disturb the stack above it, he slid it out, then sat back to read the letter from the commander, which was the first page on every one of the reports.

```
                    Intelligence report
                     Heshian border
                      5th Legion
Honorable King, please accept this report from I, humble
servant of the Aragonian Empire, General Anson Mott. The
border between Hesh and the great Empire remain closed, as
they have for the last four days. The Hessian border guards
tell us that there is a disturbance in their capital, but
refuse to elaborate. Our operatives inside the country
continue be silent, this is of great concern, we fear they are
captured, dead or compromised. We need more intelligence
before any further information can be given.  Request
contingent of Rangers be dispatched and permission given for
those rangers to extract our operatives.
                              In Service of the empire
                                            Anson Mott
```

He sighed, and then called for an attendant. The door cracked open and a small man poked his head around it, "Please send a messenger up, immediately, it is very important." The attendant nodded and left. He withdrew a yellowed sheet of parchment from the top drawer of his desk. Dipping a quill in black ink, he started scratching a response to the report. His orders could not be put in writing, lest they fall into the wrong hands. No, the message was a simple call for the ranger commander to report to him. Rolling the paper up, he dripped red sealing wax onto the scroll, then pressed the sigil of the king, a crown floating between two towers, into it. Below that, he dripped blue wax and sealed it with his personal house sigil.

He looked up as a small, mousey, man walked in. Messengers were not warriors, they were small and their diets were strictly controlled so they remained that way. Speed was their most important attribute; any excess bulk affected that speed.

The man walked to his desk and he handed him the sealed scroll, "Place this directly into the hands of Commander Wybb, do not leave it with anyone but him. I want you to report back to me to confirm delivery. Are these orders clear?"

"Yes sir." the messenger saluted and ran out of the room.

Chapter 36

"NO!" Jakes screamed. He came around the corner as Teridon took the blonde man down. He sprinted to his friend and grabbed the massive arm just as the blade was about to sink into the man's neck.

Teridon reversed the hold, flipped his arm on top of Jakes' and pulled the arm into his viselike grip. He wipped to find that arm belonged to Jakes, who was down on a knee, trying to take the pressure off his shoulder.

"Teridon, it's me." He was just able to get the words out through clenched teeth. Teridon immediately let his arm go. He stood, rubbing his shoulder in a vain attempt to loosen the knotted muscles.

"Jakes, I am sorry, I didn't know it was you."

"It's alright, I know, I shouldn't have ran up behind you, given the situation." He was stretching his shoulder, and his arm was starting to move normally again, "This man needs to be punished, not killed."

"You're right; I let my emotions get the better of me. Something is up, and I'd like to see him questioned."

"Fair enough, I'll question him myself"

Teridon nodded, and stepped over the prone man, kicking him in the side as he did. Jakes stepped in, "by the authority of the city of Capuamundi, you are under arrest."

He grabbed the prone man's right hand, and pulled it into a chicken wing lock, pinning it behind his back. Pulling iron shackles out of the small pack he carried on his belt, he clapped them around the wrist and fastened it with a small clasp lock. After securing the left hand, Jakes pulled him to his feet and shoved him into motion.

Teridon took a deep breath, his anger had subsided for the most part, but it still percolated. He had been ready to kill that man, and, in truth, he still wanted to. Luckily, Jakes tempered him, just like when they were growing up. It was a good thing he was here tonight. The man had singled him out, trying to bait him into a fight. It may have been a random encounter, but he was not about to take that risk. Teridon needed to know this man's agenda.

Teridon hung a step or two back, letting Jakes push the man along as they walked the short distance to a guard station. The man hung his head and went willingly.

***

This station had light streaming from within, and was manned, as it should be. Jakes pushed the heavy wooden door open. The captain looked up from the paperwork he was doing, and stood from the tall desk, saluting Jakes.

"Captain, this man is under arrest for attempted assault and inciting a riot. When is your pickup scheduled?"

"The wagon is due within the hour, sir, I will be sure he is on it."

"Please do. He is to be interrogated, so he is not be transferred to the magistrate until I authorize it."

"Yes, sir, I will make the note."

"One more thing captain, has there been any trouble of note tonight?"

"None that I know of, sir. Why?"

"Because when I went to this ward's other post, it was completely unmanned. Do you know who that captain is?"

"Captain Arnold, sir."

"And, do you know Captain Arnold?"

"Yes, sir, he is usually reliable."

"Thank you captain, good night."

The captain grabbed the blonde man and sat him roughly against the wall. He pulled a chain off the floor and fastened the end to the shackles that were still on the man's wrists. The man never showed any emotion, just slumped back against the wall with a vacant look in his eyes.

He would wait for the paddy wagon, one of the many that rolled about the city all night long. They went from Guard Stand to Guard Stand, picking up the people who had been arrested and transporting them to the harbor district, where they would be placed in the holding yards. There, they would wait to be transferred to the magistrate, who was in the prison, located just outside the harbor on Prevalka Island.

Teridon's anger had cooled and, as they walked back to the tavern, he was thinking about what needed to be done, "I need to know who that was, who his associates are, and where he lives."

"I'll see what I can do."

"Jakes, next time we do this, can we just eat?" Teridon said with a feigned whine, Jakes could not help but laugh.

Chapter 37

The Holding Yard was a huge warehouse on the outskirts of the harbor district. Transport wagons flowed in and out all night long, dropping prisoners off to be housed until they can be transferred to the island prison. The guard used a large horse powered barge to get from the harbor to the island. The barge did not need any wind to make the trip out to the prison, so it went out daily, in almost any weather.

Once the prisoners reached the island, they were brought before the magistrate, who ruled on their case and handed down a sentence at the same time: incarcerated; fined and released; released outright; or executed. There were no appeals; the magistrate's ruling was final.

Prevalka Island had been housing criminals for as long as Capuamundi had been a city, probably even before. The actual prison itself, however, was a fairly modern structure. Originally there were no buildings at all. Prisoners were just left on the island. Over time, as social mores and prison techniques changed, structures were built on the barren island. The prison went up slowly, with buildings constructed as they were required. The result was a mash of buildings with disparate architectural styles and materials.

The large courthouse with its ornate brick and woodwork clashed with the stark, grey, stone box that made up the newest cell block, for example. The prison was the most secure in the empire. The island was not protected by the harbor, so it bore the full brunt of Lake Nemi's currents and storms. The only way to get there was by boat, anyone who tried to swim it would have to be insane.

The rays of the morning sun cut through the haze that hung over the lake, thin golden bars shining on the wharf as it came to life. The yard outside the great human warehouse was no different. Guardsmen ran about, preparing for the morning's transfer. Some were setting up the chain barrier that blocked off the pathway from the yard to the barge, others were on the barge checking attaching chains to the steel rings on the deck floor that secured the prisoners during transport, and still others checked the barge for seaworthiness. Part of the hull had been lifted away, and three squat horses were being walked into the barge's belly.

These horses were extremely valuable, they were bread to be short, yet powerful, and were trained to work in enclosed environment, and not be spooked by the boat's motion. Once the horses were inside and secured to the large center wheel, the shipmaster would certify all was ready, and the transfer would begin.

***

It was just as busy inside the building as it was out. Running the prisoner transfer was the most dangerous job in the city guard. Riots were frequent and assaults were a daily occurrence. The guard always responded to these riots with overwhelming force, putting them down before they spiraled out of control, but they usually ended with one or more dead prisoners.

This morning should be uneventful. Last night had been a slow one, most of the prisoners were drunks and minor thieves, and so they would likely be fined and released. If any of them were dumb enough to try and flee or fight, it would dramatically increase their charges and they would not be leaving the island. One man would not be moving this morning, a blonde man, with a short cropped beard, was segregated in a cell of his own. He had been arrested late last night for assaulting someone important. He had not been a problem, though, just sitting in the small cell, tearing at his clothes. Assuming the man crazy, the guards ignored him and went about their business. There were much more important things to deal with than some crazy prisoner who did not want to wear his clothes.

Chapter 38

Jakes lay in bed, shielding his eyes from the morning sun. Sleep had never come to him last night, the events of last night stealing that pleasure. But that was past, and all he could think of was questioning the man. He needed to know what the man wanted with Teridon, and more importantly, what the implications were for the city. He could have been a drunk, showing off for his friends, or he could try to get at the King through Teridon. If the later, he needed to wring any information he could out of the man.

He dressed quickly, donning his formal reds, blood red leather armor worn only by guard commanders. He fastened a black cape to his shoulders and started down the hill. The morning air was chill, but the sun had just poked over the horizon and warmed his face, it felt phenomenal. The day was looking to be an idyllic fall day, a light wind flowed through the city, carrying the rank stench of the city away, leaving a fresh clean smell behind it. He did not rush, either; the man was not going anywhere.

***

Jakes approached the intake officer, who sat behind a simple wooden desk. The gruff looking man was finishing the night shift, his dark, heavy, eyes belied the man's need of sleep. The clerk slowly looked up from whatever document he was pretending to look at, "Yeah?"

Jakes noticed that there was no salute, but the man needed sleep, he couldn't blame him for letting decorum slip, "I am Commander Jacob Pints. I arrested a man last night, he was ordered sequestered for questioning. I am here to begin the interrogation."

The man flipped open the leather ledger that sat on a table next to him, running his finger along the scribbles on the page, "Got it, follow me sir, your boy is the only one being held back this morning."

He followed the intake officer through the heavy iron door, ignoring the unnerving metal on metal slam of that door. As soon as the inmates saw an officer had entered the yards, the screaming started and catcalls started, they were trying to intimidate him, but he had been here many times, and they would not get to him.

Ignoring the noise, he walked down the central aisle. Iron bars ran from floor to ceiling, forming the human cages on either side. The ceiling was highly peaked in the middle, sloping down until it met the walls, at about twice Jake's height.

A long vent at the peak ran the length of the roof. It was supposed to vent the body heat and smell from the pens. It did not work. The stench of feces and urine, combined with the smell of unwashed bodies, assailed them as soon as they walked through the door. Jakes ignored it, refusing to cover his mouth, he could not show any weakness.

He stared straight ahead, following the intake officer down the center. At the end of the row, past all of the prisoners and their howls, stood the sequester cells. Only one cell was occupied this morning.

Jakes stared through the bars at the blonde man, who did not look up from the floor. He leaned against the timber wall at the rear of the cell. His pony tail had been let loose, and his hair hung wildly about his shoulders. He was shirtless and his trousers had been shredded. Only a few strips of cloth hanging around his waist remained. All told, the man looked insane. Jakes cleared his throat, trying to get the man's focus off whatever fascinating item was on the floor. The man slowly raised his head before speaking with an odd cheerfulness, "Hello officer! Can you give a message to the king's dog for me? Tell him that his master will soon be dead, but not to worry because he will join him in the afterlife shortly after." The false joy bled from the man's face and his eyes snapped wide as he became deadly serious, "A wave is coming, commander, a wave that no one will be able to withstand, least of all you and that dog."

The smile returned to his face, though it was a sick smile, too wide and with too many teeth. It did not portray joy, but insanity. Jakes rolled his eyes as he stood waiting for the guard to open the door.

The man stared wide eyed at Jakes, not blinking or even moving, "You can listen or not, commander, but know the wave is coming. Your tyranny cannot last, will not last, and the hot fire of revolution will burn that tyranny away." The man smirked, and then dropped to his backside. A makeshift noose snapped taught, but the short drop did not provide enough force to break the man's neck. His backside hung just off the floor as the 'rope' dug into the man's neck, crushing his windpipe.

Sick gurgling sounds blended with the scraping of his boots as they flailed about the floor. The man's eyes were popping out of his head as the gurgling started go quiet.

"GUARD!" Jakes screamed.

The guard started to run, the man's fat stomach shaking left and right, the fat hanging over his thighs pushed up while he ran. The prisoners started cheering when they saw the commotion. Panting from his short run, the guard sifted through a large ring of keys.

Jakes stood watching, helplessly, as the incompetent fumble with the keys; the prisoners roared, the noise hit a fevered pitch as the man's hands and feet convulsed, his face turning bright red, and lips deep blue.

Heartbeats passed, each one feeling like it took an hour, this man's life was fleeing, and the information he needed was fleeing with him. The click of the lock let him know the door was open, he threw the door open and crossed the small cell in two steps, pulling a knife as he did. Cutting the rope, the man fell, slumped over, and rolled onto his right side. He held his hand in front of the man's nose; nothing, the man was dead. He stood, ran his hand through his hair and cursed under his breath. Teridon was sure that this was part of some grand plot, and this certainly reinforced that suspicion. Why would he kill himself if not trying to hide something?

Jakes snapped around, "who was watching this man? How was he allowed to fashion something to kill himself, was ANYONE watching this man?"

The guard struggled to meet Jakes' glare, "Sir, I am sorry, but we don't keep watch on individual prisoners. We don't have the staff for that."

The man was right, of course, the Holding Yard was one of the most dangerous places in the city. The prisoners were held in large pens, with nothing separating them, and they ran on a skeleton staff, at best. The guard did not worry about what went on in the cells, they couldn't. They just did not have the bodies. Rapes and murders were common occurrences; it was a bonus if all of the prisoners survived to be transferred, a rare bonus. Adding to the trouble, the male and female cells were only separated by bars. Prostitutes were able to continue plying their wares and women that were not prostitutes were sure to stay far away from the bars.

Jakes took a moment to settle his thoughts. Once calmed, he inspected the body with a clear head; from the look of the redness around the eyes, the man may have been on drugs.

The whites of his eyes were red with blood, but, more than likely, that was a result of the trauma of his death. He rolled the body over to find a giant tattoo of a five pointed star on his back, there was no writing or anything else, just the star.

"Where is this man's property?"

"He didn't have any property, sir."

'*Of course he doesn't.*' Jakes considered the situation, the man was a zealot, that was clear; but, to whom that zeal was dedicated was the question that needed answering.

Whoever it was, they were important enough that the man would kill himself before he would risk being questioned. He did not recognize the symbol on the man's back, so he sketched it using parchment and charcoal; he would investigate it further, later.

The fat guard's heavy footsteps were followed by the scrape of a body sled. The man walked around him, dropped the handle and rolled the body onto cloth that was slung between two wooden poles, which made up the sled's structure and handles.

"Listen to me, and listen well. Take the body DIRECTLY to the morgue. I want at least one other person with you, at all times. If anyone gets in your way, kill them."

The guard snapped straight and saluted, "I understand, sir. I'll take care of it personally."

"Don't tell me, just get it done."

"Yes, sir."

Chapter 39

Preacher stood brooding in the door of the hovel. Word had filtered back that the king's dog had not taken the bait, and Grig had been arrested. It was supposed to be simple, Grig would taunt the Teridon, take his beating, and the boy would be arrested. He had given simple instructions, but Grig thought he knew better. He got in the boy's face, and made it easy for him to walk away. Grig was no real threat, and Teridon knew it. That moron did not understand what he was there to do; he thought he was there to just get into a fight.

Adding to this disaster, Grig had tried to clean up his mess, getting himself arrested in the process. The night was a total failure. His task was to get the boy away from his charge. Instead his flock would soon be down a member. They were not large enough to sustain many losses, not yet.

His plans had been worthless lately. He desperately needed something to go right. Larger aspirations needed to be founded upon the foundation of smaller successes, and, right now, that was a foundation of shit. He went to find Patrick, who, for all of his weakness, could at least follow instructions.

***

Patrick stood on the ground floor, staring out a glassless window onto the ancient road. Members of the flock milled about, moving along the road as they waited for orders.

"Hello my son."

The boy turned, greeting him with a small smile. He had recovered from his breakdown, and seemed rededicated to the movement.

"We tried, but we could not get him to take the bait. I told Grig the boy's pressure points, just like you told me, but he ignored me. Instead of going in with the weapons you gave him, he chose to go in unarmed."

"Should I talk to him when he gets back?"

"He won't be coming back, he was arrested."

He gave a small nod in acknowledgement, he knew what that meant. Preacher's standing order was no one was allowed to be interrogated, and that usually meant suicide.

"Will we need to get the body back?"

"No, Grig failed, he isn't entitled to anything more."

And, that was that. It was cold, but Preacher had no mercy for people who failed him, or the movement. Patrick considered, and not for the first time, what Preacher was planning. For some reason he had a fixation on taking down the new King, and that fixation was leading to failure. Did he really have larger plans, or was this some personal vendetta against Sir Loorie.

"My son, I know that it is easy to let doubt creep in. You look at our little group and think, what can we do? We are nothing, a collection of rabble facing the most powerful city in the most powerful country in the world; however, think on this, it is a tiny pebble falling from a cliff that starts the avalanche that destroys a mountain village; a small spark from a lantern can start the fire that burns a city to the ground; and the humble beaver pulling the wrong stick out of dam can start the flood that drowns a ship. The point is, humble people and, seemingly, insignificant can be the catalyst for great change."

"Thank you sir, I need to think on that."

Preacher put his arm around Patrick's shoulders, squeezing him tight, "You have a very important part to play in this, just stay with me."

"I will sir; I promise that I am with you."

"I know you are son, but sometimes even the most loyal need reassurances."

Preacher gave him a thin smile before reaching down and picking up a canvas pack that was slumped at his feet. Patrick untied the leather cord and looked inside. There were 30, or so, rolled up pieces of paper inside, each tied with a red ribbon.

"I need you distribute these to the usual drops."

"Yes sir."

"All of them."

That caught his attention. The request itself was not unusual, they had contacts throughout the city, and these clandestine notes were their typical mode of communication.

Over the past year, his main job was running these notes for Preacher. He usually placed one or two messages at a time.

This time, however, he was dropping a message for every operative at once. He could not help but be excited at the plans that may be finally be revealed.

"Patrick? Please make sure no one disturbs me, I am going to be busy for the next hour, maybe more."

He disappeared up the stairs without waiting for an answer.

***

Preacher sat in front of a squat timber alter in his little room at the top of the hovel. He crossed his legs and shifted until he was comfortable. His back was straight and he let his hands rest on his knees.

He stared straight ahead, trying not to let his eyes focus on anything. Just above his eye level, a simple mirror reflected the only light in the room back at him. It came from a single candle sitting on a shelf behind his head. The reflected light washed him in a very dim, wobbling light. He shifted once more, and, now, it was the time for him to have a little bit of fun.

He focused on his breathing, in through his nose, slowly out through his mouth, with every breath, he let his eyes lose more focus and he retreated further into his own consciousness. After a time, his vision blurred completely and then snapped back into focus. The mundane world of the underground was replaced by a spiraling tunnel into blackness. He allowed his consciousness to unmoor from his corporeal body and it was pulled into the tunnel.

The physical world fell away as he, or his consciousness, was thrown into in a gray sea of nothing. In this miasma, he moved effortlessly. His movement required noting but a thought. He turned and flipped waiting, and enjoying the freedom. It was not long before he saw what he was waiting for.

It was not much, nothing but a tiny pinprick of white light that blinked in, then quickly fled. But, against the solid wall of gray, that tiny pinprick may have been a sun. There was no reason to investigate any further, he had been doing this dance for the greater part of a month, and knew what he was looking for. Channeling all of his negative thoughts, all of his hate, all of his malice, and all of the venom that he could muster, and then focused the negative emotions, and like a mirror, reflected them at the point of light.

Chapter 40

Sir Loorie leaned back in his thickly padded chair. He sat in his great circular room, looking out over the city. The sun had mostly slipped beneath the horizon, leaving nothing but a burning orange sliver peeking above the sharp barrier. His tower did not have the view of the city that the others did, the other towers were in his way on one side, and the trees and old wall block his sight in the other. But, what he did have was the best view of the setting sun in the empire. He looked between the two other towers as that burning sliver got smaller and smaller. He loved this time of day, the sky's deep red and burnt orange hues were unlike any other colors, save for the brief few days before the leaves fell in the north.

He tried to focus on the beauty, but deep in the recesses of his gut, there was an unshakable feeling that something was not right. He could not point to anything specific, it was just a sense of dread, it was a feeling that was at the same time unfamiliar, uncomfortable, and confounding. Whatever the reason, the feeling was just that, a feeling. He was one of the most powerful men in the kingdom, surrounded by luxury, with servants attending to his needs. He also had Teridon watching his back, that boy was as loyal as the day was long. He was unable to find comfort in any of that, however, the feeling would not go away. So, he ignored it, as best he could.

He stood and stretched, but continued staring out the window. This time was the sole island of calm in the roiling sea that was governing this empire, and he never wasted a second of it. The last bit of the sun was about to slip out of view, when he saw a black cloud billow up from the lower city. The waves in the window's thick led glass distorted his view, so he threw the panes open.

As soon as the two panes cracked open, he could smell the faint scent of the acrid smoke. There must be quite a fire to produce that amount of smoke. He pulled the two panes shut, hoping the fire brigades would be able to keep it under control.

He would have to remember to check in on what happened, and see if he could provide any aid. His hand hung by the latch, he was about to let the small metal bar drop into its catch on the other pane, when he heard a strange, metallic, sound. It was faint, far off in the distance, but it was definitely familiar.

Throwing the window back open, the sound clarified. It was one he knew well, it was ring of steal striking steal, interspersed with faint screaming. He also noticed that the smoke was getting thicker, and blacker. The city was under attack! He needed to know more, he needed to find Teridon.

***

Sire Loorie ran into the hall as Teridon crested the stair at the end of the hall way. The boy strolled towards him crunching on a large red apple. He stared off in to space as he absently wiped the apple's juices away from his chin with a sleeve. He walked with no urgency and gave no indication that anything was amiss five floors below.

"Teridon, what is going on outside?"

Teridon responded with a quizzical look, "I don't think anything is going on outside, sir, I was just out there, nothing was wrong."

Sir Loorie was exasperated. How could the boy be so flippant? Was the boy being deliberately obtuse?

"What are you playing at, smoke thickens in the air and I can hear the sounds of battle coming from the lower city. Clearly, something is going on. Now, get out there and find out what!."

"Yes, sir, I'll go see what I can find out."

He turned and disappeared down the stairs, not showing any more haste than he had coming up them.

***

Sir Loorie's heart skipped a beat when he returned to the window. The battle had reached new city. How could it possibly be moving this fast? Where was the city guard? The city was falling, and with frightening speed. How could Teridon not see the army of heavily armed men pouring through the gates? Had he turned coat? Was he blind?

The attackers attacked with pikes and halberds, and were protected by dark gray chainmail and heavy plate. From the heavy armor to the long weapons, he guessed they were infantrymen, not that this information would help identify the attackers, the armor had no sigils and they carried no banners.

He couldn't even see what the aggressors looked like, their helms completely covered their faces, and they were tucked behind a wall of great square shields.

The tight phalanx marched toward the Crier's square. The synchronized thump of heavy bootfalls echoed through the square, it was the music that accompanied the last stand of the city guard. They formed a line in the square, steady, and ready to defend to their last man, but they were woefully outnumbered. Their leather armor and short swords were meant for policing the city, where armor was slight, if any at all, and the weapons were more than likely to be clubs and rocks. The horde poured into the square and spread out to form a line opposing the guard's. Once the line formed, pikes were lowered into place, the solid line of steel now sprouting wicked 10 foot steel toped spikes. The two lines paused for a moment, the city guard, to their credit, did not back down.

"FORWARD!" the command came from the center of the line, and the synchronized bootfalls began again. The attackers closed the gap in heartbeats; the screams of the city guards being skewered on the pikes began long before they had a chance to counter. They were not built for this and they were rolled over the like they were children.

The last living guardsman broke ranks and ran away, while the line of attackers started to form into a circle, and that circle closed around the towers of the three. After the infantry set their line, more of the black-garbed attackers began pouring into the square, though the leather armor showed that they were not infantry. The new attackers knelt, drew great black bows, and let fly. Archers had entered the fray. There was a click, and then another, and another, these clicks were sounds he knew well, arrows striking stone. He reached out and yanked the oak assault shutters closed, and then sunk down to the floor. The city was lost. Clicks turned to thuds as arrows sunk into the shutter's thick wood. A crack appeared as the steel tip of one of these arrows poked through.

Gingerly, he reached up and running his finger over the dark gray, almost black, edge. The razor tip had the signature color of Aragonian steel, but the attacker's armor looked like nothing any of their enemies, or even allies, wore. He stood and paced the room, like a caged rat. He was struggling to keep his emotions in check. He should not be reacting this way. His service trained him better.

He took a deep breath, trying control his emotions. Where was Teridon? He was desperate for any information he could get, so he went against his instincts and cracked the shutters open. His head dropped in defeat at the scene outside.

Six men slung a massive steel tipped timber between them. This was the ram they were going to use to breach the tower. The last line of defense was the front door, and the spiked cap on the ram would make short work of that. Where the hell was Teridon?

He stormed into the hall. Teridon was casually strolling towards him. What was the boy doing? He ran up to Teridon, "do you have a report? What did you find?"

Teridon gave him the same quizzical look as before. He did not understand why the knight was so angry, so he answered carefully, "I don't think anything is going on outside, sir, I was just out there, I didn't see anything out of the ordinary."

What game was this boy playing at? Sir Loorie was furious with the boy's nonchalance,

"Teridon, I gave you a direct order. Either you have are insubordinate or you are a traitor, which is it boy?"

"Look into what, sir?"

Did the boy get hit in the head?

Teridon looked at the genuine terror in the knight's eyes. It was a stark contrast to the hard determination that was usually there, "Sir, are you OK? What is wrong?" He was stalling, trying to figure out a way to placate the knight's, obviously irrational, fear.

That was the straw, Sir Loorie lost his last bit of patience, "NO, I AM NOT OK! We are under attack! You were supposed to investigate. So, either you disregarded my order, or you are in on it. So which is it, Teridon?" He punched Teridon's shoulder.

Teridon was shocked, Sir Loorie had never laid a hand on him in anger, this was serious. He bowed his head, "Sir, I truly don't know what you are talking about, you did not give me any order, but I will go outside at once and find out what is going on."

Sir Loorie was not happy with that answer, but what choice did he have. Teridon had already left, he screamed at the boy's back, "GO YOU FOOL, SHOW SOME DAMN URGENCY!"

Teridon stopped after descending two or three stairs.

Sir Loorie stepped forward ready to unload his anger. Something stopped him; Teridon was not moving, at all, was something on the stairs? Had the tower been breached already? He opened his mouth to chastise him when his back arched towards him and he flew up the stairs, feet not touching until the tripping over the top step.

Teridon crumpled, then slid across the polished stone floor, gasping for air with his arms wrapped around his chest, he tried, desperately, to catch his breath as he rolled back and forth on the floor.

He pushed up onto his elbows and started to push himself backwards, but slipped to his back on the smooth stone floor; the thud of his head echoing off the hallway's hard surfaces. Everything stopped for a heartbeat, then a large man ran up the stairs, as soon as the man's foot hit the top step; he launched himself into the air, landing heavily on Teridon's chest. He had never seen a man move like that, the man's feet were at his eye level during the jump.

The man was massive, larger than Teridon even, tall and thick with corded muscle, black hair, heavy with blood and sweat, hung over his face.

Reaching down, he closed his hand around Teridon's throat. He grabbed at the muscled hands, desperately trying to pull them off his throat. The sick bastard seemed to enjoy toying with Teridon, squeezing his windpipe and just as he was about to pass out, loosening the grip just enough to allowing him a breath.

Sir Loorie stood frozen in fear. He had felt that Teridon was a second son, and he helplessly watched Teridon's feet flailed as he punched at the powerful hands, desperately trying to get free. There was nothing he could do, Teridon was the strongest person that the knight had ever known, but he was helplessly pinned under the mass, and strength, of the man standing on his chest.

This sick game went on for a few moments before the long fingers sunk into Teridon's neck. His scream was cut short by the fingers that crushed his windpipe. With no real effort, the man yanked upward, a spray of blood following his hand away from Teridon's throat.

His hands shot to his neck. He desperately tried to stem the pumping spray, but, his hands did nothing. Blood pumped around his fingers, covering he white walls and floor.

The man stood over Teridon. He did not look up, just watching him bleed out. It was not long before the blood flow slowed from a spray, to a river, before finally becoming a trickle, which pooled around his head. The powerful man died with nothing but a weak gurgling sound.

Satisfied he was dead, the man dropped Teridon's throat to the floor, it landed in the puddle of blood with wet splat. Then it turned his attention to him.

The violence of the last several moments had not prepared him for what he saw when the long black hair fell back, and the face of terror was revealed for the first time. He had never seen anything like this thing. Despite its shape, it clearly was not human, not anymore. For the first time, it stretched to its full height and it was at least several inches taller than Teridon, maybe as much as a foot. Its face was covered with leathery black skin and had no eyes, just pools of inky blackness floating in the sockets. Its nose and mouth was a long, thin, muzzle, like a jackal's. The creature's lips pulled back, exposing the creature's fangs and large triangular teeth.

Despite having no eyes, he could feel the creature staring through him. It growled, the low, guttural, sound rumbled toward him, it was so low that he felt it more than heard it. It stretched those fingers out; blood was still dripping off the long blade like nails.

When he was young, his father had told him stories of demons, terrifying creatures that ate souls. He had always thought they were just stories, but this thing was the living embodiment of every one of those terrors.

His knees were about to give out, and his stomach knotted. For the first time, he felt true terror, not anxiety, like before battle, but the terror of being the hunted, instead of the hunter. There was no mercy with this creature. It would give no quarter. He tried to draw his sword, but it stuck tight in the scabbard. He yanked, over and over, but, matter how hard he pulled, the scabbard would release its grip.

The meager sword may not even hurt the creature, but he had to do something, after all, he considered himself a man of action. His paralysis had already gotten Teridon killed, and he would not suffer the same fate without some kind of fight. Trying again, but the sword stayed locked in place.

He allowed himself a glance; his peace lock was in place. Cursing himself for such a beginner mistake, he clicked the brass lever off the pommel, the sword scraped out of its metal casing.

The sword was halfway out of the scabbard when the creature drove into the center of his chest, its weight and momentum driving the wind from his chest and easily taking him off his feet. His skull cracked on the floor, as he slid to a stop. The creature's mass pinned him to the floor, and crushed his chest.

He could not move, even to draw breath. The creature lay on him, its muzzle right above his face, the moist, fetid, breath washing over him, long stringy hair draped over his face, it was still soaked with blood. Like it had done with Teridon, it sniffed around his face and head, investigating something. It drew one final long breath and began to stand. Once the mass lifted, wind rush into his lungs as the thing's hair left hot wet streaks across his face.

He gasped as the thing rose to its full height, blood dripping off various parts of its body, splashing on, and around, him, as it straddled him. It stared down at him, the cold stare of a predator sizing up its most recent catch. He stared into those black eye holes for a heartbeat, then two. Finally, the beast extended its savage claws, and swung down. It struck him across the face, the knife-edge of the foot long claws tearing at his cheek. It reared back for another blow, he threw his hands up in front of his face, but the creature tore right through the feeble guard. He was never able to fully draw his sword, so he had no weapon, and his armor was 5 floors down in the armory. He may as well have been a babe attacked by a lion. Even had he been armed and armored, he doubted that he could combat the monster's size and strength.

The creature tilted its head, and then slowly lowered its outstretched hand towards his neck, then pressure built around his throat, and the searing pain of the claws entering his exposed neck was the last thing he felt before he died.

Chapter 41

Teridon kicked at the bedroom door. Screams were coming from within and he needed to get inside. The door moved a bit more with every successive kick. His foot struck the door again, and, this time, it bent and around the brass bolt. He stepped back, and drove his foot towards the door with every bit of strength in his great leg. The sharp splintering of wood echoed through the tower as the brass bolt gave way, and shot across the room. The door crashed open, and Teridon crossed the room in two great leaps.

Sir Loorie tossed and turned in the bed, hands out in front of his face. Alone in the room, it looked like he was trying to defend himself from an unseen enemy.

He grabbed the man's shoulders, trying to shake him awake, to no avail. Not knowing what else to do, he shook harder, then harder still, finally shaking so hard that the man's head was actually flopping back and forth. The force finally jolted Sir Loorie awake. His eyes snapped open and he grabbed Teridon's neck, trying to close his hands around it. Even panicked, the old knight was no match for his strength. He easily swatted the man's hands away and pushed him back to the bed, "Sir, what are you doing!"

The knight's eyes were like saucers and his breathing so fast, it bordered on hyperventilating, "Get away from me! You are dead!"

Teridon arched an eyebrow. The knight was still dreaming. He had a solution. He stood and walked over to the washbasin. Pulling the large ceramic bowl out of its wooden base, he threw the cold water on the knight. The shock finally woke the man. Soaking wet Sir Loorie jumped out of bed, his thin white nightshirt stuck to him, and grabbed Teridon again, "Are we under attack?"

Teridon tried to figure out what the man was talking about. He was undeterred by the boy's reticence, "Listen son, this is important, are we under attack?"

"No sir, the city is not under attack, I was just out on patrol, and nothing is amiss." Was the man drunk?

Exasperation welled up in the pit of his stomach. He knew, now, that he had been having another nightmare, but that it had felt so real that he was having a hard time not holding Teridon responsible for the actions of the Teridon in his dream.

He walked over to his reading nook and dropped wearily into the chair, "Son, I need to tell you something, for the past several weeks I have been having terrible nightmares. The circumstances change, but in every one, the city falls and the people around me die. This one was the worst yet. The city had fallen to an invading army, and a creature, a demon, attacked both of us. I saw you die, and I followed shortly after. It may seem like a crazy question, but I need to know the city is safe."

Teridon considered his response for a minute, wanting to portray concern for the knight's situation, but not wanting to play into the man's delusions. "Sir, these dreams are a manifestation of the terrible stress you have been under. I can assure you that the city is safe, and there are no 'demons'."

Sir Loorie nodded, and slunk back into his chair, there was nothing more he could do. He could not afford to be a slave to his delusions.

Teridon was deeply worried for the man; it seemed that he was cracking under the stress of the office. He would not be the first. Unfortunately, there was no time to discuss this further,

"Sir, I hate to rush you, but we need to get moving, you are late."

***

Teridon rushed after Sir Loorie as they hustled to his office in the Kethi-Draal. They were not typically this rushed, but the events of this morning had disrupted the routine they had settled into over the past weeks. Most days were much more relaxed; Teridon was up before dawn to train. When done; he walked the tower, making sure the security measures were in good repair and that the night tower guards were in place and alert at the end of their shift. Breakfast followed and then he woke Sir Loorie, to start his day.

Typically, before the day's session began, Sir Loorie would meet with the pauper and advocate. Sometimes they would revisit topics they had slept on, others, they would just chat about the news of the day. Finally, Rosi Starling would review the schedule of hearings for that day. Today, they had missed all the meetings and would be rushing into the hall just in time to begin proceedings.

Sir Loorie stopped in front of a simple wooden door; Teridon stopping a couple of steps behind, his office was through that portal.

"Can we get out of here? Will anyone notice if we just don't show?" Sir Loorie was, mostly, joking. The knight was having a hard time adjusting to spending his days sitting on his behind.

"Unfortunately sir, they will and we do."

"Always bringing me bad news, my boy." Sir Loorie, jokingly, chided.

He had stalled as long as he could, and eased the door open and walked into the small, utilitarian, office. There was a small desk and comfortable chair, but the office was mainly meant for changing, not spending any real time.

Each of the three was expected to wear the trappings of their office while they presided over the hall, but every time he laid eyes on the hideous costume hanging to his right, he had to fight the urge to wretch, "If I was a dictator, I would burn that thing."

Teridon softly chuckled in agreement, the uniform was hideous, but it was the uniform and he knew the knight was stalling. He leaned into the hall, signaling to the nearest attendant. The hall was abuzz with activity as petitioners filed into the cavernous room and pages directed the chaos. An old attendant, bent with age, shuffled into the office. The stooped old man tried to bow, but only manage to lower his shoulders slightly. Age had taken all of the man's flexibility, "My lord."

Sir Loorie hated the trappings and titles of rank and had repeatedly told the staff to address him as an equal, something they were struggling with; old habits do not change overnight.

"Please, you don't need to be so formal."

"Yes sir" the man replied.

At least 'sir' was better than 'my lord'. He started by pulling the thick velvet pants on, they were tight in all the wrong places, and tied in the rear, which, he was convinced, was just to annoy the wearer. The attendant pulled the laces taut and tied them off.

Teridon handed the attendant the coat. He held it open and Sir Loorie slipped his left arm in, then his right. The colors remained gaudy, but the tailor's work had made the cut much more contemporary, the jacket had been tailored so it hugged his side and followed his body to the waist. The hem had been raised from upper thigh to just below his waist. He pulled the thick leather boots on.

Finally, he fastened the golden toggles, while the attendant pinned the King's sigil to his lapel, the simple hammered golden crow was a stark contrast to the ostentatious outfit. A swift pull at the hem tightened the jacket, and he was ready, or at least he was dressed, and just in time, the tower bell began to toll, the booming sound vibrated through the building, and over the city, signaling the start of the day's session.

Sir Loorie steeled himself for a day of tedium. Before taking the position, he had many ideas about what it would entail, but listening to people's problems all day was not one of them. He let out a long sigh before his face hardened into the mask of the King.

"Please rise. The three are entering the hall." the crier intoned from his perch above and behind the dais. The acoustics of the room sent his voice echoing over the hall, quieting din of the petitioners.

Attendants opened their office doors and they walked out onto the dais, taking their seats behind a large, stark white, marble table. The King sat on the left, the Pauper on the right and the Advocate sat between them, a symbol of his position as arbiter between the two. The stone chairs had no cushions, and were meant to be uncomfortable. The idea was that they should never be comfortable with power, but, in truth, it just made his ass fall asleep.

He shifted, trying to get comfortable as he looked out over the rows of people that filled the cavernous hall, and at the upturned heads and expectant eyes that stared back. He never counted, but there had to be at least thirty rows of benches on either side of the central aisle. As always, they were jammed full with petitioners.

"Who's up first?" He was itching to get things moving.

The advocate flipped through the papers that were stacked on the table in front of him, "The main road was washed out by flooding in some of the lower provinces; they have sent representatives to petition for funds to repair it."

The crier called out some names; two men left the benches, about half way down the aisle, and started words the front. The men were clean cut, with their long hair was tied behind their head, as was the style in Southern provinces.

Wearing fresh clothes, probably purchased for this event, they approached the lectern, which stood in front of the table, on the same level as the dais, showing that the three were not above the people they serve.

"Sirs, we represent the township of Wilton, in the Southern empire. The region around our village has been devastated by flooding this year. Most roads have been washed out. We have been able to repair the local dirt roads. The empirical road, however, is far too expensive for a small farming community like ours.

The damage has hampered trade throughout the area. We need to acquire funds to begin repairs."

"Deny." The pauper said

"Deny." Sir Loorie agreed. The two men's faces slackened and dropped. They looked like they were just told a family member was killed.

Sir Loorie held a hand up and continued, "Be at ease, we will not be leaving you in the lurch. I propose sending a crew of engineers from the local garrison. The engineers will affect repairs, without cost to the local community."

The pauper raised a hand in approval, "Approve." Rosi Starling sat behind him, frantically scribbling the minutes in the log for today's hearing.

The Advocate lifted his hand giving as well, all in agreement with Sir Loorie's suggestion; he turned to Rosi, "Dispatch orders and funds to the local commander, on the morrow." The plume of Rosi's quill whipped back and forth as he wrote the decision down.

"Is there anything further we can do for you?"

"No, and, thank you, sirs." The two men deeply bowed before walking back down the aisle.

Sir Loorie looked over the jam-packed hall, '*there is no getting out early today. At least those people needed actual help; it wasn't the usual squabbling neighbors.*' The crier's call echoed through the hall. The name did not register with him, but a young man left the rearmost bench and began the long walk towards them.

A presence behind him drew his attention. A hand softly grasped his shoulder and he felt warm breath on his neck as the presence whispered in his ear, "Head Ranger Wybb is waiting, sir, he came as soon as he received your orders."

"Thank you, Teridon, I will receive him in my library. Go, make him comfortable, get him some food, and I will be along as soon as I can."

Teridon nodded and left the hall.

He turned to others, "Gentlemen, I beg your leave. Urgent matters have arisen; unfortunately, they require my immediate attention."

Two of the three could hear cases that did not involve matters of state. It was allowed for one day, at most, and only with the permission of the other two.

The three turned to Rosi, who flipped through the ledger, "Nothing on today's docket appears to require the presence of all three of you."

"Leave is granted." The advocate said as Sir Loorie stood up to leave.

"Thank you. I do apologize for my tardiness this morning. Please, Advocate, you have my permission to rule in my stead. If a matter arises that requires me, I will be available in my library this afternoon." They nodded and he left the dais, toward the office that he left a short time before.

***

The attendant that had helped him dress was waiting in his office. He slammed the heavy door behind him. Despite his ambivalence to the work of office, duty was duty, and he felt like he was shirking that duty by leaving; unfortunately, people's lives were at risk. In his position, information was more valuable than a pile of gold, and he needed some, as soon as possible.

Chapter 42

Branyan Wybb waited inside the library, lounging back in a low chair in front of the great central fireplace. The man was unmistakable, short, and thick with muscle, it was a wonder he could even turn his head with his thick neck. His tanned skin was covered in tattoos, common for rangers, and his bald head reflected the fire's dancing light. As with most career soldiers, his body was covered with scars. The most visible was a large gash on his right cheek going from the top of his ear to the corner of his mouth. It was so old that it was no longer pink, but it certainly stood out. He never spoke about that scar, and no one pressed him on it.

"Branyan Wybb?" Teridon knew of the man, but they had never met.

The man stood, rising to just below Teridon's chin. His short stature did nothing to dull the man's menace. His thick neck joined with broad shoulders then tapered down to a tiny waist. The man wore no uniform, just black trousers and a loose red cotton shirt, tied at the center of his chest.

"I am, and you are?"

"Teridon Jace, it is an honor, sir."

The shorter man took his outstretched hand and shook it heartily. Branyan Wybb was high commander of the Aragonian Military's most elite special operations division, the Rangers. Teridon had stars in his eyes. He had dreamt of being a Ranger, all those years ago in Barnstable. The rangers were given all of the specialized missions that the regulars could not do: search and rescue, assassinations, clandestine operations in hostile territories.

"So you are Teridon Jace. I've been given a message for you, 'The offer to join the military still stands'. The sender told me that you would know who these words. They told me about you, and I would love the have the chance to get you in the Ranger's camp."

Teridon smiled broadly, chest puffed with pride.

"Thank you, sir, you, really, don't know how honored I am, but I owe a debt to Sir Loorie; one that I may never be able to repay. Whether I can or can't is a matter for the future, but it is a certainty that I can't repay a dead man. I intend to keep the King safe."

"That is very noble of you, but you know he doesn't share that opinion. He did what he felt was right, for him and you."

"I know, but, in my mind, it is a debt none the less."

"I understand. If you change your mind, the offer awaits."

The door crashed open and Sir Loorie came running in, pulling the stocky ranger in a great hug.

"Branyan, you bastard, how are you? Thank you for coming so quickly!"

"I am well, and don't thank me, when I get an urgent message from the King, friend or not, I make haste. Now, tell me what is so urgent."

"Please, sit, both of you. Time is not our friend, so I will be brief. The situation in Hesh is very disturbing, there were reports of a coup developing Then the passes were closed, and since then, nothing."

Branyan leaned forward; his already stern face became iron, "What do our assets in country report?"

"Like I said, nothing. Our network has gone completely silent, the border has been sealed tight for over a week, not even traders are allowed through."

The Ranger took a moment to digest this information. If Hesh fell, it would pull the empire down with it, the economies of the two counties were so closely intertwined.

"What do you need me to do, sir?"

"I need you to assemble your best, most trusted men, then get into the country and find out what is going on. Whatever is blocking the flow of information needs to be removed. Our assets need to be supported, and finally, if all goes into the privy, they need to be neutralized."

The ranger took a breath, "neutralized, Sir?"

"Get them out of country if possible, but, if it is not possible, then, yes, neutralized."

Teridon's breath caught, Sir Loorie had just ordered the murder of their Heshian spy network. This is what it means to be doing what needs to be done, he supposed.

Branyan nodded, slowly, he knew what the knight had meant, but those types of orders need confirmation, "Understood Sir, I will do my best to get them out. Please, I need any other information you can give me, no matter how insignificant."

"I have very little information to give, unfortunately. Last indications were that there was religious zealots had been pushing the government for official recognition, and were threatening violence if they weren't recognized.

The Golden Lords had been negotiating with the heads of the zealots, but the situation was teetering. The last communications indicated that the talks were not going well, and that the zealots were threatening violence if they did not get their way. Two days later the borders were closed."

"Any chance that the government is just trying keep new zealots from getting in? Until they get their arms around the situation?"

"Possibly, but the stopping of all trade and information coming from Hesh seem to indicated something else is wrong. That said, I hope that is the case, if so, get information flowing again, and get out."

"Understood; getting into the country will be a problem. Those mountains are as good as a high castle wall, better, in fact, because they can't be scaled, pulled down, or undermined. Are we sure that the passes are sealed?"

Sir Loorie nodded, "The 9th confirmed it, the message came this morning."

"Do we know who gave the order?"

"No, the ninth asked the Hesian soldiers at the post, they did not know, all they knew was the order came from Hessium, and that it bore the proper seals."

The ranger crossed his right leg over his left and leaned into the plush chair, looking up at the ceiling. Teridon moved to speak, but Sir Loorie waved him back.

He spoke, but towards the ceiling, "If the crossings were open, we could hide or disguise ourselves as traders, but they aren't. No one, to my knowledge, has ever been able to cross the peaks. Would we be able to?"

Teridon saw why he was waved back. The ranger was musing, thinking out loud, trying to work the problem out. The man was the high commander for a reason; he was the best at what he did.

The musing continued, "If it really is a coup, than the borders will not be open for some time, the new government will not risk allowing anyone in or out until it has firmly taken power. We could sneak by the border guards at night, or sail, but that could take months. I am guessing we don't have the time for a long voyage."

"No, you don't. Do what you must, all of the empire's assets are available to you, just let me know what you need, and you will have it.

This is assignment needs the utmost secrecy. Nothing is to be written down, any planning or status updates must occur in person."

Sir Loorie hated limiting communication this way, it delayed the transfer of information greatly, but the mission had to remain secret. They were invading the only significant ally the empire had, and it would be considered an act of war, if discovered. Who knows how the new government, if there was one, would react. They may be looking for an excuse to flex their muscles. If there was not a new government, the Golden Lords would be more understanding, but that understanding would certainly cost the empire money, as was typically the case, they were ally's but when toes are stepped on, someone has to pay.

"Understood, sir, with your permission, I will take my leave and begin preparations."

"Please do. Branyan, please remember, time is of the essence here, we need to know what is going on inside Hesh."

Sir Loorie looked haggard; his eyes were drawn back into his head, with dark pockets below them. His face hung slack, showing none of its usual vitality.

"Sir, I am sorry if I am being forward, but what is wrong? You look worse than when you first came to the city."

"I have not slept in a week, son, those dreams I told you about, have been taking quite a toll on me. Teridon, do you ever have these dreams? I have never remembered my dreams before. Now, I can't sleep because of night terrors."

The demon has been plaguing his dreams for the last several weeks. He knew it was in response to stress, but it was still unnerving to see someone you love die on a nightly basis.

"Yes sir, I have; everyone has, there is nothing unusual about it. You need rest, maybe a sleeping tea will help? It may dull your mind, and maybe the dreams with it."

The sleeping tea sounded like a fantastic idea. He had taken his leave for the day, so he could afford to take some time and rest, "That is a great idea, I will retire to my room, can you send the doctor up?"

***

The doctor arrived at his bedroom moments after he did. He held a steaming mug in front of him, which clacked on the saucer as he walked.

The doctor placed the cup on his nightstand and pulled the bundle of herbs that had been steeping in the water out. The herbs were tied with thin twine and looked brown and flaccid; they had given all they had to give to the tea. The doctor crushed them into a spoon, wringing every bit of the brown liquid he could out. The drink smelled nice, it had a sweet, almost flowered, aroma. The smell was a lie, he choked it the concoction down, it may have smelled like sweet herbs, but it tasted like bitters mixed with dirt and tree bark. He chased the noxious tea with a cup of cool water and then lay down in the bed.

After a few moments, his eyelids became heavy and his vision blurred. For the first time in a week he drifted off to sleep with no demons anywhere in sight.

***

Teridon slowly opened the door. The knight was snoring softly in his bed. He slipped into the room, careful not to make a sound, and drew the velvet drapes, keeping the midday sun at bay.

Chapter 43

Bisicara milled nervously about the store. Today was her first day running the store on her own. She had been confident when they were here, but they left yesterday, and her nerves were getting the better of her. In her head, she was sure she can do the job, but that did not quell the anxiety coming from her gut.

The plan was for her parents to sail north, to Queens, Lake Nemi's northern most port. From there they would visit the northern centers of trade, stocking up on: furs, leather, hides, and ivory before the northern port's winter freeze. Winter struck early, quickly, and hard, in the North, so this was the last northern supply run until spring. They were planning to be gone about a month. If they stayed any longer, they will be racing the freezing lake on the way back.

She opened the store at the usual time, an hour or so after sun up, and got to work, stocking display cases, inventorying the back room, cleaning the showroom, all of the morning rituals. While the business was a wholesaler of raw goods, it had become a bit of an ad hoc pawnshop as well. At his heart, her father was a trader, and could not resist accepting a good item for payment. While he was good at judging values of objects, it made for an eclectic showroom.

She puttered about for an hour before a local leather worker came in looking for hides. She took his order of 20 'B' grade hides. The 'B' grade indicated a good thick hide, but with cosmetic defects, they were used for boiled armor, helmets, boot soles; anything that needed good skin, but could show some blemishes.

She scribbled the order on the ledger and handed a receipt to the man, "Thank you, sir, I will send a courier along with the order this afternoon."

"That will do fine, thank you."

The leather worker left, and Bisicara grabbed a broom, continuing her puttering. The shop was clean, but working passed the time. She had just left the room to check on this morning's orders when the bell on the front door jingled.

She poked her head out of the back to see a scruffy man closing the door. His long, oily, hair hung in strands, looking like it had not been washed in weeks, and his scraggly beard had not been tended to in at least that long.

She grabbed the ledger, and walked out as the courier turned. Seeing her, his face broke into a toothless grin. The lecherous grin held no warmth, and sent shivers along her back.

The couriers her father employed were all old sailors, and, most, made her skin crawl. She could feel the heat of their leers whenever they were around her, and more often than not, she could not get their eyes to move from her breasts.

She pulled her shawl tight around her shoulders, covering her cleavage. She stood straight and handed him a sheet of paper, with the manifest and the address. She had loaded the order last night; the cart was waiting behind the building.

"Remember, I needed the manifest signed and returned once the load is accepted. I won't pay you without it."

He gave her another toothless smile; this one had some patronizing mixed in the leering. He turned and left, the door slamming shut and bell ringing again. Pushing the disgusting man out of her mind, she went to the warehouse in the back to take inventory.

Chapter 44

Jakes walked into one of the few stone buildings in the lower city. It was a plain single story building at the base of the hill, just before the west road started its incline. Though stone, the building looked no different from the rest of the storefronts in this section of the city. Underneath the innocuous exterior was another matter, altogether. A massive pit had been dug; extending several stories had been dug below ground. The rooms in the pit were cold all year long, and the coroner's office used the cold to preserve dead bodies, even in the heat of summer.

It was an ingenious solution to the problem of preserving dead bodies during Capuamundi's rapid expansion. Before, the dead could only be buried in the plane between the hill and the harbor, but that area was been engulfed as the cities grew. Once the cities merged, they had no were to house the dead, the plains outside the city were not feasible, it would eventually grow there too, and moving further out ran into the problem of decomposition, putrefaction, and the rapid spread of disease. Early city officials were forced to cremate the dead right away. That was until someone figured out that cold slowed the decomposition process. Once the pits were dug, they had days, sometimes weeks, to investigate deaths. The pits also provided valuable research tools for doctors, and spurred a great improvement in medicine. He could not imagine how much evidence was lost, and how many crimes were unsolved in the flames of ancient funeral pyres.

***

He stood in front of a counter that ran the length of the room. The reception area was empty, and furniture sparse, consisting only of a single chair behind the counter.

Jakes rang the small bell that was sitting on the counter, and waited. After a moment, a woman came out from one of the two doors that stood behind the counter.

"Can I help you?" She asked with a curt edge, not concerning herself with niceties.

"I need to inspect a body that was brought in from the Holding Yard yesterday. Is the coroner about?"

"We are not open to the public, please show yourself out." She turned to leave after dismissing him. Jakes looked her up and down, she was very pretty, shorter, and a little heavy set, but pretty. She wore light, loose fitting, clothes, which did not show her, ample, curves. He removed his commander's star, and slid it along the counter, towards her.

"Excuse me ma'am, but I am not a member of the 'public'" He added a hint of emphasis to the word 'public'.

She turned to see what the metallic scraping was, and her eyes went wide when she saw the silver star on the counter. Her face softened, and she came around the desk to shake his hand, "I am so sorry commander, I don't know how I didn't see the star..."

Jakes waved her off. "Think nothing of it, it happens, I am Commander Jacob Pints."

"Pleasure, sir, I am Doctor Stella Greene, the coroner on duty."

"If you don't mind my asking; isn't it unusual for a woman to be in your position?" Women were allowed, even encouraged, to be doctors in the empire. Coroners, however, were not doctors, in the traditional sense; they were guardsmen, guardswoman in this case. Their medical training was paid for by the city guard, and they were expected to fulfill one of two duties, field medic or coroner. The guard had ceased to employ field medics years ago, so these guardsmen served as coroners. Some chose to forgo the contract and just resume service as a guardsman, but most took the opportunity to continue learning while they dissected human bodies and investigated death and disease. They had to serve in those rolls for 10 years to fulfill their contract, and would be free to leave the guard. As guardsmen, however, they needed to go through basic training before their schooling. It was rare to find a man who had both the aptitude to be a doctor and that could physically pass the training; it was far harder to find a woman with the same attributes.

"It is sir; I am the only one in the empire. Now, you need to see one of my guests?" The pride in her voice was clear. He chuckled lightly. It seemed, despite her education, Doctor Green shared the same dark humor as the rest of the city guard.

"Yes, he was brought in from the holding yard last night, he had long blond hair, and a star tattoo covered his back. He hung himself."

"I know the one, follow me. I just finished the examination." She held the door to the morgue open and motioned for him to follow. The air started to cool as soon as he walked through the door. They started down the circular stair, the temperature continuing to drop as they descended into the pit.

Just as the name implied, the pit was a large circular hole dug into the ground. The stairs wrapped around the wall of the pit stopping periodically at a landing, each with a heavy metal door. There were six landings, and Jakes estimated that the pit was 20 yards deep. A giant metal oil lamp hung in the center of the ceiling, casting a dim light down the walls. Oil lamps were held in sconces periodically along the winding staircase to add to the light, though they did not much, there was just enough light to see the stair.

Doctor Green led him down until stopping on the fourth landing. He stood back as she pulled open the metal door, growling softly at the effort. It looked to take all her strength; the door clearly was not hollow. She disappeared into the darkness behind it. He scurried in behind her as the door had begun to close on its own.

Her torch provided an island of light in the total darkness of the hallway. Again, she motioned for him to follow and started away, the globe of light bobbing away with her.

Their thud of their footfalls surrounded them as they echoed off the hallway's stonewalls. The smooth stonewalls were broken periodically by more metal doors, these much smaller than the one out of the pit. She did not stop until reaching the end of the hallway. She waited for him to catch up before pulling the last door open, the slightly smaller door taking less effort, but still appeared to be heavy.

Jakes stood in the doorway as Doctor Green walked to the corners of the room, lighting an oil lamp that hung in each. The large lamps washed the room in light soft yellow light. Finally, she lit an odd lamp that hung in center of the room. It was attached to the ceiling by three chains, and hung a few feet down. The bottom of the lamp was solid metal, while a large convex mirror was over the flame, attached to the chains, and not the lamp. She stepped onto a stool and touched her torch to the oil, the purpose of the mirror was revealed. It concentrated and focused the light, making a small bright circle of light on the body below.

The chains allowed her to move it about, and, by sliding stays up and down the chains, the circle of light would move up, down, left, and right

That work light was illuminating the body of the blonde man, which lay splayed out on the stone table. The man's chest was laid open and pinned back. The incision looked like a giant 'Y' in his chest. He grabbed the man's face and studied it for a moment, "this is my guy."

She smiled, "Excellent. That was easy. I do need to correct your facts, however, he didn't die from hanging. He was poisoned. I found small shards of glass in his mouth, so it appears to be suicide." She held up a tiny capsule, "we see these now and again, they are given to spies and high ranking officials, anyone that would be expected to commit suicide if captured."

She pointed to the man's eyes, "see the redness around the eye lids? And the dried white spittle around the lips? Those are pretty clear an indications of poison."

"If you were going to poison yourself, why go through the pain of hanging yourself, especially the way this man did it?" he asked to no one, but the doctor answered anyway,

"Don't know, but I would guess that he wanted to make sure you knew that he committed suicide. Had he just bit on the capsule, it would have been assumed that he was murdered, not uncommon in the yards. By hanging himself, he left no doubt."

"Makes sense" Jakes said, it was a more legitimate theory than he could come up with, "What was he poisoned with? Is it anything you have seen before?"

"I can't say for sure, but given the symptoms, it was probably Conium. Made from spotted hemlock berries, It causes the throat to swell and cuts off oxygen, a death that would fit well with being strangled."

"Is there any way to tell where it came from, did a noble give it to him?"

"I am no magician" she joked, before adding, "I am sorry, I should not make light."

He laughed it off, in truth, the bit of humor was refreshing, "Didn't you say that these are typically given to important people?"

"Sorry to be unclear, but I meant a similar technique was used. I wasn't referring to this particular capsule. The capsules that are given to high-ranking individuals have a poison taken from a highly refined blue dye. It kills very quickly and painlessly. It certainly was not used in this case; strangulation isn't quick, or painless. If I had to guess, I would say he had knowledge of the technique, but did not have access to the poisons themselves. Maybe he used to be in the military? Maybe a former politician? I am just guessing, sir."

"No, no, please, any help you can give, even if just speculation, will help."

"Unfortunately, that is about all of the information I have, the man had no obvious health issues. Other than the tattoo, he had no obvious identifiers. There aren't signs of any major bone breaks or scars, so he probably was not in the military, His hands don't appear to be callused, so he was not a laborer, maybe a university student? Again, just guessing, sir. I checked with all wants and warrants, no one fitting his description is being hunted by the empire or the city guard. I also looked through the missing person reports, none fit."

Jakes leaned over the man, holding his cheeks and rolling his head back and forth, '*Who are you? Who gave you the orders?*'

"You have been immensely helpful, Doctor Green. If you find anything further, please fetch me immediately."

***

Jakes held up his hand to the sun as he walked out the door, it was high in the sky; the time was getting close to noon. He left his conversation with the doctor shaken. This seemingly normal individual had tried to start a riot, kill his friend, and, ultimately, killed himself. Jakes always tried to think positively, but his time in the guard had tempered that positivity with an edge of skepticism.

He could come up with no other conclusion than Teridon was right, this was not a random event, and Teridon had been the target. He was not sure what it all meant, but he was sure it was not a positive sign. Trouble was coming to this city; he was now sure of it, he just did not know from where or from whom. That worried him even more. He had no idea where to even start looking.

Chapter 45

This situation was a mess. Jakes needed to speak with Teridon, the largest figure in the mess. He suspected bad actors were trying to get to the King through Teridon, but Jakes had stopped assuming anything. He stood in front of the door to the Kings tower. Grasping the great steel ring, he pounded it against the door. After a moment a stout young woman answered the knock.

"Good afternoon, is Teridon available? I need to see him immediately."

He always tried to be pleasant to the staff. While he liked to show people respect in general, there was a selfish motive as well. Most of his informants were cultivated by just treating people with respect. For most of the nobility, the staff blended into the background, much like furniture. That meant that the staff was privy to the most intimate conversations, and could be a treasure trove of information. In his experience, a little courtesy went a long way with people who were used to being treated like they do not exist.

"Please wait, I will see if he is available." She disappeared back into the tower.

Jakes sat down on the stone bench next to the door, still trying to puzzle through recent events. There had to be some pattern, some common thread that he was missing.

The door opened, and short woman stepped out of the tower, "He is training, sir, you will find him in the yard behind the Kethi-Draal."

"Thank you so much," he said, flashing the woman a large smile before starting across the courtyard. He walked past the Kethi-Draal, marveling at the massive building, as he always did. It was beautiful; the façade was of white marble, dark gray granite and pure black obsidian.

Over the three sets of huge black epee doors, each twice the height of the average man, ornate baas reliefs were carved into the stone. The reliefs commemorating the Battle of Wilson's Hill, with mounted men facing great winged beasts. The beasts were roughly twice the height of the men, and attacking with claws and teeth. Wilson's Hill was the most famous single battle in the empire's history; it was the event that turned a fledgling empire into a world power.

The location of Wilson's Hill was lost to time, but the stories remained. The great General Cimean destroyed the army of the Free Nations, removing the last impediment to the formation of the empire. The Free Nations were six smaller kingdoms who banded together to oppose the first emperor, Suelmin Aragon, as he consolidated power and territory. After the battle, Emperor Suelmin was so impressed with General Cimean's performance that he adopted the man's sigil, the hammer, as the symbol of the Aragonian Military. Liberties were taken by the artisans, depicting the army of the Free Nations as beasts, but those are liberties earned by the victors. Above that battle, a large golden circle represented the sun coming up over the battle and blessing the victorious army. The circle was embossed in the peak of the gable, the edge of the dark grey slate roof framing it. On either side of the great doors, a great arch connected the building to the spires, this signature feature of the building. The circular bases, roughly 40 paces around, anchored the perfectly round columns that continued up for one hundred feet. They were capped off with cones of gold that reflected the sun back over the city. They were the pride, and sigil, of the city.

The building continued back, away from the square. Buttresses jutted out from the wall every 10, or so, paces. Each rose from the ground and connected to the top of the wall, making half of an arch between the top of the pillar and the building. He had heard that the buttresses were the reason they were able to have a large open space inside. The buttresses took the weight that interior walls and pillars would have in a conventional building.

He walked under the buttresses, feeling small next to the scale of the building. He had almost reached the rear corner when the clash of steel rang out.

Jakes rounded to corner to find Teridon sparing with a much smaller partner. The big man saw him and held his hand up to stop the session.

"Ho, friend! Come on, it's been ages since I have had a good sparring partner, let's see what all that military training has taught you."

Jakes was an experienced soldier. He was certainly not afraid of a little friendly competition. He doffed his cape and doublet, and then walked into the ring, wearing just his undershirt and trousers.

The sparring partner bowed his head to Teridon and left the circle. Teridon bowed in return before turning to face Jakes. It had been years since they had sparred and Jakes had forgotten just how imposing his friend was.

Teridon stood in the middle of the ring, looking bigger and stronger than ever. He had a bastard sword in his right hand, which was traditional, but in his left, he had a long dagger, long enough to be a short sword if held by a smaller man. The dagger was positioned so it hung down his forearm, the tip going just past his elbow.

Jakes drew his much more conventional, military issued, short sword and round shield.

Teridon smiled, "Ready, army boy?"

Jakes laughed and dropped to a ready stance, feeling his weight and balance. He approached the larger man cautiously, Teridon's reach, combined with the longer weapon, gave him an advantage. He led with his left side, placing his shield out front, moving on Teridon using combat walking, sweeping his feet along the ground in half-moon shapes. Because his feet were never off the ground, he was never off balance and always ready to strike.

Teridon stood in the center, putting most of his weight on the back leg, the toes of his front leg facing Jakes, and only lightly touching the ground. It was a fencing stance, one that he had never seen it used in actual combat. He knew Teridon, they had sparred countless times growing up, he was impatient and aggressive.

He may look serene now, but it would not take much to frustrate him and force him into a mistake. Teridon had always been bigger, stronger, and more athletic than him, but he had been able to beat him using something Teridon did not understand, strategy. He would retreat, evade and stall. Eventually, Teridon would get frustrated and overcommit. Once he did, the match was easy. He would go on the offensive as Teridon's size worked against him.

Jakes was focused. He began slowly circling, ready to begin baiting his friend. Teridon stood stone still, his left arm holding the dagger in front, protecting his sword hand. Teridon never cared much for defense. He would rather take your best blow so he could deliver a bigger one in response.

Jakes stopped circling and lunged forward with a straight thrust before skipping back, and out of range. The strike was light and quick, not intended to be a killer strike, just enough to get Teridon to give chase. To his surprise, the chase did not come. Teridon's feet never moved, he just turned the dagger, slapping the flat of Jake's sword, and redirecting the halfhearted stab past him.

He looked serene, like he was walking in the forest, his face showing none of the effort that one would associate with sparring.

Jakes made several more attempts to instigate a response, each one effortlessly turned aside. Teridon's face never lost its serenity. His friend, it seemed, had learned some patience over the past several years.

After a few minutes of feeling him out, it was clear that Teridon was content to allow him the initiative. Jakes obliged, lunging forward with a flurry of thrusts. Teridon took a slight step to the side, and Jakes stumbled right by. He quickly righted himself, surprised at the frustration bubbling up from his gut. Things were not going the way he wanted. Trying something new, he slid to Teridon's left, trying to slip behind him, but as soon as he made the move, he knew it was a mistake. He had slid forward instead of to the side, and gotten far closer to Teridon than he intended. He had created the opening that his friend had been waiting for.

Once the Jakes was open, the serenity left, and Teridon became a blur. He kicked Jakes in the upper thigh with his front leg, quick and precise, with just enough power to send a shock through his lower body. His balance broken, he chopped down with his shield, desperately trying to strike the kicking leg and regain some space, he missed. Teridon did not let up. He doubled Jakes over with a swift kick to the rib, then reversing the kick and knocking the shield out of his hand, it landed in the dirt with a thud.

Horribly off balance, and his shield gone, Jakes took a desperate swipe with his sword, trying to get enough space so he could stand back up and regroup. Teridon snapped around in a spin, his sword easily blocking the weak attempt. The block did nothing to slow his spin, and he drove his elbow towards his friend's face as his body whipped around. Had this been an actual fight, he would have driven his elbow through the opponent's face, but this was Jakes, no need for anyone to get hurt.

Stopping just short of his face, he hooked his arm around Jakes' shoulders, and swept with his foot, dropping his friend face first into the dust.

Jakes lay on the ground, spitting out dirt. He was both impressed and embarrassed with the ease that Teridon dispatched him. He rolled over and saw his friend smiling down at him, holding his hand out,

He reached up and took the help to his feet, "Been practicing a bit?"

"Maybe a little."

"Where did you learn that? It isn't like any other styles I have seen."

"That is because it isn't like any styles. I have been taking parts of other styles and combining them into my own mishmash of what, I think, works. Once I'm done, I'll be glad to show you. Now, for the obvious question, what are you doing here? Aren't you on duty?"

"I am, but I couldn't wait to speak with you, this is too important. It's about the blonde man from the other night. He is dead; he killed himself in the Holding Yard-"

The smile drained from Teridon's face, "What do you mean? He's dead? I thought you were going to protect him?"

"I was. I had him sequestered. When he saw me, he said something about a fire burning, and hung himself. He made a noose out of his pants. After the coroner examined him, though, we found out that he hadn't died from hanging, he had actually poisoned himself. He ate a small glass vile that was filled with the poison."

"Who was this guy? I've seen a lot of surprising things over these past couple of weeks, but someone killing himself over a fight takes it. Was he a politician, or someone who would have had to kill themselves?"

"The coroner didn't think so. She thought he could have been ex-military, they would have known of the technique. But, the poison was wrong, that's why she felt it may have been out of the military, they used the technique, but couldn't get the right poison. Teridon, we might be looking at a possible coupe, or even worse, the military may be compromised. I think you were right, they are trying to get to the King through you."

"I have to tell Sir Loorie. Jakes, be careful, we don't know who we can trust."

"Shouldn't you be telling yourself that? You're the one that does the stupid things, not me." Jakes teased.

Teridon laughed deeply, the levity taking the weight of circumstances off his shoulders, if only for a brief moment. Unfortunately, however, the statement was too true.

Chapter 46

Sir Loorie awoke refreshed for the first time in weeks. He would need to thank Teridon for the suggestion. The tea had dulled his mind, and he had been able to rest peacefully. He threw the thick duvet off, and slowly rose, while stretching the stiffness that sleep brings an old man out of his, well-rested, muscles as he did. He was still rubbing sleep out of his eyes when Teridon burst through his door.

"Teridon! Thank you, my boy! The tea was just what I needed, what time is it? How long was I out?"

"It is late afternoon, sir, the sun will be going down soon."

He looked out the window, reveling in the rested feeling that had been eluding him lately. Behind him, Teridon ran about. Going from window to widow, throwing the curtains open, and looking out each one.

Once the sleep had left his mind, Sir Loorie took notice of Teridon's actions. The normally stoic boy was completely frantic, he kept running from window to window, eyes wide as he stared out each window.

"Teridon, what is going on? What is wrong? I have never seen you frantic."

"I just spoke with Jakes, the guard commander. We cannot hide this anymore, there is trouble brewing, and we think you are the target, sir." He recounted the events of the night before, and of his conversation with Jakes.

He held out his hand to stop him, "Teridon, you need to take a breath, calm yourself, boy, everything is just running together. Now, you said that you found a necklace and that it is the same symbol as the tattoo on this man? Is it possible that the two are a coincidence?"

He already knew the answer, only a fool would believe this a coincidence, but, conclusions must not be jumped too, rash decisions lead to terrible consequences. He believed in gathering as much information as possible before he decided on a course of action, even if some of that information was far fetched. "It is always a possibility, sir, but the symbol is not a common one. Jakes had the guard's Keeper of Records look at it. The symbol was used by Capuamuni's last truly successful cult. They almost brought the city down about two hundred years ago.

It was in response to this cult that the three of the time passed the laws against cults and finally took the last step to outlaw religion completely."

Sir Loorie nodded in agreement; the boy's instincts were sharp, "Well son, you seem to have a good handle on things, where do we go from here? What's next?"

Teridon was taken aback; the knight was asking him for advice? He considered his answer carefully, "right now, we can't do anything. We just don't have enough information to make any moves. Jakes is going to look deeper into things, but whoever is pulling the strings seems to be very good at covering their tracks. All we can do is be extremely careful until things shake out. Please, for the next couple of weeks, be extremely vigilant, and report anything out of the ordinary."

Sir Loorie laughed, out of the ordinary? What wasn't out of the ordinary? Two weeks and a day ago, he was a simple retired soldier; two weeks ago he was sworn in; and today he felt himself being pulled into intrigue. Still, the boy's heart was in the right place, "Wise advice, son, I will keep my eyes open, Please take your own advice."

Teridon nodded, it was all he could ask for. The King had to remain visible, so he could not hide. All they could do was be careful. Sir Loorie felt for the boy, he had been going nonstop for weeks, even on a night off, trouble had found him. Teridon needed real down time, "Get away, you have been thinking about this day and night for the past several weeks and you are starting to get paranoid."

Teridon never turned, and did not respond. He continued out the door, leaving the knight by himself. Sir Loorie may not think that there is anything to worry about, but he knew better.

It was possible that his intuition was wrong, but both himself and Jakes? He thought it highly unlikely. Things were beginning to swirl and he was at the center of the rapidly forming vortex. He needed more information. He needed to see Jakes, to see if he had been able to find anything new. He walked down to the new city, unsure of where he was going.

Chapter 47

Bisicara was in the back room pulling orders. She had just closed the shop for the day, and it had been a good one. There were a few orders for leather, the furrier had placed a large order for pelts, and she had even sold a few of her father's knickknacks. In all, the first few days of her business career had been a resounding success. She stood on a small ladder, pulling heavy leather bales from the shelving. The bundle of tanned hides landed on the wooden floor with a sharp clap. She broke the banding on the bale and started to load the hides, one by one.

Ellen walked in as she threw the last off the hides into the wagon. She had completely forgotten, they had plans to go out tonight, "Oh, Hey Ellen." She avoided her friend's eyes, looking more past, than at her. Ellen walked up, casually looking into the back of the wagon, "You forgot, didn't you?"

"I did, I'm sorry, Ellen, things have been so crazy. Give me a few minutes to get ready." Beyond being stiff and sore from loading the wagon, Bix had so much on her mind. Trivial things, like a night out, had fallen to the side.

"That's OK, we aren't in a hurry, go ahead and get ready."

"Thanks Ellen, I'll be quick, I promise, go ahead"

***

Ellen waited in the shop while Bisicara disappeared upstairs. Ellen was wholly ordinary, average height, average weight, not beautiful but not ugly either. The two girls had been friends their whole lives, growing up on the same street. She was killing time, wandering around the store and idly playing with the junk that Bix's father had collected. A bell jingled lightly as the door creaked open behind her. She turned to see a hideous man walk through the door. The man was about Bix's height, with long, oily, hair, a scruffy beard, and an odd, toothless grin. His eyes were cold and emotionless.

"I am sorry sir, the store is closed." She said, trying to calm her nerves, her gut was telling her this man's intentions were not good. He did not move, and just kept staring, "Can I help you sir?" She had started to back out of the room, hoping she would be able to get to the stairs.

"Well yes, yes you can." The man spoke with a slurping sound; he was trying to keep spittle in his mouth, "I am looking for the patroness of this store, a young woman named Bisicara."

"She is not here; I'm watching the store while she is out." Ellen swallowed hard. Whatever his intentions with her, they were not honorable, "can I take a message for you?"

Without warning, He ran across the store, the hunched old man was gone, and he easily cleared the distance in three long steps. He roughly grabbed her around the neck. The cold eyes had become wide with rage. He breathed heavily as he ran a finger along her neck. Terror shattered her cool facade.

"Tonight is your lucky night, you little slut. I really wanted that blonde, but I can have her another time. I don't mind breaking two of you in."

The man licked his lips, his right hand dropped to her side and slid up from her waist towards her breast, sliding her shirt up with it. Tears started to flow as she quietly begging him to stop; she could not muster the wind to scream.

"You will do nicely, you aren't pretty like the other one, but when one has needs, well, any port will do." He chuckled in her ear, apparently thinking the comment witty.

This man was making jokes? He was about to rape her and he was joking around? Her whimpers became sobs, and tears flowed freely, which only pushed the man further, he seemed aroused by her suffering, "Please, no." She muttered again and again, as the man's hand found the soft curve at the bottom of her breast.

"LET HER GO, YOU PIG!" Bisicara stood at the base of the stairs, holding a large kitchen carving knife. The man dropped Ellen and turned on her. She stood tall, she was not going to back down from this filth, "I have called the guard, they are on the way, get out... now." It was a lie, but it was the only thing she could think of to get the man out.

The man did not move, just stared at her with a disgusted look on his face, "What the hell is wrong with your face? What are you? A damned witch?" He stared at her for a heartbeat before fleeing the store. Ellen collapsed into her arms. That man had always given her the creeps, but she never thought he would try anything. Her father was gone and he had been emboldened by her, assumed, vulnerability.

"Ellen, are you OK?

"I'm fine, just shaken. Bix, what is wrong?"

"Wrong? There is nothing wrong, I'm worried about you, though."

"Bix, your eyes were glowing bright gold, he ran when he saw them getting brighter as he faced you."

Chapter 48

Teridon passed through the western gate. He did not care about making a scene this time, and wore his weapons openly. The guards eyed him as he walked through the gate, but there was nothing they could do. After the events of the last few days, he could give a damn about the fragile ego of the city guard, he needed to be armed.

He moved in a daze, his thoughts preoccupied by trying to puzzle through the events of the last couple of days. Before too long, he found himself nearing the harbor district. His home, Barnstable, was totally land locked, and he had never actually been to this, or any other, harbor. Maybe now was a good time to visit. New scenery might take his mind of things.

He pushed through the crowded streets. The harbor was Capuamundi's center of commerce, so it was usually crowded. On the other side of that coin, the area had a vibrant nightlife and there was almost always something going on.

He twisted to and fro to move through the crowd, his broad shoulders making it difficult to navigate through crowds. He suddenly began to feel very claustrophobic. The bumping and pushing of the crowd was starting to feel oppressive. He was focused on moving forward, but had he been paying better attention, he may have noticed the man shadowing him through the crowd.

He reached the bottom of the hill, still lost in his thoughts as the road flattened. Suddenly, a scream snapped him out of his fugue. Before he had a chance to think about what he was doing, he ran towards the sound. It had come from a narrow ally across the street. The small entrance was framed by tall tenement walls, making it feel very confined. He did not paused at the entrance, just ran in, the alley was too deep to see then end, anyway. Sliding to a stop, he relaxed when he reached the brick wall at the end. He felt the rough surface; it was solid, what was going on? There was nothing here. Was he losing his faculties?

"*Sir Loorie is right, I need a break.*"

He took a quick second look to make sure he did not miss anything. The wall was solid, it was three or even four times his height, and so there was no way to climb it. The scream must have been in his imagination.

"Please, put your weapons on the ground!"

He snapped around, two city guards were advancing on him, swords drawn and shields extended towards him. One was young, about Jakes' height and a little pudgy. Clearly not confident, the guard approached him cautiously. The other guard, tall and skinny, was a step behind and stood over the leader's left shoulder. The two held their swords so tightly that he could see the veins popping in their arms. They had obviously never actually used those weapons in anger. A true swordsman knows that the key to swordplay was to relax, taut muscles led to slow reactions, a lack of power, and poor aim.

Teridon spread his hands wide, showing that he was not going to draw his weapons, "Officers, what can I do for you?"

"Please, put your weapons down." the guard repeated with more force, voice shaking a bit less.

He did not want to cause a scene, so he unbuckled his sword belt, rolled it around the scabbard, and placed it on the ground at his feet. There was no doubt in his mind that he could take these two should things turn ugly, armed or no.

"Sirs, I must ask again, what can I do for you? I am authorized to be armed. Can I show you my Identification, I need to be on my way?"

The guards did not stop advancing, "You are under arrest for assault and robbery."

The lead guard pulled a pair of shackles from a pouch on his belt.

"Sirs, surely you are mistaken, I've not assaulted anyone, I have only been in the district for a short while."

The vortex of trouble that had been swirling around him for the past week had just tightened further. He needed to make sure it did not strangle him altogether.

The guards parted, revealing a smallish, unkempt man. He had been beaten bloody, his left eye was blackened, his lip was bleeding, and he was hunched over, holding his side. The man stepped in front of the two guards, walking towards him with a noticeable limp.

"This man has accused you of beating, and mugging, him." The guardsman stood straighter, speaking with more confidence now that Teridon was unarmed.

He had to chuckle softly at the guard's stupidity, he could kill the man with ease. He had cooperated thus far, but things were taking a turn, he needed to play his biggest card to head the trouble off, "I am the head of security for the King, Nidan Loorie. I have assaulted no one, why would I assault a beggar?"

"I know who you are, but it doesn't matter, you were accused. Your guilt is a magistrate's decision, not mine. Please, come with us."

Teridon's first instinct was to fight, but he had to remember his station. As a newly elected member of the Three, Sir Loorie could not afford his head of security assaulting two city guardsmen. Besides, given what happened the other night, an assault may be exactly what these two wanted.

He turned and folded his arms behind his back, offering his wrists to the guard with no resistance. The lead guard cautiously fastened the shackles around his right arm, then his left. For all the trouble he was in as a youth, this was the first time he had ever actually been in shackles, the cold iron clasps were fastened by a steel bar, holding his wrists a few inches apart. Padlocks hung off the outside of the clasps; clanking as he walked, like he was a cow with a bell. The lead guard still moved cautiously as he picked up his weapons and pushed him towards the road.

The skinny guard took the lead as the chubby one pushed him along. If they were trying to intimidate him with their rough treatment, they were failing. He went without trouble, but that was his choice, he did not want to do anything that would besmirch Sir Loorie's reputation.

The skinny guard was still taking the lead, and the chubby one prodded him until they stopped at a squat stone building tucked between apartment buildings.

The chubby guard knocked at the door. It took a brief moment for the knock to be answered. The door opened and the skinny guard pushed him inside.

He was could not believe how stupid he was, after lecturing both Jakes and Sir Loorie about being careful, he wandered through the city with his head stuck up his ass. If he had been paying better attention, he may not have walked into such a simple trap.

`He stood just inside the door while the guards spoke with the captain on duty.

"This man was arrested for assault..."

Teridon stopped listening and assessed his situation. The room was windowless; the only light came from oil burning in sconces along the walls. An old blackened fireplace dominated the back wall; it looked like its fire had gotten away from it more than once. A huge black leather bound book sat on top of a slant top desk, off to his left. The cell door stood half open to his right, the heavy iron door had a huge tumbler padlock hanging from the hasp. It looked to be empty, so Teridon would probably be the only guest today, and he was not getting through that door without a key.

The two guards took their leave. The captain pushed the cell door open, the hinges whining as it swung. He pointed into the cell.

"Get your ass inside. Sit quietly and you'll go to the magistrate, like everyone else. If you give me a hint of trouble, there will be serious trouble. Got it?" Teridon nodded and quietly walked into the cell, now was not the time anger the captain.

There were no lamps in the cell; the only light came from a thin opening cut in the top of the wall, and the barred square opening in the middle of the door.

His first instinct was to get out through the slit at the top of the wall, but that would not work, it was far too narrow, and, even if he could fit, there were bars across the void.

A stone outcropping jutted out from the back wall, the only place to sit in the austere cell. The door wooden door slammed shut and tumblers clicked as the lock engaged. He was now a prisoner. Bootsteps echoed into the cell as the guard walked away. He ran to the door, wanting to keep an eye on the man.

The guard sat down at the desk, the stool's three legs creaking as they took the man's weight. He took a quill from the well at the top and began writing in the large leather book, which Teridon assumed was the register of arrests and incidents, or the ledger.

Every guard station in the city had an identical book, all of the guard's activities were entered in it, and when it was full it was placed in the city's central archives. They were the housed and kept in perpetuity. Supposedly, there were records going back to the founding of the city.

Once he had sat for a moment and calmed, the reality of the situation hit him. He was in trouble, but worse, every second he was in here was a second his friends were vulnerable. Not content to just sit and rot, he went to the cell door as the captain folded a piece of paper and started towards the door.

"Please, I need to get me get a message to the King."

The guard did not turn, he just kept walking. The city guard had rules on how prisoners were to be treated, and he had a right to send a message.

"Guard, I would like to send a message. It is my right as a citizen of this city."

This got the man's attention, "Guard? My rank is Captain. As for your rights, you will have the opportunity to send a message after you go before the magistrate, just like everyone else. Now, mind your manners, or you WILL regret it."

Panic flooded over him, Sir Loorie could be in danger and he would have no way to get a warning out. If he was not there, could the city guard be trusted to intervene?

There were so many thoughts running through his head, all underscored by one fact, he needed to get out of this damn cell, and get out now.

"Captain, Sir, I am the King's head of security, he is in danger. I need to get back to him as soon as possible."

"The kid who brought you in told me who you are, but I don't care. I got news for you, I don't care if you are noble or not, you will be treated like any other prisoner. NOW SIT DOWN and SHUT UP!"

Teridon cursed under his breath, Sir Loorie needed to be warned, but he had no way to do it. Plus, he needed to tell his lord what really happened. Lies tended to race ahead of truth, and he needed to stay ahead of them.

The captain snapped his fingers in Teridon's face, "Listen to me, you prick, try and pull rank like that again, I will make you suffer. With your connections, I expect that you won't be here long. Whether your time here is easy, or hard, is completely your choice." The man spun on his heels and walked towards the door.

Teridon was smart enough to take a hint and know when to stop pushing. But, he needed to know one more thing before shutting up. Making sure to feign deference to the man, "Captain, sir, May I at least have your name?"

The guard did not turn around or slow his walk, but did give a half-hearted answer, "Captain Anderson."

'Captain Anderson?' That name meant something, but why? He would think on it, he knew that name from somewhere, but could not place it. The captain left the station, slamming the solid black epee door behind him with a thundering boom that echoed throughout the building.

Teridon had to blink a few times, the bright sun had flashed into the room when the door opened, and he was trying banish the spots that hung in his eyes and to get his low light vision back. He went back to the bench and allowed his head to fall back against the damp stone, alone with his despair.

Chapter 49

Preacher knelt in front of the squat alter, his face illuminated by the dancing light of the candles burning on it. His eyes were closed, and he spoke with words that were much too quiet to be for anyone to hear. This was how the man slept, if you could call it that. It was really more of a trance than slumber. Whatever it was, Patrick knew not to disturb it. He had lived in the underground with Preacher for the better part of the last 4 years, it had become his home, and the rest of preacher's followers had become his family. Growing up, his family life was horrible, his father was an abusive piece of dung and his mother stood by and watched the abuse happen. If his father's wrath was focused on him, he was not beating her. Preacher may have had his fits, but he treated him like a son, at least more than his real father ever had.

Preacher went out recruiting a few times a week. He always returned with one or two new recruits. The group had already filled up the old apartment building, and now spilled to the other buildings along the old street.

They had grown so fast, and space was becoming a premium. They were not going to fit down here much longer. Unfortunately, they had not been able to find another place as anonymous, and secure, as their underground sanctuary.

He had tried to talk to Preacher about it, but the man's only response was, 'That is a different worry for a different day." it was usually accompanied by a lecture reminding him to focus on the now, let later come as it will.

Preacher's recruits were from disparate backgrounds, some were rich, some poor, some were educated, some not, but they shared one common trait, their lives had been empty and they longed to be part of something larger then themselves. Preacher gave them that larger cause, with him they were no longer misfits and castoffs, no, and they were part of something.

He wandered around the building for a while longer. There was nothing going on, so he went to his room to lie down. He was about to doze off when the lookout's bell chimed. Shooting up, he ran down two flights of stairs and out into the street. He looked up to the entrance and saw a man climbing down the ladder from the entrance.

He wasn't afraid, had this man been there to arrest any of them, he would have brought an army.

No one would be crazy enough to try and arrest a whole group by themselves, especially given the security of the underground. Besides, other than Preacher getting harassed every now and again, the group had done nothing to draw the focus of the guard.

The man dropped the last couple of rungs and landed heavily, dust puffing out from under his boots. The dark grey uniform and tower sigil on the breast, confirmed the man to be a guardsman. The black cape marked him as a captain.

Patrick wrapped his hand around the hilt of a short dagger, tucked in his pants at the small of his back, then started towards the guardsman. He was not much of a fighter, but he knew enough to be able to defend himself. He also had a crowd of people behind him up. Crowds always gave cowards courage. He stopped just out of the other man's reach, "Hello brother."

The guardsman looked right passed him, "I need see Preacher, right away." From the rolling eyes to the clenched jaw, the annoyance was written all over the man's face. He must have seen Patrick as one of the rabble, and thought himself above him, a notion that he was going dispel, "Preacher isn't here, is there a message I give him?"

The guard rolled his eyes again, and started to walk around him. He stepped to his left; blocking the man's way. Dipping his shoulder, he tried to push past, but Patrick held firm. He could feel the group gathering behind him.

The guard sighed, realizing he had to at least pretend to show the boy deference, "We caught the dog."

Patrick was shocked. Preacher would want to know about Teridon's capture immediately. Separating Teridon from the King had been his number one priority. It had become clear that Teridon had to be removed before any serious moves can be made against the King.

The first attempt had been a miserable failure. Teridon had shown maturity and restraint, two things he did not have when they were younger. In the wake of Grigg's idiocy, Preacher had told the group that he would order no further attempts.

Instead, he made it open season on Teridon. Their brothers and sisters could make attempts at Teridon, but would not risk the greater group. It was important that any failed attempts were not be traced back to Preacher.

Patrick dropped his attempt at authority, this was too important for such silliness. He motioned for the guardsman to follow, and walked into the apartment.

***

They reached the top of the stairs. Preacher still sitting in front of the alter. He was not talking any longer, just breathing deeply and slowly. Waking him from this trance was unpredictable, he could come out of it relaxed or raging, there was no way to know. He was not quite ready to risk the man's wrath, so he paused. Preacher saved him the trouble.

"Let the man speak for himself, Patrick. Captain Anderson, tell me why you have come down to visit us"" Preacher had not moved a muscle, but somehow, knew who was standing behind him. Following Preacher's direction, the guardsman sat cross-legged on the straw mat next to him.

"We have caught the king's dog"

There was no embellishment needed.

A huge smile spread across Preacher's face, he draped his arm over the captain's shoulders, and pulled him tight to his side.

"Truly? Tell me how you did it. Was it you, alone, or did you have help? Tell me everything."

"Sir, I wish I was the one who captured him, but, I was not. We had two brothers at the Western Gate. They saw him heading down to the harbor, and threw together a plan. They grabbed a beggar out of the holding cell, and offered him his release if he went along with the plan. When he agreed, they beat him, and ordered him to report the assault to my guard post. Then, they lured the dog into an alley, and the beggar fingered him for the assault, then he was arrested, and they brought him to me to process."

Preacher was visibly struggling to keep his excitement in check, "Where is he now?"

"He is locked in my station, waiting to be transferred to the yards. The wagons haven't started running yet, so he will be in the holding cell until tonight."

Preacher stared into space for a moment, considering the next move.

"Have you entered the dog's name in the ledger yet?" The guardsman smiled while he shook his head no. If he was following preacher, Patrick was not.

"So, if a name is not in the ledger, than there is no record of the arrest. Correct?"

The man gave another nod, "that's right, sir."

"And, would it be odd to the arresting officers if there was no name in the book?"

"It would be extremely unlikely that they would even know, they are stationed at a different post. Besides, the commander controls the ledger. It would be unusual for them to check on the ledger of their own post, leaving alone another."

Suddenly, it hit Patrick like a bolt of lightning. They were going to kill Teridon. If there was no record of his arrest, they could eliminate him without drawing any attention to the group, preacher, or any of their brothers.

"Would you like to see him?"

Preacher hesitated for a moment, "No, I can't have him seeing my face. I need to be careful. I don't want the boy eliminated just yet. I want him knowing his failure before he dies. Can the he be held?"

"Yes sir, for a time. I am on duty tonight, so there is no rush to transfer him until tomorrow morning. The incoming captain is not one of us, and will want why a prisoner has not been entered in the book and was not transferred to the magistrate."

"I understand, my son, you have shown great resourcefulness. I have no doubt you will continue to do so. Soon, the King will have larger problems to worry about. He won't have time to wonder where his dog has gotten off too. Get back to your post captain, keep the boy hidden. I will send someone with orders shortly"

"Yes sir." The guardsman clapped his fist over his left breast and ran out of the room.

***

Preacher clapped Patrick on the shoulder, still beaming, "Can you believe this, son? This movement may have gotten off the ground with fits and starts, but this is what we needed to begin our major move, that boy was the bulwark that kept the king safe. That bulwark has just cracked, and is about to fail completely."

Excitement radiated from the man. Patrick shared it, but for different reasons. He was finally going to see Teridon get his. He was still dubious that the stupid farmer was as an important figure as Preacher did, but important or not, he would enjoy watching Teridon die. Patrick started to speak, but Preacher cut him off.

"You have never let go of your hatred, have you? Good, hold the hate, use it, let it forge your will for what is ahead. But, you cannot help dealing with him. There is far too much risk. You are too important to my plans." He put his arm around Patrick's shoulders, pulling him tight. "I cannot risk losing you, yet."

Chapter 50

Nidan sat heavily on his bed, sinking into the soft feather mattress. Teridon had not returned yet, but the boy was young and good looking, maybe he had found a nice girl at a tavern. He leaned back into the pillows, smiling, '*maybe he was out at a tavern and found a not so nice girl.*' If anyone deserved a night of debauchery, it was Teridon. The boy had been working nonstop for weeks.

He loved the night air of early fall, the chill made it smell so crisp, so clean. He slept with his window slightly ajar, allowing the chill into his room. Breathing deeply, he pulled the thick duvet to his neck, and drifted off to sleep.

'BANG! BANG! BANG!'

He shot up and jumped out of bed. He cracked the door open to find a guardsman standing in the hall. The man had his dress black uniform on, polished metal, hung from his belt, faced his grieves and made the star on his breast. Even in the dim light of the hall, the metal gleamed. His eyes were still heavy with sleep. Even those tiny points of light hurt.

The guardsman was panting, his brow shined with sweat. One of his tower security guards had just reaching the landing at the end of the hall. The tower guards were provided by his station, the only security he had personally hired was Teridon. They tried, but no one actually expected for them to have to do anything. The tower guard ran down the hall and grabbed the guardsman. He took a step back into his room and tried to figure out what was going on. The sleep started fading from his mind, but it was still a confusing scene unfolding.

The guardsman shrugged the grab off and doubled the tower guard over with a kick to his gut. He turned back and spoke quickly, before the guard could recover.

"Please, my Lord, my name is Jacob Pints. I need to speak with you immediately."

The security guard was up again, and moved on the commander, sword drawn, "Jakes?""Yes, my lord, I am from Barnstable; I grew up with Teridon Jace."

The security guard grabbed Jakes' shoulder, and yanked him away. Sir Loorie stepped forward and stopped the security guard with his hand.

"Release him, I know him, he is no threat. Thank you for your quick response, but you may leave us."

"Yes, Sir"

The guard clapped his fist over his heart in salute and did as he was ordered, the clicking of his boots on the marble floor hanging in the air as he disappeared down the stairs.

"Please, son, I need a moment to get composed and dressed. Go down to the library and I'll send some refreshments along, I will be down as soon as I can gather myself."

***

Jakes sipped slightly chilled red wine from a crystal goblet. Between the fire's heat and the good wine, he had begun to calm down. The large double doors creaked open and the King entered; his, previously disheveled, hair was slicked backed and tied in a ponytail, and the flannel night shirt had been replaced by light cotton trousers and a heavy shirt. He began speaking as soon as he saw Jakes.

"What can I do for you, son? You are lucky Teridon spoke so highly of you, that situation could have ended very differently."

Jakes nodded, the man spoke true, "I understand, my lord, and I apologize, but it was vital that I spoke with you right away. The guards would not let me in, so I had no choice but to push past them."

Sir Loorie dismissed Jakes's, unnecessary, apology with a wave of his hand, "Enough with that 'my lord' crap, please, I am tired of it. Now, son, tell me what is so important."

"Teridon has been arrested."

"WHAT!" Sir Loorie leaned forward, suddenly awake and engaged, "I need to know everything, now."

"Well sir, what I know comes from his accuser, a beggar, in custody for pickpocketing. I had just arrived on duty when he was brought in for processing. He came in bloodied and bruised, looking like he was badly beaten. When I asked him what happened, he told me quite a story."

The old knight sat on the edge of his chair, looking at him with unblinking eyes. This was a man of action. Jakes could tell he was getting ready to move. The man waved his hand towards himself, biding for Jakes to continue the story.

Well, he said that he had been arrested earlier in the day. Several guardsmen had offered to let him go free if he took a beating, then finger the person who gave it to him. The person would be whoever the guards told him it was to be. When he described who the wanted accused, it was Teridon, no doubt it. I would have come right away, but the man was a beggar, I needed see if he was lying. I asked around. I was able to confirm that the man had been arrested earlier that day, and that he matched Teridon's description. So, I went to the station where he was arrested." He paused for a heartbeat, "They would not let me. Sir, I am a guard commander, I can't be ordered around by a captain. This man refused to let me in, and then when I ordered him to open the door, he just slammed the window in my face. Something is wrong, and I assume the captain would not let me in because I would ask questions about the prisoner. I needed to get help, and did not know who else to turn to. The guard has been compromised, and I don't know who I can trust."

"Thank you son, you made the right decision." There was edge in the King's voice.

"Teridon and I went to dinner earlier this week, did he tell you about the problems we had outside the Poisoned Monk? Did he tell you about how the guard post was empty?"

Shrugging, "He did, he said that a man tried to start a fight with you two, and that you had him arrested. He may have mentioned the guard post in passing."

Jakes nodded, "I expected as much, he doesn't know our protocols. A guard captain is required to man his post at all times. They need to intake prisoners, take complaints, dispatch guards for investigations, and facilitate prisoner movements. They are only allowed to leave their post in times of great need. The post was empty that night, and there was nothing that would have required a captain's attention, I checked. The captain on duty that night, Anderson, was filling in for the normal captain."

Sir Loorie sensed where this was going, but he let Jakes continue anyway.

"The captain, that would not let me in this afternoon, was also named Anderson. I don't know if it is the same man, but I don't believe in coincidence."

Sir Loorie stood, not needing to hear anything further, "Nor do I, son, it will take me a short while to get ready, meet me outside in a few moments."

***

When Sir Loorie came out of the tower, the king had been replaced by a soldier. His hair may gave been graying, and his skin starting to wrinkle, but there was no doubting the hard eyes and set jaw. He wore a padded doublet, dark leather leggings tucked into high boots, a bastard sword hung at his left hip. The clothing was not armor in the traditional sense, but the thick leather and padded cotton would give some protection if any trouble found them. Sir Loorie was ready to get his hands dirty, and, for that, Jakes was grateful.

"Sir."

Sir Loorie rolled his eyes, "Kid, enough with the damn titles. We are going to break someone out of jail, not going to a ball." Jake smiled broadly; it was clear why Teridon loved this man so much. He was a soldier playing at politics. Too many were politicians playing at soldiering. They started out, heading towards the west gate. The old city was empty at this time of night. The government was shut down, and the residents were either asleep or playing down the hill.

***

They approached the gate; it was lit with three large oil lamps, each several feet across, one on either side, the third hanging from large chains in the middle of the gate's arch. The night shift at an old city gate was one of the guard's most uneventful postings. Guards aimlessly milled about, looking to be more interested in whatever gossip they were discussing than the two approaching men. Jakes wanted to keep Sir Loorie's profile as low as possible. It would not do for a guard commander to put the King in danger, though he feared danger was coming no matter what he did. Still, keeping a low profile was always advisable. There would be no questions asked if they did not know who was standing in front of them.

"Sir, stay here, just outside the gate's light. You need to be visible, but don't let then see who you are. We don't know who to trust, and if any of the guards at the gate are compromised, we can't have them knowing the King is in the lower city."

"Don't worry about me, son, it's not the first time I've had to keep a low profile. Do what you need to, I'll play along."

Jakes strode up to the nearest guardsman; he walked with purpose, and held his chin up, with hard eyes, projecting the authority of his rank.

The guardsman started when he saw his rank. *'Perfect!'* The more they focused on him, the less they focused on his companion. He squared on the man, who snapped to attention, "I am escorting this man to the Holding Yards. His son has been arrested, and he has requested a personal escort to the Yard so his son can be released tonight."

The lie spoke to an unusual situation, but not an unheard of one. Sometimes, when a member of the aristocracy was in trouble, their family would ask for a personal escort to the Holding Yard. The yards were a dangerous place for anyone, but they were doubly so for someone with money. These people typically wanted out as soon as possible. Everything tended to move smoother when there was an officer present. The guard looked over his shoulder, at Sir Loorie, who was standing just outside the gate's circle of light. He was close enough that they could make out his face, but not so close that the light would reveal any real details.

He rolling his eyes, tapped his feet, held his hands up and appeared generally annoyed. He was playing the part of an arrogant noble perfectly. The guard wanted no part of the pair, questioning people like this tended to end badly for low ranking individuals. He signaled for his fellows to open the door, and then waved them through.

Once through the gate, they casually walked down the hill, anyone who saw them would not think they were in any particular hurry. Sir Loorie leaned into Jakes, asking quietly, "Are you sure which guardhouse he is being kept in?"

Jakes shook his head, "No, I think I know where he was. But, I have no way of knowing if he is still there. For obvious reasons, I doubt the usual intake procedures have been followed. If he is allowed to go before the Magistrate, they would have to explain why there is no warrant, and why the accuser cannot be produced. I can't imagine the responsible people want those questions asked."

Once they were out of the gate's view, both men started running, if Teridon had not been moved, he would be soon.

***

Teridon took off his cloak, rolled it up, and laid his head on it. The bench was hard, damp, and uncomfortable, but he was in a cell, it was not supposed to be comfortable. He stared numbly into the darkness that enveloped the ceiling, the uneasy feeling in his gut building.

Something terrible was brewing, a child could see that, but beyond that, was all he saw was a wall. Figuring things out, seeing patterns, those were Jakes' strengths, not his. His strength was action, and right now he was stuck in this forsaken cell.

Even if he was good at seeing patterns, it would not help. Facts were in short supply, all he knew was that he had been set up by a random stranger, the city guard was not following procedures, and he had been alone for a while. He allowed himself to wonder just how long that while was, if the sun was still out, where the captain went. There had been a knock on the door a while ago. It had been followed by a heated exchange, but the thick door had blocked the sound enough that he could not make out words, only two men yelling. After the confrontation, the captain had come back in, grabbed some papers, extinguished the lamps, and then left him in blackness.

He had tried every way he could think of to get out, and he was on the brink of giving up. All of the bars were firmly embedded in the ceiling, and the door was securely locked. His only option was fighting his way out. Currently, however, there was no one to fight, and even had there been, he had no way to get to them.

He was jolted by the metallic crash of iron shackles against the bars of the cell door.

"Did you miss me? I hope you're ready to move."

The heavy sarcasm in the voice was trying to get a rise out of him, but he did not take the bait. He turned his head slightly, confirming the captain had returned, and was standing in the cell door. He jumped up and ran to the door, not caring if desperation showed.

"You have orders? Who is giving those orders? Which commander? Where am I being moved, when?"

The captain took a step back, just out of his reach.

"Are you really dumb enough to think I take my orders from the guard? I have already sent one commander on his way."

'He had turned a commander away? Was that the argument he heard outside? Was Jakes looking for him?'

He dismissed the thoughts quickly, there were many commanders, and they could have been there for any reason. He had to focus, not wander off in flights of fancy. He was desperate for any information he could get.

"Fine. Captain, can you at least tell me where you are taking me?"

"Well, we are leaving this rat hole, but after that, who knows."

He wanted nothing more than to beat the life out of the smug little man, but knew that his mouth will just make things worse, so he bit his tongue.

The captain threw the shackles through the bars; they hit the floor and slid into his feet. He looked down at the shackles and then looked back to the cell door, staring through the captain.

"Where are you taking me?"

"Does it matter? You are going, whether you like it or not. If I have to come in there to put them on, it will just make things worse."

The thick wood and steel that separated them stoked the captain's bravado. This little man seemed to have an outsized ego. Suddenly, the way out of this mess hit him.

"You know, captain? I am tired. Do you think we can do this later?"

"What are you doing? GET UP! I gave you an order!"

Teridon sauntered back to the bench. He stretched and lay gently down on the stone bench, letting his head rest on his cloak. He shifted to get comfortable, and making no move towards the shackles. The Captain was staring to breathe heavily, his anger clear as he pushed his face against the bars.

He responded to the captain's anger with deafening silence, not even acknowledging that the man was still standing at the bars. The captain pushed up against the bars and struck them with the iron key, his belt buckle thudded against the wooden door as he slammed his body forward.

"MOVE, YOU SHIT! I GAVE YOU AN ORDER!"

Teridon groaned loudly, then made as how of rolling over, and turning his back to the door. The show of disrespect pushed the captain from simple anger to red hot rage.

"YOU WILL PAY FOR DISRESPECTING ME, PUT THE DAMN SHACKLES ON!"

The captain was pinned against the bars; the door was clinking in its frame as the captain shook it. Teridon responded to the captain with exaggerated sigh. Ignoring the man was getting the exact reaction he wanted.

The Captain took a deep breath, as he backed away from the bars; he took a moment and exhaled slowly, "I will give you one more chance. Put the shackles on, and we won't speak of this insolence again. Don't, and there will be serious trouble." He spoked softly, but through a clenched jaw.

Not bothering to roll over, Teridon held his open hand up and waiving the captain away. While he was trying to get this reaction, the man's threats bordered on pathetic. The captain hissed as he grabbed his keys. The keys clinked against each other as the key slid into the lock, then it fell open with a click. Teridon stayed facing the wall so his huge smile did not tip his hand.

"You WILL wear those shackles you arrogant prick. Give trash like you a little power, and you think you don't have to obey your betters."

The captain threw the door open and stormed into the cell. The door slammed against the stone wall. The captain had opened it with such force that he had to block the ricochet so it did not hit him in the face.

The captain grabbed his arm. As soon as the captain's fingers tightened around his forearm, the little man got his wish, he moved. He savored the thought of the captain's ego deflating when he realized the grave mistake he had made.

Teridon rolled his hand over, and clamped his hand around the captain's arm, engulfing the entire circumference of the smaller man's forearm. The shocked man tried to pull away, but, unfortunately, his arm was caught in the vice that is Teridon's grip. Controlling the captain's arm, he flipped it so the elbow faced the ceiling.

The captain struggled, jerking backwards time and again, but even with his whole body weight, the weak attempts were not enough to overcome Teridon's strength.

He paused for a few heartbeats, giving the captain a moment to think the situation, and his mistake. Then, he rolled over, trapping the captain's arm between the bench and his body, his bulk putting pressure on the man's feeble elbow. The captain screamed as Teridon's weight forced his elbow to bend opposite of nature's intention. He dropped to a knee, desperately trying to release the pressure that Teridon was putting on the joint. It was useless attempt; Teridon was just too damn strong and held his arm firm.

The captain doubled over, then dropped to his hip. His shoulder twisted further, but he was trying anything to relive the pressure on his elbow. Unfortunately, for him, his arm was locked firm.

"Let me go, you are assaulting an officer of the Capuamundi City guard, a crime punishable by death. Let go, and I won't pursue charges."

Teridon did not respond to the captain's pathetic threats. They both knew that none of the guard's protocols had been followed, and the captain would not be reporting this to anyone. Once the threat fell on deaf ears, the captain returned to his desperate attempts at yanking his arm away.

Teridon had enough of the little captain. He rolled while pinning the man's wrist in place, against the stone. The captain screamed again as his elbow bore Teridon's full weight. The pressure was far too much, and the elbow collapsed. The captain shrieked when the joint snapped tendons and ligaments tearing as Teridon bore the man to the ground.

The two men landed side by side, but the captain's mangled arm was trapped under him. He stared at Teridon. His eyes were unfocused and glazed with tears from the pain. His mind could do nothing but focus on the excruciating pain radiating from his elbow. He tried to move, but his arm was trapped.

Teridon met the guards stare. He allowed himself a brief moment to gloat, then rolled his hip and, drove kick into his face. Shrieks of pain followed as his foot broke the man's nose. He ingnored the spray of blood from the guard's nose, and used the kick's momentum to pull him over.

He popped to his knees, straddling the guard's chest. In a mount position, he was in complete control. He had been previously controlling his rage, but he allowed it to begin trickling out. The pathetic little man would already be dead if he had not been controlling himself.

He bent and drove his forearm into the guard's throat, pathetic gurgles and wheezes squeezed from the guard's mouth as his weight crushed the man's windpipe. He leaned on the arm and bent close to the captain's ear, whispering, "Captain, this can be easy or it can be hard. You will answer my questions, or you will die painfully, it is completely your choice. Who hired you? Who do you work for? And, who is giving you orders?"

Even though he gave the man a choice, but, in truth, his rage wanted blood. The captain moved his mouth, trying to talk, but only producing a faint gurgling sound. Annoyed, he lifted up, allowing the man a breath. The captain used that breath to wheeze out one word, 'Preacher.'

Teridon fought to keep his calm, "Who is the preacher?"

His arm hovered just above the man's neck, all he had to do was drop and the man was dead, they both knew it. Teridon looked the man in the eyes as the man lay there fighting for any breath he could take. Would the man die to protect a preacher? He was going to test that dedication. He dropped his forearm down onto the man's throat, forcing another gurgle out. He leaned his weight on the man's throat and whispered into his ear, again.

"One name, that's it. Are you really going to die protecting a preacher? You know I have no issue killing you, right? Give me your preacher's name, and I'll let you go."

He lifted up again, allowing him a breath and a chance to respond. The captain began sobbing, all his bluster gone.

"He's not a preacher, that's his name. It's the only name I know. A runner brought me money once a month. They asked me to do small stuff, help people through the gates, get people out of minor trouble, and leave my post if needed. It was easy money, and they never asked me to do anything bad, so I never pushed back.

By the time they told me what they were planning with you, I was in too deep, I had no choice. I never thought it would come to this. They told me to hold you until I heard further. That's all I know, they never told me names! They never told me anything!"

"Liar! That wasn't the song you were singing when you were making threats through steel bars, no, you were a 'captain' and I had to respect you. Now that you are begging for your life, you are some low level flunky. I will give you one more chance, who is Preacher?"

"I do not know, I never met him, I only dealt with runners."

Teridon had enough; he growled and dropped his arm back onto the captain's neck, not bothering to keep any of his weight off the man this time.

The captain's lips silently opened and closed, but he had no wind to make any sound. Teridon pushed harder, making sure it stayed that way.

The captain punched with his good arm, but the light taps on his thighs did not even faze him. The punches did not start with much force, and they were getting even weaker. He let up and drove his elbow into the captain's throat, collapsing the windpipe. He stood and watched the captain grab his throat, then his body trembled and relaxed, the light leaving his eyes as he died.

Teridon walked out of the cell. He was free. His weapons hung on a wooden rack next to a couple of other swords and shields on the far wall. He grabbed them and fastened the belt around his waist. He looked around the room, trying to find some information. He flipped through the last couple of pages in the ledger, not surprised that there was no entry for his arrest. He had suspected this to be all a scheme to separate him from Sir Loorie. He also suspected that he was supposed to end up dead. While, this seemed to confirm that, it also pointed to something even more disturbing, the guard had been compromised. He would tell have to tell Jakes, maybe he could find out the extent of rot inside the guard.

Chapter 51

Jakes pounded on the door. The thick epee door was reinforced with steel banding at the top, middle, bottom, and around the latch mechanism. Epee, also known as iron wood, was deep black, with very little visible grain, it was a beautiful wood, and as the name implied it was very hard, and very strong. Jakes pounded the door's large circular knocker into a round iron plate embedded in the wood, the metal sending vibrations through the thick door. If he knocked with his hand, no one would hear a thing. After three knocks rang off the plate, he took a step back and grasped this hilt of his sword. Sir Loorie had positioned himself off to the right, hidden from anyone opening the door. The latch moved, and Jakes unclipped the stay on his sword as the door creaked slowly open.

His hand fell away from the hilt when Teridon peaked around the door, wearing that crooked smile of his. He should have known that his friend would not be laid low such a simple setup. Teridon's smile widened.

"Hi boys, how's the night been? Pardon my manners, come on in!" He swung the door wide, and stepped out of the way. Jakes walked in and looked around.

"Teridon, where is the Captain? I need to question him."

"The captain had a little bit of an incident. I tried to help him, but he was just too far gone. His ego had grown so big; it broke his arm and crushed his throat. It is the craziest thing, but the poor man died from the malady."

Only Teridon could find humor in this situation. Jakes shook his head then began his investigation. The captain lay dead on the floor, his lips were purple and his tongue hung out of his mouth, the man had suffocated from the crushed throat. His arm was bent at a sick angle, the elbow was bent up instead of down, hand lower than the elbow. He blanched a bit when he saw the corpse, the man's death must have been horribly painful.

Sir Loorie chided Teridon, "Well, I guess he won't be giving us any information."

Teridon ignored the knight, "Does the name 'Preacher' mean anything to either of you?"

Jakes shook his head no, "No, Should it?" while Sir Loorie stood behind, shaking his head no, as well.

"Because 'Preacher' was that little man's boss. Or at least that is the name he gave me while I interrogated him. I am not an animal; I gave him the chance to die quickly if he told me more, but was a good soldier, and died slowly."

Jakes loved Teridon but the ease that he spoke of killing this man chilled him. He was taken aback at just how cold his friend could be. He pushed the thought down, and focused on the task. He grabbed tore a page out of the ledger and, using the quill from the desk, scribbled 'Preacher' on it. It was a name he would not want to forget, but, unfortunately, meant nothing.

Stuffing the paper into his pocket, he looked around room. It was a fairly standard guard station, the only difference were the walls were stone instead of wood. The furniture was austere but functional, as was the norm. The ledger book was also standard issue, roughly half full. He flipped through the last couple of pages, finding nothing out of the ordinary, beyond the fact that Teridon's arrest was not recorded. Captain Anderson had opened the last page in the ledger when he came on duty, and there was no doubt the man was a traitor. Suddenly, something stuck him.

"Does the captain have a tattoo?"

Sir Loorie stood next to Teridon, in the cell, when Jakes asked the question. He reached down and tore the captain's light shirt open, then kicked the body over, so he could see the back.

"No, he doesn't have any tattoos."

Jakes cursed softly, he had been hoping to draw a link between the blonde man, Captain Anderson, and the pendant that Teridon had found. Unfortunately, it was not going to be that easy.

Teridon walked out of the cell,"Find anything?" Jakes shook his head no, the captain had been careful not to leave any evidence.

"Did any other people come while you were in the cell?"

"No, the captain left for a while, and he argued with someone outside the door, but I couldn't tell who it was. No one but the captain ever came in."

Jakes was frustrated. He had a talent of seeing patterns as they formed, and while he could feel something was wrong, but when he tried to figure out what, he ran into a wall. He was looking for patterns, but all he saw was random dots, like someone had flicked paint on a wall.

Teridon was done with this place, the stone felt like a mausoleum, and he swore they were starting to close in, "Have you looked about enough? I need to get out of here."

Jakes kicked the desk's stool across the room in frustration.

"Yeah, there is nothing here, let's go."

The three men left the guard post. The oil lamps were burning along the road, and some tenements along it had already gone dark. It was well past dark.

Jakes turned to the men,"I need to report the captain's death and get this post covered. I'll report that I found it on a routine check. There will be an investigation, but I looked around, there is nothing pointing to anyone in particular. What are you two going to do?"

Teridon looked at Sir Loorie, who answered,"We're going back to the tower. We need to get our arms around events before they spin out of control. Right now, we don't know what is going on, and we need more information, badly. If you find something, Jakes, let me know immediately."

"Yes sir."

"Jakes!" Sir Loorie addressed him

"Yes, sir?"

"What did I tell you about that all that sir crap?"

Jakes and Teridon burst out laughing as they split up.

Chapter 52

Branyan Wybb led four of his most trusted Rangers as they rode through the rolling fields that surrounded Capuamundi. The city was no longer visible when he signaled a stop. The orders he was about to give were beyond secret, and he could not risk them being overheard. He preferred these plains for such sensitive conversations. There were too many eyes and ears inside the city, and out in the plains no one could lurk around without them knowing.

The four rangers circled their commander. Dangerous missions, like the one he was presenting, had to be voluntary, and protocol required that he give the men an opportunity to decline. With the regulars, some may walk, but rangers were not the regulars, they were their owe breed. Still, they were soldiers, protocol was their master, and that master needed to be served.

"Men, we are out here because I could not trust the ears in the city. This mission is as sensitive as it is important. I have very little information for you, but the little information we have indicates that the government of Hesh might have fallen."

The statement hung in the air, shocking the four hardened soldiers. There were no wars anymore, the world had been stable for so long. The commander continued.

"The borders have been closed, trade has stopped, and contact with our assets in the country has ceased. Our mission is to get into the country, make contact with our assets, assess the situation, and get them out, if possible."

The four men looking back at him nodded. They understood what the other side of 'if possible' was.

"As usual, if any of you have any reservations, you can back out, but if you commit, there is no turning back."

He was not surprised when all four stepped forward; they were Rangers, and Rangers do not back down.

"We will ride hard for the border. We need to be there in days, not weeks."

They mounted up and spurred the horses on, heading south and east, towards Hesh. The ride will be hard. The rolling plains would give way to steeper, and rockier, hills as the land rose towards The Crags. The importance of this mission meant that they might need to sacrifice a few horses to move as fast as possible.

Chapter 53

A gruff old guardsman manned his post. He was supposed to be watching the crowd but if anyone looked closely, they would see that his eyes were glazed over. He looked through the throng more than at it. The man jumped when he saw a man in black push out of the crowd, and walk towards him with purpose. The commander was not running, but he was walking fast enough to make his cape billow behind. He snapped a hasty, and sloppy, salute when the commander stopped in front of him. Jakes had much more important matters than an old guardsman slacking on the job.

"At ease, guardsman, I need to speak with the captain on duty, right away."

The man nodded, and ran to fetch the captain.

The captain rushed from the stand to meet him.

"Sir, what can I do for you? We have the ledger is inside. Would you like to see it?"

It was commonplace for commanders to drop in on stations and check in while out on rounds. Finding something strange while making rounds would not be unusual, a murdered guardsman was another matter entirely.

"Captain, we have a grave situation. My last check was at the guardhouse up the hill. I found the captain's body in the cell, he appears to have been murdered. The investigation needs to begin at once, please have your men secure the scene, and send for the inquisitors so they can begin their work as soon as possible."

The captain's eyes were wide, "Yes, sir, right away!"

He snapped a salute and ran inside. Two guardsmen came running out immediately after and heading up the hill. After a brief moment, the captain came out of the station holding a scroll sealed with the guard's sigil pressed into black wax, and called for a runner.

Usually teenagers, runners stood throughout the city waiting for messages that needed to be sent quickly. Along with scroll, he handed the scrawny boy a slip of paper with the address and a gold coin. Messages sent without a coin tended to get lost. They would get to their destination eventually, but there would inevitably be a problem that 'delayed' the missive.

Satisfied with the captain's response, Jakes had a personal matter to take care of.

"Thank you captain, do you mind if I take a second, you just reminded me of a note I need to send."

The Captain waved his hand towards the door, "Sure commander, you're welcome to whatever you need. Do you know where to find the supplies?"

"Yes Captain, I can manage, thanks."

The Captain snapped another salute, which Jakes reciprocated before going inside.

***

Jakes locked the door behind him, and then sat at the captain's desk. He closed the ledger, and took a sheet of paper from the draw below the desk's slant top. Dipping the quill in the desk's inkwell, he scratched a quick letter. This situation was beginning to spin out of control, he needed assistance, so he turned to his oldest friend on the guard, the only guardsman he could be sure was not compromised, Marie Pepon. She was the highest ranking female guardsman, and they had known each other since meeting in basic training.

Once the letter was done, he rolled the letter and used a candle to drip black wax onto the scroll. He pressed the sigil into the wax, this time; however, he cut an 'X' over the silhouette of the Kethi-draal. The 'X' will alert Marie that something was wrong; he would fill her in on the details later.

***

He left the pose and grabbed another runner, a small black haired boy who looked to be about thirteen. He handed him the note, Marie's address, and a coin. The runner started to move, Jakes grabbed him, pressing a second coin into the boy's palm.

"This is to ensure that Ms. Pepon, and ONLY Ms. Pepon, receives this."

The boy nodded and disappeared into the crowd.

Things were about to explode, he could feel it. Foul energy hung so thick in the air, it seemed a small spark would ignite it. Even more concerning, there seemed to be an unseen party itching to provide that spark.

***

He ran home, focused on getting his family out of the city before it exploded. If he waited any longer, they may not have the chance to leave.

His home was a small two story wood building, about three quarters of the way up the hill, just off the north street. The hour was late, so it was dark, both his wife and son were asleep. He slammed the door open and ran up the stairs. There was enough moonlight coming in through the windows that he could make out the online of Nydelis beneath the thick blankets. He lit a lamp then shook her awake, she rolled over, heavy eyes questioning what he was doing.

"Ny, you have to leave the city, right now, tonight."

Still addled by sleep, she did not comprehend what he was trying to say, but he would not wake her up if it was not serious. She tried to follow what he was saying, but he was talking so fast.

"The city is going to explode, and we don't have much time, please, you need to get Terry, and go."

Rubbing the sleep from her eyes, she got out of bed, and started gathering clothes and travel gear. She was moving stiffly, still trying to actually wake up.

He felt horrible, and wished that this could wait until tomorrow and he could fully explain what was going on, but there was just no time. Things were moving much too fast for that kind of delay. If they waited until tomorrow, there might be no escape.

He followed her around the room as she prepared.

"I have secured an escort for you. I don't know who to trust, some of the guard has turned coat. While I am sure some, maybe most, will remain loyal to their oaths, we have no way to know who they are. I have a few fellows that I know I can trust, but that won't be enough to turn the tide. I'm sorry this is so sudden, but if you are here, I can't focus on my duties, and I would be putting all of us in even more danger."

Tears touched the corners of her eyes; her initial feeling that this was an elaborate prank was gone. She understood, he had his duty, his oaths. Ever since Jakes took the post, she had always hoped serious trouble would not find him, but, she knew that her hopes were naive. That time, it seemed, had come. Tears wetted the corners of his eyes as well.

"Marie is going to meet you at the north gate. She will have a carriage waiting, and will escort you, and Terry, out of the city"

"Where are we going?"

"Getting you away from the city the most important. I have a friend who owns an inn just outside the city. Spend the rest of the night there, then go back to Barnstable, stay with my family until I can come for you."

"I don't want to leave you." She was sobbing now, unable to keep the tears at bay.

"Listen, Ny, you have to go. There is nothing you can do to help, and staying here will just put you and Terry in danger. I cannot have you here, not with what is coming. The last couple of days have shown something is being planned by a brazen, and powerful, actor. We don't know who, and I need to find out.

I cannot focus with you two here. Please, go with Marie, she'll keep you safe, I have already arranged everything; I will come for you as soon as I can."

He was practically begging now, but he did not care, he just needed them out of the city. She looked at him through eyes glazed with tears, which began flowing freely.

"I am going to gather what loyal guardsman I can find and carry out our duties. I'm going to make the traitors pay for this."

She sobbed, and all she could come up with was a simple "Be careful."

She was going to leave, relief flooded through him.

"Thank you, Ny, thank you. I am going to say good-bye to Terry, then you two need to get moving. Marie will be waiting for you."

The dull circle of lamplight slid onto Terry, who was sleeping peacefully in his small bed. He allowed his mind a moment to wander; he had made that bed with his own hands. He brought the hemlock back from Barnstable, milling and cutting the boards out of the logs. It was his way of connecting with his son while he was away for months at a time. Terry lay in the bed in a odd way that children do, across the head of the bed, pushed against the headboard, feet resting on the wall. The boy was his world. He would die if it meant the boy would live, it was something he said before, but the proposition suddenly seemed very real.

He bent and gave the boy a soft kiss on his forehead. Finally, he answered his wife's final request softly and to no one in particular, "I will."

Chapter 54

Preacher was at his modest desk, nothing but an old door on some sawhorses, reviewing final plans. Patrick fought to keep his excitement in check, this was the day that he would finally hear Preacher's grand plan. It was going to be the culmination of his years following the man. He knew that Preacher had more followers than just the group living in the underground, but as he looked over the packed street, he realized that he had no idea just how much recruiting the man had been doing. People had been trickling into the underground all day. They had been instructed to come in waves, so as not to draw unwanted attention.

He stared out the window, trying to count how many people were stuffing into the underground. He had gotten to two hundred when Preacher spoke to his back.

"Is everyone here?"

Patrick had no idea; he never met any of the other groups. He paused, still pretending to stare out the window.

"I will take your silence as your answer."

He cringed.

"It's alright son, if you don't know, then you don't know."

"Yes, sir, thank you, I can tell you that there are a lot of people here."

"Excellent, then let's begin."

Preacher got up and walked towards him, a serene half smile on his face. He paused, nodded slightly, and then disappeared down the rickety stairway.

***

Preacher pulled a simple brown robe over his head, and then tied it around his waist with a black cord. He gave the image of a poor man, one of the people. The image was carefully crafted, and even more carefully maintained. He never told anyone his true name or spoke of his history; they were a secret known only to him.

He ran his hands through his hair, pulling it into a tight ponytail, and securing it with more black cord. The robe was oversized and ill-fitting, giving the illusion of bulk to his slim frame. The poor fit was like the rest of his image, carefully constructed to look accidental.

It also served a purpose, allowing Preacher to pull the robe off and suddenly, the thick man was gone, and a pursuer would not be looking for the slim man who replaced him.

"Son, are you ready to turn this city inside out?"

Patrick responded with an enthusiastic nod. This is what he had been waiting for. He took a brief moment to think about the empty husk that had deserted the military, and the chance meeting that set him along this path. After all those years, the day was finally here.

***

A small balcony overlooked the street. It probably was built for decoration, but it was large enough for one man to stand on, but only just. It gave the perfect platform to address the gathered crowd. Preacher paused at the window, then walked out onto the small balcony, the rousing cheers of hundreds of onlookers greeting him. He held his hands high, the crowd fell silent.

"Welcome."

He spoke conversationally, there was no need to raise his voice, the acoustics of the underground gave his voice sufficient volume. He could have been whispering anyway, no one dared make a sound when he spoke.

"You all have been following me based on promises. You had no reason to believe those promises, but, you did not need a reason, you had faith, faith in me, faith in you brothers and sisters, and faith in our movement. You accepted that you are part of something larger then yourself. For too long, you have had a boot on your throats. For too long, you have been beaten down by a lie. That lie, my children, is freedom and its bastard child, choice. You have been told that you are free, but you aren't.

You have been told that you have a choice, but you don't. How can you have a choice when you are forced into the system that they have constructed?"

There was rumbling as he said that. He held his hands high again, silencing the conversations that had kicked up.

"You came to me because, deep down, you knew that the choice society gave you was false. You may not have known why you felt that way, but the feeling was there.

The choice society really gave you was simple, submit or die, whether by the force of the city guard, the boot of the military, or the starvation of poverty, you must play their game or succumb. You follow me because you know that these are not choices; they are threats. You are here because you would not bend to those threats. No, you chose a third way, you chose to pull yourself out of their construct and join our movement. Now, I will admit, that this movement has started slowly. But, like the foundation is the most important part of a building, this movement is no different; the foundation is the most important part. We needed dedicated men and women who were willing to give their all for their brothers and sisters."

The crowd was enthralled, Preacher's voice rose and fell, and the crowd would cheer as it rose and lean, silently, in when it fell. These vocal theatrics were all deliberate, and extensively rehearsed.

"Tonight, children, your faith begins to pay dividends. This movement is not me, or any single one of you. NO! It is the brother to your left, and the sister to your right. You have thrown back the shackles of the individual, and found salvation in something larger. I know that every one of you will lay down your lives for your brothers. I know that each and every one of you puts the movement above your own, single, well-being. None of you are selfish enough to let you brothers suffer while you thrive. I will not lie to you..."

His voice trailed off as tears glistening in his eyes, touching the corners. He grasped the railing and his shoulders slumped, as if a weight had fallen on his shoulders, his voice cracked as he continued.

Patrick had watched him practice these overly dramatic displays; they seemed so silly when done in front of a mirror. But, in front of a crowd, they were amazing; they drew the crowd in kept their rapt attention.

"No, I can't lie to you, some of you may be asked to make that very sacrifice."

He steadied himself against the rail, letting out a large, exaggerated, sigh. After staying in this position for a heartbeat, his shoulders straightened. Throwing the imaginary weight off, he stood straight, as if he had gotten a surge of vigor.

"BUT KNOW! Know that you will not have given that, most precious, commodity for nothing! No, it will be given for your brothers, your sisters, and the movement. You will be venerated as a hero.

A hero because you will have paid the ultimate price to give the gift of freedom to your fellow man, a hero for having freed your fellows of the lies that this society has been selling for hundreds of years. Nothing can stop this boulder once it begins rolling, and just like a boulder, this movement started slowly, but its momentum will build. Tonight is the kick that will get that it rolling. Be sure, our movement will pick up some clingers, the rest... well... they will be crushed."

He slammed his fist on the railing for emphasis. A piece of the brittle railing broke and fell to the ground. It was unplanned but helped drive the point home.

"This country is a pig, a pig that has fattened itself off of you, your sweat, your effort, your blood. Tonight, the head of the pig, this hole of a city, gets cut off. Then, we will peel the fat off the pig's back and give it back to the people."

He gripped what was left of the railing, knuckles white as his head slowly swept left, then right, looking over the leaders of his movement.

Patrick stood with his mouth agape. Any doubts had melted away, and had been replaced by that feeling in his gut. The same feeling he had when he first saw Preacher speaking in that little square, the same charge, and the same excitement. He could hardly contain himself as Preacher gathered his robes and left the balcony, walking right towards him. His heart was racing, but a deep breath calmed him just as Preacher stopped in front of him.

"Follow me son, our night is just beginning."

***

Preacher spent the night meeting with small groups of his supporters, Patrick following him the whole time, running messages to various groups. Finally, as Preacher was wrapping up one of those meetings, Patrick mustered his courage.

"Sir, what is my roll? I have been following you all night and you haven't said what I am going to be doing. Am I just to going to be a puppy dog? Or am I going to do something?"

He cringed, he could not believe the words that had just came out of his mouth, he never spoke like that. But, to his surprise, the response was just a smile, a brush of his cheek, and a simple, "Just a bit longer my son, come, follow me."

A lone shaft of light streamed in from the underground's entrance. The meetings had taken the night, and morning had broken. The light will shine for about an hour after sunrise, and then the underground will return to pitch black. He followed Preacher to the second floor, and watched him return to the balcony.

The crowd stared up at him with bleary eyes; there were no conversations to stop this time, the exhausted faces showing that everyone was ready to sleep.

"Brothers, sisters, it has been a long night, thank you for your patience and attention. You have your orders; carry your missions out to the best of your abilities, and if you give your best efforts, we will bring this system down. Remember, your orders are for you, and you alone, speak nothing of them, even to your brothers."

Preacher was the only person who knew the totality of his plans, there was no way the plan would be stopped, even if the group had been infiltrated, the spy would not have enough information to stop them. Cheers followed Preacher as he returned to the solitude of the building. He lightly touched Patrick's shoulder.

"Let's go, my son, our preparations must begin.

Chapter 55

Sir Loorie sat up, groaning as his face hit the the shaft of light streaming through the window. He had forgotten to close the curtains, again. His head throbbed and his eyes fought his attempts at opening them. Last night's rescue had kept him up until the small hours, and times like this reminded him that he was not a young man anymore. Teridon had done most of the work, but his old bones still felt the lack of sleep.

Last night had confirmed that he was right about the oversized, and over egoed, boy all those years ago in Barnstable. Teridon was self-sufficient, aggressive, intelligent, and most of all, a hell of a fighter. He had said it that night, and the intervening years had proven him correct, the military's shortsighted loss was his gain. The boy had been a passable squire, but he had not recruited Teridon to be a squire, he had recruited him because he refused to see the boys potential wasted.

He swung his feet out of the bed, stretching the night's stiffness out of his old joints. He swayed a bit; his head was in a fog, like he had drank a little too much last night. Unfortunately, there was no such fun, the aches, stiffness, and slow-wittedness, were just old age.

He studied himself in the mirror, staring at the bags under his eyes, his peppered stubble that needed shaving, the hair standing all over. He splashed cold water on his face, trying to smooth the rough face that stared back at him from the mirror. The last thing he wanted to do was preside over the council today, but it was his duty, and duty was a word he took seriously.

He had delayed for as long as possible, so he leaned into the hall, calling a servant. It only took a few moments for the young man to arrive with his clothing for the day. The boy helped him tie the light shirt while he tied the black wool trousers. Dressed, he stood in front the wash station, wet his unruly hair down, and pulled it back into a tight ponytail, finally he pushed his finger through his wedding ring, and then pulled both signet rings on. It was time to start another day.

"Son, Please fetch Teridon, tell him to meet me in the library."

***

"What are you reading, son?"

Teridon flipped the book he was holding over and back. "Oh nothing, I was thumbing through 'A history of the empire', I have never had much of a reason to care about it, but after recent events, I figured maybe similar things have happened before, and there is some guidance in history."

The depth of the boy's thinking shocked him, sometimes he had to be reminded that Teridon was more than just muscle and swords. He sunk into the couch across from the boy.

"Those are wise words, words I wish others would consider. History forgotten is history repeated. Unfortunately, history is also dirty, ugly business, so it's usually easier to forget. We can't let that scare us, though, it is vitally important. You've picked a fine place to ask your questions. This library is one of the empire's best and most complete. Even better, it has original documents, not some egghead's interpretation of the events." Teridon face flushed with embarrassment, he had never gone to school in Barnstable. He had to work the farm. He looked down at the book, flipping pages, not making eye contact.

Sir Loorie knew that look, "Don't be embarrassed, you did what you had to do, there is no shame. Ask your questions, there won't be any judgment."

Teridon nodded, "Why did Emperor Telemin step down? Why would he give up power? There was no reason for it. He was the proper heir, and raised, from birth, to be king. One day he just decided to give it all up; why? I know the legend says that he loved the people so much that he turned the empire over to them. I'm sorry, but it doesn't take a scholar to see the lie in that, especially because he died so soon after breaking the power."

Sir Loorie shrugged, "I wish I had an answer for you, but you are asking a question that has been struggled with since he stepped down. He left nothing behind that gives those answers, so all we have is theories and supposition. I can give you my thoughts, but they are just that, my thoughts."

"I would love to hear them."

"Well, I have always thought that the church was angry over the Proclamation of Man. At the time there were two competing powers in the empire, the monarchy and the ecclesiastical. There had been a struggle between the two for centuries.

Throughout the centuries, the church's power waxed and waned depending on the circumstances at the time. At the time Telemin issued the proclamation, the church's power was on the rise again. He cut that off rise off in one stroke of a quill. With the proclamation, he did what none of his predecessors could, strangle the church, and end the struggle for once and all. Shortly after, he abdicated and broke power. Now come my suppositions. I believe the church killed him, so he could not come back and re-claim the throne. It assumed that a council made up of ordinary citizens will be easily intimidated and controlled. They could be pushed into overturning the proclamation. If they wouldn't they could be eliminated and replaced with someone who would. Of course, they miscalculated. Once power is obtained, it is not easily given up, if at all."

"Ok, but it still doesn't explain why he broke power. There just seems no reason for it. If he is worried about the church, why weaken empirical power as well?"

Shrugging again, Sir Loorie responded, "Again, this is a question that Telemin left no answers for. There are three main theories, all centered on him being unmarried and childless.

The first was that he wanted to marry his most favored courtier, Lilly, and stepped down, breaking power to end the monarchy, negating their stations; because there was no more royalty, he was free to marry her. The second was that, because he had no heir, he was the focus of an assignation plot, and broke power as a defensive move. The last theory was that Lilly found out that he was homosexual and was threatening to expose him if he did not step away from away. There has been no evidence to put one over the others, so pick your favorite."

"Where did the Proclamation of the Man come from? Was it just to cripple the church?"

"Not quite. He wanted to cripple the church, true, but not because of the monarchy's battle with the church. No, he had come up with a theory that worshipping gods, the church's very existence, was holding mankind back. Scholars continue to research to this day.

Unfortunately, most of his writings were before the proclamation, and he left very little writing explaining what he was thinking. The little we do know is that he based the theory on a document called the Hawk Treatise, but we don't exactly know what it said, the text was lost with Telemin. There are scholars who have dedicated their lives to finding the document, but, to date, all that has come of it were a scant few references in other texts."

"With respect, none of this makes any sense. It seems that there should be more information about such a major event."

"Like? Don't stop your thoughts, son."

"I have never heard of this 'Hawk Treatise', what is it and why wasn't such an important document saved."

"Most of his predecessors were warriors, but as one of the few scholarly emperors, Telemin spent most of his time in the great library at Laine. The story goes; he came across the tome while searching the old, lower, archives. He consumed it, becoming obsessed, reading it over and over, so often that after a month he no longer needed the book. It was written by a philosopher named Hawk, who we know nothing about, other than he wrote this one book. All we know about that book is that he used mathematics to prove the gods did not exist, and postulates that belief in the gods held man back, and was in the way of progress. We don't know the math, the theory, anything about the author, where he came from, anything more. But, the reason you don't know about it was because the document has never been made public, only academics know about it."

"This makes no sense, modern government is based on this document, and we know nothing about it?"

"Yes, unfortunately. The theorem was ancient when Emperor Telemin dug it up, which was hundreds of years before today. Even in its day, it was largely discredited and ignored, so few copies were ever printed.

By the time of Telemin, there was only one copy of the book remaining, and that disappeared after the emperor's death. We only know about it because of the notes that he left when he wrote the Proclamation of the Man. There have never been any other copies discovered, despite thousands of scholars looking.

For me, it makes a stronger case that the church threatened and killed Emperor Telemin, then destroyed the book. They were too late to stop the proclamation, but they could destroy the source material."

Sir Loorie saw the frustrated look on the boy's face and leaned forward, "Sorry for dumping all that information on, my boy, but, you did not ask simple questions."

Teridon laughed, "There is no apology needed. I know the questions I was asking were not easy, and remain, unfortunately. Thank you, sir, for answering straight and not talking down to me, but I will have to keep reading, I want to know more."

"Good! That's the spirit never take anyone else's opinion as a fact, no matter who they are. The questions you ask are the ones that people have struggled with since Telemin's death. Historians have struggled, and failed, to explain his abdication, the breaking of Power, and his death. As you have discovered, his actions don't make any logical sense. You will learn, son, that people, nobility or not, rarely make logical sense."

"I know. This has been fascinating, but we are very late, and need to get to the hall."

Sir Loorie's head dropped. Some days he practically had to drag the man to his post.

"I thought you would forget."

***

The warm sun on their face punctuated the unseasonably warm fall, it felt more like late summer, and it felt wonderful. Teridon had spent most of his life in the harsh north, and he would take a long summer over a long winter every time. He lifted his head as they casually strolled across the courtyard, enjoying a brief moment of peace and the warmth of the sun. No one that saw them would guess they were late.

***

"Teridon, grab the Jacket while I pull these damn pants on." There was no time to wait for an attendant. He slipped the jacket on as Teridon pulled the trousers tight and tied the leather cord. The boy squatting in front of him would not be the most comfortable position to be in if someone came into the room.

Once to cord was tight, he pushed past Teridon, leaving him on his backside, as he hurried into the audience chamber.

He walked into the hall casually, pretending that he was not hurrying, but he was still fastening the jacket's toggles, showing the truth of his tardiness.

He was about to walk onto the dais when he realized that, in his rush, he had forgotten several things, including his sword. It was part of the uniform and he was expected to wear it.

He waved Teridon over, "I forgot the sword. Can you go retrieve it from my bedroom?"

He nodded, and ran out of the hall.

Sir Loorie took a breath, letting Nidan Loorie go and embracing the King. After taking his moment, he took his seat on the dais, next to the advocate. He turned to them, "accept my apologies, gentleman, I was held up."

The other two were already seated, and were rolling their eyes in annoyance.

The advocate waved Rosi from the back of the dais, "let's begin," barely covering the agitation in his voice.

"Who is first up?" Sir Loorie asked, trying to engage, unusual for him.

The day's first petitioner walked to the lectern, and stated his petition. He was asking for an increase in military presence to help the local constable police the area around his home. He lived in a border community that was having problems with thieves crossing the border, and fleeing back across. They were unable to give chase because of empirical law. All operations on foreign soil must be carried out by the military. He was petitioning for a garrison to be stationed in the area until the problem is brought under control. Sir Loorie listened half-heartedly. The conversation with Teridon weighed heavily on his mind. His gut was telling him that the boy was on to something, but what?

He realized that he was not listening when the man stopped talking, and he did not know the petitioner's name or town, but he had heard that bandits were crossing a border, so soldiers seemed reasonable. He moved that the petition be approved and the pauper concurred.

Rosi's quill waved back and forth as he scratched the decision in the day's ledger. The Advocate gave the decision to the hall, "Dispatch one garrison to help the constable, any crossing of the border must be reported to the local governor."

The treaties with their neighboring countries allowed for sporadic border crossings for purposes of policing, but one man's police action is another's act of war.

The man thanked them profusely as he stepped back and walked back to his seat.

Rosi finished writing and then called the next petitioner's. He did a great job keeping things moving, not that it was a surprise; he was as good at these types of things as Teridon was at fighting. He was smart and organized; he kept things moving along and in order. A couple moved up to from the long benches and started to walk up to the dais, they were younger, a man and woman, he estimated them to be in their late twenties. Their daughter had been kidnapped and they were asking for a tracker to help them find her. This request was approved; they would dispatch a ranger to help the couple.

He sat back and shook his head, his heart went out to the couple, losing a child was beyond terrible, but this was not a matter the military, especially the rangers, should be handling. The military should be training for war, not rescuing random people. He hid his reservations, however, and approved the request.

The rest of the day had plodded on, just like this, one person after another making their petitions, and him half listening. Teridon had brought the sword later that morning, and, as was the usual routine, he released him to train. There was no reason to subject him to this tedium.

The room had started to darken, as the sunlight was no longer streaming in through the colored windows. It was getting late in the day, the session would be ending soon. He looked off to his side, surprised Teridon had not returned yet. He always returned shortly before the session ended.

Rosi stepped forward and called the last petitioner. A frail old man stood up and slowly shuffled towards the four men. The man was hunched over, walked with a cane, and shook of palsy. The scrape of the man's shuffle echoing through the empty hall. This was the last petitioner? He almost asked Mr. Starling if this was a joke, but held his tongue. The man seemed like he slowed with each labored step. His arm was quaking even more as he reached the front of the aisle. While the man labored up the aisle, he took the opportunity to look around, again. Where was Teridon? He was never late.

The old man finally reached the dais. He moved very deliberately, leaning his cane against the lectern, then grasped it tightly, stabilizing himself, wheezing from the effort of walking up the aisle.

After waiting for the man to catch his breath, the advocate leaned forward, "How can we help you petitioner?"

Nidan appreciated the Advocate's effort to move things along. He was tired and hungry, and he was getting more and more curious about the whereabouts of the head of his security.

The old man paused, hands no longer shanking. After finally gathering himself, he looked up; Sir Loorie was taken aback, the frail old man's eyes were not white or dull, they had the bright shine of youth. Where was Teridon?

***

Teridon pulled on the small door at the back of the Kethi-Draal, it was locked tight, just like all the other doors, even the giant front ones. He ran around the outside of the Kethi-Draal, desperate to find another way in. Most of the windows did not open, but there has to be some other way to get in. The council was still in session, the building should not be locked.

Something was going on; he had to get into the hall. As he ran back to the front, it suddenly struck him how empty the square was. Other than a few guardsmen, the square was empty; it was usually flush with people at this time of day. He checked his sword and dagger, which had become a habit when he was nervous, the cold power of the steel reassured, and settled, him.

The ill winds, a strong breeze since the swearing ceremony, were starting to coalesce into a tornado, and he knew what those winds preceded; the vortex would tighten until the pressure crushed him.

***

The Pauper, King, and Advocate sat on the dais, looking down at the old man. The man, who had just struggled to shuffle down the aisle, now stood straight, his eyes clear and focused, the frailness gone, even the quaking in his hands had stopped, thought he did grip the lectern with both hands.

The man's hair was bright white; he had a short beard, also white, and wore a simple brown robe. He did not speak, just stood at the lectern, staring at each of them, in turn. The three men looked at each other, unsure what was going on. Under the table, Sir Loorie unclipped the stay on his sword, just in case. For several minutes the man's eyes moved between the three of them, never singling one out, but looking through all. Finally, after staring at them, he finally spoke, his voice scratchy from age, but still strong.

"Thank you, good sirs, for taking the time out of your busy days to see a humble man such as myself"

The pauper leaned forward, "We are here to listen to the concerns of all the empire's subjects, so please, speak your piece, sir, do not be nervous."

"Thank you for your kind words, Damon Maxk; they lift the spirit of a poor, old, man."

The three looked at each other again, shocked, referring to them by their given names was a massive breach of protocol. While the hall was in session, they were only addressed by their titles. They were trying to get a handle on the situation when several booms reverberated through the hall. They jerked around, and saw back doors of the hall were open.

The boom of the doors opening seemed to hang, then fade, replaced by the sound of boots clicking on up the stairs that were behind the doors. About 20 city guardsman, fully armed and armored, marched through the doors, into the hall. Sir Loorie glanced at Rosi, who was white with terror, his head swinging left to right, eyes wide. Well, at least it doesn't look like any of the other three men were involved in this.

'Where is Teridon? Where is that boy?'

Those thoughts fled quickly, Teridon was perfectly capable of taking care of himself. He had to focus on his current, and much more pressing, situation.

The soldiers fanned out, ringing the dais, there was nowhere for them to go, they were trapped. There was also no more doubt that the city guard could not be trusted. He let his hand fall from the hilt of his sword. He was not going to be able to fight his way out. He was the only one with military experience; he needed to be the rock that the other three men anchored themselves to. He spread his hands below the table, signaling the others to stay calm. Once satisfied that they were not going to lose their heads and do something stupid, he turned back to the old man, taking the lead.

"Well, sir, you certainly have our attention. If you were worried about us listening to you, you needn't have gone through all this trouble, we listen to all. Why don't you tell the guardsmen to go back to their posts? The city needs them; we can discuss your concerns without endangering the rest of the city."

He was trying his best to keep things light, the last thing he needed was to push the man to anger. If the guardsmen were ordered to kill any one of them, they would be able to do so without much effort.

The old man smiled back at him, the smile that did nothing to put the knight at ease, it was too wide, had too many teeth, and did not touch his eyes. Long ago, he had learned a smile that does not touch a man's eyes is not real. More importantly, he had learned never trust the words when the body language did not match those words. Just because the man holding a club over your head was smiling does not mean that he does not want to cave your skull in. These lessons applied here, this man was trying to portray a kindly old man, but his hard eyes showed that evil lurked behind the thin facade. They were cold, so very cold, there was no spark of life in them; yet they shone like they were polished glass.

Still smiling, the man still spoke casually, like this was a daily occurrence, "Well, thank you for your kind words as well, Nidan Loorie; that is pleasing, coming from such a decorated officer. If you please sir, I prefer to have my soldiers stay with us, I do hope you understand."

"Of course, if you like... I do not believe we have your name."

"No, sir, you do not, and thank you for your kindness allowing my soldiers to stay."

Sir Loorie looked around, these were city guardsmen, but the old man referred to them as 'his' soldiers. Were they real guardsman, and traitors, or were they impostors with stolen uniforms? The old man was being so bold, if they were real guardsman, it had been infiltrated to a frightening extent.

He was desperately trying to figure a way to get out of this. Unfortunately, those thoughts kept running into a wall of armed men.

"Sirs, I suspect that you are wondering why we are here, why I have kept you past the end of the session. Well, first let me apologize for the inconvenience."

The old man continued, his voice deadpan and devoid of any emotion, he was trying, and failing, to keep them at ease by keeping his speech light.

"I fear my reasons for being here are, well, unusual, but I am here to help you. I am here to relive you of the burdens of power. It places so much pressure on you three poor men. Please, sirs, allow me to relive that pressure, you fine men will be finally able to breath."

He had to fight the urge to jump back in shock; the man was talking about a coup, though he sounded like he was speaking of lunch. Sir Loorie glanced at the other three men; their heads frantically looked between the old man, the soldiers, and him.

After giving a breath for the demand to settle, the old man continued, "Please, allow me to explain. I stand before you representing the oppressed people of the Aragon Empire. You three have been sitting up here, on your secure hill, for too long, you are woefully out of touch with the people you allegedly serve. Do not despair. It is not your fault. No, fault lies with the system that you rule, and serve, as we all are forced to do, even powerful men, such as yourselves. It is a system that steals the fruit of the people's labor, and uses them to support your lavish lives. The people you have stolen from are left with nothing. I don't blame you, though. You do not know any other way; you probably don't even think of it as oppression."

"Well, allow me to show you that there is another way. I implore you on, behalf of the people you crush, to take the opportunity I present. Take the opportunity to become one of the people again. Take the opportunity to live outside of the padded life you currently live; the opportunity to feel again.

The opportunity to suffer again. The people you rule feel, they suffer. Why should you be different? Seize this opportunity to be like the subjects you claim to empathize with. Please, do the right thing. Abdicate your positions, step down, become part of this glorious revolution."

The old man paused for a moment, He groned, as if the effort of speaking was draining him.

"Or, do not and die. I don't care which you choose, but you must choose. You may take a moment to consider, but please, do not take too long, my master awaits your responses."

The old man dropped onto the front bench, slumping his elbows to his knees, his weakness did not appear a ruse, just the effort of standing, to deliver his speech, exhausted him. Nidan almost laughed at the foolishness of considering someone backed by 20 soldiers weak. It did not matter if the man could walk or not, a simple command would be all it took to end their lives.

The four men huddled, the three looking at him with wide, expectant, eyes. He was the only one with any tactical experience, so they must expected that he would come up with some grand plan to get them out of this.

He shook his head sadly, that was not going to be possible. There are times to fight, times to retreat, and then, there are times when surrender was the only viable option. This was one of the last; they would be slaughtered if they tried to fight. Officers must accept that surrender is a viable option. Sir Loorie motioned them to tighten the circle.

"Gentlemen, I know you want a plan, but there isn't one. We have choice, we have to surrender. There is no other option."

They other three hung their heads in unison, the reality of the situation becoming clear for the first time.

"We are surrounded by armed guardsmen, while we counter with one armed, and old, man. Even if these men are completely incompetent, one man against twenty is not a winnable contest. We need to accept the terms, get out of here, then regroup. We can stage a counter assault if we can find some loyal guardsmen, but first we must to get out of this hall."

The three men could not argue with the knight's logic or judgment, the situation was untenable. Fighting meant dying, and dying meant that the city, and probably the empire, was lost. The pauper summed up the feelings of the other three, "I understand, and agree, surrender is our only viable option."

Sir Loorie nodded, relived that the three saw things his way, "Do not trust these people, make no mistake, this civility is false. They want us dead; don't let your guard down, but don't give them a reason to harm you either."

None of the men were soldiers, but both the pauper and advocate grew up on the streets of Capuamundi, their intuition had been honed to a fine point.

They knew when things were right and things were wrong; Sir Loorie was hoping that intuition would keep them breathing.

"We are in agreement? If you have any reservations, speak now." He looked at the three men in turn, each nodding yes in response. He stood; the soldiers moved a step closer. He raised his chin, and stared directly at the old man, like he was announcing his retreat to an enemy commander. This was a strategic maneuver, not a defeat.

He unbuckled his sword, wrapped the belt around it, swallowed hard, and then laid the sword at his feet, "we surrender." The words felt like acid coming out of his mouth.

The old man started, he had been silently staring forward this whole time, Nidan assumed him listening, but he seemed to be genuinely startled by his voice.

"Excellent, please step down from the dais and leave your trinkets of office on the table. Then, please lay down on your stomachs so my men can search you for any hidden weapons."

The three men each put their portion of Telemin's staff onto the table, then stepped down and lay on the ground, arms and legs spread wide. After a rough pat down, the old man came near, satisfied that they were unarmed.

"You will be escorted back to your towers. You will stay there until we are ready for you. There will be guards, so don't do anything stupid."

Sir Loorie managed to get his head turned a bit, "Who is we?"

The old man ignored the query, "get them on their feet, we need to move"

The four men were pulled to their feet, and were escorted out, three guards per man.

Sir Loorie looked around as they left the building, seeing Teridon peaking around the corner, off to his right. He allowed himself a slight sigh of relief; the boy was OK. Teridon's muscles were tense, he was going to attack. This was not the time; even someone with the boy's prowess would be slaughtered.

Subtly as he could, he waved over his shoulder; relived when the boy took the sign, stood down, disappearing around the corner.

***

The old man leaned heavily on his cane as he left the hall, struggling to navigate the short stair in front of the Kethi-Draal, he almost collapsed, but managed to right himself. He was exhausted; all of the day's walking had drained him. It was easy for anyone to see that he was an old man, but only Preacher knew how old.

There was a small wagon outside the hall, hitched to a single mule. He could not walk up and down this blasted hill any longer. So the carriage and mule were his transportation. He climbed into the driver's seat, clicked his tongue, and the mule started away. His swollen joints radiated pain.

He used to be a vibrant man, full of piss and vigor, but those days were long gone, and age takes everything. These days he fought just to hold his piss. The mule walked down through the east gate.

He navigated the carriage to the small area behind his house, and tied the mule off. Once done, he hobbled into the small home, needing to lie down. His palsy worsened as his energy waned, even holding something was not stopping his quaking limbs. He pushed the door shut and turned, seeing a solitary man sitting in the flickering light of a single candle, staring at the doorway. He did not jump; he had expected his master would want to know the details personally.

"Was your trip up the hill productive?"

He didn't answer, just threw a burlap bag onto his master's lap. The contents of the bag spoke for themselves, even in the dull candle light, the polished golden pieces of Telemin's staff gleamed,

"And? The three?"

"As you expected, they surrendered. The old knight is wiser than I gave him credit for. He knew that there was no fighting their way out. The other three took his lead. He is more practical than I would have thought."

"Well, most officers are learned men, a true leader does not send people . You have done very well sir, your talents were so badly needed. I could not trust the lowborn scum to carry out such a delicate mission, the last thing I needed was a bloodbath in the seat of government."

"The people cannot see this as a coup, that is key to the rest of my plans. We need to be seen as intervening on their behalf, as protectors, liberators even."

"Thank you my lord, what are we going to do with the three now, you aren't intending to actually let them free are you?"

Preacher just smirked as he left.

Chapter 56

Teridon had waited all afternoon in a small nook between some hedges and the wall, listening to the sounds of construction coming from the Crier's Square. Now, with darkness cloaking his movements, he could finally see what was going on, and was thankful that whoever was behind the insurrection did not post any patrols. He crept in the Kethi-Draal's shadow, using the great building to further hide his movements.

The courtyard was abuzz with activity. People were worked all over the square. But, the bulk of the activity was in the courtyard in front of the three towers. A long, thick, timber connected the top of the king's tower to the top of the Pauper's tower. Two thick ropes were tied to in the middle of the timber, and lazily hung slack as they disappeared into the top window of the Advocate's tower. Below the timber, Men erected a stage. It looked like they were getting ready for a concert, though, as far as he knew, events like that did not take place in the upper city. Whatever was going on, it was well planned; the stage wasn't being built, just assembled. He was stuck in the same situation as before, in desperate need of information.

Trying to stay in the shadows as much as possible, he started towards the King's tower, using the wall to break his silhouette, making him impossible to see from a distance.

The front door was guarded by a couple of city guardsmen; lamps on either side of the door lit the area. There was no going in through the front. He needed to go in through the servant's entrance. Stepping lightly, he continued along the wall, he was able to pass the guards, unnoticed. Once clear, he allowed himself a breath before peaking around the corner of the tower's base. He thanked his luck for his enemy's incompetence; the servant's entrance was unguarded. Finally, something went his way. Kneeling, he swung his feet over the wall, and dropped a few feet to the ramp below. Pulling on the elaborate lock, it did not budge. No matter, he had designed this entrance, lock and all. He inserted his key into the lock, he turning it slowly, not wanting to make any loud noises. This was too easy, this entrance was meant to be a trap, and he could be walking right into it. But, there was no other way, he drew his sword and kicked the door open, driving into a pitch-dark room. He slid along the wall and lit the oil in the sconce.

Light filled the room, he gripped the sword and swung around to find, nothing. The room was empty. There was no trap.

Leaning into the stairwell, light shone onto the landing at the top of the stairs. He padded up, and looked into a mirror on the far wall, seeing that, like the basement, it was empty and unguarded. He quickly crossed the landing and continued up the stairs.

He reached the second floor and, again, found the landing empty. He continued on to the library. Slowly cracking the door, he saw Sir Loorie lounging on a chaise, his face lit by the dim flame of the great fireplace. He looked up, smiled, and motioned Teridon over.

"Relax, my boy, there is no one in the tower, the entrance is guarded, but they are woefully inept at keeping a prisoner."

Teridon sheathed his sword, but did not relax.

"What happened, sir? I tried to get into the hall, but the building was locked tight. Then, you were being led out in shackles. What is going on?"

Sir Loorie sighed, then recounted the tale, in as much detail as he could. As Teridon listened, he seethed, but unchecked anger was counterproductive. Closing his eyes, he briefly meditated with deep, slow, breaths. Cool air filled his chest with each long breath in, the anger leaving with ever long exhaled breath. When he opened his eyes, he was ice; cold, sharp, and focused on the task at hand.

"Sir, we need to get you out of here."

The knight shook his head, "Not yet, we can't leave until the master of this rabble makes himself known. We don't know what their intentions are, and if this is a larger coup, we need to know who is behind it. Besides, the other two have been taken as well; twe need to free them before we can flee. The government needs to be complete, and running again, as soon as possible. There is an emergency hall in Grenbryr, a small town on the other side of the lake. It was built there so it could be quickly accessed and the government can continue to function if the capital fell. Order needs to be maintained, and we need to make sure our control of the military remains. This coup has compromised the city guard, but if the military remains loyal, we can put these people in their place, prison or grave. But, if the military is compromised..."

"Sir, with respect, staying here is suicide, they could come for you at any moment!"

He respected that Sir Loorie was dedicated to his oaths, but he was focused on saving the man's life. Still, the man was in charge.

Anxiety tightened around the knight's gut, the boy was right, of course, but he did not have a choice, he had bigger worries than himself.

"Teridon, I can't just flee. I took an oath. I have a responsibility to the people of the empire, of this city. If I were to leave now, this insurrection will fester and spread. If they can take the capitol, they will have what they need to take over the military, and I can't let that happen. I need to sit tight until the leader makes himself known. It does no good to flee and allow the man to have the security of anonymity. Once he is revealed, we will gather the other two and make for the harbor. There, we can secure a ship and get across the lake."

"Yes sir."

Teridon did not like sitting still, his leg shook, he squeezed the hilt of his sword, fire ran through his arms, and he fidgeted in his seat. Sitting in the stuffy library was the last thing he wanted to do, the dust and mold from the papers bothered his senses, which were heightened by the excitement of the moment. He wanted to take the fight back to these cowards. Men fought one on one, in the field of battle. Cowards hid inside groups. Being an anonymous part of a crowd did more to embolden cowards than even the strongest drink.

"Sir, can we at least move to the higher rooms so we can monitor the situation outside?"

***

Teridon paced back and forth in front of the master bedroom's window. He was a cat stuck in a cage, wanting a fight, but with no fight to be had. Sir Loorie was in charge, so he had to follow the man's orders, but that did not mean that he had to like them. For the next hour nothing changed, he paced, Sir Loorie read, and the work continued outside.

After a time, Sir Loorie started to get antsy as well. He wandered over to the window. There were fires burning below, lighting the stage, and people streamed into the courtyard.

Word had spread, people were coming up the hill, some to participate, some were curious, and still others were scare. There was a nervous energy in the gathering crowd; it was palpable even five floors up.

Sir Loorie opened the window, the thick glass was muffling the sounds from the square, and he wanted to hear what was being said. As soon as the windowpanes cracked open thick, acrid, smoke wafted into the room. The two men looked over the city, a glow rose from the new city. Sir Loorie's knees went weak, he had to grab the sill for support, the city was burning. Until now, he refused to believe this was really an organized coup, but there was no more denying it.

With the window no longer muffling the sounds from below, they heard the screams of terror were coming from the houses around the square. Flames were starting to poke out from the upper floors of some noble houses. They could only assume that the mob had gotten out of control.

Teridon felt utterly helpless, and hated it. He was angry at the scum in the street, blaming their lot on others, and helpless because they were trapped in this tower. He stared out the window, at the spectacle. The smoke was growing thicker, the glow was getting brighter, and he feared that the city was moving beyond the point where it could be saved.

"Sir, please, reconsider, let's go, now, before this gets any worse."

"Son, you know I can't leave. We will stay until the person, or people, behind this are revealed."

Then, almost as if on cue, a robed man appeared on the stage. He was hooded, but even in the hood, you could see his head was high. He walked with authority, with steps that were heavy and confident, this man was no follower. No, the leader had just been revealed. The robed man stopped at center stage, looking over the quickly building crowd. His face remained sunken inside the hood, and he just stood in the center of the stage, hands folded surveying the crowd.

Chapter 57

Bisicara was done for the day, but she had to wait for the deliveryman to return with wagon before she could actually go relax. She had to ensure everything had been delivered and accepted by the customer. If you sell a better product with better service, you can charge more. Her father had pounded that lesson into her. He prided himself on selling the highest quality materials, and if the buyer felt that the order did not meet those standards, he would take it back, no questions. It was one of the reasons the store had done so well.

She sat on a stack of furs in the storeroom, reading a book. It was tripe, a romance novel, light reading, but she was not looking to educate herself, just pass the time. Where was he? These men were so unreliable, and they were pigs to boot. Young and pretty, she understood that there would be quick glances, but the way these men leered. She lost herself in the book and was not paying attention when the delivery driver walked in. She started and threw the book to the floor.

"Where were you? I have been waiting."

"Sorry, I was held up outside, streets are crowded. There is trouble brewing."

"Whatever, did everything get accepted, do you have the manifests?"

Her father never accepted excuses, why should she?

"Yes ma'am, right here."

He handed several papers to her. She thumbed through the pages, checking the bottom of each page. They had all been signed. Satisfied, she dismissed the man with a wave. She hated treating anyone this way, but these men would eat her alive if she appeared weak. The man did not take the hint, he was still standing there.
She looked at the man over the stack of papers, "Can I help you with something else, sir?"

The man paused for a second.

"Ma'am, there is trouble in the streets; you would do well to leave."

She let out a small sigh of relief, having thought he would ask her to go for a drink, or something even worse.

"Thank you for your concern, but I will be fine."

The man shrugged and left. When the door opened, faint yelling and screaming wafted in, and now that she was paying attention, there was also a faint smell of smoke. Taking the delivery man's warning more seriously, she ran into the street, and looked down the hill, towards the Harbor.

There was yelling, but she could not make out any individual words, it was too far away and blended into one unintelligible mass of sound. Smoke rose from the harbor and she could see the glow of the fires below.

The sound grew as the crowd neared, and the mass of sound separated into individual voices. A man on horseback led the crowd up the street, using a cone to amplify his voice, he rode back and forth, whipping the crowd into a frenzy, "Take it, take what is yours! Take this city back from the tyrants, strike at the heart of their tyranny. Show them the power of democracy."

He stopped and allowed the crowd to wash around him, continuing his yelling as the people flowed by him. She was shocked, these men were telling the crowd to destroy the city, destroy property, destroy legitimate businesses, and these people were doing it! She did not know what to do. The crowd was close enough that she could see the faces of the front line in their torchlight. Her heart raced, she needed to save the store. Her family had built this business, and this mob was going to destroy it. She ran into the safety of the store, slamming the door behind her.

Chapter 58

Preacher stood, still as a stone, at center stage, dwarfed by the towers, framing the stage. People were still filtering into the upper city, but the Crier's Square had been filled and the roads leading up to the square will be filled in moments. Word was spread faster than the fires, and people were coming to see. They did not know it yet, but all of these people were part of his glorious revolution, whether they wanted to be or not. He allowed himself a small smile of satisfaction, though it was hidden inside his deep hood. Things were going better than he could have ever imagined. It may have started slowly, but momentum was building, and building quickly.

He turned to look at the towers looming behind him. The ropes still cut that low, lazy, arch from the timber to the center tower's highest window. A faint glow emanated from the window, but there did not look to be any activity inside. He knew better. He turned back to the crowd. The glow from filtering over the top of the wall grew brighter. His minions had done well. He wanted to bring this city to its knees, make the population beg for deliverance, beg for his strong, stable, hand. From the looks of things, they had succeeded.

Preacher turned slightly to look at the window again, a shadow was waving in the window, all was ready. This will be recorded as the true beginning of the revolution, everything else that had happened until this moment was all part of the foundation. He pointed at the Criers Rise, the long, low, tone rang out from the great gong. The crowd quieted down some, but there was still a steady hum of voices. Preacher stood stone still as the men on the sides of the stage stoked the fires, lighting the stage completely, and throwing the crowd, mostly, into darkness. The crowd quieted further, but still not enough. Using a bit of theatricality, the men stoking the fires threw small bags into the fire. The sulfur flared bright white. The blinding light silenced the crowd. He lowered his hood and stepped to the front of the stage. "Welcome." The crowd was silent, but the acoustics of the area amplified his voice so the whole square heard him.

"I am sure you have heard rumors about what is occurring throughout the city tonight. You may have heard that the city is being taken down, the empire is under attack. I am here to tell you, those rumors are all true."

A rumble from the crowd built like a wave. He held his hand up, as if quieting a child, and stopping the wave.

"Do not fear, it is not an end. NO! It is a new beginning. Like a forest renewed by the cleansing heat of a fire, this city, and this empire, will be renewed through the cleansing fire of revolution. For too long, we have been wedded to old, broken, ways. Each of you need to ask yourselves, have the old ways worked? Have they? How hard do you have to work for scraps you are allowed to keep."

He turned and swept his hand from left to right.

"They sit here, living in these giant houses, but they don't work for these fancy houses, YOU DO! It is the fruits of YOUR labor that finances their lives. Is that fair? Is that equitable? You work yourselves to the bone, while your rulers to sit on their asses and order you about. I ask again, is that fair? Is that Equitable? NO! Of course it's not fair; of course it is not equitable. These three call you free, claim that you have choice, but we know that is not true. No, friends, I am here to tell you what you are, you are SLAVES. You are slaves to those three pigs. They feed from the trough that your labor fills and expect YOU to thank them for stealing from you. I am here to propose a new way, a way where everyone gets a say in the government, a way where the majority is no longer subservient to a small minority. I am offering you the end of hunger, the end of homelessness, the end of want, and the end of need. You will be part of a new grand, egalitarian, society. We can come together and set ourselves free from the tyranny of the individual."

The crowd pushed forward, trying to hear Preacher's words. His well practiced speaking techniques enthralled the crowd, his volume rose and fell, and his had a timbre and cadence that just drew people in. He walked left and right across the front stage, surveying the crowd for a moment before he returned to the center. Silence was another trick he used, the crowd kept focused, wanting to hear what was coming next. He was sure to wait a moment before giving it to them.

"I can see the questions written on your faces, Why? What caused this revelation? What can I do?"

He stopped talking, and he took a step back. He acted like he was gathering his thoughts. The man understood that politics, and public speaking, were mostly theater, how things were said being far more important that what was being said.

People needed to feel what you were saying, in their loins. It was how to spur people into real action. If people truly felt what you were saying, the words were irrelevant, they would follow.

Thoughts gathered, Preacher stepped back to center stage, he began again, voice shaky and quiet, and he was looking down at his feet.

"My next words will be hard to get through. Hard, because I thought him to be an honorable man, as did all of you, when he was elected. It brings me no joy to reveal the man's true nature, but I feel it my duty. Whether he had planned this from the outset, or if he became drunk with power, we may never know. Either way, the King, Sir Nidan Loorie, is under arrest by, and in the custody of, the free people of Capuamundi. That was man was elected as an honorable knight, but in truth is an oath breaker. In front of all of you, he stood on that stage and swore an oath that he had set aside his military ties and serve the people of the empire."

Preacher continued the theatrics, holding his hands in front of his mouth, shaking his head in disbelief. The crowd was eating up his show.

It had pushed forward until the front row was touching the stage. Once satisfied the crowd had taken the bait, Preacher screamed, stomping his feet.

"Today, his betrayal was completed. He had soldiers place the Advocate and Pauper under arrest!"

The crowd gasped and an angry rumble started to move through it.

"You heard correctly, HE ARRESTED YOUR REPRESENTATIVES! He was going to kill them if they did not name him emperor and rejoin Telemin's staff. He intends to undo hundreds of years of progress, throw us back to the days of the emperors, and stomp out the small bit of freedom that you have. He had a small army at his back, and, brave as they are, the other two had only two choices, submit or die. It was after hearing witness accounts that I decided this could not stand, and I could no longer sit idle. I would not watch this liar take power for a corrupt military."

"I needed to do something. I love this city, and my country, far too much to watch that happen. So, I gathered a small group of men, and we chased the coward into his rathole in YOUR tower."

Preacher paused, gathering his thoughts again. His voice began to quiver again.

"Unfortunately, we failed to free the prisoners. The military remains' loyal to that snake, and we were no match for trained soldiers. Now, with the support of you, the people, we now have the strength to take them back! The soldiers may be a match against a few of us, but they cannot stand against the might of the people! Come! Help me free the Pauper and help him put things right."

He lowered his head and placed his hand on his chin, as if trying to hold back tears.

***

That was the signal! Patrick turned away from the window, looking at the two men lying bound on the floor. Just a few hours ago these were two of the three most powerful men in the world, and, now, they were at the mercy of a nobody.

"Get them on their feet."

Soldiers moved in and pulled the men roughly to their feet. Their hands and feet were bound with cord. Thick ropes came in through the window, ran along the floor, ending at nooses hanging loosely around the men's necks.

They held their chin high, trying to portray strength, but their eyes betrayed their terror. Patrick nodded and the solders pushed the men towards the window.

They tried to push back, but their feet found no purchase on the dusty wooden floor. The window loomed large as they were pushed towards it.

"The crowd needs to see you, make sure the crowd sees you!"

The soldiers held the Pauper and Advocate in the window, their polished armor gleamed, even with the dim light from the square below. There would be no mistaking who they were, even from a distance. After a moment's pause, giving the crowd an opportunity to see them, Patrick gave the signal.

The pauper saw the motion and tried to defend himself, but his efforts were cut short by a boot to the center of his back. His head snapped backwards as the soldier kicked him out the window; the other soldier did the same to the advocate.

The two men dropped until the ropes snapped taught, violently jerking before beginning to swing out over the stage. They were dead by the time they swung over Preacher's head, heads lolling sickly on broken necks; bodies limply swaying as the morbid pendulums hit their apex and began to swing back.

***

Nidan Loorie watched in horror as the two men died.

"We need to go, right down, I will meet you on the first floor in five minutes." He took one last look at his colleagues swinging slowly above the stage before he went to his wardrobe to grab his go bag.

Teridon had been ready to go since he arrived. He did not need the order, he was already moving.

***

Preacher held a hand to his heart and dropped to his knees as the two bodies swung over his head. The crowd gasped, as one, when men were thrown from the tower, the hanging was so public, and so violent. They fell most of the height of the tower before the ropes tightened and snapped their necks.

The crowd did not see the small cords that ran from the large ropes to the men's waists. Without these, the force of the fall would have torn the bodies from the necks, and robbed Preacher of the macabre spectacle that framed his speech. Two soldiers, with their shining metal armor stood in the window, shaking hands and congratulating each other. The crowd pushed forward, against the stage, the impact causing the poorly built structure to quiver. The people packing the square cried out as one, thirsting out for revenge. These were no longer independent, thinking people. They were an emotional mass, caught up by the wave of hysteria. The stage swayed as the crowd started beating against it, chanting for blood.

Preacher was still on his knees, facing away from the crowd, looked up at the swinging bodies with feigned disbelief. They were longer limp. Their death throes had begun, causing the bodies to violently twitch and spasm, the ropes going slack then snapping taught, as their arms and legs shook and twitched, held in place by the cord.

The bodies started to swing in lazy circles. The boy had done his job spectacularly. The two men were dead, and the crowd believed Sir Looire had ordered their deaths.

The mob was behind him, the chanting's intensity was increasing and they were pushing harder against the stage, which was starting to shake and sway. He was beginning to fear that they would push it over in their zeal to be close to him, it would not take much.

They were primed, he had set the boulder in place, now was the time to kick it into motion, and there would be no stopping it. He slowly rose back to his feet, turning to the crowd with his arms wide open. He shook his head, then his eyes snapped up, voice strong and full of life.

"Look! We thought this man honorable, but look what he did to your representatives! Your men! These men came from the lower city. They came from the same wards and districts that you do. They rose themselves up. This could be any one of you hanging by your necks. He killed them because you dared to speak your mind. He held them responsible for your speech.

The military, through that want-to-be tyrant, wants to INTIMIDATE you into silence. Will we be intimidated? Will you be silenced?" Preacher asked, voice hitting a crescendo.

"NO!" The crowd answered in unison.

Preacher turned, his arm sweeping over the city, "Go then, this city is yours, TAKE IT! Take what is yours! This is the start of our new society. The start of a grand new state where no one is above anyone else. Everyone here is brothers and sisters now, and keeping things from you family is greed. Greed, in our new society, will be punished harshly."

He turned to the Kings tower, most the crowd dissipated, starting towards the new city, going to carry out his charge to riot and loot. But, some remained behind, more interested in revenge than looting, the chant of 'COWARD' building from the crowd.

Chapter 59

Teridon met Sir Loorie in the basement. The crowd was pounding on the front door, screaming for the knight's head, the pounding on the thick would door filling the tower with its angry vibrations. They needed to get out of this death trap, and the servant's entrance was the only way out that would not get them killed. Ready to leave, Teridon pulled hard, and his heart caught in his throat, the door was locked. That was impossible, he had left the door unlocked, and it could not be locked from the outside without a key. His arms bulged, veins popping, as he pulled at the handle, but the heavy door did not budge. He took a breath, and calmed himself, the door was locked, but he had a key. He slid the key into the lock, but it stopped half way in. He pushing harder, bending the flat iron key. The lock had been jammed and now there was no getting out. If the key would not work, the door was too strong to be knocked down. The irony was not lost on him, all of his security measures were doing just as good a job at keeping them in as they did keeping people out.

He could not stop himself, he yanked at the door, and with every futile pull, despair came closer to overtaking him. His choices were going to get Sir Loorie killed. He was losing the battle with himself, his stomach knotted, and wetness welled in the corners of his eyes. *'Stop!'* He scolded himself, *'you can beat yourself up later. For now, you have to get Sir Loorie out of this forsaken city.'* He allowed himself a moment of self-pity before he pushed the thoughts away and began thinking clearly. He swung a torch to the knight, "We need to get to the upper floors and climb down."

In the torchlight, for the first time, Sir Loorie looked like an old man, he was hunched and his face was slack in defeat. He grabbed the man's arm, and started up the stairs, the knight gave resistance, and allowed Teridon to lead.

***

Teridon pulled the knight across the first floor landing, and started up the stair to the second floor when the tower shook. Their heads jerked in unison, and Teridon jumped back down the stairs, clearing the three steps he had climbed. He landed in the archway to see the front door bow in, splintering along the center a little.

They had a ram! BOOM! It bent again, more splinters falling off the door.

The mob had hit a fevered pitch and the riot was in full swing. After the two more booms, a crack appeared across the center, and the door's cross bracing started to crack, and a high pitch screech pierced the air as the iron nails gave way. They had to move, the tower would be breached any minute, if they were here, they were dead. He pushed Sir Loorie towards the stair, but the old man shrugged his hands away, avoiding the push.

"They don't know you're in here, they only want me. Go, get out of here."

"What are you talking about? We can still get out sir, please, come with me."

He was begging more than asking, tears were starting to well up in the corners of his eyes. The knight gave him a rueful smile as he shook his head slowly.

"No, we can't, but you can. I'm old; I can't climb down that rope. If the mob has their ounce of flesh, it may be placated, and lives can be saved. Consider it my last act as king. Tell anyone who will listen that I died trying to save what is left of the city."

This was insanity, Teridon had to get the knight out of this tower, the stress was turning him daft.

"You know this won't work, they will kill you and roll over your body. They don't care about you; once you are dead they'll move on to the next person or burn the next building. They are a mob."

Tears ran down his cheeks, his stomach was knotted so tight he was surprised he could stand up straight. His head spun as he desperately tried to think of a way to change the knight's mind. He needed him; the man was the only father he had ever known. The knight grabbed him, a hand on either side of his neck, "That may be, son, but I have to try. I took an oath, and whether the rabble outside believes it or not, I take that oath seriously. I need to put the empire above myself.

If there is a chance I can save this city, I need to take it. Listen, Teridon, you have grown to be a good, strong, man. I thank whatever controls these things that I was able to find you. You have exceeded even my wildest expectations of what you could be. Your place is not here, sitting with an old man, waiting to die. You needed to spread the truth, and cut this cancer out before it spreads. It won't be easy, but we are the only ones that know the truth of what happened.

One of us must survive to get that truth out. Don't die with me, live and spread the truth. You must be the counter to that man's lies. People won't want to hear it, and they will reject it at first, but tell them anyway, then tell them again, and again, until they listen."

Teridon dropped his head and looked at the man, he reached out, and hugged Sir Loorie tight, crying softly. The man had made up his mind, there was no changing it. As hard as it was to let the man go, Teridon ran up the stairs towards safety. The last thing he heard was the crowd noise exploding as Sir Loorie opened the door. He could not bear to look outside. He could not bear to see that man die.

***

Teridon stood just inside his bedroom door, wiping tears. He needed to focus, or Sir Loorie's sacrifice would be for nothing. There would have time to grieve, but it was not now. He ran to the window and slid the emergency rope from under his bed. The weight of the thick rope cut into his palm, the course fibers stuck his skin like small pieces of metal.

He took a breath and threw it out the window, it dropped and snapped taught. He let a breath out, glad he had remembered to install these ropes, at least one of his decisions was worth a damn.

In all of the chaos, he had been focused on escaping. Now that he was about to climb down a wall, his focus wavered and his hatred of heights seeped back into his thoughts. He took moment to steady himself before gingerly climbing out onto the rope. The moon was but a sliver in the sky; he was lucky, any larger and the moon would have lit his escape for the mob. As it was, he was able to climb down the rope undetected.

His feet touched the knot at the bottom of the rope, and he dropped to the soft tar roof. He let a small breath go, but this was not done, the ground was still two stories below.

A rope had been installed for this as well; unfortunately, it was meant escape a fire, not flee a coup. It was on the front of the tower, and would drop him right into the heart of the mob. He swallowed hard, there was only one way down. Kneeling down, he slowly looked over the edge.

The soffit was about two yards wide, it would be impossible for him to climb down the wall. He made a quick, and if he had thought longer he would call it stupid, choice, dropping to his stomach, he pushed back, then over, the edge.

Catching himself, he hung for a moment, trying not to think about what he was doing. It was no use, so he stopped trying, and dropped.

He landed hard, tying to absorb the drop with bent legs, but it was too much force. His legs buckled and he fell hard to his back, knocking the wind out of him. He lay, gasping, trying to catch his breath, his vision fuzzy from hitting his head on the ground. I took a moment for his vision to clear, and see the face hanging over him.

"Get up, you lazy ass, " Jakes reached down and smacked him across the face. With Jakes' help, he stood on shaky legs, cobwebs robbing his equilibrium. Jakes wrapped an arm around his friend's shoulders, helping steady the big man.

"These things have stairs for a reason. What happened?"

Teridon groaned, trying to stand on his own, "Yeah, thanks, I'll remember that next time. What happened? That's quite a question."

Jakes stepped aside to reveal Rosi Starling, who had been standing behind him.

"He already filled me in on the beginning; right up until his boss fell out of a window."

Teridon was immediately suspicious; this man was one of the four men that left the hall this afternoon, three of which were now dead.

"How is he here? Why weren't you executed with your boss?" Forgetting about his fall, he stepped up, looming over the much smaller man, "how did you get away?"

Jakes pushed between the two, he shared some of his friend's suspicions, but Teridon was unable to keep his emotions out of this.

Rosi took a step back, trying to put space between him and the huge man. The look in Teridon's eyes chilled him to the core; it looked like he was going to be held personally responsible for the death of Sir Loorie. Terdion stepped with him, and it felt like he was looking straight up at a giant. He stammered and tried to explain, "I am a commoner; they assumed I would be with them. They took Mr. Maxk out, and let me go. I tried to follow them, but they went into the tower and threw me out. I saw Mr. Maxk get pushed from the window and was frozen with horror after that.

Once the riot actually started, I was just kind of pushed along. I was finally able to get out of the wave, and I ran back to the towers, where it was relatively calm. I hid against the tower until Jakes found me."

Teridon calmed himself, while his suspicions were not placated, they were no more than suspicions, and there were more important matters to focus on, besides, Sir Loorie trusted the man, "I am sorry about Damon"

"Thank You," Rosi sniffled and spoke while barely holding back tears.

Jakes, always the pragmatist, brought to two men's focus back to the matter at hand, "We need to get out of this city, right now."

Teridon could not agree more, "I know, the city is on fire, but things are just getting going, it is about to actually explode. But, Jakes, what about your family?"

"I got them out of the city." Jakes replied, the relief written clearly on his face and in his confident tone. Teridon looked to Rosi, "Do you know how to use a sword?" The man hung his head in response, confirming what Teridon had already suspected, the man was a scholar, not a warrior.

"It's OK, we'll get you a dagger or something easy." He nodded towards Jakes,

"Make sure you keep a watch on his back, he'll need it when you two are going through this crowd; they are looking for blood. Jakes, take off your ornaments, don't risk them knowing your rank."

Jakes removed the badge, "what do you mean? You're coming with us, right?"

"No, I have some business to take care of, Sir Loorie is dead, and someone is going to pay for it. The man on that stage is going to die tonight."

"Teridon, don't do this, come with us, the time for revenge will come, but it's not now."

"Thanks for your concern friend, but this must be done. Don't worry about me, I don't plan on dying tonight. Go to the gate, I will meet you there in an hour."

"Teridon, what if he wants this, what if he wants to be a martyr? Just come with us, we can regroup and get reinforcements."

"If he wants to be a martyr, than he will be one. Go to the gate, if I am not there in an hour, leave this city. Don't wait for me, get to the harbor, get a boat, and get out of the city. Do not trust anyone, the guard is compromised, the military may be too. Once you are out of the city, it will be up to you to spread the word of what happened."

"Please, come with us, you can't do this."

"Jakes, go, now. I will see you in an hour."

Chapter 60

Preacher walked off the back of the stage. His robe hung in ribbons; it had been torn to tatters by people pulling on it, wanting to touch him. He had meeting with his protégé in a little while, but he gave himself a moment to savor the night. Patrick had two tasks this night, hang the two, making sure that the crowd saw the 'soldiers', and to lock the three towers' servant entrances. The first was accomplished spectacularly, and given the scene outside the King's tower, he had been successful in the second, as well. The boy was weak, but he was dedicated, and that was enough.

They were meeting in the King's tower. Patrick had thought it overconfident, but he was confident that the king would be taken care of by the time of the meeting. If he was not, they would be dead anyway. But he had no more thoughts of failure. The night had been a rousing success. He had known the people were hungry for the strong hand of a true leader, but he found that they were not just hungry, but famished. The façade of democracy will be washed away and the natural order of humans will be restored. The weak are ruled by the iron fist of the strong.

The building blocks of this revolution were laid two hundred years ago, when Telemin broke his power and created the three, passing ultimate power into the hands of the common people, and the fickle whims of democracy. Over the intervening years, the stupid elected the, slightly less, stupid, always looking out for their selfish interests instead of trying to keep the empire strong. It took several generations, but the empire's power was now on the wane. And he would be the man to stop that wane

While the first act in the breaking weakened the government, it was his second that tore the soul out of it, The Proclamation of the Man, and the banning of religion.

As long as the people had religion to fall back on they would never fully embrace him as their new emperor, they would always run back to the church, to what was comfortable. But, because they did not have that foundation, the people walked as empty shells, longing to be filled. Had Telemin not issued his proclamation, that space would be filled with faith, but, because he had, it could be filled with more base emotions, hate, envy, want. It was up to him to ensure that these emotions were cultivated, and that he gave them an outlet.

Tonight, he had taken those people and offered them the relief of revolution, allowing them to release the hate. Preacher laughed again, a deep, hearty laugh that shook his body, after all his time and effort, it was real, and he had led the movement that took down Capuamundi. This was just the beginning; he would pick up the reins of power, and from his new capital, lead the empire's fall.

Pride was a luxury he rarely indulged in, but he thought it appropriate to allow a moment of indulgence. Taking a deep breath, he felt intoxicated by the cleansing smoke that hung over the city and he revealed in the sooty aftermath of the fires. Fire was both a destroyer and a creator. This city will be destroyed, but a new, stronger, city will rise in its place. It was only a matter of time until he did the same to the empire at large. With his strong hand and ruthless nature guiding it, the empire will return to what it once was, instead of the empty name it had come to be. Enough dawdling, he had an appointment.

***

He walked into the common area behind the three towers. His security detail was late, they were supposed to be waiting at the base of the tower. He looked around, the grass clearing was empty. He did not have time to wait, things were moving too quickly for him to stand around. He started across the grass.

He rounded the tower, and in a circular clearing, three men were splayed out on the ground. Cuts ran ear to ear across the men's throats. Blood still flowed from the slashes, running down the men's necks and pooling under their heads, staining the green grass, which looked black in the dull light.

It did not take much imagination to figure out what happened. They were sloppy, and paid for it with their lives. Oh well, he did not tolerate incompetence and these three saved him the trouble of punishing them. He walked into the center of the servants walk, behind the towers. He smiled; tonight was going to get even better.

***

He walked slowly into the center of the clearing, "DOG! Come out, you killed a bunch of incompetents, but, do you have the courage to come out and face me. I can assure you that you will not find me such easy prey."

Teridon slid out from the shadows that surrounded the clearing, walking towards him with slow, deliberate steps. Focused on his steps and breathing, he was fighting his rage, fighting to stay centered and focused.

Teridon drew his sword; he hadn't bothered to clean it after dispatching the three men, so blood ran down the blade, streaming over the pommel and onto his hands. He walked around preacher, dripping a circle of blood as he spoke,

"You started this. You killed a good man, while you dragged his name through shit. He lived for this country, for its people. He died with those people believing that he was tyrant. They may be stupid enough to believe your lies, but I see what you are. This ends, tonight."

Preacher didn't move as Teridon stalked a circle around him, not even turning his head to follow the circle.

"Boy, if you think I am going to apologize, you better turn around and leave. Your master died a just death. Sir Nidan Loorie was a member of the nobility. He had lived on the backs of the people for his whole life.

Those people took their revenge. He may not have intended to be a tyrant, but once he sat on that council, he became one."

Teridon stopped his circle directly in front of the man, about two paces away, "I am not here for an apology."

One large step closed the distance, and his self-control evaporated. All of rage was focused into his right arm, to his hand, and powered a massive sweeping cut at the unarmed man's throat. This fight would be over quickly, there was enough force in the strike to complete severe a man's head, and probably a second if a man stood next to him. He never fought with emotion, but they were running so strong, there was no keeping them in check.

Preacher casually stepped back, drawing a sword from underneath his robe as he moved. He snapped the slim curved blade up just in time to intercept the savage strike. Preacher looked like he moved so slowly, but the sword came up so quickly. He held it at an angle, the blade redirecting Teridon's powerful swipe harmlessly over his head, without so much as a grunt of effort from Preacher.

Teridon stumbled as his strike was turned aside. He was off balance and overcommitted, while Preacher maintained a perfectly balanced stance, sword out front, at the ready. Surprised at how fast the man was able to get the sword out, and that he even had a sword under those robes, he skipped, caught his balance, then spun away from Preacher, the space gave him a moment to take a deep breath and gather himself.

Preacher stood stone still with his strange curved sword held at about his naval, extended towards Teridon at an angle. His hands were split on the grip and face serene, if he was intimidated by Teridon, there was no indication of it.

Preacher's blade was so thin, an inch at most, Teridon was sure that he could break it with a square strike, but his first strike was deflected. He drew his Main Gauche and prepared to attack.

"NO!" Both men turned as Lueless ran into the light.

Preacher held up his open hands to stop him, "Patrick, be at ease, I will take care of this." He turned back just as Teridon exploded into action. He stabbed at the Preacher's heart, holding the dagger in front of his face for defense.

Steel clashed as Preacher swatted the strike off to the side, he seemed to barely move, just moving the sword enough to deflect the stab, his body did not move at all. His face still showed no emotion as he shuffling forward, slicing downward, then turned the blade and sliced up, shuffling towards Teridon with each slice. Each move was calculated, every step forcing Teridon further back onto his heels. The man fought like nothing he had ever seen, striking with quick slices instead of powerful thrusts. Everything strike was circular. Preacher held his sword with two hands, his strikes should slow and heavy, but the man struck with unbelievable speed. The sword was barely a blur as it whistled through the air. Teridon continued his retreat, still on his heels, desperately trying to get a feel for the man's timing. The blade sliced down, he jumped to the side, barely avoiding it. The blade sliced across, steel rung out, as he just barley caught the slice with his dagger, which dug deeply into his forearm. He despite the slight sword and the thin man wielding it, the power behind that strike was breathtaking.

Teridon took that power into his arm, stopping the blade, and using the slight opening, he punched at preacher's face, hoping to knock the man back and give himself some space to work. He hit nothing but air, Preacher bobbed his head slightly, just enough to avoid the strike.

Teridon went on the offensive, needing to change the dynamic, he swung out at the Preachers's head with another wide strike, the curved blade snapped up to block. Teridon pressed, driving forward with the swing, as sparks flew from the edges of the two blades, he spun the dagger in his hand, so it was now an offensive weapon, and stabbed at Preacher's exposed belly.

Preacher seemed surprised by the change, it was the first time he seemed off balance, though it was only slightly. He did not try to block the stab; he just bent inward, sucking his stomach in. He was not able to completely avoid the blade, however, and the blade sliced through his robe, cutting a shallow slice in his abdomen. Blood started to seep from the superficial wound. It was a minor sting, nothing more, easily ignored.

Teridon pressed further, slid left, then right, trying to find another opening, something that would allow him to actually hurt his opponent. Unfortunately, Preacher saw what he was doing, and was not about to give him that second opening. The boy got him once; he would not get him again. Teridon continued left and he mirrored the move, sliding right and sliced downward, at the boy's shoulder. He was not trying to maintain serenity anymore. He grimaced with the effort of the big overhead slashes. He slid forward with every cut, the fast slices turning to great cuts, slower, but much more powerful. He started on the offensive, causing Teridon to desperately jump and slide, just barely avoiding the flashing steel.

Doubt crept into the edges of Teridon's conscience, this was not the way he had envisioned the fight, and he was not accustom to being the inferior fighter. It was only a matter of time until he made a mistake, and he had no doubt Preacher was ready when that moment came.

Teridon dropped to a knee to avoid a slice at his head. He did not stand again, he knelt, head down, neck exposed, pretending to pant, hoping to bait Preacher into a finishing strike. The other man obliged, raising the curved sword high over his head, he stepped in for the killing blow.

Teridon pushed into the ground and slid backwards, just enough that the slice whistled by his head. The power of the strike buried the tip of the sword into the soft soil. Preacher took one heartbeat too long pulling it out. He jumped to his feet, and swung with all he was worth, the razors edge of the sword easily cutting through Preacher's wrists.

Normally, his hand felt like an extension of his arm, swinging it was natural, easy, effortless, but now, it felt heavy in his hand, like a machete, the last bit of strength going into cutting Preacher's hands off. He dropped it to the ground as blood sprayed from preacher's stumps.

Preacher looked past him, to a donkey pulling a small cart into the square, the old driver bouncing in the seat. He dropped to his knees, this could end. Teridon stood and picked up his dagger, he had no strength to swing his sword. He grabbed Preacher's hair and pulled his head back, exposing the man's neck.

Preacher looked at him with a slight smile, "Do it Dog, end this."

Teridon was happy to oblige. He stabbed through the man's adams apple, and turned the blade around the man's neck. Preacher's head fell back, lolling on the still intact spine. Blood exploded out of the stump, he jumped back to avoid the spray. The body knelt for a heartbeat before falling limply to the ground. He was drained completely, the emotion he was running on gone completely.

***

Patrick ran towards him, as he slowly turned. The idiot gripped a knife tightly, and took a weak swipe, even unarmed; Teridon easily blocked the pathetic attempt. He grabbed his wrist, and then dropped him with a swift punch to the face, ending the meager threat. He reached down, and picked up his sword, not even turning to see where Patrick landed. .

Before leaving, Teridon looked at Lueless laying on the ground, "I'd kill you, but you're not worth it my effort. Besides, you got to watch your new daddy die, and I was the one that killed him. Have a nice life, Lueless."

Pathetic sobbing followed him as he walked out of the square.

Chapter 61

Bisicara pushed anything she could find up against the door. The stone building could withstand some fire, but it would be only a matter of time before the fire jumped onto the wooden roof, and the flammable tar that sealed it. She was dead if that happened. The riot had been going on for hours, but the momentum continued building. The smoke grew thicker and people sporadically pounded on the front door as they ran by. Her time was running out, it was only a matter of time until one of those knocks was someone who wanted to loot the store. The only thing she could do was block the door, so she dragged the heaviest item she could move, her father's wooden desk, in front of the door. Putting her back up to the desk, she slid it tight against the door. Stepping back, it did not look like it was enough weight. She grabbed a few heavy wooden chairs and stacked them on top of the desk.

Desperation turned to terror as a boom came from the door. That was not a knock; it was louder, deeper, like someone trying to open the door. There were no windows on the front of the shop, so as long as her makeshift barrier held, everything might be ok. She slumped to the floor and pushed back against the desk, adding her weight to the blockade.

***

The desk shuddered, the chairs creaked as the stacks swayed slightly from the impact. The door shook again, more this time. She pressed her feet on the floor, pushing her back into the desk, trying to brace it. Another boom and the pile of chairs swayed further, as the desk slid, just a bit, pushing her with it. She tried to push harder but her feet found no purchase on the lacquered floor.

Her heart thundered as she was pushed across the floor, inch by painful inch. Her weight was not enough, the desk slid with each boom, and the stacked chairs swayed a bit more every time the desk moved.She peaking around the edge of the desk as another knock hit the door. The door had cracked open enough that one of the attackers was able to get a hand inside. Acting on instinct, she grabbed a granite paperweight from the desk and smashed it into the back of the hand. There was a scream, and the hand was quickly retracted. Another boom and the desk moved again.

So focused on the door, she did not notice how much the chairs swayed above her head. Another boom, and her world flashed white then went black.

***

Teridon walked into the square, thoughts elsewhere as he waded into the riot, allowing the mob to engulf him. He considered the events of the last hour. He thought killing Preacher would give him a sense of satisfaction, but it did not. Killing the man did not bring Sir Loorie back from the dead, and it did nothing to stop the chaos that had taken the city. In fact, there was no stopping this chaos now. Preacher had lit the fire, and that fire had flared far past the control of one person, it was self-sustaining and needed to be extinguished, or burn itself out. He pushed against the tide, both figuratively and literally, trying to get to the gate before Jakes left. The crowd was crushing up to the towers, and the only way through the square was through its heart. He twisted his shoulders right, and left, squeezing through the crows, when he felt a bump on his shoulder. He turned on a scrawny teenager who had his right fist up, left grabbing at Teridon's sword. Was this idiot really trying to steal his sword?

"Give me that!" The boy swung again. He had to laugh, *'so these were the muscles a crowd gives you huh, boy?'* The mob may make someone brave, but it also did not care if one person lived or died, once you join the mob, you lose that individuality. Easily blocking the teen's punch, Teridon stepped forward with a short punch from his hip. He struck the boy's solar plexus, right in the center of the boy's skinny chest. It was important to defend himself without overtly attacking the boy.

The Teen doubled over and dropped to his knees. His back rose and fell in quick bursts as he held his chest, and gasped for air. Shaking his head in amusement, Teridon moved on, continuing his push towards the gate. It was a few moments later when the crowd opened up and released him from its grip.

Free of the press of people, he looked around, assessing his situation; the gate was directly in front of him. A thick haze of smoke hung in the air, burning his eyes, nose and lungs. The city was cloaked in an eerie glow as the lower city's wooden buildings burned.

He was staring off over the new city when a hand closed around his shoulder; he swung around, and relaxed when he saw it was Jakes, who was dragging Rosi by the arm.

"Is it done?" Jakes asked simply.

"It is, Sir Loorie has been avenged, though it doesn't mean much, he's still dead."

"Teridon, there was nothing you could have done, you need to focus, we need to go, now."

"You're right, let's move, "He took the lead as the three men passed through the gate, moving towards the harbor.

***

Her eyes fluttered open, her vision was still blurred. Through the haze, someone straddled her, yelling and pointing deeper into the store, from the depth of the voice, it sounded like a man. She struggled to get up, but her hands were tied and the man stood so his legs pressed her arms against her sides. Worse, her head was still fogged from the blow, and she was having trouble focusing.

The man, not noticing that she was conscience, was laughing heartily.

"Look around boys, I see a whole lot of silver in those cases. Preacher told us to take what we want, and I see a whole lot I want in here."

He looked down at her and licked his lips as he said that last bit, sending a chill through her. Glass started smashing as the other criminals opened the display cases. Her vision had finally cleared, she saw three other men emptying the cases into burlap sacks. The man standing over her looked down at her again and flashed a grotesque, toothless, smile at her. It was HIM! The deliveryman that tried had tried to rape Ellen. She began to really struggle, desperate to get out. He just laughed at her, while tightening his legs, pushing her arms painfully into her sides. Her struggles just emboldened the sick man, confident that the others were busy looting the store; he turned his attention to her.

He cocked his head, "Remember treating me like I was nothing? You remember acting like you are better than me? I tried to love you. I tried, baby, I did. But you spit in my face, you cold bitch. Then, you got jealous when I was going to take that pretty friend of yours. These mixed signals are enough to drive someone insane. It doesn't matter though, Preacher is in charge, and members of his revolution get to take what we want." He dropped to a knee and grabbed her face, the smell of rotting teeth assaulting her nose and mouth. He looked in her eyes for a moment before whispering in her ear.

"Well Sweetie, I want you, a nice young blonde to bring home and play with. When I am done, bitch, you'll wish you had given yourself to me, and I wasn't forced to take it."

She turned and spit in his face. The man may take her physically, but he would not break her. He just smiled and pulled a knife from his belt. He let the tip of the knife fall to the base of her neck, not putting any pressure on it, just allowing the weight of the knife to push down the edge into her skin. Bix kept her chin up, not really sure what else to do, the man could end her life with a simple slice. He was still smiling at her as he started to slide the knife down her chest, not cutting her, just putting enough pressure on the blade to leave a red line. She was focused on his repulsive face.

A bead of sweat rolled down his cheek, and fell off his chin. She watched it until it splashed on her face. The moisture ran down her nose into her mouth, the salty taste making her want to vomit.

She screamed for help, there had to be a semblance of humanity left in this cesspool of city. The knife was against the collar of her shirt, one cut and her breasts would be exposed.

The man was laughing, he enjoyed torturing her, knowing the power he had over her, and knowing that there was nothing she could do.

Chapter 62

"No, no, no." Patrick lay on the ground next cradling Preacher's, mostly, detached head, openly sobbing, his tears pouring down. The man, that had become his surrogate father, lay dead, killed by a nothing farm boy. The head he cradled was still attached to the body by the spine and some flesh around it. The mouth hung open and blood flowed out of the head and neck, running soaking into the ground. The man never cried out, he was too brave to give Teridon that satisfaction.

"Get up you pathetic wretch, " the old man stood over him, disgustedly shaking his head, "Seriously, kid, get out of my way."

Patrick did as he was told, standing and stepping away from the body, "You knew him longer than me, how can you not have any emotion. You are just standing there, don't you even care!"

"You have no idea what you are talking about, so shut your mouth and get out of my way."

The old man gingerly knelt next to Preacher's body. He started speaking softly, placing a hand on Preacher's chest.

"What are you doing?"

"SHUT UP BOY, Let me work."

The old man never turned around, just went back to the soft chanting. He moved his hands around Preacher's chest, never touching the dead man, but hovering just above. After a moment or two of chanting, Patrick barely could hear the words, the ones he did hear were no language he had ever heard, then the old man pulled a knife and cut Preacher's robes open, exposing the dead man's pale skin. The old man's chanting quickened, and got louder, as it intensified. He touched his hand to preacher's chest, just over his, now still, heart. Now that the chanting was clearly audible, it definitely was not a language Patrick had ever heard. Preacher's death fell out of the forefront of his mind, and he became enthralled with the scene in front of him. Even with the trauma of the last moments, he could not turn his eyes away. The chanting continued as an eerie dark violet haze formed around the old man's hand, the haze seemed to absorb all the light around it, yet it still was visible. He had never seen anything like it.

The tone of the chanting changed, each, unknown, word was emphasized, drawn out, and with a pause between them. With each of these pointed words, the haze pulsed, and with each pulse tentacles started moving out from the haze, and drilled into Preacher's chest.

Not moving his left hand from Preacher's chest, the old man pulled a cloth package out of his pack. Unwrapping the package revealed a solid gold dagger, shaped like a long needle, the golden blade had silver runes running along it. The butt of the handle had a five-pointed star with a ruby sunken into the middle. The gold was offset by onyx inlaid into the legs of the star. As soon as he revealed the dagger, tentacles shot from the haze to engulf it, connecting his hand to the dagger and preacher's chest.

The old man stopped chanting, but the haze continued its pulsing, like it had a heartbeat of its own. The haze silently pulsed for one beat, then two, then three, after the fifth pulse, the old man plunged the dagger into Preacher's chest and the ruby in the handle flared with an intense red light of its own. The light was so intense that it blinded him, white spots hung in the air, as the purple haze ran from his hand and disappeared into the ruby.

The old man withdrew the dagger, the blade was clean, no blood sullied the brilliant golden blade. The runes were no longer silver, but they glowed with the same violet color that engulfed his hand, still pulsing with the heartbeat of his own. He ran his hand along the razor thin blade, and motioned for Patrick to help him up.

He grabbed the old man under his arms and pulled him to his feet. He did not know where they would go from here, but the old man did not seem to be concerned by Preacher's death.

"Patrick, Preacher has been telling you that you had an important role to play. Are you ready to fulfill your duty to the movement?"

This was the first time that the old man ever addressed him with anything less than disgust. Patrick nodded dumbly, not really sure what his response should be. He had no idea what he just witnessed, and was not sure he wanted to know.

"Excellent, know that Preacher foresaw this, and had already made plans in case he fell. You are the bulwark of those plans."

Patrick's heart leapt, was he that contingency? Was he going to be put in charge of the movement? Preacher had always told him that he was his most loyal follower. He beamed, so hungry for Preacher's approval, he did not care what the duty was, he was ready, "I am ready to take my place."

"Excellent, Patrick."

He still beamed with pride when the knife sunk into his left side. It was so sharp, he did not know what it was at first, but the shock wore off quickly and his side exploded in pain as the blade slid past his ribs, towards his heart.

The old man renewed the chanting and ripped Patrick's shirt open, running his hand over Patrick's chest, just as he had done to Preacher moments before. The same violet haze engulfed the old man's frail hands, with the same tentacles growing out of it. The tentacles hung in the air and pulsed before driving into his chest.

Patrick had never felt true pain until the violet tentacles dug into his chest. The pain was more than just physical, it was like his very essence was being torn from his body, he tried to scream but no sound came out. He grabbed at the old man for support, darkness was threatening to take him as the pain increased, and his very essence felt like it was being torn apart.

***

He ignored the sounds of anguish, and pushed the dagger deeper, towards Patrick's heart. This part of the process was delicate, he had to pierce the boy's heart but only just, go too deep and the boy would die before the ritual was complete, and then all was lost. He had done this ritual many times over the centuries, and his deft hands never hesitated. One last push and the dagger struck home, the needle tip of the dagger piercing the boy's heart.

As soon as the dagger struck home, he spoke the words gain, as before, deliberately, with a pause between them, making sure the pronunciation was perfect. When he finished, the ruby flared, again, even brighter than before, and then the light shot back into the stone, which went dark, all color gone from the burnt out gem. He withdrew the dagger, all the light was gone from the runes as well, which had returned to their bright silver.

The blade was as clean as it was when it was removed from the wrapping, and the wound in Patrick's side sucked closed, and healed soon as the blade was removed. All evidence of the ritual was gone as soon as the wound healed.

***

Patrick was losing a battle for his soul. The violet tendrils were inside him now; they had entered through his heart and were using his blood to travel throughout his body. He was losing the battle of attrition with the invader, the battle becoming harder with every inch he gave the tendrils. He felt his consciousness being pushed into the background. Pain wracked his body, he felt every move the tendrils made, the pain increasing as they took more and more of his body.

His limbs were no longer his own, the pain had taken them from him, and it was moving up his chest, towards his head. He gasped; the tendrils flowed through his neck, and into his head, surrounding his mind. He tried to fight, his consciousness was being ripped from his mind, but there was no way to overcome the power. It was only a matter of heartbeats before he gave up, allowing himself to be torn out of his own mind.

Time froze as the violet tendrils closed around him, forming a bubble of violet pulsing power, a prison for his soul. The last thing he saw as the bubble closed, was the burning red fire that followed the tendrils.

***

"My lord?"

"You have done well, I knew this wretch would be easy to break, and, as I thought, he barely put up any fight. Come, we have things to do."

Patrick carried a knife in his belt, he used it to cut the head off Preacher's body, severing the spine, then tossed it to the old man, "make sure this is properly preserved, we have the martyr we need to push things along."

Chapter 63

Teridon, Jakes, and Rosi ran hard towards the harbor; it was only a matter of time before the mob started burning ships. The guard had sealed the city, so if they could not get out on a ship, there was no telling when they could get out of the city, if they even survived to leave. Ships, however, were symbols of wealth, and were not long for this night.

"Do you hear that?" Teridon asked as he slid to a stop on the slick cobbles.

Jakes grabbed Teridon's arm, "Come on, we don't have time for this, we need to leave!"

Teridon twisted his wrist, easily breaking Jakes grip. "Don't you hear that screaming?"

Jakes did hear the screaming, but they were standing in a riot, there was screaming everywhere. Hadn't he learned anything from his last attempt at playing hero? This could delay them long enough that they cannot leave the city, or worse, it could be a setup.

Jakes did not have to say anything; Teridon could read his friend's mind. "Listen, Jakes, I know we need to leave, but if we can't protect one person, than what good are we. The whole point of this riot is to strip this city of its humanity. It doesn't matter if one person lives or dies, as long as the mob survives. It may be a small gesture, but if we let someone that can be helped die, we are just as bad as they are, maybe worse. The counter to this madness needs to start somewhere, my friend, why not here and now?"

***

"You think anyone is going to save you? Preacher said we can take what we want, and I want you. I've seen you playing at keeping shop, acting like you are a man, but you're not. Like every one of your kind, you are a whore, and I am going to remind you of the only thing that a whore is good for. And no, bitch, no one's going save you.

This filth was not satisfied with just raping her, he wanted degrade her as well. He was going to strip her of her humanity before he took her virtue. She had to do something. Giving the man her most comely smile, trying to make things easy on herself and stop fighting.

He dropped down to a knee, and smiled that grotesque smile, showing her those black, rotten, stumps of teeth. He licked the front of his lips as he drew close to her again, whispering in her ear.

"come around little Bixy? I'm glad that you finally realize your place. Now, tell me what you want."

"I want you to die."

Something had snapped inside her, the anger and pain had coalesced into a raw energy. She concentrated on her bindings, the energy flowed to her arms, and they burnt up, and then fell away. She was not going to be this pig's, or anyone's, victim. She bit the man's ear, tearing it clean off his head. He grabbed the side of his head and screaming to the ground, flailing his legs. Freed of the pig's weight, she jumped to her feet.

Having never felt anything like the energy in her chest, she grabbed the man's neck and released the fire burning in her chest. The energy surged out of her, leaping from her hands and disappearing into the toothless man's chest. His eyes shot wide as the energy flowed into him. He let out a terrified shriek, which seemed fitting, given what he had planned for her. His eyes began glowing as she allowed more energy to flow into his body. She had no idea what was happening, how she was producing the energy, or how long it took, but the glow in the man's eyes turned to sparks that started arching to his mouth.

This man was not deserving of her mercy, and up until now, she had been holding back the full weight of her rage. She completely removed the block, and released the full force, allowing the torrent to flow out of her arms.

His eye's exploded, his jaw locked open, with sparks flying from it, lighting the room; finally, once the full brunt of the energy was forced into him, he man's arteries exploded from his neck and the sparks flew from them as he fell dead.

She stood over the dead man, completely emptied and drained. The call of 'WITCH!' came from behind her as she lost consciousness and collapsed.

***

Hot liquid splashed on her face, waking her up, along with gurgling and screaming. She rolled to see the tip of a sword cutting through a man's throat. Hot spray from the neck covered her as the man's head fell off, landing next to her. She jumped back from the dead eyes that stared at her.

Tearing her eyes away from the leering head, she focused on the sword that killed him, eyes following the gleaming steel to a giant of a man.

Teridon kicked the man's body away before it hit the ground, then stepped over her, and intercepting the other men that had charged to avenge their dead companions. The first swung a long silver candelabra at his head, gripping the makeshift club in both hands, Teridon easily avoided the clumsy attack, he slid left, driving his elbow into the attacker's face. He caught the man under the chin, driving the head back; he took the man clean off his feet, and dropping him like a sack to the floor. Teridon stomped on the center of the man's chest, using his mass to pin the man to the ground. The man flailed and punched, trying in vain to get Teridon to move, but his leg may as well have been rooted to the ground.

The man to his right attacked; unfazed, he flipped his sword out straight, thrusting between the man's lower ribs. The sword drove through the man's lung and his momentum pushed the sword deeper. He was dead by the time the last man reached Teridon.

Trying to draw his short sword as he ran at him, he was off balance and out of control, and ripped over the dead man's body. As he fell to the floor, Teridon drove his knee into the falling man's face, breaking his nose, and driving his head backwards. The force of his head going back, while his body fell, broke his neck and he fell limply to the ground. Finally, Teridon looked down, to the initial attacker, still pinned under his boot. The man stopped struggling and started begging, "Please, please don't kill…" Teridon drove the tip of his sword through the center of the man's neck before he was able to finish that statement.

***

Jakes helped the woman up, her eyes were glazed over and she was unsteady, he had to support her as she swayed on her feet. Her shirt had been ripped wide open; her breasts were covered by nothing but a thin corset.

Teridon pulled a shirt out of his back, and threw it to her. She caught the cotton shirt, then pulled it over her head, it was massive on her, hanging almost to her knees, but she was covered.

She cautiously took Teridon's outstretched hand.

"Are you OK?"

She stared numbly at him. She was still undecided as to the fresh group of men's intentions. They had saved her, but why?

Teridon saw her trepidation, and tried to put her at ease, "My name is Teridon Jace, this is Jacob, Jakes, Pints and Rosi Starling is the man trembling in the doorway. May I ask, Ma'am, your name, and what, exactly, you did do to that man? He deserved it, of course, but it was... frightening."

"Bisicara, people call me Bix, and I have no idea."

She was measured, careful about giving to much information. After what she had just went through he understood her hesitance, but he could not leave her, or anyone in this city, "Pleasure Bix, now, let's get out of here."

"I can't leave."

Teridon was stunned as he looked around; she stood, covered in blood, among four dead men, including the one that she had burnt from the inside out.

"I'm sorry? You can't be serious, if you think this is ending tonight, you are mistaken. This is just beginning; it will get darker, and bloodier. If you stay here, you will die."

Bix fought her tears, this was all her family had. If she left, all they had built would burn.

Teridon walked over to her and softly grabbed her chin; pushing her eyes to meet his.

"Look at me, this shop is destroyed. There is nothing to be saved, only rebuilt. Once everything settles down, feel free to come back and do that, but come with us now, save yourself. You can't rebuild anything if you are dead."

"But my father-" she whispered

"Would rather have his daughter than some trinkets."

She gave a subtle nod in agreement. She knew he was right, staying would not save the business, and would, probably, cost her life.

***

The harbor was relatively quiet, this area had already been consumed, destroyed, and the mob had moved on. They had to get out before the riot came back down the hill to get the ships they had missed.

Moving along the great half-moon of the harbor, they ran toward the city wall. On either end of the harbor, the city wall ran continued off the shore, forming a half-moon in the lake that left a small space in the middle, barely large enough for two ships to pass through side by side. The walls doubled as breakwaters and were massive, with tops wide enough to march four men abreast. The walls ended at two massive round towers, each housing the garrison assigned to the walls.

They also housed the massive chain that could be pulled into place to blockade the harbor. Port Mundi was the largest harbor in the world, bigger even than Southport and Winterheart, the largest ocean ports. It was the city's center of commerce and the harbor reflected that.

None of them were sailors, so the large sailing ships in the piers were worthless. Besides, they needed to be able to get out without drawing attention to themselves. The smaller fishing boats were beached at the far ends of the harbor. They reached the beach, a small sandy section between the stone wharf and the wall. They cut the ropes of the nearest boat and pushed it into the lake. The boat was small, with six rowing stations and a small cargo area in the back, along its transom. The four took positions at the oars and started into the harbor. They were not sailor, it would be a long row out through the cut and back to shore outside the city, but it was the only way.

Chapter 64

Nydelis walked out of the Inn. Jakes had set them up at the Dancing Horse, he was friends with the owner, so she had been able to rest easy knowing they were safe, for one night. Marie, their escort, was already awake and packing their things away into the wagon, getting ready to leave and be away from the city. In other circumstances, this would have been an ideal early fall day, perfect for some spiced cider and griddle cakes with syrup. She let out a long sigh, it seem that it would be some time before she would have that luxury again.

"Good Morning, Ma'am" Marie called. For a soldier, she was very pleasant. She was a beautiful woman with tan skin and long jet black hair.

"Good Morning, Ms. Pepon" she called back.

The inn was only a mile outside of Capuamundi, so she could see the smoke that engulfed the city, coalescing at the summit and rising as a large black column into the sky. Jakes had been right, and she owned him her, and Terry's, lives. Though, he got to be with her, so he had almost evened the score, she laughed softly to herself, "Ms. Pepon, what are your plans?"

"Well Ma'am, your husband had asked me to take you to Barnstable and I intend to do that very thing. He provided enough money for supplies and the carriage. We do need to move soon, the city will only contain that for so long, we need to be away."

"Ok, and Marie, thank you so very much, we would be dead if you had not come for us."

"You are welcome ma'am, but please save the thanks for when you are safe in Barnstable."

***

Nydelis went to see Terry, who was inside finishing his breakfast, a simple berry muffin, "Honey, we are going to visit Grandma and Grandpa in the country."

"I don't want to go, I want to see daddy." He was far too young to understand what was wrong, and he had just begun making friends in the city.

Her face softened, she stroked his back, "I know, sweetie, but we have to, we can go home soon, but for now, we need to go to the country so we can be safe."

"Yes mother." He said, sullenly. He allowed her to take his hand and lead him to their room. Dragging his feet the whole way.

***

About a half an hour later, the carriage eased away from the inn and started along the road. A chill hung in the air, the sun had not risen high enough in the sky to chase it away. For now, they pulled thick woolen blankets tight around themselves, and set in for a long ride.

Chapter 65

Teridon's arms, shoulders, and back burned as he strained to pull the oar through he water of Lake Nemi. He, like the other three was weakening, and the boat was covering less distance with every disjointed stroke. The boat had slowed to a slow crawl by the time they neared shore. Not waiting, Teridon jumped into the frigid water, and dragged the boat onto shore. The curved prow grinding loudly into the stiff sand. They did not bother to tie the boat off; they were not coming back, and did not care if it floated away.

Once secure on dry land, they collected their packs, and the three gathered around Teridon, looking for him to take a lead. He was careful not to give the others orders, where they went from here was their decision to make.

"I am going to Sir Loorie's estate. I need to tell his family what happened. The news needs to come from me, not second hand. None of you need come, this is my burden."

He was surprised when the three others slung their packs and followed after him, making the decision without talking about it. In truth, they had nowhere else to go, but there was more than that; something that was drawing them to the large man, though they could not identify what that was.

***

The first step was getting horses, they could not walk to the estate. Stables were common along the main road, horses frequently needed to be changed, especially when ridden hard. They became even more frequent as you neared the city. The only stables inside the city were reserved for the City Guard, so most people needed to store their mounts outside the walls.

It was a short walk to the first stable. The stable house door hung open; five horses grazing in the corral. "Hello!" Teridon called, there was no response, the interior was dark, and appeared empty. He hated thieves, but there was no alternative, He horses and there was no one here to deal with. Besides, he had no money. Gathering four of the horses, he led them out to the road. The others had gotten the tack out of the shed, and saddled the horses, before setting out down the road. They rode in silence, the clicking of the horses's shoes the only sound that broke the silence.

***

It was early afternoon when Teridon stopped the group, a few miles out from the estate.

"Please don't follow me any further, this is something I have to do on my own. Camp here, if you wish to stay, but don't stay out of obligation, you have none to me."

Jakes started to speak, but reconsidered. Teridon was an adult, if he felt he needed to do this on his own, then so be it. They dismounted, and Teridon helped them set up camp before he rode off towards the manor house.

***

"We are really going to let him go alone?" Bix asked.

Jakes was already unpacking his bag, "Yeah. This is something he needs to do. He didn't ask us to stay behind lightly. Respect his decision."

Bix huffed, and then went to work at starting a fire. She snapped at Rosi, "Can you do something? Find some wood."

She stormed over and pushed him towards a stand of trees, taking her frustrations out on the meek man, who did not put up a fight. Life on the road was new to him, he never had to gather firewood before, he did not even know what made good firewood. He rooted around in the leaves, picking up small sticks, cutting his soft hands while carrying them back.

He had spent his days in the comfort of a library; books did not require callused hands. He dropped the pile at the feet of a disgusted Bisicara.

Jakes stood off to the side, a wide grin on his face, she will be a valuable addition, he thought, Rosi needed toughening if he was to survive what was coming. It would be better received from the pretty blonde woman than from he or Teridon.

Chapter 66

The boy, closer to a man, that used to be Patrick Luless, walked to the former King's tower, still basking in the night's success. The lower city was a burnt out husk, but the buildings of the old city were stone, and had fared much better, some could even be lived in. He could not say the same of the noble born who owned them, they had, either, accepted the will of the people, they died, or worse. He took a deep breath, taking in the smell of the destruction he had inspired. Most would find the smell of smoldering fire disgusting, but he found it intoxicating.

He had waited so long for this moment, had spent so much time in laying the ground work. That investment of time and work had finally paid off, in spades. He had taken the empirical capital down, he now had control of the largest port, most of the banks, and the treasury, but he was just getting started, the city was the capital of the empire, while important, it was not the empire. The number, and concentration, of people in the city had made recruiting easy. Bringing the rest of the empire under his thumb will be much more difficult. It will be much harder to foment dissension among people who have little interaction with the government. But, those were worries for a different day.

He slammed the library door open. The old man started up from his slumber on a couch within.

"I cannot believe it, I knew this day would come, but it is hard to believe that it is actually here. We have given the country back to the people"

The old man smiled but did not rise, "now what happens, will you ask the people? Will you hold a vote?"

He threw his head back, and laughed, a deep hearty laugh, that came from deep inside him. "The people have already spoken, they have their leader. Why do they need to vote?"

"I am sorry, but no vote has taken place, who has been elected, and when?"

He shook his head, "Naivety is not a becoming trait for someone of your experience. They have elected me, of course. After all the work I have put in, do you honestly think I would let this rabble govern itself? They would destroy themselves. They need a strong hand to lead them. That hand will be mine. Do you have the object?"

"I do. It was packed in salt, it must be kept in the salt or it will rot." The old man pointed to the small chest sitting on the table.

He cracked open the chest and smiled, 'Preacher's' face stared back at him. The face will be the new symbol of the movement, a martyr that will prove what would happen if anyone crossed the new government. He intended to give them one choice, submit to his salvation or suffer death by the military's spear. They did not have to know that the spear was just being held in his opposite hand.

Chapter 67

The wagon rumbled along the road, the metal bands on the wheels scraping the stones as they had for the last several days. The ride from Capuamundi to Barnstable is a long one, but, usually, pleasant, the scenery in the northern regions was beautiful, deep evergreen forests, interspersed with low mountains covered in the red, amber and brown, as the trees prepared to drop their leaves for winter. The mountains in the north were much lower and less severe than the Crags to the south. The summits tended to be gentle and round, without the sharp cliffs of the south.

This trip north, however, was much different. Nydelis could do nothing but brood, Jakes had said that he would get her when things settled down, but she had no way of knowing when that would be, or if he was even still alive. She had seen the column of smoke rising from the city, and could only imagine the death and destruction that caused that great column. The ride seemed interminable, like it was taking weeks.

Marie had been a good companion so far. She helped with Terry and arraigning their accommodations at night, they had hopped from inn to inn, only having to camp outside a few times.

Things had started to look up, however. Several days ago, the rolling plains had started to give way to straggling trees, and today, the trees closed around the road; they had reached the outskirts of Westin forest. It would only be another day or so before they reached Barnstable. Being there would not ease her mind about Jakes; his family might help her feel like he was near.

The carriage was swaying and her mind was wandering, she was drifting towards sleep. Through heavy eyes, she saw a huge panther sitting at the tree line; the cat was black as a moonless night with a huge pink scar breaking up the inky fir on its shoulder. The cat's bright yellow eyes bored through her as its massive head followed the carriage. She had though these giant cats were merely legends of the forest, stories told to keep children from wandering too far into the woods, it seems she was wrong. The cat just sat staring, but not showing any aggression. She did wonder how it got that scar, it was a single cut so it had to be a blade, and it had to have been deep, the fur never returned after the wound healed.

Her thoughts were interrupted by soft words, "The forest has awakened, momma."

She smiled, where had he learned those big words? She turned and screamed in horror. A creature that looked like her son was staring at her. It stood and stared at her with ink black eyes, they were open, but the orbs that floated where his eyes should be were just black. There was no white, no color, just dark black orbs, "Why are you screaming momma? What is wrong?" The thing spoke in a monotone voice, there was no emotion in it at all, yet it had a slight sing song quality. She felt her head getting foggy as it spoke.

"Where is my son?" She asked drowsily. She was struggling to hold onto her thoughts.

"NYDELEIS!" She was shocked to her senses by Marie who had thrown the door open and had her sword in hand, "what is wrong? You were screaming."

She looked at Terry, who was sleeping softly, bundled in his wool blanket, as he had been for the last hour or so. What was going on? Was the stress getting to her? "Did you see that panther, Marie?"

"Yes, Ma'am, it was amazing, I never thought I would actually see one of the giant cats. I thought I would only hear about them in stories."

She let out a sigh of relief, the cat was real, she was not going insane, "I am sorry Marie, the cat surprised me, I had never seen such a thing.

Marie gave her a tight hug, "I understand ma'am, please don't worry, I am here to protect you and I intend to make sure you get to Barnstable in one piece."

"Thank you Marie, truly, thank you." The woman slammed the door and the carriage rumbled off. Continuing towards Barnstable.

Chapter 68

Teridon passed gardeners working on the flowers beds, and farmers working the fields. Riding by these fields brought back so many feelings. He recalled the first time he rode up to the manor, and the awe he felt. He smiled as he passed the tack shed, remembering learning how to repair a saddle's girth strap. He rode past the blacksmith shop, were he learned how to sharpen a sword and maintain armor. Those were great memories, but the news he was here to deliver prevented him from enjoying them. Sir Loorie was dead, and he was responsible.

The house loomed, it was usually beautiful, but today it looked ominous and dark. He pulled back on his horse's mane, stopping in front of the door. He jumped off the horse and stretched, both his body and time, walking slowly to the door. He gripped the large iron doorknocker, but the door opened before he had a chance to use it. He did not know the butler who answered, "Can I help you?"

"Yes, I am here to see Krys. I didn't think I needed an appointment."

"Was the lord expecting you?"

The man spoke with great formality, a marked change from the last time Teridon was here. Sir Loorie had taken pride on the informality of his manor; he felt that the employees should feel that they are part of the household rather than slaves to it. Sir Loorie actually scolded new employees for calling him lord; so to hear Krys being referred to by that title was strange, to say the least. This man was new, though, he may not know the traditions. He will play along, the reason for his visit was more important than teaching a servant a lesson.

"No, but it is important that I see him; please tell him that Teridon Jace is calling. This is important, I have to see him right away."

"Please wait here."

The door slammed in Teridon's face, he had to jump back so he was not hit his nose. Alone, there was nothing to do but wait. He suddenly remembered why he had never rode bareback, he was sore in places that should not be. He pulled a piece of jerky out of his pack and dropped heavily onto the top stair.

Ripping a piece off the slab of jerky, he chewed more out of boredom than hunger. He was not a patient man, and the wait gave him time to dwell in his thoughts. The guilt continued to tear him apart.

He waited for some time, the sun had moved about an hour before the latch clicked and the door opened again. The butler motioned him inside.

Walking into the great room, and he too a deep breath, the staff may have changed, but the house had not, and he loved this house. Allowing himself a moment to enjoy being home, he stated upstairs to get his task over with. The butler stood at the bottom of the stair, blocking his way, and trying his patience.

"What are you doing? Please, get out of my way. I don't have time for servants who don't know their place."

The man did not move, setting his shoulders against the weight of Teridon's presence.

"Master Loorie has instructed me that he would receive you in the hall."

Teridon was taken aback, what was going on? This was certainly not the reception he had been expecting. The Butler pushed past him, and he numbly followed.

"Please wait here."

The butler motioned to a bench next to the receiving hall's door. He waited on the little wooden bench for a while, until a guard came out of the hall to gather him, "the master is ready to receive you now."

For the first time, Teridon felt truly slighted. Maybe it was exhaustion, but he had attributed his reception to a new staff member who did not know him. This was different; Krys had sent and armed guard to get him. He had to remind himself why he was here, "So he sends an armed man to fetch me like a criminal?"

"I am sorry sir, please don't read anything into this, I just happened to be free." His defensive posture revealed the lie of his words. Teridon pushed past the man without answering, the man's armor clanking as he rushed to catch up. Teridon had expected to see Krys in the dining hall, where his father had received guests. In the five years in Sir Loorie's employ, he had never seen the formal receiving hall used.

He shook his head in disgust, the meeting would take place in the receiving hall, Krys did not intend this to be an informal meeting.

He gave a questioning look to the guard, who leaned in and whispered, "There have been a lot of changes, since Master Nidan turned things over to his spawn." Disdain dripped from the man's words.

***

Teridon walked through the gaping double doors, and moved up the aisle, passing benches on either side, approaching the raised chair at the head. The chair and dais was an ode to the old empirical throne, oversized and ornate, with gold-leaf accents, intended to make people feel small in its presence. It was one of the many reasons Sir Loorie never used it.

Krys sat on the throne, playing at being a lord, adorned in all the trappings the station. His father did not need all the accouterments to prove he was lord of the manor, but, then, Krys was far from his father. He wore a torque, adorned with the sigil of house Loorie, a hawk extended talons, he also wore a silken sash, blood red and trimmed with white tassels. Teridon shook his head; the idiot didn't even know what he was wearing. That was not the sash of a lord, it was the sash worn by veterans who had been wounded in battle. The other sash was purple, and that was placed on the bodies of soldiers that had actually died in battle.

His father wore it because of his service, not his title. Most galling, however, was that he had already taken the position of lord. He did not even know his father was dead. Traditionally, laws of succession dictated that a regent could not assume the chair of the lord until the terms of the regency were met.

He had anticipated a happy meeting, but it seemed that Krys' head had swollen with his new position, and this meeting would be anything but. He strode to the front of the hall with purpose. Krys sat with his elbow resting on the arm of the chair and leg tucked up under him, making no move to stand and looking completely uninterested, "Krys, it's bee-"

Krys shot forward, squeezing the arm of his chair, anger flashed across his face, he was suddenly very interested.

"You will address me as 'my lord.' I know you have been away for some time, so I will allow the lapse in decorum, once."

Teridon's jaw clenched, he really was going to continue this charade, "What is going on here?" pausing, he spat "my lord", through clenched teeth.

Krys smirked, "I don't know what you are talking about, my father made me lord of this house, and I am merely acting as such. This station deserves a measure of respect, and, you will show that respect, to the title, if not to me."

He was not made lord; he had been installed as a regent. Teridon was barely able to hold down the bile that was building in the back of his throat, he wanted to take the boy off the chair and beat Krys' head back to its normal size. Instead he swallowed his pride and ignored the slights, refusing to dishonor Sir Loorie's memory.

"My lord, I come bearing terrible news. Capuamundi has fallen. Revolution has taken hold; the city is in flames and the government fallen. It is only a matter of time before the insurrection spreads to the rest of the empire. However, that is not the worst of it."

Krys' eyes narrowed as he leaned forward with as scowl, "and, what is the 'worst of it'?"

Teridon's shoulders' relaxed and dropped as he discarded the pretense, he stepped up and grasped Krys' hands, addressing him as a friend and brother, "Krys, your father is dead, murdered by the mob. I am-"

Krys jumped off the dais and backhanded him across the face, "IT IS MY LORD! You will address me with proper respect, commoner. It's only out of respect for my father's memory that I sullied this hall and granted you this audience.

You will remember your place, or you will suffer for it." He paused, composed himself, and looked up at Teridon, "I am sorry my old friend, the stress must be getting to me."

Teridon did not respond; Krys' aggression had put him on edge, and he regretted not coming armed.

Krys came close, placing his hands on either side of Teridon's neck, squeezing his shoulders and staring up, into his eyes, wearing a large smile, which did not touch his eyes, "Thank you for coming all the way out here to tell me this terrible news. My father's death is a tragedy that the empire will feel for years to come. He was a good man and a great leader."

Sincere or not, what he was saying was absolutely true; Teridon nodded in agreement.

Krys continued, "He loved you like a son, more than his real son, if we are being honest. He also trusted you; so much so, that he brought you to the city and made you head of his security. Giving you a position that you had absolutely no business occupying. He trusted that you would grow into it.

I'll never know why, he saw the same things I did, a lowborn oaf with more muscle than brains." He paused and took a large step back, "Anyway, he was too trusting, and that drove him to stupid decisions, stupid decisions that led to his death. I knew about his death, friend, and hold you personally responsible, GUARDS!"

Epilogue

Five rangers had been riding hard; they had left the ease of the roads, choosing to travel the most direct route to the Heshian border, across the countryside. They traveled as lightly as possible, only carrying enough supplies for the ride, the plan was to get fully provisioned when they reached the garrison and then push into Hesh from there. They had been pushing their mounts hard and traded them for fresh yesterday, allowing them to continue pushing and make the fort this week. Their destination was the seat of the 5th legion, Fort Telemin. The fifth patrolled the hessian border, and they had requested the support. This mission was going to be exceedingly dangerous; they were going to be crossing into hostile territory with no information regarding the country's situation. All of the ways in were treacherous, at best, and if caught, they would be certainly be executed.

The worst of it was, even if they were successful, they might need to kill the Aragonian operators in Hesh; the situation was a mess, and there will be no support, from the Fifth or anyone else, but that was what the Rangers were about.

The sun had passed its apex and was headed towards its rest. They had been able to see the Crags for the past two days, while the plains had begun giving way to foothills, and the terrain was becoming rockier and rockier. They were getting close.

The sun was about to slip below those peaks when the fort came into view. The massive structure darkened the sky ahead of them. The fort was built for another time, a time when this was a contested border. The walls were fifty feet high and broken every thirty feet by a tower, leaving no blind spots for attackers to exploit. Inside the fort were giant trebuchets, which were constantly maintained but had never been used in the modern era. The fort was ancient, even during Telemin's rein; it had been renamed in his honor after the breaking of power. The five men slowed their approach.

The fort should be bristling with activity, but no soldiers patrolled the walls or grounds, the great iron gates hung half way open, as if they guards were interrupted while closing them. Continuing the slower pace, they noted that the walls were blackened, like the fort was a rock that had been thrown into a fire.

But that was impossible; nothing could burn that high or hot. Proceeding cautiously, they entered through the open gates to find, nothing.

There were no bodies, the buildings stood empty; there was no blood, nothing. The entire garrison had disappeared and the fort stood empty.

END BOOK 1